The Far Northern Land Saga Book II

The Heir of Lemminkäinen

David Allen Schlaefer

Printed in the United States of America
Print ISBN: 978-1-953910-79-0
eBook ISBN: 978-1-953910-80-6

Library of Congress Control Number: 2021921629

Published by DartFrog Plus, the hybrid
publishing imprint of DartFrog Books.

Publisher Information:
DartFrog Books
4697 Main Street
Manchester, VT 05255

www.DartFrogBooks.com

Join the discussion of this book on Bookclubz. Bookclubz is an online management tool for book clubs, available now for Android and iOS and via Bookclubz.com.

For Dan and Jeanie

Acknowledgements

I first became interested in Finland and its heroic tales as a child. I owe this interest to my parents, Dan and Jeanie, who collected an odd assortment of amazing books on all sorts of subjects. One such book was a *Reader's Digest* special on folklore of the world, which introduced me to Väinämöinen and the Kalevala. The other was part of a Time Life series on World War II and battles in Scandinavia. My interest whetted, I read everything about Finland I could get my hands on. Many years later, I had the opportunity to serve in Finland as an American diplomat, fulfilling a life-long dream and setting the stage for the Far Northern Land Saga.

My Finnish teachers, Anuliinna Santry and Anna-Mari Barrineau, provided inspiration and amazing instruction. The staff at the Gallen-Kallela Museum in Espoo, Finland, generously gave their time and patiently answered the strange American's many questions. I was encouraged throughout the writing process by many friends, but Heikki Hämäläinen, Vera Stah, Marja Sevón, and Ulla Anttila stand out among them; I thank them profusely.

The gorgeous map of the Far Northern Land that accompanies this volume was created by Misty Beee, as was the map of Pohjola found in the third volume. The creative process that led to the final version was one of the most rewarding experiences of my artistic career, and I encourage those interested in fantasy cartography and design to visit her website.

Finally, no author worth their salt can fail to acknowledge the support of their family, and I'm no exception. My incredible wife, Raluca, and children helped me in so many ways and I am grateful to all of them. Gaddison, Christian, Anastasia, Viktoria, Maria and Klara, I thank you all, with love.

Notes on Names and Language

The stories that appear in the Far Northern Land Saga are inspired by Finnish folklore, especially the famous work *Kalevala* by the great compiler of Finnish oral poetry, Elias Lönnrot. In addition to his expertise in medicine, ethnography, and many other fields, Lönnrot was a philologist and loved language. Having had the unique opportunity (for a foreigner, at least) of studying Finnish full-time for an entire year and then live in Finland for almost half a decade, I naturally incorporated Finnish into my work when I set out to write the series. Beautiful in phonology and structure, it is not an easy language for non-native speakers to acquire and I beg patience of readers who find themselves confronted by pages of unfamiliar words and letters with no mentor like Väinämöinen to guide them as they journey.

The chief peculiarity, at least to English speakers, is the extensive use in Finnish of diacritics: the letters ä and ö. These letters represent distinct sounds, and their use is governed by the process of "vowel harmony." This, and the multisyllabic, compound structure that encourages long words with lots of double consonants, can be a challenge. But the recompense is that readers will catch a glimpse, however dim, of the sounds that Ulla, Egan, Väinämöinen, and the peoples of Iron-Age Finland actually used and heard, and which they bequeathed down the centuries to their contemporary descendants. I believe this glimpse is worth the challenge.

By necessity, I have been inconsistent throughout my stories. For any violence done to the Finnish language, I can only offer sincere regret. Most words in the Far Northern Land Saga used to represent the speech of its inhabitants at the time the events occurred are contemporary Finnish. But I have "antiqued" some to better match the feel of the age in question. In a few instances, I have purposefully dropped diacritics, which Finns will quickly notice (*Etela* vice *Etelä*). Perversely, I have added them to one word. Most egregiously, in a very few instances, I have used incorrect case: a cardinal sin. I can offer only apologies and the feeble justification that as Väinämöinen taught Ulla, balance in all things is ideal, and to strike a balance between fidelity to the language and accessibility to non-native speakers was my intent. Undoubtedly, I sometimes failed, but I hope the sincerity of effort warrants forgiveness.

Finally, to assist the reader, I decided to spell out a few phonetic pronunciations of some of the chief characters and places, and a glossary of some key words is here at the onset of the book. The proto-Finns who lived in the Far Northern Land at the time of this saga were divided into many clans and kinship groups. The chief groups each had their own totems, which often appeared in the clan's name or the name of its homeland. There are exceptions. The great kingdom of the south was *Etelamaa*, and its people were the *Etelalaiset*, which literally translates as "Southland" and "Southerners." However, their totem was the swan (*joutsen*) and they were colloquially called the Swan Folk by the other clans. Since these names can be confusing at first (and second and third, etc.) encounter, I set them out below and encourage readers interested in such things to thumb back whenever needed to this page to refresh their memory of who was what and lived where. The map will also offer assistance.

Proper Names

Väinämöinen—VĪ-na-MOY-nen—(the great singer)

Lemminkäinen—LĔM-min-KĪ-nen—(ancient hero and high king)

Löhi—LŌ-hee—(the Witch of the North)

Länsimaa—LĂN-si-maw—('Westland')

Ulla—OOL-la—(the girl who bears the Mark of the Clan)

Egan—Ā-gun—(King of the Swan Folk)

Kirsikka—KEER-sik-ka—(Ulla's friend)

Mielikki—MEE-e-LĬK-kee—(the Lady of the Forest)

Pohjola—PŌ-ho-YŌ-la—('Northland')

Kuupää—KOO-pă—(the 'Moonface')

Homelands and Clans of the Far Northern Land

Karelia—Karelialaiset—(the Reindeer Folk)

High Länismaa—Karhulaiset—(the Bear Folk)

Deep Länsimaa—Hirvilaiset—(the Elk Folk)

Etelamaa—Etelalaiset—(the Swan Folk)

Tavastia—Tavastialaiset—(the Hare Folk)

Akkala—Kotkalaiset—(the Eagle Folk)

Susila—Susilaiset—(the Wolf Folk or Lost Clan)

Pohjola—Pohjolaiset—(the Northerners or Löhi's Folk)

Itäläiset—(the Easterners)

Table of Contents

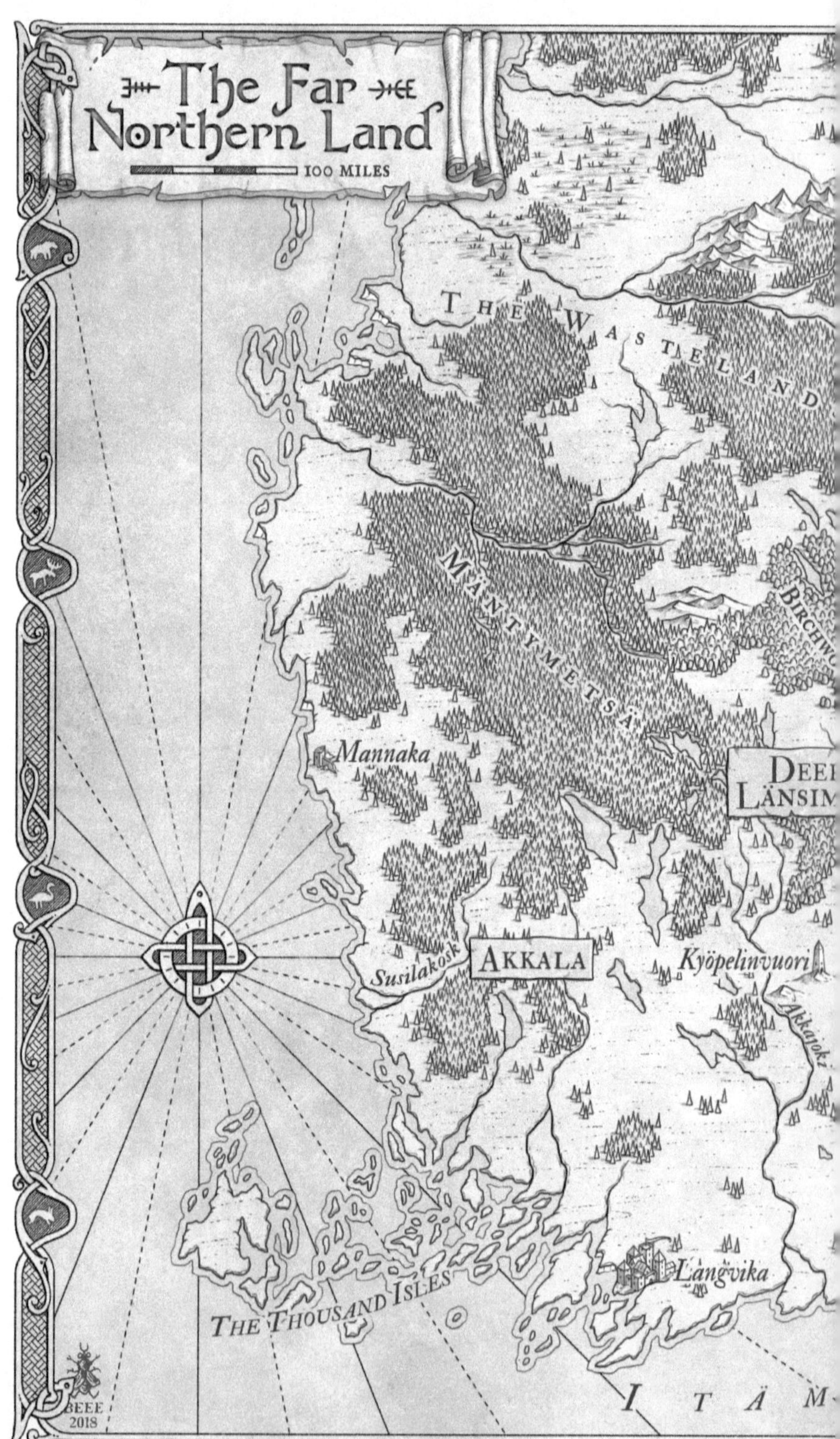

The Far Northern Land
100 MILES
THE WASTELAND
MÄNTYMETSÄ
BIRCHWO
Mannaka
DEE
LÄNSIM
AKKALA
Kyöpelinvuori
Akkajoki
Susilakosk
Längvika
THE THOUSAND ISLES
ITÄM
BEEE
2018

NORTH MARCHES
Grankulta
Gamla
Ilkeakosk
LAKE SUURIJÄRVI
Metsäposti
KARELIA
Väinölä
ENCHANTED VALLEY
Joukzi
HIGH LÄNSIMAA
Keskimaa
EE
EE
Siinesaare
innavuori
THE WALL OF THE GIANTS
ANISKITA
GREEN VALES
NECK
Kotanrannta
Rajavesi
ETELAMAA
Tapiola
Haamerouksi
VASTIA
LAKE ETELAJÄRVI
Stone City
E.rannta
Harmaaniemi
Sepällä
I   S   E   A

CHAPTER ONE

The Hiisi on the Hilltop

The sun smiled down on the Far Northern Land like the face of a daisy set against a pale blue sky. Cold wind still whistled through the evergreens, and patches of icy snow streaked the ground and hid in dark hollows. Spring was coming, however, and all the north stirred with life. Melting ice brought swift floods and opened waters. Birds and animals moved again among the forests and lakes. The trees bloomed and slender shoots waited just below the surface, ready to sprout up through the frozen earth. Spring brought hope to the folk of the Seven Clans, as it did to people everywhere, but hope was not always enough—with summer's toil and autumn's harvest yet to come, winter's stark power always waited to contest whatever it could.

A small figure darted about the bramble atop a thickly wooded hill. It slipped quietly from shadow to shadow, as if playing hide-and-seek with an invisible friend among the firs and pines. It took care not to linger in places where it might be spied from afar. To a watcher in the fields below or perhaps to a hawk circling above in the clear cloudless heavens, the figure might seem slight: some mortal child, a little girl or boy, flitting amidst the green. But this was no mortal child of the Kaamoslaiset. The diminutive shape on the hilltop was a Hiisi from Pohjola.

The goblin lifted its head, peering at the yellow sun with its white eyes. It had come again to the hilltop, the highest point along a line of scattered bluffs, to gaze down upon a small valley below, through which a lazy stream bent round and round. The Hiisi reached the tree line and slid down into a dank, muddy hole beside a fallen fir tree. A clear, unobstructed view of the dell lay before it. It was risky coming to this place; enemies were all around, and, even from a distance, the Hiisi could feel the magic that lay over the little valley, protecting it from wizardly *sight*. Only once before had the goblin risked coming so close, but now it had little choice. It would soon be spring, when the roads would fill with traffic. The Hiisi needed information before it left the hills near Kyöpelinvuori and made report to its mistress, the queen.

The dark-skinned goblin, clad in ragged clothes and with a tattered cowl about its head, had been hiding in the nearby woods for many weeks. It had journeyed far before that. During the dark winter months, it had been sent south from Pohjola by Löhi, who had instructed the goblin to spy on the valley and the little village that lay within: *Laulavalaakso*. There, the mortal singers gathered and the Erilaiset taught them songs and spells of power. But the heroes' magic was strong. Their spells protected the little valley so not even Löhi could see what happened within.

Seven years had passed since the Battle of Linnavuori, where Työ had been slain through Väinämöinen's treachery, blunting Löhi's first great assault. The Witch had bided her time, leaving nothing to chance, and all the while her red star rose ever higher in the heavens for all to see. Each year, great raids had been made along the Marches. The battles over the northern border of High Länsimaa had left most of its villages in ruins. Now Löhi deemed the time right for her next move; she felt the world's change hastening and her own time growing short. Many large clans of the Itäläiset gathered beneath her banners, and new legions of Hiisia, formed after the debacle at Linnavuori, would soon be unleashed. First, however, she needed news of her enemies, especially the old singer of the Erilaiset and the mortal girl whose birth Mielikki had foretold—and, though the Witch's *sight* was long, still, she could not see everything.

So the Hiisi on the hilltop had left Pohjola with two companions. They had made their way south, passing through the wilds of Deep Länsimaa, hiding from the mortals they encountered. Near to Siinisaare, they came upon several scattered farms, distant from other villages, and had found some children playing by a brook. Against the goblin's wishes, its companions took two of the children and tormented them for sport, so that one died and the other fled back to its folk in terror. The mortals were wrathful and came against them, and there were many more of these nearby than the goblins had known. Through the woods, the Kaamoslaiset hunted the two Hiisia that had taken the children, caught them, and then slew them in vengeance. Such was their reward, for they had disobeyed their queen and strayed from their mission; Löhi's anger would be great.

The lone goblin had continued and, in time, come to Kyöpelinvuori where the old mortal crone dwelt in her tower and where the Erilaiset had made their new dwelling. It had lived in the darkling woods through the long winter months; famished and starving, it spied on the Erilaiset and mortals, watching all that transpired. But now the harsh time in the wild all alone had come to an end.

With spring on its way, the Hiisi was commanded to leave its lonely vigil and go north. There, on a tall, barren hill in the fens and marshes above the Blue Lake, it could reach out its mind to its mistress, who awaited its report. She might even come herself, as an *etiänen*, and read the very pictures in its mind.

For this purpose, the goblin risked the hilltop one last time. It took a final measure of the village below, to see, if it might, what manner of folk gathered there. The Hiisi blinked in the golden light, scanning the horizon. At Kyöpelinvuori, in the distant northeast, the old, mottled tower reached skyward. Seldom did the mortal crone leave her crumbling keep, but twice the goblin's sharp eyes had spied her on the path that led to and from the valley. Closer to the Hiisi's vantage point on the high bluff lay the valley's gate, the stream's glittering water issuing from its opening and running south until it disappeared in the haze of the hill's lower slopes. The view toward the valley was perfect; in the crisp, clean air, the Hiisi could see all that it desired.

A grove of trees lay in the valley. Beside the running water sat a long hall built of dark wood, smoke rising from its several chimneys. Bonfires were lit in a little clearing nearby, where the singers often gathered to weave their mysterious spells. The goblin had spied folk of all kinds: men and women, old and young, and Erilaiset, too. It had heard deep voices chanting in the ancient tongue as red flames danced about and watched wizards with wooden staffs spread their arms skyward in invocation; it had listened to drums beating during the long winter nights.

The goblin knew that one of these wizards was surely Väinämöinen and another Turi the Changer. And it had spied a young girl with pale skin and raven hair, like to the one Löhi most sought news of. But no mortals stirred on this day, no Erilaiset gathered around a fire or near the hall; a single figure sat beside the stream, watching over a herd of goats. All was quiet in the peaceful grove.

The long hall stood in the middle of the little valley, with cottages and *pirttis* scattered here and there among the woods and along its slopes. Some resembled the cottages of the Tavastialaiset, but others, fashioned strangely, looked more like the cabins of Karelia than Tavastia. Smoke rose from many hearths into the clear blue sky, and soon people moved among the trees. The goblin could see a woman with long blonde hair beside one *pirtti*, fetching water, perhaps, or tending to some small beasts too distant to be seen. She wore a bright blue dress, and as she moved, the sunlight glinted off the silver chains pinned to her clothes and belt. The Hiisi felt the valley's magic and power as surely as if it sat before a roaring fire, basking in its heat and glow. But while it could see these things from its hilltop vantage point, the magical net protecting the village from wizardly *sight*—the net that exuded the magic the Hiisi felt so strongly—dimmed Löhi's vision; it would not allow Lovêatar to enter therein, or other spirits of Pohjola, for such was the power of Väinämöinen and the Erilaiset.

The goblin, watching the woman in blue with its sharp eyes, suddenly became aware of sounds in the woods below—faint, but coming from the hillside itself, not from the valley or fields beyond. It pricked its ears and listened. The barking and whining of dogs was plain to hear.

Caught after all this time! Dogs on the hillside, the blue-eyed hounds of Tavastia with faces like wolves'. Surely their mortal masters had set them to search. Somehow it had been seen, and now the hunt was on!

The goblin scrambled out of its muddy hole and ran through the trees, slipping on patches of melting, icy snow and ripping its tattered clothes on trailing branches. Famished and weak, the Hissi cried out in anger and fear for its now desperate plight. What had it done to deserve such a fate? Had it not endured pain and hardship, starvation and suffering for its mistress? Why was it the lot of its folk, its own lot, to know such torment and misfortune?

Not far from the Hiisi's hiding spot ran a game trail. Löhi's servant made for it now, hoping to outpace the mortals and their dogs, then escape down the bluff's blind side. Despite the sunshine, the air was cold and snow still covered the woods, but the dogs with their keen noses could track a scent even in winter's chill and frost. The goblin cursed all mortals as it ran, calling on the queen's mighty spirit to afflict them with all manner of misery, ruining their lands and towns. It received no answer, however. Löhi was not there, and the Hiisi was alone with its enemies.

Halfway down the rolling slope, the barking became louder, mingled with the shouts of men. The dogs had caught its scent and cut across a great fold of mossy earth, hoping to come at it sideways and catch it unawares. It glimpsed them in the distance through the trees and knew it now had no escape; the hounds ran swiftly, their braying and growling echoing throughout the woods while their masters tried to catch up. About to give up and turn to face its pursuers, the goblin spied an outcrop of grey stone cutting like a dark narrow ribbon down the hillside. The stone fell a great distance, covered by an icy coat, clear and slick. Without hesitation, the Hiisi leapt upon the icy stone and slid down the slippery stair, crashing through bracken and bramble, then dropping many feet into a mossy pit below.

The dogs barked excitedly in the woods above, but could not slide down the same way. The sound of the hunt changed as they turned to make their way round a twisting fold of earth and so descend to the foot of the hill. The goblin did not intend to wait for them.

Battered and bruised, its leg hurt in the fall, it scrambled to its feet and sped down the even slope as fast as it could. The slope ended abruptly, opening onto a long patch of flat meadow, but opposite the meadow grew a broad, thicker wood with many trails and streams. The Hiisi had often hid in these woods and knew them well; it hoped to move quickly through the trees and come to places where the dogs could not follow, where it could elude its pursuers. It reached the bottom and paused, gasping for breath.

The sounds of its enemies grew faint above it. A low, crumbling wall of stone, an ancient marker of some border long forgotten, made a sharp turn; beyond it, the meadow stretched out before it. It faced a long run to the safety of the woods, out in the open, an easy mark for watching eyes— but there was no other way. It would have to take the chance. If only the westering sun shone in their eyes!

The goblin drew its only weapon, a long, curved knife. With a low howl, it ran along the stone wall and round the bend, ready to race to the tall trees in the distance. The Hiisi stopped short.

There, waiting just around the bend, sat an old man on a speckled grey horse.

The old man's ruddy face was calm. His long white beard stood out against his colorful garb: a bright red tunic, its hems sewn with clever, multi-colored designs, and high yellow boots wrapped about his legs. A wooden staff lay across his lap, but his hand grasped a long sword glinting in the golden sunlight. His horse took a step back and snorted.

The Hiisi, its face twisted with rage and anger, spat on the ground before it.

"Curse you!" it screamed in the tongue of Old Talvimaa. "Curse you to the dark pits of Tuonela! May Tapiola wither and never be renewed!"

The goblin raised his knife and sprang forward, intent on slashing the horse, if not its tall rider. But the old man called out a single word, "*Pysäyttää!*"

The knife fell from the goblin's hand.

With a swift stroke, Väinämöinen brought down his sword, *Jääpuikko.* The goblin fell to the ground, its dark blood staining the snow that still clung to the hill's lower slopes. The horse jumped, but the old wizard reined it in. He looked down at the dead goblin. His enemy was vanquished, but Väinämöinen's face reflected neither triumph nor joy of victory, only a distant sadness; for though need may require stern choice, such grief brings no delight.

The old man sighed and bowed his head. The sound of barking dogs came closer, and fleeting birdsong incongruously filled the air.

And so no report from the Hiisia she had sent forth ever reached Löhi, nor did she ever learn of their struggles and sacrifice, of the suffering they endured to further her dark designs—but what did Löhi care? The Witch of the North was strong and botherered little about the fate of the meanest of her servants.

Chapter Two

The Valley of Song

Nested inside a gentle dell within the old tower's shadow lay Laulavalaakso, the Singing Valley. The power of the Erilaiset rested upon it. Green in springtime and golden in summer, the valley hosted many hearths, which sent smoke into the dark sky in autumn and winter. A winding ribbon of a clear, glistening stream ran through it, and cottages hugged the easy slopes on either side among the trees. On one side grew firs and pines, while a stand of white birches graced the other. But close by the long hall that the Erilaiset had built grew rowan trees that bloomed year-round and, in the winter months, were heavily laden with berries. Väinämöinen had chosen the spot after the battle seven years before.

When mortals began to gather at Kyöpelinvuori to learn the ancient songs and rituals—which, though almost forgotten by the Seven Clans, were still remembered by the Erilaiset—they needed a place to dwell. Väinämöinen had chosen the dell in part because of its peaceful green among the tilled fields of the Tavastian countryside but chiefly for the beauty of the rowans, which reminded him of those at his home in Väinölä in far-off Karelia, where the heroes lived and where Mielikki still dwelt.

After Tyë, Löhi's great captain, had been defeated and his forces scattered or destroyed, Väinämöinen had agreed to the Seer's plan, though he little trusted her. But Mielikki, daughter of Tapio and child of the Vanhalaiset, whose mind saw farthest of any being yet alive in the Far Northern Land, gave long thought to the matter. She sang in her garden, calling upon her father to guide her and upon Ukko the Creator to illuminate the uncertainty that darkened their counsels. Then knowledge came to her; she understood that, for good or ill, they must seek the path that ran through Kyöpelinvuori and thus the mortal Seer's friendship. If there was any chance for the Seven Clans to return to the Old Ways and to stop the Witch's last, great attempt to subdue them before her time faded, the Seer must play a leading role. And the Seer had discovered Työ and his jewel, a great thing that could not be forgotten.

So Väinämöinen and the Seer had traveled to Tapiola, the chief city of the Hare Folk, the Tavastialaiset. They came to the heart of that fair land of golden fields and blooming trees, the land that long ago had been the first homeland of the Kaamoslaiset ere they were sundered into the Seven Clans and spread throughout the Far Northern Land. King Egan of Etelamaa went with them, and Teemu, High Lord of the Elk Folk—and, of course, the little girl with dark hair, Ulla of the Karhulaiset, who bore the Mark of the Clan on her shoulder and whose coming had been a sign for mortals and Erilaiset alike.

There they spoke with Asikkas, King of Tavastia, and with other great lords of the land. Bergil, Lord Captain of the March Wardens of the Far Northern Land, and Ilkka joined the debate. The lords and captains took counsel then about the battles in the north, the coming of Löhi, and the return of the Erilaiset to mortal lands, considering what they should do to protect their people and homelands. Mielikki's prophecy was unveiled to the Hare Folk, and Väinämöinen urged Asikkas to join with them in common cause.

Now the Tavstialaiset were wary, for the old wizard's tale seemed incredible to them and many of them distrusted the Erilaiset. It had been long since the people of Tavastia had followed the ancient ways. The customs of their forefathers now seemed remote, like dim legends from the misty past. But the Seer of Kyöpelinvuori, to whom Asikkas had often turned, spoke this same counsel, warning him that the Seven Clans would be overcome one at a time unless they united and looked to the singers for wisdom. So in the end, Asikkas consented, and his nobles, too. Tavastia, Etelamaa, and Deep Länsimaa made a pact to join forces against Löhi. Soon the folk of High Länsimaa and Karelia joined the pact as well.

Väinämöinen and Ulla returned to Kyöpelinvuori and found Mielikki there before them. She hallowed the ground of the little dell that the old man had chosen, close by to Kyöpelinvuori as the Seer wished. Then, ere she returned to the Enchanted Valley, Mielikki spent many weeks with Ulla while mortals and heroes built the little village together, gathering within the sacred grove. The ancient songs were heard once more in the Far Northern Land. And the people had come.

From all corners of the Far Northern Land they came, from every clan and folk of the north. Each year in the spring and early summer, they arrived in the Singing Valley, driven by the same strange dreams and burning compulsions. Some were poor folk of the land or fishermen or hunters, as poor as Ulla's people had been in Grankulta and the hardscrabble villages of the Marches that were no more. Others were craftsmen and traders and there was even a scattering of nobles from the great kingdoms of the south. Many men came, but each year several women also reached the Singing Valley, even some with children at their skirts. Man or woman, rich or poor, they told the same tale when at last they arrived beneath the old tower's shadow.

Dreams had come to them during the long winter months, when snow covered the Far Northern Land and the pale sun showed her face for only a few hours each day before dark night settled over the frozen lakes and woods. In some of the dreams they heard Mielikki, singing softly, her melodious voice making pictures in their minds, showing them the path to take though they knew not why. They left their homes and the lives they had known to come at last to the old Seer's tower. There, the Erilaiset welcomed them to the gentle valley and taught them songs and spells of power—for indeed, they all had been born with this gift, the gift of magic, and needed only the ancient heroes to awaken it within them.

During all this time, Löhi's power had grown; her spirit waxed for a final season. The winters grew colder; great storms of snow and ice troubled the Seven Lands. The Itämeri Sea froze solid all winter long, and the shorter growing season left the folk of the Seven Clans little margin for comfort. The shadow of Lovêatar appeared in many places, terrifying people and spreading pestilence and disease, disappearing for a time only to reappear again in a new place far away. And other spirits, too, came out of the north, ghosts borne on a black wind from Pohjola to freeze mortal hearts and spread despair.

But where the *tietäjää* appeared—the mortals who followed Mielikki's call to become singers and shamans under the tutelage of the Erilaiset—the Witch's power lessened and many evil things might be righted. They brought healing to the sick, as the ancient rituals of field and fertility brought healthy crops or rich bounty from the waters. Spells of ward and protection brought safety, freeing folk from fear, unease, and madness. Löhi's power might not be broken, but it could be contested, giving the Kaamoslaiset respite from her deadly assault.

In the bright sunlight of a new day, Ulla stood blinking in the doorway of the small *pirtti* she shared with Kirsikka. She yawned and stretched her long arms above her head. A trickle of water from a little spring above ran through a stony channel beside the *pirtti* and on down to join the stream below. Ulla stooped and splashed her face with the icy water, shivering from the shock. Fully awake now, she breathed deeply, savoring the strong evergreen smell mixed with the light scent of hearthfires. After a few moments, she grabbed her green hooded cloak, which was made of thick, coarse hemp after the fashion of the Reindeer Clan, and wrapped it about her shoulders. She wanted to talk to Väinämöinen this morning. Ulla knew exactly where to find the old man on such a day. He would be sitting beside the strangely shaped *seidi*-stone on the opposite side of the dell, staring out at the trees and grass, thinking.

The little girl with dark hair had grown during all this time. Her dark brown locks fell past her waist, though she was as tall as many grown women. Her skin was still as fair and pale as ever, her limbs were long and lithe, and she skipped quickly down the path from her *pirtti* to the stream. She had stayed with Väinämöinen at Laulavalaakso, seldom leaving the Valley's narrow confines, for seven years. Still restless at heart, she loved to travel, but had gone only once to Karelia and the Enchanted Valley since the Battle of Linnavuori, twice to the Stone City in Etelamaa, and twice again to Tapiola in the south.

In some ways, Ulla's life at Laulavalaakso was like her life in Grankulta. She did the chores and women's work she was given—tending animals, learning to spin, knit, grind, and bake. But never did she forget that the Singing Valley, for all its charms, was not truly her home. Never did she forget the face and voice of her father, whom she still loved with the heart of a child, nor the family that had been torn away and never found. Never had Ulla's will been broken by these things, but the sadness of her trials lingered, setting her apart from other folk. Yet her sharp mind and spirit grew strong.

She seemed a village girl in some ways, but she was not, of course. Ulla, the child of Mielikki's prophecy, bore the Mark of the Clan. Nobles and lords still came to the Singing Valley to see the bear's claw on her white shoulder, but Ulla no longer cared or felt reluctant to show them. Now she recognized the power this gave her over them; she enjoyed their surprise, fear, and wonder. She had learned many things that few girls ever learned in those days, which did not wholly please Väinämöinen.

Turi gave her lessons in how to shoot a bow until Ulla could hunt like a Warden in the wild. Her clear sight and true aim made her a match for men much stronger and larger. And in Etelamaa, Egan had taught her to use a sword. At first he did so in jest, for the young king had become a great swordsman, and it humored him to fence with the little girl armed with a long knife atop the Keep. When she proved a natural with quick reflexes and instinct, he drilled her in earnest. Ulla loved the thrill of wild swordplay and the sound of iron against iron.

As a gift and remembrance, Egan gave her *Pohjanpiiki*, Työ's sword, which he had taken as a trophy from the field of Linnavuori. Ulla kept it in her cottage in a leather scabbard set with amber stones. She practiced handling it, long and heavy as it was, in secret—for she knew the old wizard disapproved, and feared he would take it from her. But she was wise enough to recognize that the great singer of the Erilaiset doubtless was aware of all she did.

She did not just excel in swords and darts, however. From the day she sang the spell to weave Tulikki's cloak, the great power within her was evident. She had the power of a mage and singer, one who might wield magic and make the *loitsu* of the Erilaiset. Väinämöinen recognized this strength, but was wary of the young girl's following the path of singers too soon. He had not foreseen her future as a witch or wizard, and though he tried to divine the girl's destiny, it was hidden to him. Yet a shadow seemed to darken his heart when he considered it. The old man had come to love the girl as if she were his own daughter, his own flesh and blood, and he grew terribly anxious for her safety. Ulla bore the Mark of the Clan, a sign unto all the folk of the Far Northern Land, and he wished her power to be manifest in that sign alone. He feared that, as a warrior, wizard, and rival to Löhi, her life would be spent in deadly peril and strife. More than anything else, he simply feared to lose her and knew that he would never forgive himself if anything bad ever happened to her.

Still, he did not deny her knowledge, and the old singer of the Erilaiset taught the girl with dark hair many things. Although the heroes did not normally instruct children in the magic of the Vanhalaiset—few enough had ever shown Ulla's skill or promise, save perhaps Lemminkäinen in the days old—Ulla often learned from Väinämöinen or other Erilaiset who came to Singing Valley to teach mortals the songs and the meaning behind them. And Ulla did not forget what she learned.

To make these spells, a singer needed power and knowledge—knowledge of where things came from, of their nature and names. The wound caused by the iron sword might be healed by a singer who knew iron's origins, and golden fields of wheat ensured by a singer who knew the nature of the seed, of the earth in which it grew, and of the sweet rain that watered it. Fire could be sparked with a single word by those who understood that it was lightning, the striking of Ukko's hammer on the anvil of the heavens, that had first brought flame into the world below. But a singer drew on the Old Powers of the earth, the *Vanhalaiset*: Ahti, Lord of Waters, Akka, Mother of Earth, Ilmatar, Mistress of Winds, and old Tapio, Lord of the Forests and Mielikki's sire in the depths of time. The words were but links in a chain.

The Vanhalaiset each ruled their proper domains, while the singers and wizards merely acted as vessels, channeling the powers of the gods and drawing on their strength, matching that strength with the knowledge, words, and songs taught to them when the world was still young and its sadness yet far removed. But even the Vanhalaiset served Ukko, the creator and master, who, with deep, unknowable design, had fashioned the earth and the sky and the very stars in their courses in the blackness before time began.

Wizards worked much magic for protection, healing, warding off danger, or increasing yield. Väinämöinen taught Ulla how a wizard might master a disease or misfortune with knowledge of it. By reminding it of its origin and of its weaknesses and remedies, a wizard might banish the evil thing or even trap it in a stone or hole, commanding it to remain in place and thus freeing its victim. But the old man was quick to warn her about the dark side to such spells. The evil magic of Pohjola, the sorceries that Löhi and her servants used, called *kalma*, were the reverse of such *loitsu*. Instead of healing, they brought curses, disease, and misfortune; other *kalma* might summon dark spirits from Tuonela into the waking world.

Ulla thought on these things now as she came to the clear stream that divided the Valley. Few of the mortals who came there had the skill to learn the great spells. They mastered the ancient songs of the clans, and maybe learned the rituals of fertility or simple arts of healing and other such *loitsu*, and then returned to their folk. Only the strongest, in whom the flame burned brightest, mastered the deeper spells. The next step in their journey involved something strange, a great mystery that neither Väinämöinen nor Turi would speak about. When they had learned all they could, the men and women who might become wizards went on a journey into the wild with the

Erilaiset, sometimes travelling all the way back to their homelands. It was whispered that they hunted or tried to trap their clan's totem and did other strange rituals far from spying eyes. Only then were they made wizards, the *tietäjää* of the Seven Clans, and given staffs as signs of their station.

For two years Ulla had begged Väinämöinen to let her make the hunt. She already had the strength and power of any mortal *tietäjää* and had learned wisdom from Väinämöinen himself since she was small. She truly wished to be a singer and magician like the Great Ones of the Erilaiset and help save her folk. But the old man remained silent, except to say she was still a child in the eyes of the heroes and should be patient.

A line of brown stepping stones had been set in the stream and Ulla crossed them nimbly, careful not to slip into the chilly water. On the opposite side, several people lingered near the long wooden hall where the folk of Laulavalaakso gathered and where the singers' fire always burned. Urho, an Erilainen of Karelia and a powerful healer, spoke with two men, mortals only recently arrived in the Valley. Urho waved to her, and Ulla waved back, but the girl continued into the birch wood and shortly began to climb a gentle slope.

Not far up the slope from the hall, she found Väinämöinen. The old man sat atop the seidi-stone—a strangely shaped grey stone rising abruptly from the ground with a flat top like a rocky cap on a giant's head—with his kantele at his side and a clay jug of *sahti* in his hand. Stretched out, he looked up at the white clouds in the sky with his long legs in their great yellow boots dangling over the side.

"I thought I'd find you here," said Ulla. "You are always on the stone on bright days in the springtime."

"And why not?" answered Väinämöinen without looking at her. "Here is a good place to be. It is pleasant to sing here and play music and watch the winds toy with the clouds up above."

"And drink before it is even noon?"

"Most assuredly," said Väinämöinen, sitting up now and smiling. "Home brew's best in the morning before it's sat too long. Here, come up here, child, and sit beside me! It is a fair day, at least for this day, whatever else the winds of the world may betide." The girl with dark hair scrambled up onto the stone next to him, while the old man took up the kantele, playing a soft, melodious tune that was new to her.

"I've never heard that," she said, and the old man laughed.

"I only made it up just now. I don't make new tunes very often, like I used to. You know my way; the old songs are best and, after all, there are so many of them. But something about this morning called for something new, so there it is."

"It is very lovely." She listened to the old man's strumming until it trailed off and he was silent again. The girl swung her long legs up and down, blinking at the yellow sun.

"How many people have come to the Valley already?" she asked.

"Six so far," said Väinämöinen. "And one's a Karelian woman with her husband and children in tow. They left the forest last summer and spent the winter near to Keskimaa. The Karelians usually go to the Enchanted Valley, you know; after all, it is right there in the heart of the forest and they have never left the Old Ways or forgotten the songs. Strange that they would come all the way here, but that is what Mielikki's song put in the woman's heart."

"How many do you think will come this year?"

"There were twenty last year—perhaps the same. It is very hard to say, child. I still don't understand all that is happening. Hey there, stop kicking your legs or you'll knock my jug off! You're not so little anymore, more's the pity. Aye, you'll be grown soon. It's a blessing when a child lives and grows, but it's a sad thing, too. I'd have kept you as you were, a little imp, if I'd had the power."

Ulla tucked her legs beneath her and ran her hand across the smooth seidi-stone; she could feel the power within it. She had come to tell the old man something and to ask him something, too, but now she hesitated. She wished that she could simply spend the bright day sitting in the sun with him.

"The Seer asked me to come see her," she said at last. "I am going to Kyöpelinvuori today. Kirsikka is coming with me."

The old man's smile vanished in an instant and a sour look crossed his face. "Did she now?" he said. "Well and good. And what does the old crone want?"

"Who can say?" said Ulla, smiling as she used one of the old man's favorite expressions. "Perhaps she wants to know more about the Hiisi you slew on the hillside last week. But I think … I think that she will ask me what she has asked me twice before: to come to the tower and be her apprentice."

The old man shook his head and sighed. The shadow of a cloud seemed to pass over them; where all had been bright about the seidi-stone, the light dimmed.

"She does not give up easily," he said. "But her wits are clouded from gazing into that looking glass, that crystal ball of hers, night after night. And what will you tell her, child?"

"I do not wish to be her apprentice; you know that, Väinämöinen. Not that you would let me, even if I wanted to. But there is, well …." Ulla looked down at her feet, clad in shoes of soft, tanned leather.

"But what?"

"I am stronger than she is!" said Ulla suddenly. "I am stronger than any of them or, at least, I could be. You know that I can work the spells and make the songs as well as any wizard—even Mielikki says so. Can I not make the hunt this summer? Will you not teach me the final songs and show me the trail? Why must I sit here, year after year, while others come and go with your blessing? I am not a child anymore, whether you wish it or no. And— and *I* bear the Mark of the Clan."

"Aye, you do," the old man replied evenly. "And that is part of what worries me. The way I see it, you were meant to unite the clans and bring hope to us all in a dark hour, not divide them, or become the enemy of Löhi, like Lemminkäinen of old. There is no coming back from that path once you take it. Already many in Akkala, and even Etelamaa and Deep Länsimaa, speak of the witch-child who took the Dark Elf's jewel and who lives with the singers. The children of the Far Northern Land were not taught magic in the days of old, neither by mortals nor by Erilaiset. It was taboo, and with good reason: *Send a child on an errand, but follow along behind.*

"There is more to real strength than just power or force. There is wisdom; that comes with time and patience, and honoring those who have seen more than you by listening to them. It's a difficult lesson for the young, to be sure.

"But not all have accepted the Old Ways again; in Akkala, they remain forbidden. The clans must still be united. You are still young, little one. Let the future bring what it will. If that path is appointed you, there will be ample time and I will always be there to guide you."

Väinämöinen hopped down and took up his staff, which had been leaning on the seidi-stone. The girl looked at him and shook her head.

"And I am not a man, but a woman; is that not also a reason?"

"Few women among the Kaamoslaiset become wizards, this is true. Or at least, few women follow the Old Ways and the Vanhalaiset, rather than acting as simple witches, mixing what little true magic they know with superstition and mischief. Then, too, there is Löhi. But the same can be said for most men. And what of Unaja the Golden, your friend? She has grown very strong!

"Most women who come here will be daughters of Akka, singing songs for the harvest and richness of the earth. This is their calling. But is Mielikki not the greatest among us, and is her magic not the deepest and most powerful, save for Löhi's madness in Pohjola? Have patience, Ulla! What will be, will be! Do not rush toward the future. There is no need for haste; it will still be waiting when at last you come to it."

Ulla dropped from the stone and gathered her cloak about her. The old man's keen, piercing eyes could be daunting, but she met his steady gaze without blinking.

"I must be going now," she said. "I need to find Kirsikka, and already the morning is passing. We have a long way to go to Kyöpelinvuori, and I hope to be back before dark. Good-bye!"

The shaman watched as Ulla set off down the well-worn trail back toward the stream. Her long hair hung down her green cloak and her feet stepped smartly around the muddy rocks. Väinämöinen sighed and brought his hand to his neck as he watched her slowly dwindle in the distance. The old man's heart was breaking, but he could not stop time nor even delay its steady march, singer and mighty wizard though he was.

***

Ulla crossed back over the stream by the long hall. More people were about now; most of the dozen or so Erilaiset who lived in the Singing Valley would be gathered inside the hall, teaching, or going about their daily business. She started up the fir-clad slope on the other side, but only a little ways from the hall, she heard a clear voice rising above the forest sounds, piercing the still air with a loveliness that sent shivers down her spine. Ulla followed the enchanting voice and, there, in a little glade not far from the silver stream, found Kirsikka.

The red-haired girl stood by two shaggy ponies, already saddled and bri-dled, brushing their flanks as they nibbled the short, new grass and singing an old song of Etelamaa. She smiled when she saw Ulla, dropped her brush, and came forward to meet her.

"It's about time you got here," she said. "If I'm going with you, I'd just as soon get started and get it over with. I don't wish to be stuck at Kyöpelinvuori after dark. You know how that tower makes me shiver."

"How did you get the ponies?"

"Unaja made the stabler give them to us. There are five or six down in the stables now. Aren't they pretty? A little skinny maybe, but they'll fatten up soon enough when the grass comes in. We'll get there—and back—much faster if we're riding."

Though matched for height, Kirsikka was a year older than Ulla. She wore her red hair tightly braided in the elaborate fashion of Tavastia, shot through with golden thread and covered with a fine, sheer veil. Her red-and-white dress showed off an apron hemmed with spirals of bronze sewn onto the fine cloth, while chains of silver and bronze hung from the clasps at her shoulders. Her yellow belt of soft leather held a short knife, given to her by Väinämöinen, forged in Seppälä and made winterfast by the smiths. Though still covered in freckles from head to toe, she had grown beautiful.

Not only her coppery hair and bright green eyes set her apart, however. Kirsikka had come with Ulla to Laulavalaakso after the battle, and the two girls had lived together like sisters in a little *pirtti* surrounded by fragrant pine. But while Ulla learned the magic of the Erilaiset or played at being a warrior, Kirsikka discovered a different gift. Her wondrous voice became more musical and beautiful as she grew. Rich and rolling, like the fertile fields of Tavastia, it could soar like the tall firs reaching toward the sky on the snowy heights of the Wall of the Giants. It could be sonorous and deep as the dark blue waters of the Far Northern Land's many lakes or as light and playful as a cuckoo's trill in the Green Vales of Etelamaa. When Kirsikka began to learn the songs of all the Seven Lands and Seven Clans, she enchanted mortals and Erilaiset alike.

No wizardly magic filled her song—she had not that gift; she was no shaman or mage. But the purity and clarity of the girl's fair voice when she sang filled all hearts with joy and delight. Her fame grew in the lands about Kyöpelinvuori, so that folk came to listen to her at festival times and sought her songs for weddings and glad occasions. Many gifts she received, fine clothes and chains of precious metal and other delicate things, which pleased her greatly. Asikkas himself had heard her and offered to take her to Tapiola where she might live in plenty, singing before the highest nobility of the Hare Folk. But she would not leave Ulla or Väinämöinen.

"Let's go then," said Ulla. "I haven't packed any food, but I see there's a bag on that pony."

"Unaja," said Kirsikka. "She gave me two loaves, a cup of butter, and two white cakes that Kappi, the Menninkainen, baked only yesterday. They are very sweet!"

The girls mounted the shaggy ponies and set off to the north, following the line of the wandering stream as it meandered back and forth through the dell. The valley widened and the ground on either side grew more level until, finally, as they rode round a stand of tall pines, a clear plain opened before them. The stream bent sharply to the west, where it flowed on into the distance, feeding the grasslands in that direction. A well-marked cart path ran ahead over the slightly tumbled plain and, some ways to the north, beneath the blue sky, they could see the hill of Kyöpelinvuori with the Seer's tower on top. The girls struck the path and rode now between dun-colored fields.

The fields, worked by the serfs of Kyöpelinvuori, fed many folk in the lands nearby, though the Erilaiset tilled their own fields near the southern bluffs. There were few people about; two or three peasants digging rocks from the earth scarcely looked at the girls as they rode by.

"Did you ask him again?" said Kirsikka as they bounced along in their wooden saddles. Ulla snorted.

"Of course. And, of course, he said the same thing—nothing. You are too young, it is unclear, there is yet time, and all the rest. Not that I had much hope; I can almost read his mind now, at least, what he thinks about me at any rate. But I thought that when he heard the Seer wished to see us, he might change his mind."

"She wishes to see *you*, not me; I am just keeping you company. When the old woman looks at me, it's like I'm not even there. But you should have told Väinämöinen that you'll accept her offer unless he gives you a staff. They all know how strong you are, anyway."

"I couldn't do that," sighed Ulla. "Besides, he can read my mind, too. He'd be more likely to take me to Karelia and lock me in Väinölä than anything else if he thought I'd really become her apprentice."

"Väinölä! There are worse places," said Kirsikka. "But Väinämöinen has been strange lately in any case, especially since they caught that goblin. Did you see it? I heard they burned its body in the woods and buried the ashes."

"I saw it," answered Ulla. "I hadn't seen a Hiisi since—you know, since Linnavuori. It was very ugly. Väinämöinen said that it was spying on us and a sign that Löhi is stirring. But he wouldn't tell me anything else when I pressed him."

"Well, that's Väinämöinen," the red-haired girl said with a laugh. "He won't say anything at all or he corners you for hours with lessons and instructions. All or nothing is his way. But look here, Lumikki—" Kirsikka suddenly kicked her pony and shook the reins. "I'll race you to the tower!"

Her pony shot off and, with a cry, Ulla followed. Ulla chased her until just before they reached the hill, then she charged ahead of her friend. They pulled up together, panting no less than the ponies, which weren't meant for racing. They stared up at the old, mottled tower.

"Ugh," said Kirsikka, her freckled face as red as her hair from the race. "Let's get it over with. But you owe me for this, Lumikki; I'll decide exactly what you owe me later."

The girls rested the shaggy ponies for a bit in the shade of an old, half-ruined rowan and then slowly rode up the hill of Kyöpelinvuori, three times round, climbing ever higher on the winding road until they reached the tumbledown keep at the tower's foot.

The crumbling keep remained much the same, but, on one side, the wall had been repaired and several new chambers built of smooth black stone. The Seer had requested this of Asikkas, and the king of the Hare Folk had sent men from Tapiola to build them. The chambers housed the *Tornilaiset*, the singers and magic-users who pledged fealty to the Seer.

Every year, as the mortals from the Seven Clans arrived to learn the magic and wisdom of the Erilaiset, the old crone of Kyöpelinvuori walked among them. She took a liking to some mortals and, if they were not chosen to become true wizards, invited them to Kyöpelinvuori to learn the Seer's wisdom. They formed a separate order, the Servants of the Tower. Some went to Langvika, the capital of Akkala, and others to Tapiola and Valkeakosk, or even to the Stone City of Etelamaa and the other chief towns of the Seven

Clans. Though Väinämöinen and the Erilaiset did not like this, they could do naught to stop it.

Servants waited for Ulla and Kirsikka when they reached the hilltop; they took the ponies, then led the girls through the ancient archway and up the old tower's stair. Ulla had been to the tower many times, but she never grew used to the dark, narrow passage. She always felt the same sense of stifling suffocation as she climbed, and she always felt glad when at last she reached the great black door between the guttering torches and strange tokens.

The door stood open this time, which was unusual, and light spilled out into the stairway. When Ulla and Kirsikka stepped into the great round chamber, their legs aching from the climb, the Seer of Kyöpelinvuori was there to greet them.

She looked older, perhaps, than when the girl with dark hair had first seen her some seven years before. The lines in her face were deeper, her nose sharper, and her braided and threaded hair was the color of snow. But her eyes, grey as Väinämöinen's, still glittered with a glassy sheen. She made a gesture of invocation, bending slightly so that her long black robes brushed the polished floor.

Beside her stood a thin young woman with chestnut hair and long, clever hands below her dark sleeves: Siitsa of the Karhulaiset, Chief of the Tornilaiset, and closest in the Seer's counsels.

"Welcome, Ulla," said the Seer in her thick Tavastian accent. "Not since the Night of Fire have you come to the tower; you have been missed. As have you, Cherry, though I have heard your golden voice from afar, growing ever more beautiful as the seasons pass." Kirsikka blushed deeply but didn't speak.

"Come and take the refreshment that has been prepared for you," said the Seer, motioning to a small table set with plates of brown cakes and cups of juniper berry wine. "It is a long way from the great hall where the singers dwell, even for riders."

Ulla bowed her head, and the girls came forward to the table. With the shutters open, the room was very bright and the golden Sampo shone like yellow flame.

"Have any more spies been found?" asked Siitsa. "We have asked for more news, but it seems that little comes to us from Laulavalaakso these days. Doubtless you are very busy. But goblins so near to Kyöpelinvuori, in the very heart of Tavastia, portends some evil this year, or so my heart tells me."

The young woman smiled at Ulla, but, as always, her tone was faintly mocking. One of the Karhulaiset, just like Ulla and Kirsikka, and only a few years older than the girls, she came from a wealthy merchant family in Keskimaa and not the poor villages of the north. All her folk had been slain by the Itäläiset, however. Held captive, Siitsa had suffered great torment at their hands ere the Swan Folk rescued her. She had come to Kyöpelinvuori five years ago and learned much from the Erilaiset, though she did not become a *tietäjää*. But she knew many songs and was skilled in the deep arts of enchantment and summoning.

For a long time now, she had dwelt at Kyöpelinvuori with the Seer. She greatly desired to be the Seer's apprentice, but she was too old. The witches on the haunted mountain had never chosen such a one, already grown to womanhood. And yet Mechtil still hoped to have Ulla as an apprentice, and the dark-haired girl from the Marches was also older than any apprentice had ever been before.

"There have been no more spies," answered Ulla. "Just the one. Väinämöinen searched for some time and made many spells but found nothing. He is worried, too, I think, but has told me no more."

"Such is his way," said the Seer. "The great singer can see many things, but is chary with what he shares, unless it be with the other Great Ones of the Erilaiset. And why not? He is wise beyond measure and his knowledge stretches back to the youngest of days. We are all indebted to the heroes of the Far Northern Land and, yet, we of the Seven Clans are a race apart, are we not?

"But come, Ulla. I will take counsel with Väinämöinen when next I see him, and together we will discuss what must be done for the good of all, Erilaiset and Kaamoslaiset alike. I wish to discuss your future now, as well you know. Tell me, child, what are your own plans? What will the one who bears the Mark of the Clan do now?"

The Seer came closer, leaning on her short black staff, but moving with no sign of age or infirmity. She smiled; Ulla saw her black teeth.

"Well, I don't know for sure, mistress," she said, her heart speeding up as the dreaded conversation began. "I will go where Väinämöinen goes, but I do not know what his plans are."

"It would seem there is much he does not discuss with you," said the Seer. "Yet I know well what you desire. You have great power within you, my child. And you are the chosen one of the prophecy of old. Why should you not join the greatest mages and make the hunt? Have you not asked this of Väinämöinen?"

Ulla sighed. "Yes, mistress, you know I have. But—but I am still too young. And there may be other reasons besides."

"Ah, yes. Indeed, Väinämöinen may have many reasons. He is very wise and subtle. But does that not tell you something? There are other paths appointed you, perhaps, paths that he knows or senses even if he stays silent. Twice have I offered the path of Kyöpelinvuori to you, Ulla; twice you have said no—or Väinämöinen has said no for you. Too young you may be for the Erilaiset, yet you will soon be a grown woman and a child no longer. I offer Kyöpelinvuori to you for a third time, but it will be the last time. For, when the seasons come round again, you will be too old to become my apprentice.

"For centuries have my mothers seen farthest of all in the Far Northern Land," said the Seer, going now to the Sampo and standing within its golden glow. "And so I foresaw the rise of Löhi and the need for the Seven Clans to unite again with the Erilaiset. The return of our folk to the Old Ways is as much my doing as Väinämöinen's. The crowns of Tavastia and Etelamaa turn to my looking glass for counsel, and the Lords of High and Deep Länsimaa acknowledge my *sight*. I have read the fortunes of many mighty lords and kings, giving them counsel in their times of need. And things are moving now in other places, even Akkala, things that only the power of Kyöpelinvuori can affect. You are of mortal race, Ulla; you bear the Mark of the Clan. You can become mighty among the Seers of old, mightiest of us all, perhaps; your strength may defeat even Löhi and send the Witch to sleep again, a sleep from which she will never, ever awaken."

Then the Seer walked about the round chamber, pointing to various beautiful and precious things among her hoard, telling Ulla their stories and of the deeds of her mothers. At last she came to a stand made of dark, polished wood. An embroidered cloth lay upon it, red with a hem of golden thread. The old woman lifted up the cloth with her bony hand, revealing a sparkling globe, the Seer's magic crystal ball, the looking glass of Kyöpelinvuori.

"Only the Seers of Kyöpelinvuori know the art of using the glass," she said. "And, with the glass, we may answer those questions the lords of the clans need answered. The power of Kyöpelinvuori is greater even than that of the Erilaiset, Ulla—at least for those of mortal race. And it may be the instrument of your revenge against the one who has destroyed your family and taken all those you loved from you. Look into the crystal ball with me so that I may read your fortune! And then together, perhaps, we may divine your fate and plot your future."

Ulla started at this, turning first to Kirsikka, then scanning both of the strange women in turn. The Seer, lips pursed in a thin smile beneath her sharp nose and glassy eyes, returned her gaze, but Siitsa finally broke the silence.

"Do you not yet understand that my mistress can read your heart and desire?" she said. "And why should you not desire revenge on those who wronged you? I, too, have seen all my folk torn from me. I would see those who did these things suffer in kind and Löhi thrown down in ruin. Consider well your choices, Ulla."

The crystal ball suddenly went dark; it seemed to beckon her as if from an impossible depth. A strange feeling took hold of Ulla, and, though she was yet a child, it seemed that thoughts and words came to her from another, unbidden. An image of the starry sky above the Enchanted Valley and the rowan trees of Mielikki's garden passed before her eyes.

"Kyöpelinvuori is indeed strong, mistress," she heard herself say, "and the magic glass is a great boon to the Kaamoslaiset. But all such strength ultimately comes from the Old Powers of this world, and the Vanhalaiset are the instruments of Ukko. Even Löhi does no more than pervert and twist this power for her own dark purpose. It is difficult to see what path I should take when that wisdom is still hidden even from Tapio's daughter, to whom the streams of wizardry flow through the very earth and waters of the Far Northern Land."

The moment passed. Ulla, herself again, blushed deep red as she stood before the Seer. Kirsikka kept her head down, staring at the half-eaten cakes on the wooden table. Siitsa made no sign, still smiling, but a look of displeasure flashed across the Seer's face. The old woman came close to Ulla and reached out to touch her long, dark hair.

"I can see you have wisdom of your own," said the crone, her voice as steady as ever. "And this is all the more reason for you to make your decision yourself and not be swayed by the counsel of others. I will say one thing, then speak no more about it. If you become my apprentice, all that you see will be yours. One day you shall surely have even more: power, respect, strength, and all the secrets that your heart desires. This is the prophecy of the Seer of Kyöpelinvuori.

"But go now and be of light heart. We shall always be friends, whatever the future may bring. I will soon go myself to Singing Valley to see the folk who have come to us this spring and to speak with Väinämöinen. Many things are moving now; we shall soon have fair guests. Perhaps we will speak of this again then."

Suddenly embarrassed, Ulla felt like a stupid child. She bowed her head and, not knowing what else to say, stammered, "Thank you, mistress." She quickly made her way to the door with Kirsikka in tow. A servant already waited in the open doorway to escort them. The girls went down the narrow stair as quickly as they dared, leaving the Seer and Siitsa in the turret chamber high above.

They mounted the shaggy ponies and set off down the path, but neither said a word until they traveled well down the hillside; they knew all too well that they could be seen from the tower.

"That is the *last* time I am going up there," said Kirsikka finally. "You can go by yourself next time—or with Väinämöinen."

"You didn't even say anything," replied Ulla. "What are you worried about? I am the one she wants to come live in the tower."

"Say anything?" exclaimed Kirsikka. "I couldn't breathe, let alone speak. I could barely move until the old woman told us to go, and then I felt like a cage had been opened and I was free to run again and talk and sing. I am never going up there again!"

The dark-haired girl rode silently for a while, but, as they came to the hillfoot and rode onto the path toward the Singing Valley, she turned to Kirsikka and said, "Well, if I became the Seer's apprentice, you'd have to come see me all the time. And soon enough, perhaps, I'd *be* the Seer and you could live there with me."

"You are not going to become her apprentice!" cried Kirsikka. "Surely you're not really thinking of it? How could you?"

"Well, no. But then again, why shouldn't I? I don't want to live with the Seer and leave the Valley, but what else can I do? Go back to Karelia with Mielikki? Väinämöinen won't let me make the hunt; he doesn't want me to be a singer. At least I would learn more, and . . . well, she's old, she's not Erilaisen. It can't be that long before she dies."

"Väinämöinen!" exclaimed Kirsikka. "He will *never* let you become the Seer's apprentice, so you might as well stop talking about it."

Ulla laughed. "Didn't you tell me just this morning that I should make him think so?"

But Kirsikka, red-faced, didn't reply. They rode the rest of the way in silence, listening to the sounds of spring about them, the birds calling one to another and the quiet buzz of life stirring anew in the green and golden fields of mighty Tavastia, the land of the Folk of the Hare.

✳✳✳

The girls came back to the gentle valley as the westering sun made long shadows creep from the trees along the ground. Kirisikka took the ponies to the stables on her way to the long hall, where she wished to sit beside the fire and sing. But Ulla, who often wished to be alone, walked slowly through the pine trees back to the *pirtti* they shared.

It grew cooler as evening came on. A light breeze moved the resinous branches and whispered about her, filling all the air with spring's fresh scent. Tiny midges and mayflies flitted about the pinecones and white blossoms; here and there a cuckoo's call or the trilled song of a woodjay broke the forest's calm. The girl with dark hair picked her way through mossy flats, balancing on grey rocks and skirting the stinging nettles that grew in the tangled brakes where the ground folded upward. At length she came to a trail of white stones, round and smooth, running below a low shelf and back to the *pirtti* with its rough walls and roof of turf.

About to go inside, Ulla heard a bleating in the trees just beyond and changed her path, walking behind the little cottage. In a small clearing, green with new grass, she saw four small brown goats and, with them, a tall woman dressed all in blue with hair the color of the golden sun at the high noon of a summer day.

"Unaja!" she cried. The woman saw her and smiled. Leaving the goats to graze in the grass, they sat down together beside the spring-course on a great, flat stone.

In the Singing Valley, folk called her Unaja the Golden because of the richness of her long, golden hair, surpassing that of even the princesses and noble ladies of Tavastia and Etelamaa. And she was tall beyond the measure of most women in the Far Northern Land, almost as tall as Väinämöinen or Ilkka the Warden. Unaja came from the northwest of Akkala, near the shores of the western sea, from the region once called Susila, the land of the Wolf Folk. All that people were tall and fair, with yellow hair and bright blue eyes.

But in the time of the Witch's War, there had been much fighting in the west. Löhi's armies invaded Susila, and fierce warriors from across the western sea raided the coasts. They burned and laid waste to Mannaka, the city of the Wolf Folk, and destroyed their ships. Then Löhi had taken all that land, enslaving the Susilaiset save those who fled south and sought refuge with the Kotkalaiset in Akkala. And Mannaka was deserted, and the ruins became the abode of ghosts and evil things. The last army of the Wolf Folk had fought in the van of the host of the Seven Clans at the Great Battle. Proud men and brave in combat, they drove against the ranks of the soldiers of Pohjola. But Löhi's sorcerers confused them and her servants attacked them, destroying them almost to a man.

And when the Witch was thrown down, the survivors returned to Susila but found no folk there; whether all were slain or taken to Pohjola or to the lands of the Itäläiset as slaves, none knew. So the Clan of the Wolf was then called the Lost Clan, and Susila was no more, and the remnant of the Susilaiset joined to the Folk of the Eagle. Centuries later, the descendants of the Susilaiset still dwelt in some few villages in northern Akkala, and they remembered their past and their legends.

Unaja was born in such a village by the shores of the sea, to fisher folk, weavers of nets. She had lived with the sound of breaking waves in her ears all her life. When she was twenty years old—or so they guessed, for who counted days among the mean folk of villages and towns?—she was betrothed to a young fisherman. They would marry in the spring, for she was already late to marry among her people. But the dreams of Mielikki came to her during the long winter nights, until she was troubled and found no peace. When spring came, she fled the village, leaving the young man and all her friends and family behind. She made the journey, dangerous for a maiden all alone, across the length of Akkala. At last, half-starved, she came to the tower she had seen in her mind's eye, the tower of Kyöpelinvuori. None in her village knew what became of her; they said she had gone mad and died alone in the wild.

So Unaja came to Kyöpelinvuori in that very first year after the Battle of Linnavuori. There she met Väinämöinen, and Ulla, too, as they returned from Deep Länsimaa with the others. Quick to learn and eager for knowledge, she was strong, especially in the mysterious spells of creation and command of the elements. She studied much with Väinämöinen and Turi. She was the first mortal woman to become a *tietäjää*. With Turi, she traveled north into Akkala where she hunted the grey wolves in the wild. Now, at times, Unaja wore a cape and cowl made from the wolf-fell of the beast she had slain. The golden-haired woman of the Wolf Folk, the Lost Clan of the north, became a powerful mage, but she did not leave the Singing Valley nor return to her home in Akkala. She lived in a simple *pirtti* near to Ulla and Kirsikka, watching over them as they grew.

Unaja put her bare feet into the icy water and shuddered. The sun slipped behind the trees, but its light still peeked at them through the branches and boughs.

"Where is your sister?" she asked Ulla, her accent so strange to the girl's ears that, even after many years, she often felt Unaja spoke a different tongue. Indeed, she mixed many words and odd phrases in her speech that Ulla could not understand.

"She took the ponies to the stables," answered Ulla. "And then went to the hall afterwards."

"You did not wish to go?"

"No, not really. Not after a day like this day."

Unaja nodded. "And how is the Seer?" she asked. "Did she ask what you expected?"

The girl sighed. "Yes, of course she did. She said the same thing that she has said before, and made the same offer. She spoke of the power of Kyöpelinvuori and of the looking glass, and of all that she might teach me and all that I might have when I become Seer. Siitsa was also there, and she, too, urged me to accept the offer."

"And what did you answer her?" asked Unaja.

"I didn't; not in so many words. She said we would speak again when she comes here. And she said I am almost too old and that this offer would be the last."

Unaja took her feet from the water and dried them with the hem of her blue cloak.

"Does this not make you happy, *tana*?" the woman said, using one of the words that Ulla had never heard from any other living soul. "Never have you wished to become the Seer's apprentice. Perhaps you need not refuse her ever again."

Ulla, silent, stared off through the trees as the light about them dimmed.

Unaja touched her hand, then gathered herself as if to stand up. "I'm sorry. I see that you wish to think on this and not discuss it. Let me leave you alone, then, and give you time to consider what you must."

"No!" said Ulla, stirring. "Please stay. It's not that. Really, I do not want to go to the tower and become like Siitsa. Or grow old in there, staring at that glass year after year."

Unaja laughed, a clear sound like cold water running down a fall. "What then do you want?"

"You know what I want, Unaja: to be a singer and a wizard like you. I asked Väinämöinen about it again this morning, but he still said nothing or, rather, the same thing: I am too young."

"Too young for the Erilaiset, too old for Kyöpelinvuori," said Unaja. "Here is a riddle to ponder."

"Won't you speak to him, Unaja? Please? He'll listen to you; you're one of the few he listens to."

The young woman laughed again. "Of that, I'm not so sure," she said. "Say rather that he *listens* to all, but follows his own heart. Who am I to say what lies within it? But Väinämöinen loves you as a father, Ulla. There is worse still to come in this war. He does not wish you to carry a burden even greater than the mark upon your shoulder. Be patient, my precious child! All will be made clear in time."

"Now you sound just like him," said Ulla.

"Then all the more reason to listen," smiled Unaja.

Ulla thought quietly for a while, then spoke again. "The Seer said something else. She said that with the magic of the looking glass, I might find those who hurt my family and take revenge on them."

The golden-haired woman's smile disappeared. "I see. And do you desire this? Revenge? It will not bring back those whom you love and have lost."

"The Easterners drove me from my folk," said Ulla slowly. "But that was long ago. Many battles have been fought since then. Those who came to Grankulta may be dead, probably are dead; I used to think they all died at Linnavuori. What hope would there be in searching for faceless men across the long miles anyway? But I thought—well, no one knows what happened to my family. Maybe they are still alive. Ilkka searched for them and so did Turi, but no one has ever found them . . . or my father and brother. You know the story of what happened. It was so long ago now. Unaja, maybe the looking glass of the Seer might find them or at least tell me what became of them! Maybe it could be so!" The girl spoke excitedly, with great passion, but Unaja's face was calm and sad.

"Powerful is the Seer," she said at last. "Oh, most of her magic may be weak. She is no healer or changer, but well she knows the arts of enchantment. Her *sight* is long, and she has the glass. She saw Tyë when you were a small child and I was alone in the wild. Perhaps the Seven Clans survived only because of what she told Väinämöinen. That is no small thing.

"But, Ulla, I do not think she can see so far as to glimpse what was or peer into Tuonela and beyond. They call her a fortune teller and so she wins renown. Mortals, who seek advantage over their enemies and friends alike, put their trust in her. I wonder if all that is due to the *sight* that her crystal ball gives, *sight* that can pierce night's shadow or the snows and clouds. Can she really see the future or divine that which people would know or seek? She may see much of the world that is, but she cannot look back into time itself. That, she cannot do."

Shadow grew all about them. Unaja suddenly stood up and put her hand on Ulla's head.

"Night is coming," she said. "My goats have strayed and I have yet to prepare my supper. Will you come with me or wait here for Kirsikka?"

"Go on," sighed Ulla. "I am too tired to do much and I'm not hungry."

"Very well," said the tall woman. "Rest and be at peace, *tana*. What will be, will be. But remember that you are loved by many and this will never change."

***

When Unaja had gone, Ulla sat a while by herself as the darkness fell and the air became chill. At last, she went inside the tiny *pirtii*. She took a lamp that sat just outside the door and sparked a flame with a single word, even as Väinämöinen did. "*Tuli.*" The lamp cast long shadows inside and filled the *pirtti's* single room with a yellow glow.

The small, timber-cornered cottage was simply furnished, little different than the cottages of the poor farmers and fishermen in High and Deep Länsimaa. Two low beds stood against opposite walls, near several wooden chests filled with clothes, furs, blankets, and everything else the girls possessed. A small table stood to one side of the stone hearth with two white birch stools; a bronze basin filled with water sat upon it. Cloaks and hats hung from pegs on the wall, with long skis and a birch broom leaning next them to them.

Ulla took off her cloak and set the lamp down on a little box beside her bed. The box held her most prized possessions, the figures of her brother and herself and the jewel she had taken from Tyë, now set in a silver pendant. She lay down without changing her clothes and watched the shadows play upon the roof while the cool air flowed in from the open window. There was no fire in the hearth, but Ulla didn't care. She knew Kirsikka would stay at the hall that night and Ulla liked the cold upon her skin. She lay very still for a long time, thinking of all she had seen and heard that day, then simply listening to the sounds of the woods outside the *pirtti*. She fell asleep like that and didn't awaken until the morning's light streamed in from the window.

She opened her eyes and ran her fingers through her tangled hair. Her mouth was dry, and she was very thirsty. She lay still for several moments, trying to summon the energy to rise, then finally popped up from under the blankets. Väinämöinen was sitting at the low table, staring out the window.

"It's about time; I was just about to wake you. The sun is already climbing and it looks to be a fine day, fine and warm. There's much to be done; aye, there is. And songs to be sung tonight beside the fire. Akka is reborn, and her rising brings all things again to their youth, greening the fields and meadows.

"I brought you sour milk and black bread, just as you like it. Eat, then, and let's be off."

Very surprised, Ulla stood up, rubbing the sleep from her eyes and peering at the old man sitting at the little table with his great boots and staff across his legs. He looked like a giant in the little cottage. A fire crackled and smoked in the hearth.

"I thought we weren't going to the fields for several days yet," said Ulla sleepily. "There's still snow on the ground and it's very muddy."

Väinämöinen's grey eyes, the eyes of an Erilainen, shone brightly. "So there is," he said. "But that shouldn't trouble a man of power—or a woman. And we have much to talk about, you and I, and little time to do it if we're to take the journey together that you have long wished for."

Ulla stood blinking in a shaft of yellow sun.

"King Egan has reached the Rantavesi and will come to Kyöpelinvuori in a few days' time. Important things will be discussed. But pack your bag and be ready, for, afterward, we will go up into the high woods of your homeland, you and I. And we will hunt *karhu* and bring her strength back with us for you to use for your folk all the days of your life."

Chapter Three

The King of the Folk of the Swan

Egan tossed back his blankets and let the room's chill air flow over him. Freezing, he soon began to shiver, but he didn't mind. Tired and sleepy, he would lie abed for most of the morning unless the cold woke him. At last he sat up and ran his hands through his thick, sandy hair. He could tell by the yellow light in the room that it was still early morning, but passing quickly. The young man jumped up and went to a silver basin filled with water beside his dressing table.

It was always cold in the old castle within the Keep of the kings of Etelamaa, and the chamber Egan had taken to be his own—the chamber of the king of the Swan Folk—was no exception. Richly appointed with woven rugs on its floor, well-made furniture of polished wood, and, above the soft bed, a great engraving of the Swan of the Etelalaiset, it held many other fine things made of silver or gold, set with garnets or amber. But it was a stone chamber and looked mostly to the north, while the small hearth gave off little warmth unless constantly tended. Now the embers scarcely glowed because Egan had ordered his servants not to enter the room while he slept or was alone. The fire often burned low, but the young king didn't care. He valued his privacy and silence more than a morning blaze. In fact, he often slept in the smaller chamber down the hallway, his childhood room and the place where he still felt most comfortable.

Egan washed his face and hands in the basin, then tried to comb out his tangled locks. He quickly put on the clothes laid out on the dressing table: white breeches, a long sky-blue tunic with embroidered hem, and a matching cloak clasped with silver at the shoulder. He slipped the breeches' loops over his feet and stepped into a pair of knee-high black leather boots, soft and supple. But he would meet many people today and confer with his counselors, so there was yet one thing missing.

An open casket stood on a great oaken table beside the half-shuttered window. Within the crimson folds of its crushed velvet lining rested a round filet set with a single pale amber stone. He took the filet and set it on his head, then looked at the fine wood carving on the wall beside the shutters: an image of his father.

Nigan, Lord of the House of Joutsen and King of the Folk of the Swan, had been struck down in the prime of his life by the Winter Plague borne on the wings of Lovêatar, Mistress of Disease. Not a day passed that Egan failed to think of his father. He felt Nigan's presence with him always, watching over him. Sometimes Nigan came to him in dreams and spoke with him, considering his options and counseling on the path he should take. Egan, wisely, never spoke of this to anyone save old Väinämöinen. Although the young king was popular throughout the kingdom, especially with his knights and men-at-arms, some still whispered against him and the clan's return to the Old Ways. They needed no more fuel for their gossip.

The young man had proven a worthy leader of his clan and, after Linnavuori, Egan never again doubted himself. He recaptured the confidence and precocity of his youth, tempered with loss and experience; and such is the path to wisdom. He felt lonely sometimes, for apart from his family, he had no friends such as before he became king, except perhaps Väinämöinen, Turi, and others of the Erilaiset. They seldom visited the Stone City, however. Egan saw them only when he rode north in the summer to the battles and raids along the Marches or when he went to the Singing Valley. The young king, filled with a sense of mission, devoted himself to saving his people and destroying Löhi. His purpose took the place of friends, perhaps, but his good nature and boyish sense of humor could never be suppressed for very long.

Egan adjusted the filet, then strapped a belt around his waist, girt with a straight, short sword—not the Sword of Legend that he used in battle, the sword that tamed the rebels of the coasts, but a light blade of burnished bronze. He opened the door, stepped into the chilly corridor, and stopped short.

A white-haired old man slumped in a chair beside the door, snoring softly. Old Orvo, Egan's manservant, despite his age and growing decrepitude, refused to retire to a house in the Green Vales or anywhere else he wished, but insisted on serving the royal family as he had done all his life. Egan smiled and shook his head. A heavy blanket lay on the floor beside a small copper of hot water; the king knew the old man had come early to his room to give him these things, as if he were still a child, and had fallen asleep while he waited. He spread the blanket over the old man and hurried through the castle's narrow passages, making his way down to the kitchens.

The servants bowed to their lord as he came in, then went back to their work. The cooks and scullery maids were used to Egan's presence since he often came to the kitchens and ate there with them, even as he had done as a child. Egan had known many servants in the household all his life and he had an easy, natural manner with them. Today he chatted with them while he took a light breakfast of honey-sweetened porridge and bread. Afterward, he went directly to the Great Hall.

The Hall of the Swan was unchanged from his father's time, even if Egan himself was not. The slender young man was deceptively strong for his size. Hours spent handling the long sword of Lemminkäinen had built muscle on his arms. Egan's sandy hair had grown darker, perhaps, and a thin brown beard outlined his face, but his bright eyes remained the same, sea-blue and sparkling. His wit and intellect shone through for all to see.

In the bright sunlight, the white vaulted ceiling of the Great Hall seemed a canopy of cloud. The young king walked across the colored flagstones toward a group of men already gathered near the dais, a breakfast set out before them upon a table. The men bowed, and Egan greeted each in turn.

Toiva Merikainen was there, the chief of his household counselors, and Sinio. A young man, not much older than Egan, stood with them—Kolkka of Palojärvi, a wizard and singer, chief of the *tietäjää* of Etelamaa. Juvari, Egan's captain, was there, too, and beside him the Captain of the Wardens of Etelamaa and an older man, richly dressed in fine clothes of blue and green, with a square white beard and clean-shaven lip, leaning on a polished stick with a knob of gold. This was Isku, none other than the Master of the Shipwrights' Guild, just arrived from Langvika in far-off Akkala where the Guild's chief shipworks lay. The Guild, like a clan unto itself, carried much of the trade of the three great southern kingdoms on its ships, protected by its war galleys. The Shipwrights had grown rich beyond the measure of all others in the Far Northern Land.

The Etelalaiset had been waiting for Isku and the message he bore from Airiki, King of the Eagle Folk of Akkala. The master had not waited for the frozen waters of the Itämeri Sea to open, but journeyed far across the snowy fields and ice to reach the Stone City as quickly as possible. Several assistants came with him, as well as the Shipmaster of Etelamaa, the master's chief agent in the City.

"Welcome, Master Isku," said Egan. "And welcome, all of you. It is an honor to have you again in this Hall. It has been many years, I believe, since last you were here among us."

"Many indeed," said Isku in the thick accent of the Tavastialaiset. "I last journeyed here seven years ago at Sunwelcome, when your father was still king, in the very year that troubles beset the Far Northern Land again. I thank you for your welcome, king of the Swan Folk. You have done well, by all accounts. Your sword is sharp and you have won renown in the battles of the North Marches. You have kept the peace among your own folk unchallenged, which few thought to see. That is no small feat. Strife is ever the enemy of prosperity, especially in these evil times."

"Strife brought you to the Stone City then—the Witch's strife, though we knew it not," replied Egan. "And Etelamaa has been at war ever since. But now that same evil compels your return, does it not?"

"Evil and dark magic," said the master. "And war besides. Last summer was the worst yet. There is mischief on the other shore of the Itämeri Sea; our trade is sorely disrupted, as you know. Many ships have been attacked, and, some weeks before *Kekri*, raiders attacked a long galley from Langvika. They sank it near the Thousand Isles. The officers and crew who manned that hundred-oared ship now rot in a watery grave in Ahtola and wait for the world to be renewed. But these troubles alone do not bring me to Etelamaa, dragged behind a sled in winter's darkness rather than sailing over the open waters. There is a new king in Akkala, a strong king. He has put down those who opposed him, and only in the northern woods of Mäntymetsä do any still deny his claim; they are weak and unimportant. Airiki rules now in Langvika as king of the Clan of the Eagle. He bade me come to you with a message."

The Swan Folk looked at one another with wonder, but Sinio spoke first.

"Of these things, much is already known to us," he said, though, in truth, little news came to the City from Akkala. "But what message does Airiki send? And what dark magic afflicts you? More than the raids of pirates or strife with the Vartilaiset who live across the Sea? Two years ago, warriors from the Vartilaisen clans came up the narrows of Etelajärvi and assailed our forts. The king defeated them while Juvari was on the Marches in High Länsimaa. What else is it that afflicts you, then, in Akkala?"

"The dark magic that afflicts us and Airiki's message are entwined," answered Isku. "There have been reports for some time of strangers along the border marches of Akkala—strange men of strange race, perhaps even the Easterners who assault High Länsimaa. And other things, darker things, twisted and grotesque to mortal eyes. They are spies, it seems, searching the approaches to Akkala."

"The Bear Folk reported such things before the Witch attacked them," said Egan.

"I do not know," said Isku. "But, most importantly, there is this. Even as Airiki put down the last of his rivals, a terrible thing appeared in Langvika and other towns nearby. Winter came early, and with it a black shadow on the north wind. A wizened old crone appeared on the streets and wharfs, her ghastly cries echoing in the long hours of the night. Folk who heard these cries grew ill, and many of those have died; there is pestilence, despite the cold, along the shores of the Sea."

"Lovêatar!" cried Toiva. "Tuone's daughter! The Witch of the North released her into the world again. She has spread sickness and death from Etelamaa to the North Marches, including the Winter Plague that killed Nigan and many others."

"So I was told, though few believed it then," said the master. "But, indeed, that name fits this foul ghost. The Eagle Folk are sore afraid. It seems the troubles of the other clans have come even to Akkala."

A silence fell then and, in that space, Egan strode to the dais and took the throne of Etelamaa.

"I am sorry to hear these tidings," said the king, "though it was only a matter of time before Löhi turned her gaze upon Akkala. The Witch desires the ruin of all the Seven Clans and to rule over all the Far Northern Land, even as she rules in Pohjola. So what then, Master Isku, is the message of King Airiki to the king of the Folk of the Swan?"

Isku hesitated a moment, surprised by Egan's lordly manner and speech.

"Just this, Your Majesty," he said slowly. "He desires to speak with you and with Asikkas of Tavastia as well. He deems that you may know more of these things than he, and he would take counsel with the other great clans of the south in this season of doubt and distress." Several of the Swan Folk began to murmur and whisper, but Egan held up his hand.

"I have sent word before to Akkala that the union of all the Seven Clans is the surest means to save our lands," said Egan. "But there has never been an answer. Has the shadow of Lovêatar at last convinced the Eagle Folk that Löhi's threat is real?"

"I can only say that Airiki was not king then," answered Isku. "I am not his counselor that I may speak for him. I am responsible for the affairs of the Guild, affairs that have made the Seven Clans rich and kept peace among them at times. But I will venture to say this—the Seer of Kyöpelinvuori aided Airiki in his victory; it is said that Torvald, who last ruled in Langvika, lost the Seer's favor. It may be that she has counseled the king in this, for it is known the Erilaiset now dwell at Kyöpelinvuori and that the Seer has embraced their religion."

Egan smiled. "Not only the Seer," said the king. "All the clans save the Eagle Folk have returned to the Old Ways, as well you know. The songs give us hope against our great enemy."

"Indeed, the only real hope," said Kolkaa in a deep voice, resonant with power. "The prophecy of old tells us many things: that Löhi shall return a final time, but also that the child who bears the Mark of the Clan shall be a sign for all the Kaamoslaiset that the Witch may be resisted. It tells that, if the songs and rites of the Vanhalaiset who made our lands are heard again throughout the Seven Lands, Löhi's storm shall pass. She will slowly fade and we may again be at peace."

The master opened his mouth as if to speak, but hesitated, then remained silent.

"The Old Ways of the Seven Clans are proscribed in Akkala," Egan said at last, "And the Erilaiset, or anyone who works magic, are outlaw. Are the Kotkalaiset ready at last to listen to the songs again?"

Isku looked hard at Egan. "That I cannot say, Your Majesty," he said. "I am only a messenger in this matter. The message of Airiki remains the same: he would meet with you. The same message has gone to Asikkas of Tavastia. I will stay in Etelamaa, attending to interests of the Guild, until the seas are open. Then I shall sail to Langvika. If you wish, I will bear a message to the king of Akkala."

The young king rose from the black throne, standing before the master and his men. He put his hand on the older man's shoulder and smiled.

"Very well, Master Isku," he said. "The Swan Folk thank you for your journey and your help. As ever, you are welcome in the Stone City, and I hope to see you many times ere you sail. You arrived only yesterday; go now to your fair house and rest. I will consider these things with my counselors. We shall speak again soon, you and I."

Isku slowly bent his head, a curious expression on his face, and said, "Very good, Your Majesty; we will do that." Then, taking up his polished stick and motioning to his men and the shipmaster, he left the Hall of the Swan as the bright light streamed down around them.

The king and his chief counselors retired to a smaller chamber to debate the message and what it might mean. Egan was excited and flushed. His youth often worked against him, so he practiced and considered his manner and speech with other men to lessen their advantage and gain what he might for his people. And Sinio had cautioned him about his dealings with the Mariners, for the Master of the Shipwrights' Guild was a sober man of reason, always calculating. Certainly, he had come to Etelamaa not only as a messenger but also to take the measure of the young king and the strength of the Swan Folk.

"How did I do, Sinio?" asked Egan in his easy way, for he had known these men since childhood and felt no awe of them. Sinio smiled.

"Quite well, as always, Your Majesty. The master is unsure what to make of you, and this is wise. Let his counsels be unsure while ours are clear."

"But now we must make our counsels clear," said Toiva. "If this Airiki has indeed put down his rivals and is willing to enter into league with us, it may be a powerful stroke in our favor. But we must know what cost there may be for his friendship. Alliance with Akkala has always come with a price."

They discussed their plans thoroughly, since it would soon be full spring and they had no time to waste. Egan had intended to travel with his knights to the Tavastian border to meet Asikkas and perhaps Väinämöinen and other Erilaiset. Afterwards, he had planned to go north with the main army of the Swan Folk, grown to well over a thousand men, into High Länsimaa to await Löhi's assault.

Each year, save one, since that first raid along the North Marches, the Witch had sent Easterners and goblins into High Länsimaa to burn and pillage. Many battles had been fought about the Marches, and as far south as Lake Suurijärvi had become a contested land, half-deserted by the Bear Folk. The men of Tavastia and Etelamaa had held the line, however. Löhi had never regained Keskimaa or threatened the southern lands since Työ's defeat.

But Airiki's message changed these calculations and could not be ignored. The Eagle Folk, a great and warlike people, largest and strongest of the Seven Clans, sailed far, both raiding and trafficking. They had little fear for their own homelands. If they joined with the other clans, the union of the Kaamoslaiset would be complete. Then the folk of the Far Northern Land could truly hope that they would weather Löhi's assault and outlast her new dominion, for though she had done much evil, her minions and servants had failed to break the clans, and it seemed the Witch did not have the same power as in the days of Lemminkäinen.

So now Egan decided to go first to Tavastia, seeking the counsel of Asikkas, the Seer and the Erilaiset at Kyöpelinvuori. And if it seemed good to them, an embassy would be made to Langvika so that Egan could meet with Airiki, King of the Eagle Folk. But Juvari and the main part of the Army of Etelamaa would march to Keskimaa as planned, in preparation for the long days of summer and Löhi's assault.

Some strength of men-at-arms would remain near the Stone City to challenge any force of the Vartilaiset that might come up the narrows between the Sea and Lake Eteläjarvi. Messengers soon came from Asikkas in Tavastia with this very counsel, so Egan hastened to prepare all that was needed. Even as the ice melted upon Ahti's waters and the fishermen and traders readied their vessels, large and small, for the open waves and grey billows of the sea in early springtime, the king made ready to leave the City of Etelamaa.

The night before his departure, Egan went to Vendla's chamber in the old castle. The queen of the Swan Folk had been distraught over her husband's death and fallen into a black gloom for many months afterward. She removed to her own family's ancestral lands near Poronlinna for a time, but the very next winter her own father, Egan's grandfather, had died as well. Then a change took place within her heart and soul.

She returned to the Stone City, focusing her energies on her younger son and her daughter, Eglano and Marjatta. Some whispered that she had been visited by an Erilainen, perhaps even Mielikki herself. Vendla feared for Egan when he rode to war, as any mother fears for a child in danger. She was proud of her son, however, and not once did she doubt his judgment or high destiny.

Egan found Vendla with her daughter and handmaids, weaving at a fine loom. He paused and watched her for a moment. Her face was more careworn, her blonde hair streaked with more grey, and sadness still wrapped itself around her. When she looked up and smiled at him, the young king's thoughts fled far away; he saw only the beautiful woman he had known all his life.

"So you did not forget your mother after all," she said, still smiling. "Is everything prepared?"

"Almost everything," he answered, sitting beside her. "Lord Kalevi will command the City while I am gone. Toiva is with him. And Kolkka will see that the spring songs are rightly done throughout the kingdom, and Akka and Ilmatar remembered."

"And will you still go first to Kyöpelinvuori?" asked Vendla.

"I believe so," answered Egan. "We will meet Asikkas of Tavastia along the border first, but afterwards, yes, we will go to Kyöpelinvuori."

"Your brother awaits you in Kotanrannta. Are you still resolved to take him with you?"

Egan dreaded this part—for Eglano was now a full-grown man and eager to try his skill at arms in the battles along the Marches with Löhi. Egan knew his mother must be doubly worried, even though she had kept her voice steady and even.

"Eglano has come of age, Mother," said the king. "I cannot keep him at home when duty calls. But do not worry. I will watch over him and keep him near."

"Ever duty calls men to war," said Vendla. "And ever the lot of women is to wait and wonder. Which is the harder task? But what must be, will be. It is useless to try and trick fate. I know my sons will overcome any obstacle. I will wait here, watching the sun dance with the water of the bay and listening all the while for your return."

The room fell silent save the women working at the loom. Then Vendla spoke again.

"It is a shame that you leave so early this year," said the queen. "Aura, Lord Tyssi's granddaughter, is coming to the City this spring with many other ladies as well. Sinio would see you make a fine match before the year is out."

"Aura is very beautiful," said Marjatta, pushing aside a strand of pale blonde hair that escaped her veil. "I met her last year in Etelarannta. Her skin is white as snow and flawless, and her lips are very red."

Egan rolled his eyes and shook his head. Sinio had indeed urged him to marry soon and produce an heir. The granddaughter of one of the lords of the coast would make a good match and strengthen his position, but he had little thought for such things while his people remained in danger. He reached down and stroked the fur of the shaggy dog that lay at Marjatta's feet.

"The Witch will not wait idly by while I tarry to meet Aura or any other girl," he said. "This year is perhaps the most important of all. We must be ready to help our kinsfolk and meet a great assault."

"And yet it is still a shame," said Vendla. "I was already married when I was your age, and you were born not long thereafter. The river of life flows swiftly. Who knows what tomorrow brings?" Egan put his hand on her head, and she smiled again.

"It will bring no evil, only joy," he said. He did not speak again, but sat there beside the women as they wove the weft through the warp and back again, as women of the far north have always done.

***

The tall black horses stamped and steamed in the crisp morning air just outside the City's first gate. Thirty knights waited in formation beside a few servants and retainers, with Egan before them all. Sinio would ride on his left, and Juvari and the captain of the knights, Garin, on his right. With a smile on his face and a quick glance back at the stone gateway, Egan slapped his horse's rump. They set off down the Kingsway.

They rode slowly at first, since they found snow on the ground in some places and muddy slush in others. Yet the horses, swift and strong, shod with iron, the best steeds in the Far Northern Land, steadily made their way north. The king's party stopped at Nummela for two days, saddle-sore and weary. They met with a few nobles from the surrounding countryside, but soon set off again, striking the northern way through the heart of Etelamaa.

Now they rode through rich, fertile land with well-tended fields and well-ordered villages inhabited by hardy, prosperous folk. Dikes, ditches, and hedgerows marked the farmlands' borders. The villagers grew barley and rye in the summer, oats in the fall, and turnips, cabbages, and greens in springtime. Orchards of apple trees and other fruit sprang up beside the berry bushes. The people of those parts also raised many animals: horses, cattle, shaggy goats, swine, and great flocks of sheep.

That part of the kingdom had suffered less from the pestilence than others. It had changed little from Nigan's time, though there were fewer young men about. Many had joined the Army of Etelamaa and already gone to their musters, or else had done so in years past but never returned.

Egan had been born in the City and spent much of his life along the shores of Lake Eteläjarvi or among the Green Vales, but he loved the rich farmlands of the plain best of all. It made him proud now to ride through them as king, to see and hear the village folk call out to him as he passed by. They made a delightful sight dressed in the colors of their hamlets and districts, the men in their belted tunics and the women and girls with hemmed skirts and blue veils decorated with bronze and silver chains.

Indeed, as they approached Kotanrannta, Egan found himself wishing that he might stay there for the summer, with his mother and sister soon to join him as they had in his childhood. But such was not his fate, and well he knew it.

Kotanrannta, the great Duchy of Etelamaa, lay on the northern end of the farmlands beside a clear river and its several tributaries. An ancient settlement, like the Stone City it had an old castle within its walls. The walls here were wooden, though, and the castle little more than a great, round tower. Kotanrannta had been fashioned more like Keskimaa than the fortress-ports of the Stone City or Langvika. But many fine houses and beautiful buildings graced its streets, and Kotanrannta's people were much more prosperous than the Bear Folk in Keskimaa.

Eglano waited for Egan outside the city on a rise overlooking the river. Their cousin Aldon waited with him, for Alder, Egan's uncle, had died some years before after a long illness and Aldon had become lord. Aldon had changed when his father died, even as Egan had. He grew silent, even somewhat grim, but had proven himself in battle along the Marches several times. No childhood jealousy or rivalry remained between him and the king. But Eglano was now the Grand Duke of Etelamaa, as the king's only brother, and by tradition the Duchy of Kotanrannta would one day become his.

Egan rode to the hillock with Juvari and Sinio, meeting his brother and cousin at the top. Eglano, taller than Egan with darker, chestnut-brown hair, more closely resembled Aldon in some ways, with his long hair, straight features, and full beard. But when he smiled, it was with the same smile they had both inherited from their mother, and his rich laugh and voice could have been Egan's own.

"It took you long enough," said Eglano. "Your herald arrived days ago. You haven't exactly hurried, have you?"

"I have bad news," said Egan with a sigh. "I bring our mother's greetings, but also a promise: she made me swear an oath that I'd leave you in Kotanrannta where you'll be safe. I was afraid to bring such bad tidings, but I know you'll understand. After all, a promise is a promise."

A look of shock and disbelief crossed Eglano's face, but Egan burst out laughing. The other men laughed, too. Eglano shook his head, but grinned.

"Well, brother, you could chain me up, I suppose, or throw me in the tower; but I'd still find a way to ride after you just the same."

"Indeed," said the king. "And how are things in Kotanrannta, Aldon?"

Aldon looked over his shoulder at the sprawling town below, tucked within the river's bend.

"All is fair, cousin," he answered. "There was Plague to the west this winter, but it soon burned out. The farmers are about their fields digging rocks and ditches, and beasts are stirring. The men-at-arms are mustered to the north, and all is ready. Only the singers wait to make the spring songs calling on Akka to bless the land. Will you wait for them before setting out?"

"No," replied the king. "I'm afraid we can't. Asikkas awaits us and then Kyöpelinvuori. It looks to be a busy year with little time to spare."

"There is important news from Akkala, my lords," said Sinio. "But it can wait until we reach your halls."

"All is prepared," replied Aldon.

"Then let's ride to them now and end this leg of the journey," said Egan. "I like riding, but it takes time each spring to grow used to long days on horseback. I can barely walk or bend my legs. We had to lift Sinio onto his horse this morning. Three days we have to rest in Kotanrannta, but no more, so let us go!"

They rejoined the knights and servants, riding swiftly to the town, where they rested three days as Egan had planned. As he could not avoid it, the king held a feast in Aldon's hall for the nobles, merchants, and fine craftsmen who lived nearby, with his aunt and cousins from the Green Vales joining him at the high table. But on the fourth day, they set out with Eglano and Aldon riding beside the king at the front of the line.

At first they travelled through land much like the farmland south of Kotanrannta. Field after field, dike after dike, they passed homesteads and little villages where folk were already hard at work in the muddy earth. Soon the land changed, however. The tilled fields failed, and stands of white birch and other trees pressed against the road. Streams and brooks frequently crossed the winding path as the land grew wilder and less tamed. They soon came to parts where few men dwelled.

Finally they reached a place where the ground rose before slipping again into a wide-bottomed dell. To the north they could descry the first, easy slopes of the Wall of the Giants. The road ran on toward the gap of the *lansikita* and other, smaller passes into High Länsimaa. But they turned west and took a trade road that rambled through a district of short grasses and green brush until they suddenly struck the Rantavesi, the river marking the boundary between Etelamaa and Tavastia.

Messengers from Asikkas met them on the road, for the king of the Hare Folk awaited them at a manor some miles from the river. The manor and village were called Pikku Niittuset, the Little Meadows, because of the fair, grassy fields nearby where flocks of sheep grazed. The king's party rode over a sturdy wooden bridge and so, at last, came to Pikku Niituset even as night began to fall.

Asikkas greeted Egan warmly, for the two clan chiefs had met many times since the Battle of Linnavuori and Löhi's return. The Tavastian lord and his nobles had been wary at first of Väinämöinen and the Erilaiset, but the Seer urged them to listen to the old singer's counsels. The attacks of the Itäläiset and reports of the March Wardens, many of whom were Tavstialaisen, dispelled their doubts.

Asikkas had proven a loyal ally, and the strength of the Tavastialaiset helped stem the black tide of Löhi's servants, succoring the folk of the Seven Clans. Slowly the Hare Folk returned to the Old Ways, coming to trust Väinämöinen and his friends. Ulla played a vital role in these matters, for the girl with the Mark of the Clan on her shoulder amazed Asikkas. He believed in her sign, and his wife, who had many dreams about Ulla's portent, urged her husband to take Mielikki's words to heart.

Older than Egan, Asikkas had a similar build,—though, unlike the young king, his brown beard grew thick and curly while he was quite bald on top. His face was scarred by pox-marks from childhood illness, but his dark eyes glistened while he spoke with Egan about Airiki and the surprising message from Akkala. Bergil, Lord Captain of the March Wardens, rode with him, and the Warden had recently returned from Langvika bearing the same tidings.

Asikkas took the news warily, mindful of the strife and conflict between Tavastia and Akkala in the recent past. The Eagle Folk had scorned the Tavastialaiset when they welcomed the heroes back into their homeland. But now the two kings agreed to seek the counsel of Väinämöinen and the Seer. Indeed, they had many other things to consider, matters of war and of battle, since Löhi would surely attack in the summer.

They stayed one day at Pikku Niittuset, resting from their journeys, then moved on. They now made a great party, arrayed in many fine colors, for Asikkas brought a large guard of cavalry with him and Bergil rode with a company of twelve Wardens. They rode into the Neck of Tavastia, sending swift messengers before them to Kyöpelinvuori to herald their coming.

The last snows melted, even in the woods and dark places, while birdsong and cries filled the air. It seemed to Egan that the spring's promise was brighter than for many years. The fear and disquiet that had troubled his heart—all mortal hearts—since Löhi's return somehow felt lessened.

The sun shone in a clear blue sky and the green meadows glowed. Egan and Asikkas splashed across a little stream and saw the hill of Kyöpelinvuori in the distance. Messengers soon arrived to guide them, not toward the tower, but to the Singing Valley where a great pavilion had been pitched and many folk gathered. All the people from many miles around had come to celebrate *hela*, the Spring Festival, and to hear the Erilaiset sing and bless the land. The pavilion, painted part red-and-white for the Clan of the Hare and part blue-and-white for the Clan of the Swan, was set in a fair field near the wooden hall where the great fire burned.

Väinämöinen came to greet them, his long white beard forked and twined with golden thread, dressed in a long red tunic trimmed with gold and green, and wearing a flowing crimson Karelian cloak clasped at his shoulder. Indeed, dressed in such fine clothes of rich color, he looked every bit like a mighty hero of old legends brought back to life. Unaja came with him, and Ulla, Kirsikka, and several Erilaiset.

"Welcome, my lords, to Laulavalaakso!" he cried. "Too long has it been since you graced our presence! It will now be doubly joyous to celebrate spring's return to the Far Northern Land, for never have two clan chiefs been with us and many others besides." The old wizard bowed deeply.

"Well met, Lord Väinämöinen," answered Asikkas. "You have been absent from Tapiola for too long—you are missed. But perhaps that may be amended in the coming year."

"Perhaps it may be," said Väinämöinen. "And yet, my lord, I think we must do other deeds ere the year is out."

"No doubt we must!" exclaimed Egan. The young king's joy at seeing the old singer again could not be contained. "But, for all that, I feel there is a change in the air. This year will bring good things to the Seven Clans."

Väinämöinen turned, motioning to Ulla and Kirsikka, and the two girls stepped forward bearing bouquets of flowers wrapped about with holly and red berries to the kings. Both were clothed in festive dresses, their hair braided and covered with gossamer veils after the fashion of the Hare Folk. Ulla's dress was no less beautiful nor her dark hair less fair than Kirsikka's, for Väinämöinen had prevailed upon her to put aside her plain Karelian things, at least for this occasion. The old man watched approvingly—after all, he loved such pomp and ceremony—as Kirsikka gave her bouquet to Asikkas and Ulla, self-conscious, handed her flowers to Egan.

The king had not seen Ulla for almost two years, and she looked very different now—tall and stern for one so young, but with the same fair skin, sparkling hazel-green eyes, and freckles dotting her nose and cheeks.

"Surely this isn't little Ulla, my sparring partner!" he cried. "I would have taken you for an Erilaisen princess from Karelia with those eyes if Väinämöinen hadn't given you away just now. I'm very glad to see you!"

Ulla broke into a wide smile despite herself and blushed beet red, causing Egan to laugh. "Thank you, Eg—Your Majesty," she replied, still smiling. "It's quite nice to see you as well. I trust your mother and sister are well."

"Very well," said Egan. "And they send their greetings to you and to this other princess with the flowing red locks."

Kirsikka beamed. "Why, that's so kind of them," she said. "I was just telling Ulla the other day how nice it would be to go to the Stone City again and then we were remembering the time when Marjatta came to our chamber that morning—the morning of her birthday celebration—and all those little boats had set sail below the Keep, and—"

Väinämöinen cut her off, shaking his head and noisily clearing his throat. "There will be time for reminiscing later, perhaps. Now let our guests refresh themselves in the lodgings prepared for them, while we tend to their tired beasts, too. Tonight we will feast and celebrate the spring together."

Asikkas and the others were shown to the tents pitched especially for them nearby, but the old wizard took Egan to the small *pirtti* where he had stayed before. They spoke together as they moved through the trees. Väinämöinen was anxious to learn more about the messages from Akkala.

"You look well, Egan," said the old man, putting his hand on the king's shoulder while they walked. "And all I have heard from Etelamaa seems good. You have proved a wise chief, even as I said you would. The Sword is indeed in the hand that was meant to hold it."

"I have done my best," said Egan. "But I have missed you and your counsel. The miles are long between the City and the Valley, and I don't have the *sight* of the Erilaiset to keep in touch with old friends."

Väinämöinen laughed. "One can't have everything!—though perhaps the smiths may again learn the art of crafting looking glasses. I could use one myself. I can see little north of the Marches and, when Ulla has tried out that jewel of hers, it falters beyond the Wall and goes dark. But tell me; what is this message that you and Asikkas bear and how did it come to you?"

"You haven't heard?" asked Egan.

"Only what your messenger told us," said Väinämöinen, "that this new king, Airiki, wishes to see you."

"Do you know him?"

"Airiki? How could I? I haven't been to Akkala in two hundred years, give or take a few dozen. They might cut off my beard, or worse, if they caught me there! No, I heard of him for the first time only last year. There was strife again among the Eagle Folk, and several lords claimed the crown—all too common in Akkala where the Vanhalaiset are dishonored!"

Then Egan told Väinämöinen about Isku's journey and the message from Airiki: that the king of the Eagle Folk, the Kotkalaiset, wished to take counsel with the other clans and that Lovêatar was awake in the southwest spreading sickness and despair. The mage was surprised, for, of all the clans, the Eagle Folk were the most warlike and proud, and they had long scorned the heroes and the Old Ways. He had thought perhaps that Löhi would spare them, waiting until all the other clans were subdued before turning on Akkala at the last. But he said no more, for they would hold council later to consider what their next steps might be.

As a gentle evening descended upon the little valley and a cool, pleasant breeze moved the birches' green tops, all the folk gathered near the long hall for the feast. The Seer arrived with Siitsa and others of the Tornilaiset. Asikkas, Egan, and all of their party dined within the fair pavilion, along with Väinämöinen and the Erilaiset. A great meal was set before them: white bread of the Erilaiset, baked by Kappi the Menninkainen; sweet cakes made with honey and cream; mutton and pork; and pickled foods from the past year's bounty.

Berries grew in a thicket all year round since the enchantment of Väinämöinen was upon it. They feasted on those as well, with sweet, white mead and beer to drink. Colored lamps of the Erilaiset, blue and white and green, swayed from the tree limbs as the wind blew from the south and bright stars twinkled overhead. Such a feast had not been held there in all the time that mortals from the Seven Clans had sought Laulavalaakso.

When the royal parties had finished feasting, they came out of the pavilion. Many folk gathered about; farmers and peasant families from the lands close by played music, singing merry songs beneath the night sky. Väinämöinen went into the hall with the two kings and their chief counselors; the Seer and Siitsa went with them. The long, low hall, built after the fashion of the Reindeer Folk in Karelia, glowed with yellow light from many candles. Fresh green rushes covered the earthen floor. Unadorned save for a few benches and stools, the hall held one long table set with bronze vessels filled with water or cool mead.

At one end of the hall, a bright red fire, constantly tended and never extinguished, burned in a great firepit with a chimney of stone and clay. Wizards looked within that fire for their knowledge and deep patterns. Before its sullen glow they instructed their mortal charges, chanted songs, and wove magic spells. Ulla had learned many things in the smoky hall.

When they all had seats, Asikkas and Egan spoke of Airiki's message and how best to respond. But it seemed the Seer already had knowledge of these things, more so than Väinämöinen.

"Airiki is strong and clever, unlike Torvald who came before him," she said. "It remains to be seen if he is wise as well. Wisdom and strength are not always mixed in equal measure."

"Have you met him?" asked Asikkas.

"Only once," said the Seer. "He came here long ago with his father, before Löhi troubled us. He was very young. His father put many questions to me about the politics of Akkala and the great raids he planned against the folk who dwell on the southern shores of the Itämeri Sea. Since then I have exchanged messages and counsels with Airiki in other ways." Despite the Seer's soft, measured voice, her eyes shone, reflecting the pit's fiery glow.

"It would have been well if you told me this before," said Väinämöinen.

"Many folk look to Kyöpelinvuori for wisdom and counsel, Lord Väinämöinen. Some require discretion. I have been careful in my dealings with Airiki. Patience was needed; I did not wish to put him off with ready pressure. But, indeed, I recommended this course to him. And this is what I told him: long will be your rule in Langvika, fertile your fields, and gold shall flow through your hands if you join your power to that of the other clans; but all is dark and doubtful if Akkala stands alone. This is the prophecy of Kyöpelinvuori."

The fire crackled and smoked in silence for a while, then Egan spoke. "So this message and invitation are his response? The Kotkalaiset are the largest clan of the Far Northern Land. Their aid would be a boon beyond hope. But even if we can trust Airiki, can we trust his people, his nobles?"

"That is my question, too," said Valso, one of Asikkas's counselors. "The Kotkalaiset are a great folk, you say, yet they are divided among many home-lands. It has not yet been a year since Airiki took up his rule in Langvika. How strong is he? Can we trust that he speaks for all his people, or do we risk becoming entangled in Akkala's strife even as we face the Witch along the North Marches?"

"A fair question," said Väinämöinen. "And I would add to it. The swords and axes of the Kotkalaiset would be a heavy stroke against the Witch, and I deem she fears it. For all of the Seven Clans would again be united against her, and thus was she defeated in the days of Lemminkäinen. But we also know that not swords alone will turn Löhi aside. Will Airiki return his folk to the Old Ways? Or does he offer only aid in battle?"

"Magic and sorcery are proscribed in Akkala," said Sinio. "The Erilaiset are outlaw in that land and have been for many lives of men. Can Airiki change this after so long?"

"I will not ally to any clan that persecutes the Erilaiset," said Egan.

"Yet their strength is not to be lightly refused," said Asikkas. "What say you, Lord Väinämöinen? Can you convince the Eagle Folk to take up the Old Ways of the Vanhalaiset, which you and your kin have brought back to the Seven Lands?"

The old man walked close to the fire, putting his foot up on the hearth's edge and staring into the flickering flames while shadows played upon the walls.

"Who can say? But I shall certainly try, if Airiki suffers my presence."

"He will," said the Seer. "One of the Tornilaiset has been in Akkala. He reached his mind out to Siitsa and, just last night, gave her this very message." The old crone motioned to Siitsa.

The thin young woman robed in black bent her head and spoke. "This is what I heard from afar, my lords. I heard that Väinämöinen or others of the race of heroes, the Erilaiset, may enter that land without fear, for he wishes to speak with them. There was no more, but it seems hopeful, as far as it goes."

"There is indeed hope," said the Seer. "Hope, but no certainty. I have done all within my power to set the stage, but it must be for others to finish. You may indeed enter Akkala, Lord Väinämöinen, yet I cannot see what the Kotkalaiset will do in the end. But if you would have my advice, I would say to go to Airiki in Langvika. Then his chieftains and followers may hear this message, too. And Ulla must go with you, for the words of the prophecy and rumor of the girl have been heard even in Langvika. She is the best proof that our chosen path is the right one."

Väinämöinen, still staring at the fire, felt the Seer's gaze upon him and turned toward her. Her eyes looked straight into his as she continued. "And it may be that Ulla will make certain choices soon, which will lend even more weight to our counsels."

The old wizard started but held her gaze. He took the meaning of her words as she intended them. If Ulla became the Seer's apprentice, the girl would go to Airiki as such; the Seer's counsel would be doubly meaningful and her value to the clans and Erilaiset ever greater. So the union of the Seven Clans would be completed.

"The girl will certainly go," he said steadily. "But the words of Mielikki and the Mark of the Clan are proofs enough."

All paused then for a moment while the old man and old woman, hero and mortal, singer and seer, faced each other in the dim, smoke-filled hall. To the others, it seemed a great tension filled the room, threatening to explode all about them. Suddenly the Seer bowed very deeply and the moment passed.

"It is in your hands, Lord Väinämöinen," she said, almost whispering. "Whatever will be, will be!"

The sounds of horns and bells came from outside, for the people were singing their last songs and would soon go rest before the early morn and day of ritual to come. Bergil the Warden then spoke, his voice rich with the accent of the Kotkalaiset, for he had been born near to Langvika.

"If I understand these counsels, then we are agreed. I will send a messenger tomorrow to Airiki with news, unless someone here can send the news more swiftly by other means. But we have more to decide. The campaign season will soon be here and Löhi will doubtless attack. She has always come through the land of the Karhulaiset, down either side of Lake Suurijärvi where there is good ground, but the reports from Akkala and Deep Länsimaa are troubling. What if she comes that way next?"

"What is the land like?" asked Valso.

"There is marshland north of Valkeakosk—a place of lakes, reeds, and fens. And the woods are thick north of Akkala, except by the sea. It does not seem a place the Itäläiset would favor. Still, who can read the mind of Löhi?"

"We may have news soon," said Väinämöinen. "Turi the Changer knows that land well. He left here some weeks ago to find Ilkka, the Chief Warden in High Lansimää, and to scout along the Marches. Perhaps his report will influence our plans, but, wherever Löhi strikes, the chief question is if you are ready. Are you ready, my lords?"

Egan suddenly drew his sword. The long blade of Lemminkäinen flickered orange and red. "Etelamaa is ready!" he cried.

"And Tavastia!" cried Asikkas.

The old man smiled grimly and motioned to the Seer.

"Well and good. Then let us take the measure of this new king of the Eagle Folk! And as for me, I will return to Akkala alongside you."

***

The next day dawned bright and clear across the fair fields of Tavastia. That part of the Land of the Hare Folk was known as Häme. All the people in Häme came out into their fields and meadows to welcome spring, seeking Akka's blessings for the year to come. The Erilaiset rose early and, with Egan, Asikkas, and the other noble guests, made a procession out of the little valley southwards. All the Tavastialaiset from miles around came to meet them, and together they stood beneath the Far Northern Land's blue sky.

The Tavastialaiset were dressed in fine clothes: the men in their best breeches and coats, the women wearing dresses of red and white with colorful aprons and veils upon their braided heads. Maidens and little girls wore green sprigs of birch twined about their hair. The young men called out to their favorites and danced with them around tall poles made of pine, newly cut and fresh-scented, like the forest itself. Children ran and played, their parents and elders laughed and sang, and, for that time at least, Löhi's evil was forgotten.

Väinämöinen stood before the people and raised his hands in invocation, then a woman of the Erilaiset called Viljatoive came forth. She was a powerful singer and disciple of Akka who had journeyed all the way from the Enchanted Valley to celebrate *hela* with her kinfolk in Laulavalaakso. Viljatoive chanted many songs as the warm sun shone down upon her; she called upon Akka, mistress and mother of the living earth, to bless the fields of Häme, bringing increase and health to the gathered folk.

For Akka ruled all things that lived and grew upon the earth; she made the ground rich and fertile in the harsh northern climes, and she made the cattle and beasts have many offspring. With her blessing, children might be born healthy and strong and survive the ills and misfortune that afflict mortal kind. The singers drew on Akka's great power for many *loitsu* and charms; but even Akka the goddess could not protect against all ills or guarantee against all evil chance. For the world is marred and Ukko's design flawed by the wickedness of men.

Unlike Unaja or Mielikki, Viljatoive was a slight woman, scarcely taller than a Menninkainen. She stood before them, dressed all in spring green, as green as fresh rushes newly gathered from a northern pond. Her hair was not golden like Unaja's, but flaxen pale, like the sun shining through thick mist after a sudden shower. Her eyes were as blue as fresh berries, deep and clear, and when Ulla had first met her in the Enchanted Valley, she thought them beautiful beyond words. Her voice sounded almost like a child's, merry and gay, although she had lived in the Far Northern Land for years uncounted, reckoned among the Great Ones of the Erilaiset.

After Viljatoive completed the rites and blessed the land, many people led their beasts through a green arbor, shot through with white flowers, to ensure fertility. Ulla stood beside Väinämöinen, holding a white egg that the old man gave to her. But before the ceremonies ended, the seven mortal singers who had come to Laulavalaakso the previous year and would go forth as *tietäjää* throughout the Far Northern Land came together. There were five men and two women in that number. And according to the ancient traditions of the Seven Clans, each swore an oath before their people: to do good and abjure evil, to help the sick and infirm, to protect their folk and work for their increase, to never use their power selfishly or for personal gain, and to honor the Vanhalaiset, keeping the rites and rituals of time and season sacred. All who stood there felt the power of Akka move through them; even the proud Seer of Kyöpelinvuori bowed her head in reverence.

The Hare Folk then made a simple meal of sweet mead and fresh loaves in the fields, but the two kings and their retinue returned to the Singing Valley, sitting in the pavilion as dusk fell and the stars came out. Last of all, Kirsikka rose, dressed all in white with flowers in her red hair. She sang a song that Väinämöinen had taught her in the ancient tongue of the Erilaiset, telling of the origins of the world, when all was new and unstained, when the heroes looked upon the seas and sky with the wonder of children. The song held no magic, no wizardly power or spell, yet the beauty of the young woman's voice held them as folk enchanted, stirring the passion of their souls.

As Eglano, Grand Duke of Etelamaa, sat beside his brother the king and Aldon, the clarity of her song pierced his heart. Her beauty captivated him. And when Kirsikka had finished, he went to her and spoke to her with halting words. Then he took her arm and together they walked long into the night beneath the gleaming, many-colored lamps the Erilaiset had hung from the trees. The colored light danced and wove among the darkling woods, until it gently faded with the dawn.

Chapter Four

The Hunters and the Hunted

uri the Changer, the great wizard of the Erilaiset and Väinämöinen's oldest and dearest friend, had left the Singing Valley while winter still held sway. Reports came to the Valley of strange things happening along the Marches of Deep Länsimaa: spies in the sedgelands north of Valkeakosk, scouts lost, and March Wardens disappeared. Then a messenger had arrived from Teemu, High Lord of the Elk Folk. His people feared that Löhi, preparing some new stroke against the Seven Clans, might raid the lands of the Hirvilaiset out of the wastes of the north, unlikely though this seemed. So Turi took it upon himself to journey to the Marches and confer with Ilkka, Captain of the Wardens in High Länsimaa. He had bid farewell to Väinämöinen on a grey and blustery day, kissed Ulla and Kirsikka good-bye as they stood shivering in the lightly falling snow, and struck out on a sled of white birch pulled by a small, sturdy beast with a cape of shaggy white fur around its neck.

The singer made for the *lansikita*. Passing through the gap in the Wall of the Giants, he turned northeast, struck the Old Trade Road, and so at last came to Keskimaa, the capital of the Bear Folk. Keskimaa had been rebuilt since the Itäläiset sacked it seven years before; the burned houses and crumbled walls had been repaired and strengthened. Its tall, proud, green-and-yellow gables still stood and men still waited for the summer's bloodrock. The red-stained stones held precious iron, the purest in the Far Northern Land, which could be shaped into weapons and other useful things, but was found nowhere else in such quantity. Indeed, the town's population had grown in recent years, for many Karhulaiset from the north, near to Lake Suurijärvi, had abandoned their lands and swelled Keskimaa's folk. Though the Witch had invaded High Länsimaa several times, despoiling nearly all its northernmost parts, Keskimaa had never again been threatened.

Turi rode into Keskimaa and went straight to the Hall of the Karhulaiset, where Janottu held court. The rich tradesman had been chosen to lead his clan after Pekka the Fat was slain by the Itäläiset. Janottu, like Pekka before him, had many interests; the trade in bloodrock and other precious things had made his family wealthy and powerful. But the coming of the Witch and the never-ending war she unleashed upon the Seven Clans changed all things in High Länsimaa. Keskimaa had been fortified and Janottu ruled wisely, raising a large army and arming his people; he welcomed the heroes and singers, ensuring that the songs and rituals of the *Vanhalaiset* were heard again throughout all that land.

Janottu welcomed the wizard warmly and shared his thoughts with him. As they sat together at night before a warm fire in the old hall, drinking and talking, the Lord of High Länsimaa told him all about the defenses he had ordered and of the disposition of his forces. The Bear Folk now kept three armies in the field to guard against the legions of Pohjola. A small force was stationed east of Lake Suurijärvi to contest the passage south and a larger one west of Suurijärvi nearer the North Marches. They had built two forts like Linnavuori, for protection and to guard the frontier. The largest army remained above Keskimaa, where its men worked the nearby fields and yet might quickly move to meet any invasion from the wastes.

Much had changed since the time when Ulla, the little girl with dark hair, lived in the dusty village along the North Road. Yet, for all the improved defenses, the Easterners and goblins that Löhi sent to raid and pillage each summer would have doubtless despoiled all of High Länsimaa had the Bear Folk stood alone.

But they did not. The number of March Wardens had been greatly increased; men tall and strong, from all the Seven Clans, now formed larger companies, each with one hundred men. Seven such companies patrolled High Länsimaa and built many strong places scattered along the Marches as refuges and redoubts. Closer to Keskimaa, men of Etelamaa and Tavastia waited in readiness to fight the Pohjolaiset, but the main armies of the Swan and Hare Folk only came north in the summer. They fought many battles all along the length of Länsimaa, and were always led by King Egan and his shining sword.

Janottu, of course, worried about the summer's fighting to come. He pressed Turi to stay with them and lend his aid; the wizard's power would be a welcome boon to High Länsimaa. But Turi held to his purpose; after counseling Janottu and instructing the two mortal wizards who served the Bear Folk in Keskimaa, he set out due north to find Ilkka, said to be in that region of the Marches.

He passed through the farmlands surrounding Keskimaa as the snows melted and winter drew toward its end; the people there, already out and about, prepared the fields and dikes for the growing season. In the rich, fertile lands in those parts, rye, barley, and even greens grew in abundance. Further north the farmlands failed and, except for some folk who raised cattle and draught beasts, the land was mostly empty. Stands of white birch and pine grew scattered along raised eskers that marched, one after another, toward the distant horizon.

Turi had come this way before, escaping the goblins and fleeing south to Keskimaa with vain tidings of ruin and defeat in the north. He had been wounded then, poisoned near to death, and on foot; but now his small, shaggy horse, sturdy and sure-footed, made good time through the lone lands. At length he struck a road that sprang from some small villages nearby a crystal-clear lake, then passed swiftly to the North Marches.

The Wardens had an encampment in that part of the Marches, near to a place called Pyhätammi. They'd built *pirttis* and cottages surrounded by a ditch set with spiked logs, which could be defended for a while if attacked. Sure enough, Turi found Ilkka there with two dozen other Wardens. They greeted the old singer with courteous words, welcoming him to their camp. When Turi had rested and bathed in the clean, cold waters of Pyhätammi's swift stream, they made a large fire beneath the night sky and sat around it bundled in cloaks and furs. As chance would have it, another Erilainen had come to Pyhätammi the previous day: Sá, an elf of Lúven's folk from the Enchanted Valley.

The power of the Erilaiset lay not in numbers but skill. Many elves toiled with the Wardens along the Marches and went into the wastes as scouts and spies to discover Löhi's designs; not all returned. But, if not for this sacrifice, even the swords of the Tavastialaiset and Etelalaiset would not have sufficed to save High Länsimaa.

"Tell us how things fare in Laulavalaakso!" said Ilkka as they sat by the fire. "How is old Väinämöinen? And my little friend Ulla? It has been too long since last I saw her!"

"Väinämöinen is as he always is," answered Turi. "Which is to say, both good and bad, as the winds of fortune blow. He weathers all storms. But little Ulla is no longer so little, Ilkka. She has grown tall and stern, proud and powerful. I think she will be a great mage if she wishes. She already knows many songs and spells that only the wise among us know."

"I don't doubt it," said Ilkka. "What she did at Linnavuori was no fluke. May our paths soon cross again!"

"Many mortals have come to the Singing Valley," continued Turi. "And they have learned the songs and then returned to their own people to help them. Some have become wizards. It seems we may all, perhaps, have weathered the worst of Löhi's storm. Yet she will not fade without a fight, and that's why I've come all this way to find you. The reports from the Marches trouble me, Ilkka. Teemu and the Elk Folk are afraid. What is happening in the wastes? What do you think Löhi is up to?"

"Her thought lies heavy along the Marches," said Ilkka, "and not only in High Länsimaa. West of here, where men seldom go and where paths are few and uncertain, one can feel the Witch's brooding like never before. It clouds the mind, filling men with disquiet and unease and turning them away. I had this same feeling seven years ago when the Witch first invaded Länsimaa and defeated us."

"And we have lost men," said another Warden. "Three failed to return after the new year; another two are late, and we're worried about them. And as for the rest of us—such great dread afflicts us in some parts that many cannot go there for fear of death or madness."

"So it is from east to west," said Sá. "Our *sight* fails in the wastes. Löhi's evil will clouds all and darkens our vision. Her power, or the power of her sorcerers, must be strong. But some of my *väki* have crept north, far north, of where the Karhulaiset once lived, above the lands where the girl with the Mark of the Clan came from. Every year the raiders come that way, always in greater numbers and with many horses.

"How can that be? How can so many gather and survive in the wastes? Do they come each year all the way from Pojhola or their own lands far to the east? I don't believe that can be true. There must be a great camp of the Easterners somewhere in that region; we have never found it. They seem to guard the ways westward, such as they are, vigilantly.

"Then there is this," continued the elf. "Nigh on a fortnight ago, a friend and I went some ways north and west of here. We came upon mortals, wandering Karhulaiset, a small group of those that make no settled dwelling but move from place to place. Even now, some few may still be found here and there. But it is early for such folk to be on the paths rather than wintering in their shelters. These were famished and starving. We helped them as we could, and they told us this—the poor folk had fled their *kotas* because their beasts were slain and they had seen devilish shapes creeping about their homes; they feared for their lives. I don't doubt it was Hiisia they feared.

"Worse still, several of them said they had chanced upon a group of many horsemen riding along a new path cut through the woods, some dragging great sleds. Then the wanderers spoke of something else, some beast or evil spirit howling in the wilds at night, which filled them with terror. The Karhulaiset said the horsemen were riding west, toward the wild lands above Deep Länsimaa, but they knew nothing more."

"What do you think, Turi?" asked Ilkka. "I was born among the Elk Folk and know Deep Länsimaa well, but the lands north of Valkeakosk are wild and uncharted. What is that region like? Can the Witch attack from that direction?"

Turi poked at the fire with his copper-shod staff.

"The lands above Valkeakosk are inhospitable," said the wizard. "The Birchwood, a fair place, lies westward. But a broad belt of sedgeland runs to the north—reeking marshes and fens where nothing wholesome grows, nor is bloodrock found there. Beyond that lie deep lakes and forests and a strange land cut by sudden ridges of grey stone and sharp rock. It is no place for horses or for an army; there is no food there for man, beast, or demon.

"Even during the Witch's War long ago, the Pohjolaiset did not pass that way. Työ led them around these wastes and came down the western coast and so destroyed Susila, the land of the Wolf Folk. I can't see how any large force can go there. Even messengers would pass more swiftly on other paths, unless things have wholly changed."

The men fell silent as the fire crackled and thin wisps of cloud drifted across the bright, waxing moon.

"Well!" said Turi suddenly. "There is only one thing to do. Löhi is clearly interested in these regions—we must be, too! Something is afoot, that much is sure. So we will go to these places and see what is there, and perhaps catch her servants unawares. Then we may discover her secret."

"Yet beware," said Sá, "lest you be caught yourselves."

They decided then that Turi and several March Wardens would scout the wastelands north of the Birchwood above Valkeakosk, where few men of the Seven Clans, not even Wardens, ever went. Ilkka would go with him, for though he was now Captain of all the Wardens of High Länsimaa, he felt this journey too dangerous and important to send others in his stead. Ilkka remained a wanderer and a ranger at heart, so the thought of scouting the wilderness excited him, despite the dangers and fear. Sá would return east to that part of the Marches where the elves kept watch and warn the Bear Folk of Löhi's approach that summer.

Ilkka and Turi set out from Pyhätammi on a fine cloudless day of fair wind and blue sky. Two other Wardens went with them: Vekka, a tall Hirvilainen like Ilkka from Deep Länsimaa, and Tapa, a shorter, stout Karelian with brown hair and ruddy cheeks. They rode horses now and made good time along the Marches but soon came to the last Warden's outpost, a small place manned by a few scouts.

Then the land quickly changed. They left the horses at the outpost and continued on foot. They had reached the lands now where Sá had found the wandering Karhulaiset. Indeed, a great fear came upon them, as if evil and unclean things were watching, waiting for the right moment to attack. Although they searched all about, climbing every ridge or hillock in sight to survey the countryside, they found nothing: no sign of men or horses and no goblins creeping through the woods. So the four men continued northwest and soon found themselves in a swampy lowland where many small rivers and streams spread out among the grasses and moss.

Fens and marshes were quite common in the Far Northern Land, even in the gentler southern parts of Etelamaa and Tavastia. In some places, people drained the wetlands or burned the marshes to make fields for rye. The marshes north of Deep Länsimaa, however, were broad and dense. No men came there save for outlaws and other desperate types who would brave a place known for disease and pestilence. If not for Turi, the Wardens might have soon become lost and come to an unpleasant end far from their homes. It took all the wizard's skill to find firm ground and hidden paths.

Sedgegrass grew everywhere among pools and bogs filled with slime and rotting things. A noisome smell filled the air and sickened them, growing even worse when the wind blew, hissing through the grasses and troubling the murky waters. The many birds in the marshes filled the stagnant air with their chirps and trills, but the men saw no beasts of any type except for small mouselike creatures darting here and there among the reeds. Mosquitos and biting flies flourished there; no cloak, garment, or spell could keep them away. Except for the birds and the wind, it was quiet. The miserable wastelands seemed abandoned and empty save for themselves—and the weight of Löhi's thought everywhere, growing stronger as they moved north and west.

At last, some seven days out of Pyhätammi, they came out of the marshes. The bogs ended abruptly and they found themselves in a tumbled, mixed land that climbed steadily up toward thickly wooded heights. Walls of stone rose suddenly beside them and great grey rocks jutted from the ground. It sometimes seemed they walked through miniature valleys, stony-sided and hidden. Now and then they came across waterfalls pouring their cold flood from streams above down many winding channels and stairs to the wetlands below. In places, such paths as they could find failed altogether, ending in blinds, dead ends, or sheer drops. There they were forced to climb, scrambling up the rocky walls as best they could until they found a path again. But the way never ran straight, so they let the land take them where it would. By their reckoning, anyone else in such lonely places would be forced to do the same.

Higher up, the trees became denser, and the travelers had to go around small lakes and streams. Late in the afternoon of the second day since they left the marshlands, they came to a river, broad and slow, flowing to the southwest. They walked some ways along its banks but found no ford or narrows, nor any sign that a passage might be near. They would have to swim across.

"This must be the river that was called the Marskijoki long ago," said Turi with a sigh. "It flows south over several falls, finally ending in the lakes and fens north of Valkeakosk. It was even greater in the old days, if I remember rightly; it seems shrunken. But, changed or not, it's still wide enough to stop us and deep to boot."

"So it seems," said Ilkaa. "But how shall we cross it? Our food will be ruined, and we need all we have left. And we cannot swim the river with swords and bows—we will lose them, or else they will drown us. Should we turn back then? We've found nothing. It seems our journey was wasted here while war doubtless gathers in High Länsimaa."

Turi leaned on his staff, silently staring across the river. The old man's wan face looked tired, and he sighed again softly.

"You are a great magician," said Vekka. "Can you not carry us across this river or cast a spell so that we and all our things stay dry?"

"You are a Metsavartija," said Turi irritably. "Can you not find some wild beast and ride on its back? If we go into the water, we shall get wet. I might make a fire on the other side to dry us, but there is no spell I know to keep us or anything else dry within a river."

"The why don't you take another shape?" asked Tapa. "You found the Easterners north of High Länsimaa in the shape of an eagle; can you not do that again and scout all these lands from the sky?"

"Better yet," said Turi, "I could simply fly back to Tavastia and let the three of you find your way to Pyhätammi.

"But come now—I am tired and very weary; my patience is thin. Forgive me, lads! I have indeed thought of changing form and searching this place like you suggest, but it is no easy thing and the spell cannot be kept up for long. And when I found Työ north of the Marches, I knew where to look and what to look for. What do we hunt for now? These wide, broken lands stretch for miles and miles. I might easily miss signs we will see on the ground. Also, if I work a change, I shall have the strength to do so only once before we turn back. You may not know it, but I have sung a spell every morning and every night to fend off the despair that Löhi's *loitsu* works on anyone traveling in these lands. I can't keep that up for much longer."

The singer paused for a moment, scanning the land about them from side to side, then brought his staff down hard on a stone at the river's edge.

"Very well," he said. "We will not turn back, not yet. I want to see what is across this river first. But I will work no change; we will go together."

"But the river?" asked Tapa.

"I said that I couldn't keep us dry if we swam," said Turi. "But we are not going to swim!" He pointed to a stand of pine near the mossy bank where several fallen trees lay. "Bring me those logs!"

The Wardens dragged the trees to the riverbank, then the wizard told them to sit in the bracken and rest. The westering sun glistened off the broad, lazy river and bathed the distant shore in a golden haze. Turi gathered the pine trunks and limbs about him and knelt beside the riverbank, touching the dry wood with both hands. He bent his head until his tall green hat slipped down, nearly covering his face; he sat like that for so long that the three men began to think he had fallen asleep. But then they heard his voice, singing softly as he passed his hands over the pinewood. The gentle south wind carried the sound to their ears, and, though Turi sang in the Old Speech of the Erilaiset, they could still understand some of his song. And, to Ilkka, it seemed that a part of it went like this:

> *Shape the sharp bow and form the wide stern,*
> *plank will be bent and wood shall be turned.*
> *Cross the swift current, all dry within,*
> *river and brook and gully and fen.*
> *Launch the raft,*
> *gain the bank,*
> *to the other side we go!*

The sun sank lower; the trees and rocks cast long shadows on the ground. But where Turi sat among the fallen pines, a glamour grew, dazzling and bright. When it faded, the Wardens rubbed their eyes in disbelief, for upon the riverbank lay a boat, a short, narrow *meloa* of the kind the Karelians used in order to cross the many rivers and streams in the forest. The three men leapt to their feet and ran to the riverbank.

"What magic is this?" cried Vekka. "You've made a boat for us to cross with!"

"I have never seen anything like it," said Tapa. "And I have often been with the elves along the Marches these past years."

Turi rose and bowed low.

"Thank you, my friends," he said. "A useful trick if you're stuck on the wrong side! Now grab the packs and let's go. We will have to use limbs for paddles, but no matter, the current is slow, even in the middle. I can help draw us to the far side with a word, if need be."

They pushed the *meloa* into the water and scrambled in, and soon crossed the Marskijoki. The bank, steeper on this side, led to a grassy lawn that stretched some ways toward a green wood. Turi peered northward while the Wardens dragged the boat up the muddy bank.

"What do you say, Ilkka?" asked the wizard, turning round. "I am tired now but still eager to see what lies ahead. I can hear animals some ways off—elk, I think. We still have a good hour before the light fails, maybe longer. Shall we push on?"

"Lead the way!" said Ilkka. "But should we not hide the *meloa* in the trees and safeguard it for our return?"

"If you wish. But there is little chance of others finding it. You may hide this boat among the trees today, but, by morning, you would find only pine logs. A true *loitsu* of making is no small thing. It takes more time and strength. This enchantment will not last the night."

Then they walked north along the line of the river and camped some few miles from their crossing point, tired and famished. The next day they found that the Marskijoki bent away northeast, so they turned west and plunged again into the strange, unknown land. Neither Turi nor Ilkka had any clear idea of what they were looking for—men or goblins, signs of trail or camp.

They found no trace of any of these, however. The countryside seemed wide and empty. Valkeakosk and the lands of the Elk Folk lay many miles due south, and all around them stretched a wild region where no folk of the clans had ever lived. Though they had left the marshes behind them, they now came across pools and lakes, which they skirted as best they could. At least beasts lived in this wilderness; herds of elk roamed through the trees, and groups of small deer darted about the woods when they approached. Squirrels ran up and down the tree trunks, and badgers scampered off to their dens. Ducks, returning to the north, lit on darkling waters that had been ice-covered only a few weeks before. The Wardens bent their bows and would have shot the deer, but Turi stopped them. There was no time to clean and dress such prey or to roast the meat, not unless they were starving and had no choice. They all knew that choice might come soon enough.

Just as the old singer was about to suggest that they give up and turn back toward Pyhätammi, they chanced upon another river at the end of an elk trail. The trail petered out atop a high esker that looked down on a narrow valley where the river ran. Jagged stones broke the surface of the river, not as wide or deep as the Marskijoki, and white water boiled around them as sunlight sparkled through a slowly rising mist. A drunken line of flatter stones stretched from one shore to the other, and the river swelled and pooled at either end, where the stones interrupted its course.

"At last we have a sign!" cried Vekka. "Surely these stones were placed here to make a ford across the rapids, or I'm no Warden."

"So it would seem," said Turi. "But, if so, the hands of mortal men did not do this thing. And who knows how long ago it may have been?"

"Shall we cross? It will be slippery with the spray and mist," said Tapa.

"It is too steep to climb down here," replied Ilkaa, looking doubtfully at the esker's slope.

"And I am too old," said Turi. "Let's explore this side, along the ridge, before going any further; we may find more signs. Then we'll find a better place to climb down and try our luck at the stony ford."

The four men turned south and walked along the ridge top among thick bushes and short pines. The sun was hot in a cloudless sky, and they stopped to pack away their thick cloaks, caps, and hats. Before long they came across what they had been looking for: signs of folk and animals passing the same way.

"And now there is this!" cried Ilkka suddenly. The tall Warden stooped beside a berry bush, digging in the earth with his knife as the others ran up. He had found black, burned wood buried beneath the dirt, and lifted a half-charred sack from the hole. "There was a camp here. No prints, but they did a poor job of hiding their fire. And it is fresh, no more than a few days old, if even that."

"Here is another," said Tapa, digging nearby with his boot in a pile of soft, sooty earth. "And horse droppings, too. Many folk have been here."

"We must be careful now," said Turi, "and make less noise. It seems we are on the right trail at last. But remember Sá's wisdom: *Beware lest the hunter become the hunted.*"

Tired though they were, they gained energy and new strength from their excitement. Drawing their swords, the scouts continued down the ridgeline, scanning the ground quietly. After a mile or so they found a trail cutting from the steep cliffside into a thicker wood. The trees in the wood grew taller and more varied, with beech, elm and others that the Wardens did not recognize stretching their green limbs skyward.

Now they walked more slowly, looking from side to side and speaking little. They had not gone far when they came to a place where two paths, wide and clear, suddenly opened up amidst the woods. One continued south, but the other turned east; looking ahead, they could see where the trees had been cut and cleared to broaden the way. At the crossroads, however, burned stumps and logs lay in patches here and there along the path, and some trees, though still standing, had scorched trunks. Tapa bent low and picked up a short link of a great, rusty iron chain.

"How do you read this riddle now?" asked Ilkka, sniffing the slight sulfurous scent on the air.

"I wonder," said the wizard. "I can feel nothing—no sign of life or hint of magic—in either direction. But that does not mean we are alone. Let us push on a bit farther!"

All along the path they found signs, both of burning and of a great concourse of men and horses passing that way. About half a mile from the crossroads, the path turned back along the ridge and again ran parallel to where they guessed the river valley lay, hidden by brush and grey boulders protruding from the esker's topline.

At one spot, a little trail ran up to a great overhanging rock. While the others spoke quietly among themselves, debating whether to continue down the path, Vekka scrambled up the gravelly height and onto the rock. After a moment, he turned and whistled like a cuckoo—the Warden's call—and gestured excitedly to his friends to join him. Tapa remained on guard below with their packs, but Ilkka and Turi climbed up after Vekka. The steep trail offered difficult footing; twice Turi slipped and slid back down, his arms outstretched above him. He finally gained the top, red and puffing, his beard torn and matted.

"This had better be important," he spluttered at Vekka, but his words died on his lips when he looked down into the narrow valley below.

The river rushed below them, swift now and speeding south with white foam and spray. Just south of their vantage point, a bridge spanned the water, and men stood on either side.

The bridge had been made of strong, roughhewn logs bound with rope and iron chains, and it was anchored with great pilings sunk into a sandy eyot in the river's center. It looked strong enough for horses and carts to pass across. Two men stood at its closer end talking together, another stood alone in the center, and several more were on the farther shore, busy at some type of work. The dark-haired men didn't look like Easterners from a distance, but it was hard to tell since sunlight glared off of the foaming river, casting everything below in a warm spring haze.

Turi, Ilkka, and Vekka watched in silence for several minutes, then scrambled back down to where Tapa stood. The old wizard slipped again and slid past his companions, landing in a dirty heap at Tapa's feet. The Karelian picked him up and dusted him off as best he could while Ilkka and Vekka described what they had seen.

"So at last we find what we were seeking!" said Ilkka. "Enemies have come here and bridged the river. Surely they plan to come down on Deep Länsimaa from the north!"

"I cannot guess how we found no sign of them until now," answered Turi. "But the land is wild, and perhaps we missed other paths as we made our way west. I might have seen this from the air as a bird, but, then again, maybe not. My eyes aren't so keen as they were a few hundred years ago!

"There's no telling how Löhi's servants passed through the bogs and wilderness to get here; perhaps she herself cleared a way for them to follow! But what does it matter? Here they are, and there can only be one reason for it. They are not passing through this land to reach Akkala. There must be a camp nearby, or several. They plan to strike straight through the marshes at Valkeakosk!"

"Then let us hasten back with this report," said Vekka. "We must warn the Elk Folk of what is coming, and the Tavastialaiset and Etelalaiset must help them, too!"

"Indeed," the wizard replied. "Hasten we must. But I would like to know more about our enemy. Who are these strange men and how many are there? Are there goblins about? And what about all this burning and mess? What say you, Ilkka—should we press on a bit and see what lies ahead?"

Ilkka looked up and down the path distrustfully. The faint sound of the rushing river came to them on the breeze.

"Our enemies are close by," he answered. "We cannot hide from them for long. And while I have the same questions, the truth is that we are already weary and our supplies almost gone. Alas, Turi, we three mortals don't have the endurance of the Erilaiset! If we are to make it back to our own lands, we shall have to leave this place soon."

"So we will, lads," said the wizard. "But let us venture this first. Vekka and I will take the southern way. You two go back to the crossroads and turn east. Scout ahead for several miles, but don't go too far! Let us meet again at the crossroads come evening. Then we can decide what way will take us back to the Seven Lands."

The others agreed to this, so the wizard and Vekka struck the path southward. Ilkka watched as they dwindled into the distance; Turi's tattered green cloak and staff soon faded in the hazy sunshine. He rounded a gentle bend and vanished from sight. "All right, then," said Ilkka. "Let's go! But keep your bow bent and be wary."

They walked back to the crossroads and turned east, moving slowly and cautiously, hugging the tree line so that they might quickly hide if any enemies appeared before or behind them. Ilkka walked in front with drawn sword, and Tapa trailed him, his bow at the ready. Many trees had been felled to clear the path through the wilderness. Stumps remained here and there, although others seemed to have been dug out, roots and all, as if to make a cart path. Yet they saw no signs of carts or wagons, no hoofprints or any other sign of beast or man. Twice they came upon spots with burned grass, scorched trees, and the same sulfurous reek that they had smelled earlier.

The path now wound this way and that, following some natural course. Ilkka noticed that the tall beeches on either side seemed to spread their broad, sweeping branches over the road like a living canopy, almost shutting out the sky in some places. It felt like a sheltered way, hidden from unfriendly eyes. He glimpsed a rocky wall through the trees to the north, perhaps the foot of some ridge or stony slope. Tinkling water fell upon the rocks or perhaps rushed through some water channel hidden amidst the woods, but no brook or stream crossed the path.

They had walked only about an hour and were thinking about turning back when a sudden noise filled the air. First one deer, then another, charged out from the woods and leapt across the path.

"Captain!" whispered Tapa. Ilkka dropped to the road as the deer jumped over him, disappearing into the trees on the other side. Even as he watched the animals vanish, he glimpsed a feathered shaft speeding past and heard the arrow's telltale whine. Ilkka turned toward Tapa; a second arrow struck the Karelian in the right shoulder. He fell to his knees with a muffled cry.

Scrambling up, Ilkka ran to Tapa and hauled him to his feet. The Warden didn't see anyone in the woods or on the path, but a third shaft passed so near his face that he felt its wind.

"Run, Tapa!" he cried. "Quick—off the path. Follow me now!"

Pulling his injured friend after him, Ilkka plunged into the trees off the left side of the road and ran madly through the woods. Tapa followed him despite the arrow in his shoulder, his dark eyes wide with fear. The Wardens slipped and tripped through the bracken and bramble; when they looked back, they saw no one following them and heard no call or cry. Ilkka drew a long knife even as they ran, slashing at the branches and vines that barred their way. A gap opened abruptly at their feet, a cut that descended a short way into a gully or dry creek bed; the grey rock wall they had glimpsed from the path lay across it.

"Come this way!" hissed Ilkka, motioning to his friend, and he dropped into the cut and crouched down. Breathless and shaking, Tapa held his shoulder, the feathered shaft still buried within, and vainly tried to keep blood from dripping onto the leafy litter which covered the rocks and stones.

"Steady, Tapa," whispered Ilkka. "Steady. We've got to keep moving until we find better cover. Can you do it?"

The Karelian grimaced and shook his head; his arm hung lifeless below the wound. "It hurts, Ilkka," he finally gasped, "Very bad."

Ilkka put his arm around him and looked down the gully. It ran on a ways to become a narrow draw, littered with dirt and old bracken, before turning sharply away from the rock wall.

"All right, lad," said Ilkka. "Just a ways more until we get out of this hole; then I'll find Turi and he'll help you. Lean on me, and let's go quietly!"

The two men started off down the draw. It was quiet now, no sound of birds or other animals could be heard, and shafts of yellow sunlight lit bright patches of ground all about them. When they came to the sharp turn, Ilkka eased Tapa to the ground and straightened, looking back the way they had come. He peered over the gully's lip but saw only woods and brush.

He turned back just as a dark figure loomed over him. He tried to raise his knife, but, with a shattering blow to his face, the world went black.

***

Ilkka came to, badly confused and disoriented. His head swam and throbbed; his left eye was swollen shut. The Warden tried to move, then realized he was standing upright, not on the ground. Cold water dripped from his face and hair. He tried to move his arms and legs, discovering that they had been tightly bound to a large beech tree behind him. A voice rang out in front of him, laughing. He started; the voice laughed again.

Ilkka blinked until his blurry vision finally cleared. He was no longer in the gully, but in a small clearing. Water rushed nearby. Not far away, Tapa lay unmoving on the ground with several black-feathered arrows sticking from his back. Three upright figures stood there. Ilkka mourned his friend but stared at the others in wonder as his head lolled back and forth.

To one side, a horseman sat atop a bony mount. Seeing his lank brown hair, drooping mustachios, and worn red-and-black garments, Ilkka knew at once that he was Itäläisen. The second man, of a kind unfamiliar to Ilkka, looked like the guards they had glimpsed at the bridge: thickset and stocky with a long black beard. Clad in rough, homespun clothing save for a black woolen cloak, he carried an iron-tipped spear. The third figure was clearly no mortal, but an Erilainen. His hood had been pushed back from his long, thin face, revealing leaf-shaped ears. An elf, perhaps—though shorter than the Haltiatar of the Enchanted Valley, whom Ilkka knew well—his features were twisted and cruel. Löhi's device, the North Star of Pohjola, was emblazoned on his black leather hauberk and vambraces. He held a long dagger in his hand.

"Are we awake now?" asked the Erilainen in a thick accent, laughing. "Good, good. I thought I'd knocked you too hard back there. But there is still time for that—time for you to join your poor friend here—unless you do exactly as I say and tell me exactly what I wish to know. Do you understand?"

The Haltia walked around Ilkka slowly, tapping the beech with his dagger and smiling. "Now tell me, my unfortunate friend," he mocked. "What is your name? And what are you doing in these desolate parts so far from the great Seven Lands of the South?"

Ilkka lifted his head and sighed. "My name is Jurma," he answered weakly. "Jurma of the Hirvilaiset. I am only hunting elk with my cousin."

"Do not lie to me!" snarled the Haltia, slapping Ilkka's face. "You are one of the filthy Wardens! And no mortals hunt in these wastelands. Now listen well! You are going to tell me your name, and how you tracked me here, and why you are here, and what you have seen. Speak!"

Ilkka dropped his head and was silent.

The Erilainen grabbed Ilkka by the hair and brought his face very close, looking him straight in the eye and leering with an evil smile. The elf spoke softly, chanting, and a shiver ran down Ilkka's spine. A strange feeling came over him. He felt a compulsion, growing ever stronger, to tell his captor all he knew and to betray his friends. Väinämöinen, Egan, Ulla, what did it matter? There was no escape for any of them anyway. He tried to look away from the elf's spinning eyes, but could not. So he fought the terrible urge as best he could.

Suddenly a sharp pain, sharper than any he had ever felt in all his life, pierced his head. He jerked back. His vision dimmed in a blast of white light. His mind burned, as if a molten spear were lodged in his brain. Ilkka cried out in agony.

He needed only to tell the elf his real name, tell him whatever he wished to know, and the agony would cease. What difference did it make, anyway? Löhi, Queen of Pohjola and of all the Far Northern Land, knew everything already. She was a goddess to mortals and immortals alike. Why resist her? Why fight her? Surely his friends would understand. Why not tell the elf what he wished to know?

He yearned for a moment's respite, whatever came afterward. He knew he needed only to begin with his name to extinguish the fire.

Just as Ilkka felt he would break under the horror, the pain vanished. Dazed and stunned, he slowly focused his eyes. The Erilainen bent over and, breathing hard, almost panting, glared at him.

"*Ka!*" cried the elf. Straightening, he spat in Ilkka's face. "So you think you can defy me? A servant of the Tower of the North? Fool! I might have let you live and even sent you back to your folk; you could be useful to us after a fashion. But so be it. My friend, you have no idea what I can do to you, but you will soon—oh, yes. I can make you beg for death on your knees, make you wish you'd never been born!" He slapped Ilkka again. The stocky man, coming closer, drove the butt of his spear into the Warden's stomach. The Easterner sat still, impassive, and made no sign.

The elf took a step back. He turned away from Ilkka, drinking from a leathery waterskin. He wiped his mouth on his arm and, turning again, considered Ilkka for several seconds.

"I have come across several of your kind before," he jeered. "The Metsavartija of the Seven Clans! What use you short-lived scavengers are I can't imagine, begging for your bread at every cottage and roaming around the swamps, poking your noses in where they're not wanted. You fancy yourself a scout, eh? What news have you ever brought back to your folk that helped them? But I can tell you this: I've met some of your friends. They gave me great sport before they died."

Coming closer now, the Erilainen flung down the waterskin and raised his dagger to Ilkka's neck. The Warden closed his eyes, waiting to feel the blade's bite. He almost welcomed death's release and an end to his torment, but his enemy had not finished with him, not yet. He drew the sharp dagger across Ilkka's throat from ear to ear. The blade scored the flesh, cutting the finest line from one side to the other. A trickle of warm blood suddenly ran down Ilkka's chest.

"It begins like this," said the elf in a soft and sinister voice. "And by the time I am finished, my dear friend, by the time I am finished, I will flay every strip of skin off you, and yet leave you alive, enchanted, hanging in the trees for the birds and beasts to do with as they will. Your ghost will haunt this place forever in anguish and regret, finding no peace or forgetfulness in Tuonela or beyond. Unless, that is, unless you see reason and tell me what

I wish to hear. Now then, who are you, Metsavartija? And how many of you have followed me? For I already know there are more than just two of you."

The Haltia shifted the knife in his hand and came close again. Even as he raised his dagger, a deafening howl shattered the forest's calm, like the roar of sudden thunderclap high in the mountains. A great wolf, huge and terrible, crashed out of the trees, leaping among them.

The horse screamed in terror and bolted into the woods. The wolf's ragged grey-and-black fur bristled like a comb along its back; sharp teeth like spikes filled its maw. It slavered and snarled in anger or madness. The wolf leapt again, slashing with its claws at the spearman. It threw him aside like a child's stuffed doll.

The elf scrambled backwards to escape the terrible beast. His dagger lost, he groped on the forest floor for a weapon in his panic and fear. Then he stopped. Steadying himself, propped on one arm with his legs outstretched, he scowled and raised his hand. With a swift gesture, his voice commanding, he cried out, "*Pysäyttää!*"

But this was no beast of the wild crouched before him, no hungry creature separated from its pack. The wolf growled, its red eyes shining. Gathering itself, it sprang full upon the Haltia with a thunderous yowl. There was a terrible scream as the wolf twisted and turned, rending its prey with savage fury. Suddenly, all was quiet again and the battle was over.

Ilkka, dazed beyond all wonder and fear, dropped his head. Calm returned to the woods as soft sunlight cast a pale yellow glow on the little glade. When he looked up again, the grey wolf was gone, but Turi the Changer stood before him. Taking the elf's fallen dagger, the wizard, his own hands trembling, carefully cut Ilkka's bonds. Without a word, the Warden collapsed into his arms.

***

This time Ilkka awoke in a small, sheltered bay on the side of a hillock not far from the Marskijoki. Turi was gone. The Warden reached painfully for a waterskin that had been set beside him. With an effort, he brought it to his lips. It hurt to swallow. His entire body ached. He lay like that for some time, staring blankly at the bay's stony wall, until the shaman finally returned.

Turi sat down with a heavy sigh. Blood spattered his torn clothes and his tall hat was missing, but he still held his staff. "How are you, lad?" he said, putting a hand lightly on the Warden's shoulder. Ilkka managed a slight smile.

"Never better," he replied, but then added, "I am not sure I will make it this time."

"Nonsense," said Turi. "You were badly beaten. You'll feel that for some days yet, but you are whole. Do not be afraid."

Ilkka closed his eyes. "Where have you been?" he asked the wizard.

"Seeing to our friends," said Turi gravely, "even as you have guessed. I buried them together in a secluded spot close to the river and sang the songs over them. They are at peace. I have hidden our enemies' bodies, too. The horse fled, but without its rider; I found the Italäinen with his neck broken."

"Then it is as I feared and Vekka is dead," sighed Ilkka. "What happened with you, Turi?"

"Much the same as with you, I deem. They ambushed us some ways down the path. I should have sensed it; the fault lies all with me. Three strange men, like the black-bearded man who attacked you. They shot Vekka with many arrows, but tried to lay hands on me and take me alive, which was their last mistake. I hurried back then, feeling that you were in danger, and took the form that you saw. It was too late for poor Tapa, but I found you just in time."

"The elf...do you know him?"

"No," said Turi, shaking his head. "Never saw him before. A Dark Erilainen of Pohjola—Haltiatar, I think, though you never know; strange *väki* serve Löhi.

But he acted a bigger fool than even I. He let his guard down, bent on his cruelty and mischief. Such is often the way with evil. He might have laid a mild enchantment on you and come looking for me or else taken you back to where his friends were and I wouldn't have been able to help. But he was eager, too eager, to draw pleasure from your pain. Let him rot forever, lost in Tuonela!"

The old wizard picked up the waterskin and drained it to the dregs.

"We shall stay here tonight and tomorrow, too. We both need rest. We should be safe here—or safe enough. I have set veils all about us, though your eyes may not see them. But the next day we must leave this place and be wary. Our report is urgent. We will go straight through the marshes to Valkeakosk and Teemu and, afterwards, to Tavastia. There will be no quick return for you to the North Marches."

"But what is our report?" asked Ilkka. "That we found Löhi's spies in the wilderness?"

"That is part of it," answered Turi. "There are hidden paths through these strange lands where none were before, and bridges across the rivers. That takes great labor and magic. And consider the Easterner. We saw no tracks or signs of horsemen when we crossed the Marskijoki. There must be a camp somewhere, or more than one. And the Witch has marshaled some new race of men to swell her ranks. I fear that Valkeakosk is in danger unless the Seven Clans move to defend it."

Ilkka made no reply. He closed his eyes again and soon fell asleep. But Turi stayed awake long into the night; he thought of past journeys long ago and of the ways they might take to escape their enemies. So he passed the hours, softly singing to himself as the stars of the Far Northern Land shone bright above them.

Chapter Five

Akkala

The men reined in their horses on the road, hard-packed with deep ruts. They faced north, the fresh, sea-tinged breeze at their backs. To their left, peasants toiled in the brown earth of fields bordered by stone; to their right were stands of oak and elm mixed with grey out-croppings of rock shaped by the wind and rain over the course of long years. Behind them, the road dropped out of sight and ran on a short way to the sea, then on to Langvika, greatest port of the Seven Clans and home to the kings of Akkala.

One of the men pointed north. In the distance they described a group of riders emerging from the green. The riders came swiftly on, and the men knew that these were indeed the visitors Airiki had sent them to meet. They saw several Wardens in the party—tall men clad in blue and white—and two women on short, sturdy ponies. Before them all rode an old man with a tall, peaked cap, his long, curly white beard spilling down his bright-yellow shirt, and a deep-crimson cloak flying behind him.

The old man led his company down the road until they checked their mounts before the waiting riders. The leader of Airiki's men raised his spear in a gesture of welcome. When he spoke, his voice was rich with the strange, full-bodied accent of the Eagle Folk.

"Welcome, my lords," he said with a bow of his head. "I am Snorri, the leader of Airiki's guard. The king bade us to meet you on his road and ride with you to his hall in the city. He commanded that I especially welcome the king of the Swan Folk, and, of course, the mistress of Kyöpelinvuori and Väinämöinen of Karelia. King Airiki waits to do you honor in Langvika."

"Well met," answered Egan, who sat next to Väinämöinen. "Lead on then! For we are eager to come to the great city."

"Indeed," said Väinämöinen, puffing out his chest and thoroughly approving of the herald's solemnity. "Long has it been since I looked on mighty Langvika! No doubt you will send one of your number ahead to announce our coming, but you may tell the king that the Seer of Kyöpelinvuori is not among us. She has sent her counselor and servant, Siitsa of the Karhulaiset, in her stead."

"We will, my lord," said Snorri. Straightaway, one of the horsemen turned and set off at a gallop toward Langvika.

The enlarged company continued down the road. Six Wardens rode with Bergil, and eight Swan Knights escorted Egan, who brought other servants besides. Sinio and Valso, the counselor of Asikkas, rode with them, and, of course, Ulla and Siitsa. Väinämöinen alone represented the Erilaiset. It had been many years since any of the ancient race of heroes had openly gone to Langvika or called upon its kings, not since the days of Lemminkäinen and the first war with Löhi.

The company had set out from Laulavalaakso soon after the spring celebration, riding southwest through Tavastia alongside the tumbled hills before crossing into Akkala at a place called Laajala and continuing south. Few folk dwelled in the northern parts of Akkala, a land of tall pinewoods and winding streams. Most of the Eagle Folk lived farther south, where the land was richer, or along the southern and western seacoasts. A broad river called the Akkajoki ran down from the pinewoods of Mäntymetsä, where it joined many tributaries before it reached the sea. The Wardens had waited for them on its gravelly banks with several long flat-bottomed boats.

They took to the boats—people, horses, and all—and floated down the river at their ease. It seemed to Ulla that the lonely lands passed by very slowly. Indeed, it all very much looked the same, but the current was deceptively swift. They made good time, coming to the southlands far sooner than they might have by foot or on horse. Ulla missed Kirsikka greatly. She had never journeyed without her since they met while fleeing the Easterners, and it felt strange to do so now.

Egan kept her company; they rode in the same boat together and talked long into the night while the slowly sinking red sun hung over the sleepy river lands, reluctantly giving way to ever-shorter nights. Väinämöinen watched them, the young king and the dark-haired girl who bore the Mark of the Clan, and it gladdened his heart.

The land of the Kotkalaiset, the Folk of the Eagle, differed from that of the other clans. The earth might not have been quite so rich and fertile as the farmlands of Etelamaa or Tavastia, but many things still grew there, especially cabbages and greens. The warm summer breeze from the sea made the climate milder. Moreover, the Kotkalaiset bred and herded cattle. As the boats floated south, Ulla watched a broad land unfold about her, studded with fields and farms where the cattle and oxen came down to the riverbank to drink. Some of the dark brown or black animals, much larger than the beasts in Tavastia or High Länsimaa, had strange curled horns atop their heads. They were branded with runes the girl did not know.

From time to time, small villages straddled the river or stretched along its banks. The boatmen would put to shore there and the travelers mingled with the surprised and curious villagers.

The tall Kotkalaiset, taller than the other folk of the Far Northern Land, had fair hair and pale complexions. Their women and girls wore dun or brown dresses with simple black designs along the hem and white aprons trimmed in yellow. They covered their flaxen hair with fine veils and pinned chains upon their breasts. Both men and women wore bronze knives at their belts. A bold people, fiercely independent, they valued their freedom above everything.

Although the king in Langvika acted as the chief of their clan, they divided themselves into many small homelands with petty lords and chiefs as leaders. There was often strife among them or between the king and his noblemen. Nonetheless, each year many men gathered in the port cities along the coast, taking to the long warships that the Kotkalaiset were known for and sailing to distant shores. They sailed to the many islands in the Itämeri Sea or to the lands of folk who were strangers to the Seven Clans of the Far Northern Land and even the Erilaiset. Sometimes they traded or exacted tribute, but often they raided and plundered, taking what they desired and killing their enemies, as they deemed them. And they took slaves.

Kotkalaiset raiders took men, women, and children of distant lands and brought them back to Akkala as slaves, greatly increasing the wealth of the Eagle Folk. They branded the unfortunate captives so that, if they escaped, they might be caught more easily and returned to their masters. Though they might someday be set free, and though they were treated perhaps less harshly than the slaves of the Itäläiset, slaves they remained nonetheless, a folk set in bondage.

The other clans found it strange that the Eagle Folk, who so valued their own freedom, trafficked in slaves. The Erilaiset believed it an evil and abomination. The Tavastialaiset returned those slaves who fled into their lands, for they wished no trouble with Akkala, but when a slave of the Eagle Folk escaped to Deep Länsimaa or even High Länsimaa or Etelamaa, they were welcomed and let be.

So Väinämöinen explained to Ulla and Egan as they journeyed southward. He stuck his long staff in the river and watched the water break around it. "*The water is the same on both sides of the boat,*" he said gravely. "What is right, is right; what is wrong, is wrong. The Easterners pillage our land and steal our children. For that we go to war, and justly so. How can it then be right to do these same foul deeds simply because it advances our interests? Think upon that before you act, my children."

After nine days, they had come to a place where the Akkajoki emptied into a large lake dotted with many small islands, then continued down to the sea by several swift ways. They could go no farther by boat, so they took to their horses and ponies, riding through the towns of the south. Rumor of the coming of the king of the Swan Folk and the old wizard of legend had gone before them. At last they came near to Langvika, where Airiki's men awaited.

They followed the road straight to the seashore, the Kotkalaisen riders in the front of the party.

"Is it not strange that Airiki himself did not come to meet us?" said Valso. "After all, when has such a company—with the king of Etelamaa, no less—come to Akkala?"

"It is wise, rather," answered Sinio. "Airiki has not long been a king, and we seek his aid. He would have us call on him to increase his standing among his own folk."

As they came to the shore, the road turned sharply. They could see the towers and stone walls of Langvika in the distance. But where the road turned, a long, rocky headland thrust out like a dark finger into the water below. Ulla checked her pony and gasped, for she had never before seen the great, open sea, only the sheltered bay and gentle swell of the Stone City.

Huge waves crashed against the cape, sending white foam and seaspray into the air as a dim mist clung to the coast, silently flowing into hidden caves and fissures. Islands loomed amidst the rolling sea, some green and tree-covered and others grey and bare save for moss or the droppings of innumerable birds. The cries of the birds filled the air as they circled above, but, louder than all else, the sea called ceaselessly in its never-ending voice of wave and water, weaving its own enchantment over mortal hearts.

So Ulla first beheld the Itämeri Sea. Her heart quickened at the sight, and she lost herself in its magic. When she turned to join the others, she found Siitsa beside her though the rest had ridden on down the path. The thin, pale girl, Karhulaisen as well, had been raised in the pinewoods of the north, just like Ulla. Her face displayed no less wonder at the grey waves, but Siitsa's expression held something more, which Ulla could not discern.

"It is so vast," murmured Siitsa in a trancelike voice. "So vast and . . . and without end."

"The Erilaiset tell tales about a great storm," said Ulla, turning back to the breakers. "It rained for days on end and the water covered all the land, but

Ahti saved some people and beasts from drowning, keeping them safe until the waters returned to the sea. Mielikki told me another tale that says one day it will happen again."

Siitsa nodded slowly, never taking her eyes off the dark water.

"Yes," she finally answered, "Yes, perhaps . . . but no!" Suddenly she straightened on her mount. "That cannot be. The mountains are too tall, and winter will freeze the seas and turn the rain to snow. That cannot be."

A fine spay fell upon their faces as the breakers crashed below. Then Väinämöinen called out from the path ahead, motioning for them to catch up.

At length they came to the East Gate of Langvika, the great port of the Eagle Folk and largest city in all the Far Northern Land. Langvika lay strung along the coast for several miles, with a strong wall of brick and stone stretched in a semi-circle around it, from one end to the other. Like the City of the Etelamaa, Langvika had grown beyond its ancient walls, spilling its folk into hamlets and villages nearby. For the most part, they built these dwellings on the city's western sides, for the West Gate of Langvika opened onto the markets and was closer to the piers. The East Gate, somewhat less trafficked, opened onto the city's oldest parts.

The great wooden doors of the city gate, banded and reinforced with black iron, swung wide. Men-at-arms and horsemen awaited them beneath the shadows of the arch and the two tall stone towers on either side of the gate. Trumpets sounded to welcome Egan, and a group of Airiki's noblemen came forward to greet him.

"Welcome, king of the Swan Folk!" said their leader. "King Airiki awaits you in his hall. Let us pass now within the gate and go to him straightaway!"

Egan rode through the gateway with all the others following behind him. A great press of city folk crowded the cobblestone road. Some threw flowers before him, yellow and white, and cried out his name, for word had passed throughout Langvika that the king of the Swan Folk was come, and the Kotkalaiset were eager to see him. Through the streets and lanes of Langvika, the procession wound its way. The city's size and greatness amazed Egan.

Thousands of folk lived in houses of all fashions and shapes; craftsmen worked in stout buildings and sheds. There were markets and open spaces for the merchants and tradesmen, and many towers and fair places. The great Hall of the Shipwrights' Guild, its golden roof shining in the sun, stretched along the wharfs. The Mariners' trading ships and war galleys bobbed in the slips beside it, and, all along the harbor, innumerable small boats and fishing *kecks* docked. Seabirds called out above.

The people shouted and pointed at Egan in his fine mail and shining helm, but Väinämöinen fell back among the many horsemen. Few seemed to notice him despite his long beard and flowing cloak. Though the city folk knew that Egan had come to meet their king, less had been said about the wizard—as Airiki wished—and few knew that Väinämöinen traveled among them, returned at last to Akkala.

The old man nudged Ulla's pony to get her attention and gestured to the crowds.

"Hundreds of years since I was last here," he said. "Aye, hundreds of years. The folk all look the same, yet it's really the grandsires of their grandsires that I remember. But I recall Langvika well enough, or at least the east end. We are taking a roundabout way to the old castle by the sea where Airiki waits in his hall. He wants to impress Egan.

"Come with me, child!" he said, pointing toward a narrow lane leading away from their route. "And you, too, Siitsa. I'm in no mood for a throng like this today. Yonder street leads to the old Square of Akkala, the center of the ancient city where the totem of the Kotkalaiset once stood. Let's see if it still watches over the Eagle Folk! From there we may still come to Airiki's hall before this procession will."

"And I will come with you," said Bergil, who rode nearby. "The Warden House of the Seven Clans is just off the square, and I wish to speak with my captains, who might be there, before I see Airiki."

The old man swung his horse around. Ulla and Siitsa followed, slipping out of the press of horses and men and riding on down the lane. Bergil and several Wardens rode close behind. The narrow street soon opened onto a large square, cobbled with broken stones worn down by long years of sea, ice, and snow. Tall buildings bordered the square with shop stalls scattered about, fishmongers on the north side and bronzesmiths and tinkers to the west. But in the middle of the square lay a round pool with a granite slab in its midst. On top sat a marble figure in the shape of a great eagle, its smooth dark surface glittering with a million crystal flecks in the sunlight. The eagle, the ancient totem of the Kotkalaiset, the Clan of the Eagle, held its wings open wide as if about to take flight, and its hooked beak screamed in defiance or warning.

Väinämöinen rode to the pool's edge and dismounted. Even Ulla could sense the power which still lurked deep within the polished stone, and she immediately thought of the wooden sentinel which guarded the Green Gate of the Karelian Forest, the reindeer of the Karelialaiset.

"So it is still here!" sighed the old wizard, setting his hand upon a mighty wing. "The Eagle of the Kotkalaiset, made by Pellervoinen of the Erilaiset long ago when the clan was founded and this Far Northern Land was yet young! There were red garnet stones set as eyes back then; they are gone now. But the strength of Akka, Mother of the living Earth, still dwells inside, even though her songs have not been heard in this place since the days of Lemminkäinen."

The old man gazed at the totem, lost in thought, until the harsh, shrill cries of birds—black crows, not seagulls—cut through the air and drew their attention to the square's eastern face. A small crowd stood about a scaffold of rough boards built there. The wizard mounted his horse and led them toward the scaffold.

Three men hung on ropes from the scaffolding. Dead, their distorted faces gazed blankly at the market square as they slowly twisted in the sea breeze. Two of the men hung close together, their arms tied behind their backs and their clothes rent and stained with blood, as if they had been beaten before they were hung. The third, apart from the others, dangled from a lower beam, his face black, his features unrecognizable. A crow suddenly lit upon this man's head, picking at his face with its long beak before hopping into the air again with a loud croak. Repulsed, Ulla still couldn't take her eyes from the grim spectacle. Väinämöinen sat quietly for a moment, then sighed.

"So do mortal men treat one another, slaying those who break their laws, yet never thinking upon the irony of repaying evil in the same coin," he said. "See, child! And this is the great kingdom of Akkala, no less."

"Have you never killed a man, Väinämöinen?" asked Bergil, who had ridden up beside them. "Are the tales about you not true? And how do you know what wickedness these men have done? They could be thieves of other men's property and animals, or murderers themselves, or abusers of women and children. Is it not right that they be stopped and that justice be done?"

Väinämöinen looked hard at the Warden.

"A man may kill for many reasons: when he is waylaid and attacked or when his home and folk are threatened. And all men become killers when war calls. But is it justice to kill a man so, murderer though he be? Or is it simply vengeance? And if it is vengeance, then I want no part of it. I've seen too much death and too many tears to thirst for revenge ever again."

"And yet maybe it is not only up to you or to the living," said Bergil. "The blood of the innocents unjustly shed may cry out for vengeance; without it they may have no peace. And do not all men know in their hearts, as surely as we know to breathe the air around us, that a murderer's own life should be forfeit to atone for his evil deed?"

"Perhaps," answered Väinämöinen. "And perhaps when you can look clearly into a man's heart and know for certain all his life's tale and why he made the choices he did, then you are fit to be his executioner. If you have not that gift of the gods, then do no deed from which there is no return."

Väinämöinen nodded to Ulla and Siitsa, and they turned their mounts, moving through the square toward the street that led to the castle. "Come, children; you've seen enough of death in your short lives. No need to linger here."

Not far from the Square of Akkala, the old castle of Merisuihke stood on a high cliff overlooking the entrance to Langvika's sound. Merisuihke was even older than the castle within the Keep of Etelamaa, its ancient walls grey and foreboding. The kings of Akkala had been crowned in its court for hundreds of years, but they no longer dwelled there, for a long wooden hall had been built close by, fashioned of dark hardwood from across the Itämeri Sea. Väinämöinen rode up to the hall even as Egan arrived with his retinue. The tall guards, dressed in brown with long cloaks over their mail, bent their knees and raised their spears in salute.

The Etelalaisen escorts and servants waited in a small courtyard, sheltered by several stunted oak trees. Egan, Sinio, Valso, and the other chief emissaries entered the hall, with Väinämöinen, Ulla, and Siitsa entering last. The old wizard, uneasy in thought and mind, mused on what had happened long ago when the Eagle Folk had turned against the Erilaiset after the Witch's War and expelled them from all the lands of Akkala.

Great yellow lamps hung from the rafters by iron chains, and a double row of tall wooden pillars, cunningly carved so that shapes of leaves and vines twisted around them, marched down its middle toward the dais. The hall, no larger than that of the Karhulaiset in Keskimaa before it burned, was much richer, built of a strong, dark timber unknown to the Far Northern Land and filled with many fine things taken in trade or plunder from distant lands. On its walls hung shields, weapons, and trophies of war, some ancient and rusted, others sharp and bright, for the Kotkalaiset were a warlike folk.

Near the dais stood a group of Ariki's chief nobles, lords who held their own lands and fields. Isku, the Master of the Shipwrights' Guild, was among them. From the lowest step, a bear of a man with long ginger-brown hair and a full red beard came forward to welcome his guests. Airiki, Chief of the Clan of the Eagle and King of Akkala, dressed in clothes neither rich nor plain, but he wore a belt of gleaming silver and gold about his waist with a long sword sheathed in a jeweled scabbard hanging almost to the ground. The king, a mighty warrior among his people, had fought bravely in many raids and battles. He had avenged his father and his homeland and defeated Torvald, the king before him, surprising Torvald's army in its camp at night and slaying him in single combat even as the sun's red arc rose above the eastern sky.

Airiki smiled and, with a sweeping gesture, bowed to Egan. "Welcome to my hall," he said in a deep voice, "and welcome to the Land of Akkala, king of the Swan Folk. Never since ancient times has Langvika been so honored!"

Airiki, perhaps only ten years Egan's senior, seemed to tower over him. The Kotkalaisen chieftains looked at the boy king of Etelamaa with curious eyes, taking his measure and judging what manner of man and leader he might become. But Egan, following Sinio's counsel, wore the fine mail of the Royal House and carried his lofty helm; his fair face was indeed very young, and his stature little more than a child's next to Airiki, but he stood, stern and proud, before the Kotkalaiset.

Egan's blue eyes sparkled in the lamplight, drawing other men's eyes to his and whispering to them of hidden power and wisdom. The Eagle Folk suddenly remembered that, young as he was, Egan had seen many battles. He had been tested many times against the Itäläiset, had defeated Työ, and Lemminkäinen's sword hung from his belt.

"The honor is all mine," said Egan in a measured voice, bowing with his hand on his chest in the fashion of his people. "It is not recorded in my land if any king of Etelamaa has ever visited this fair city, strange though that seems, making my honor and privilege all the greater to be the first in this—as I have been in other things. Hail, Airiki, King of Akkala! May the blessings of all the Seven Clans be upon you, and may the ties of kinship between our two folk be renewed and never broken!"

Airiki's men marveled at Egan's proud words, but the Akkalan king smiled even more broadly and clapped a big hand on Egan's shoulder. "Well met indeed!" he cried with unwonted, but not unwelcome, familiarity. "Let it be so! And who else graces our hall?"

Egan introduced Valso and Sinio, but when he came to Siitsa, Airiki surprised him by bowing low before the young woman.

"You are most welcome, Lady," he said. "I had hoped your mistress, the Seer, would come herself, but the gates of Langvika are open to you, and you will always have a place beside my own hearth."

"Thank you, Your Majesty," answered Siitsa. "My mistress sends her greeting. She would come if she could, but, for the present, her long *sight* is needed at Kyöpelinvuori."

Finally Väinämöinen stepped forward with Ulla by his side. The old man drew himself up to his full height. His grey eyes flashed as he bowed, and he brought his staff down hard on the floor stones. Though not so tall as Airiki, the wizard's presence and great spirit filled the hall. The Eagle Folk could feel the strength and power that lay within him, singer and maker of a thousand songs and spells since the world began.

"Hail, king of the Kotkalaiset!" he cried. "I am Väinämöinen of Karelia; I thank you and your men for your welcome and hospitality."

"Väinämöinen!" cried Airiki. "Väinämöinen in the flesh! A legend from the past come to life again! So you are the shaman of whom the old tales speak— Väinämöinen and the magical Sampo, Väinämöinen and his magical harp! I have looked forward to this meeting—to meeting you especially. You are most welcome in Akkala."

Väinämöinen, who had been pensive and somewhat grim the entire day, was flattered by the king's speech and doffed his hat in return. A hint of pleasure flashed across the old man's face; he relaxed and smiled.

"I am Väinämöinen, indeed, but I am not come to life again, for I've never been dead! Far away in the Enchanted Valley of the Karelian Forest I make my home, I and all my folk. And far away in the Enchanted Valley, among the rowans of Väinölä, I would remain had not Löhi returned to trouble the Far Northern Land again. But it has been a long, long time since any Erilainen has come to Akkala, unwelcome and exiled as we were in the ages past. Yet you seem to remember tales of magic well enough, Your Majesty."

"Such has been the law in Akkala since the Witch's War, they say," said Airiki. "These are mortal lands, the lands of the Eagle Folk, and we have welcomed none of different race or kin. Only the people of the Seven Clans, the Kaammoslaiset, have had leave to enter Akkala, and then only with good faith and intent. But I do not begrudge my welcome! I am king in Akkala and chief of the Kotkalaiset, and I change the law this very day. You are my guest, Lord Väinämöinen, and under my protection for as long as you remain in the kingdom—you and all that go with you."

"So the Wardens told us, and the Seer of Kyöpelinvuori confirmed," said Egan. "Or none of us would be here—not myself, nor Asikkas' counselor. Without the Erilaiset as our allies, Löhi would already have conquered most of the Far Northern Land, and even Akkala would be besieged."

Some of Airiki's men murmured unhappily at Egan's sharp words, but their king raised his hand and nodded.

"Then let us talk about these matters and delay no more," he said. "That is why I sought you and why you have come. But first, Väinämöinen, will you not introduce the young lady at your side?"

Ulla blushed as all eyes turned toward her.

"Your Majesty, I present Ulla of the Karhulaiset, of whom you have doubtless heard," answered Väinämöinen. "As foretold in prophecy, she bears the Mark of the Clan upon her shoulder."

"The witch-child," whispered one of the Kotkalaisen chieftains, but the old wizard heard him and answered, "Nay, she is no witch. All the same, her deeds saved all the Seven Clans, and she is Ukko's sign and instrument on this earth."

Airiki bid them all sit at a round table with many seats set before the lowest step of the dais. His servants brought food and the sweet mead made in Akkala, while the king introduced his nobles and counselors, men with names such as Biorn, Grels, and Jarl—names not used among the other clans, and which Ulla had never heard before.

Airiki asked many questions about the other clans and their policies, and about the battles fought in High and Deep Länsimaa and all along the North Marches. Egan and Valso described all that had happened since the raid on

High Länsimaa years before: the sack of Keskimaa, Battle of Linnavuori, the constant strife each summer with the Itäläiset, and the attacks on Etelamaa by strange men from across the Itämeri Sea.

"Löhi will never stop making war on the Seven Clans," said Egan, "not until we are ruined or she herself destroyed and faded into nothingness. Indeed, as the Erilaiset tell us, that is our hope. Prophecies and ancient songs tell of Löhi's return but are unclear about her ending, save that her power will wane and she will pass at last into whatever fate awaits her in a short time—unless she defeats all the Kaammoslaiset and makes the Far Northern Land her own as before. If she succeeds, then all the power and all the strength of the land will flow into her, making it a barren and hostile place with winter everlasting and little hope for men."

"But all these things you already know, Your Majesty," said Valso. "For surely the Wardens and Shipwrights have shared their counsels and concerns with you, and many of your men have fought among the March Wardens in the north. Why, then, do you now seek counsel with the other clans? Will you not open your mind up to us at last?"

Airiki took a long draught from his cup and looked at his chieftains one by one before speaking.

"It is true enough," said the king. "We in Akkala have long heard from Bergil and the Wardens about the strife that afflicts the other clans. And yet most of our folk believed this did not concern us. Clans that dealt in magic and witchcraft, as in the days of old, could expect such troubles. But that has changed now.

"Two years ago, I put down the rebels who challenged me and was crowned king in Langvika. At first, all seemed well. Soon, though, news of strange things reached the south: dark shapes prowled around our borders and spied on our lands, always near the villages closest to Deep Länsimaa. Then came even worse news of people slain and homesteads burned. We kept these tidings as quiet as possible, but rumor spread."

"And there was this," said Biorn. "My lands lie in the northeast, where these things happened. Some of my men came upon a company of spies at night and drove them away. At daybreak, they found the bodies of three of their slain enemies. They were not men but twisted, wizened shapes, folk of evil kind, like demons from Tuonela."

"They were Hiisia," said Väinämöinen grimly, "Goblins of the north. Löhi has increased their race and marshaled their strength. They spy on all the lands of the Seven Clans."

"Little do I know of these things, save the name," said Airiki, "But such it was. And last year came the worst of all. Isku the Ship Master told you of the long galley that was attacked and lost in the Thousand Isles. Others have been attacked as well. The men across the Sea with whom we trade have grown hostile. The trade we depend on has never been worse.

"Then, in the winter, the last stroke fell. Sometime after the first snows, which came early, a strange and terrible thing appeared in Torgu, a port town a half-day's ride from here. Folk deemed it a ghost or specter or a shade of the dead. To some it looked like an old hag, ugly and shriveled; its cackling and wailing filled the night with terror. And some who saw this thing were stricken with a Plague and died or were sorely ill. From house to house it went, and from the town to other villages, wrapping all the lands in fear. At last, in the dead of winter, it came even to Langvika.

"Many died here, and fear spread throughout our folk; some said it was the end of the world, when evil and strife will overwhelm the Far Northern Land like a great wave from the sea. Even I . . ." Suddenly Airiki's voice dropped. He continued in almost a whisper. "Even I heard the hag's cry in the dead of night, and it filled my heart—the heart of Airiki the Strong, King of the Kotkalaiset—with dread. And so I wonder, we wonder. Are the stories true? Has Löhi indeed returned and come to Akkala? What do you say to this, Väinämöinen?"

"That you have done well to seek counsel and friendship with your kin— and with me, too. The hag was not Löhi. The Witch uses others for her purposes when she can. Löhi sent this ghost from Tuonela to afflict your folk. Lovĕatar is her name in the language of the men of the Seven Clans—the Mistress of Disease. The same figure has appeared in other lands, to our misery."

"And the same ghost slew my father," said Egan. "He died of the Winter Plague seven years ago. You are lucky, Airiki, that you only heard Lovĕatar's wail and did not feel her sting."

"Who can say?" said Väinämöinen. "In the world of men, of which we are a part, nothing is certain but the sun, wind, and sea, and that all things will run on to their appointed end as Ukko set in motion at the Beginning. But that does not make it vain to resist evil or strive for good. The hearts of men are not set in their courses like the stars in heaven. The choices you make govern many things, your own fate not the least."

Airiki seemed to frown at Väinämöinen words but then quickly nodded his head. He gestured with his big hand to Ulla, who stood just behind the old wizard.

"And what of Ulla," he asked, "the girl spoken of in old tales? What is her part in all this?"

"You have heard Mielikki's Prophecy, have you not?" answered Väinämöinen. "And those words that came from Tapio himself, Lord of the Forests?"

> When the cold hand reaches southward,
> reaches with its frozen fingers,
> comes a child into the Northland,
> all the clans to bring together.

"She is the Child of the Prophecy, Ulla of the North. She was sent to us all, mortal and Erilainen alike, as a sign to return the songs to our people! Show the Clan Mark to King Airiki and his men so that the Eagle Folk, too, last of all the Seven Clans, may learn the truth of Tapio's words!"

Ulla went to where the king sat with his men. She felt strangely uncomfortable here. She had come to enjoy the reactions of the great men—kings and captains, lords and merchants—who stared at the mark on her shoulder with wonder or even fear when they first saw it. But that was in Tavastia or Etelamaa. The tall, grim Kotkalaiset who held slaves and hung bodies from gibbets in their own towns made her uneasy and uncertain. The girl with dark hair withdrew the pin that fastened her mantle and uncovered her shoulder down to the blade. The mark stood out, black on her fair skin.

Airiki made no sign, though several of his men stirred and crowded closer to Ulla to better see the Clan Mark. She pulled the mantle over her shoulder and went back to Väinämöinen's side while the Kotkalaiset murmured among themselves.

"The Mark of the Clan," Airiki said at last. *"By the Clan Mark shall you know them."*

"Yes," said Egan. "It is Tapio's sign to all the clans that, if we stand together against the Witch as we did of old, we can prevail."

"But this sign is the Mark of the Karhulaiset alone, is it not?" said Airiki. "The Mark of the Bear Folk. Why not the Mark of Akkala, the Clan of the Eagle?"

"The Karhulaiset were the first of the Seven Clans," answered Väinämöinen. "A small folk, perhaps, yet the eldest. All the Kaamoslaiset in the Far Northern Land honored the Bear totem. Even Lemminkäinen of Tapiola took it as his token when he became the High King. It belongs to us all, even to my own people, the Erilaiset. It belongs to you, too, king of the Eagle."

"Draw swords with us, Airiki!" said Egan suddenly, with passion. "A league of the Seven Clans is what Löhi fears most. All she has done so far is to prevent that league. Is it not strange that her attempts to spread fear and divide us have only brought the Kaamoslaiset closer together? Only your folk are missing to make the circle complete."

"Aye, it is her greatest fear," said Väinämöinen. "It may be her only fear, for she knows the ancient prophecies better than any other. If the clans unite and the Kaamoslaiset return to the Old Ways, natural to them and this land, then her time will be short. The Witch cannot defeat the Vanhalaiset nor those that serve them. She will fade, never to return while this world lasts."

"But you seek more than our swords," said Airiki. "Always you speak of the Old Ways, the old magic and lore driven from this land long ago. Akkala honors Ukko. We remember Akka and Ilmatar, Ahti and Tapio after our fashion. But the races of the Erilaiset, and their magic spells, are different."

"And is it not strange," said Biorn, using Egan's words, "that to defeat the Witch's magic you say we must use this same magic ourselves?"

Väinämöinen rose, throwing back his crimson cloak. With a swift gesture, swifter than any mortal hand, he swept out his sword and brought it down on the table before them as plates and cups clattered and spilled. *Jääpuikko* gleamed like newly wrought steel, wrapped in a pale saffron glow like the eastern sky on a cold midwinter dawn.

The men nearby jumped back; several drew their blades. Airiki, though no less startled, was still.

"See, Airiki?" said the singer. "You speak much of magic for a folk long without it. But you do not understand. Magic, as you call it—the power of the songs and spells we make—is like this sword. Is the iron before you good or evil? Does it know right from wrong? Nay, it is only a tool. Good or evil come from the heart and hand that wield it.

"A man may defend his folk and home with this blade or use it to spread death and ruin. Either way, the blade bears no blame. The power of the songs, the magic of the Erilaiset, may be used for good or evil, and yet the songs are blameless of themselves. The wizards, be they mortal or Erilaisen, simply share the power of the world itself—the wind and water, earth and woods.

"Löhi was, indeed, one of the Erilaiset; so were many foul things that still live under the sun and moon, serving her. I will not deny it. But are there not many evil men among the Seven Clans, even among the Kotkalaiset? And yet they do not define their folk. Truly I say to you, Airiki, I will never bow to Löhi. None of the Erilaiset of Laulavalaakso or the Enchanted Valley will; we will always help the Seven Clans while we live. Such is our purpose; we were born into the Far Northern Land for this."

The old man withdrew his sword. All looked at one another in silence, waiting for some sign from Airiki. The king pulled on his ginger beard, staring hard at *Jääpuikko*. At last he rose from his place.

"Is this also your counsel?" he asked Bergil.

"Yes," the Warden replied. "It is time to complete the circle."

"And you, Lady," the king said to Siitsa, who had been silent throughout all their debate, "I know the Seer's rede already; she makes common cause with the Erilaiset and would that Akkala do the same. Has this changed?"

"It has not changed, Your Majesty," said Siitsa. "The Lord Väinämöinen has my mistress's trust. They are partners in all that concerns these matters."

Finally Airiki turned to Egan. The big man broke into a broad smile and clasped the young king's shoulder.

"Let us be brothers in arms, then," he said. "I will not sit idly by while witches and ghosts torment my people and our boats are lost at sea. I will lead a host of the Eagle Folk into battle, and Löhi will again remember our name! But, although I lift the ban on the Erilaiset from this day on, I will not suffer the old songs and rituals in this land—not yet. I will come myself to Laulavalaakso and see this place where the people of the Seven Clans now gather at the foot of Kyöpelinvuori; then I will decide.

"And let us hope," he said, suddenly gesturing to Ulla and meeting her steady gaze. "Let us hope the Mark of the Clan is indeed a sign that victory is at hand and that peace and good fortune will be ours once again."

Chapter Six

Fire in the Night

There was little time to celebrate the league that united the Seven Clans against Löhi once more. Spring ran on, with summer swiftly approaching. Löhi's allies and servants would soon raid across the North Marches, striking at different places this year, seeking to pillage and burn, slowly wearing down the strength and ruining the lands of the Kaamoslaiset.

After the snows melted and the rivers went down, it took time for the Witch's armies to gather and march in that land of rivers, lakes, and fens. Löhi seldom struck before midsummer, but Väinämöinen was anxious. Egan felt it, too. They both believed that the coming summer would be decisive, and they doubted the Witch's intentions. The young king of Etelamaa was especially eager to return north and make his dispositions of the Swan Folk who would fight alongside their kinsmen.

Väinämöinen and his friends stayed one week at Langvika, though the old man went little about the city, staying mostly at the Warden House where Bergil and his captains lived. He often met with Airiki, speaking in great detail about Löhi and all her history, about the Erilaiset of the Enchanted Valley, and, most of all, about Mielikki and her prophecies.

Egan had a suite in Merisuihke, where Ulla and Siitsa had rooms as well. For Egan, used to the old castle in the Stone City, this was no great discomfort, but Ulla disliked her cramped, stony, windowless chamber, which was cold even in summer. Väinämöinen, content that his dark-haired ward was with Egan and his men at Merisuihke, let her be while he met with Airiki and the others to discuss armies, weapons, and battles to come. Siitsa offered little company, keeping to herself in her own chamber or else going out alone on whatever errands the Seer of Kyöpelinvuori had given her. So Ulla took to walking alone along the cliff wall beneath the castle and sitting on its weathered rocks, gazing out at the sound and the little islands in the distance while the seabirds wheeled overhead.

One day, Egan, standing on a broken parapet that looked seaward, saw Ulla sitting on the rocks below. He called to her, but the wind took his voice and she didn't hear him. He stood there for a while watching her, surprised by how much older she looked. It seemed strange that he only noticed this now, from afar, although they had traveled many miles together. Ulla had been a child, no older than his sister, when he first saw her at Nummela—a scrawny girl from the north with unbraided hair, clad in ill-fitting clothes from Karelia. She was very strange to him then, and still was, though he now knew her well.

Now he noticed that she had changed in many ways since those times. Though yet a girl, she would soon come of age in the reckoning of her folk. She wore her long hair braided in the simple but comely fashion of the peasant girls of northern Tavastia. Her pale face was round and fair, her white arms were long, and she was growing tall, almost as tall as he was. Standing on the crumbling wall, Egan saw her as if for the very first time. He wondered just who she was and what her destiny might be, this girl Väinämöinen had saved from death whose scars meant so much to the folk of the Seven Clans.

The young man walked down to the cliffside, and Ulla turned toward him even as he approached, as if she expected him. Egan stopped short, then broke into a smile.

"You knew I was coming, didn't you?" he asked. "You could feel my presence. It's true what they say, what Väinämöinen says, then—you have great power within you. How does it feel when you sense something like that?

What is it like? I used to wish that I had the power of wizards and singers, the power to use magic and sing spells. But I am not so sure anymore!" He sat down beside her on a slick, weather-stained stone.

"It's hard to explain," said Ulla in the easy and familiar tone she used with Egan when they were alone, almost as if she were speaking with Kirsikka. Väinämöinen had taught her well how to speak to the lords and ladies, the merchants and tradesmen, the strong and the powerful of the Far Northern Land, but she had known Egan for so long, and he treated her so kindly—more like a sister or cousin than a stranger—that she had a simple, unaffected way with him. As Ulla was a child, an orphan from a poor village of humble folk, and a girl, only the slaves of Akkala were below her station—but she sat, talked, and laughed with Egan, King of the Swan Folk and perhaps the greatest lord in the north, as if she were a princess and his equal.

"It started when I went with Väinämöinen to the Enchanted Valley," she continued, "a long time ago. I can't really remember what it was like before that. It's like the sun on your face, the wind at your back. You just . . . well, you can feel the power in things, and you can push yourself out to it, and . . . I'm sorry, I can't really explain it. Väinämöinen is the teacher."

"And is he going to teach you to become a wizard?" asked Egan. "You have lived in the Singing Valley for many years now, but you do not have a staff."

Ulla hesitated, then spoke softly, though no one lingered nearby and the sound of the sea filled their ears.

"Soon," she said. "This year or maybe the next. Don't tell anyone, especially Siitsa! He does not want the Seer to know, not yet."

Egan nodded. "No. No, he wouldn't. I understand." A great wave crashed against the cliff, leaving a fine spray hanging in the air about them.

"I've seen you sitting here several times," said Egan. "Do you like looking at the sea?"

"Don't you? It is so different here than in the glassy bay in your City. The waves are so large, the water seems so deep and endless. I used to think the lakes in High Länsimaa were big."

"You should see Lake Etelajärvi, near to where my family comes from. That is greater than all the rest of the lakes of the Far Northern Land together! Great seals live in the lake, and I remember, when I was young, we went hunting in little boats out on the water. Hundreds of them would gather on little rocky islands in the sunshine—and in winter, too. You could hunt them on the ice. Their oil is very precious.

"But you are right; the bay of Etelamaa usually stays calm unless it storms. The coast here is much wilder."

"There is music in the waves," said Ulla. "The songs of Ahti, Lord of the Sea. I can hear them. Väinämöinen said that when Ukko first made the world, water covered it. For ages, there was nothing but the song of Ahti, the first of the Vanhalaiset sent into the world; at least, there was nothing until Ukko raised the land from the seas. Can you feel Ahti's power in the waves?"

"Yes," said Egan slowly. "Not the same way that you do, perhaps, but, yes, I can feel the power of Ahti."

Ulla narrowed her eyes and gazed at the islands, both within the sound and in the distance. Egan had sharp eyes, but Ulla's were sharper, and she had learned to use *sight* to see better—even without her jewel. She could see things farther off which were hidden and unclear. There were many islands before them, some little more than grey rocks jutting out of the sea, others green and grassy with trees and moss. Some of the rocky isles had red and orange flowers growing in their brakes and white birds fluttering about on the wind.

"I would like to visit those islands," she said at last. "I wonder what it would be like to live there? Nothing but the wind and the tides, always the same, never changing from year to year—I think that would be very nice."

"Those islands," said Egan, "are the closest of the Thousand Isles, as they are called, whatever their number. Off the coast of Akkala, to the south and east, they stretch far out into the Itämeri Sea. A fisherfolk live among them. They are reckoned among the Kotkalaiset, but they seldom come to the mainland, living their lives by their own ways in the Isles. There is a large island, greater than all the others, very far from here, nearer to the lands of foreign men than our own shores. They say the folk of that island speak a different tongue. Lemminkäinen hid there for a time, long, long ago."

Egan fell silent then, but he and Ulla, the young king and the girl from the north, sat together as the afternoon faded and the grey waves broke upon the cliffside, wrapping it in clouds of mist while the south wind blew upon the face of the old stone castle of Langvika.

***

Väinämöinen, Egan, and their company left Langvika swiftly one night after the sun sank and darkness finally fell. They planned to strike the road to the north and ride as quickly as possible back to Tavastia. Airiki would join them on the road later, for he, too, was riding north to a great muster of warriors that he had called. The men of Akkala would fight that summer alongside the other clans, though neither Airiki nor Väinämöinen wished that news spread among the Eagle Folk, where it might quickly reach Löhi's ears; so they departed Langvika without fanfare and did their best to avoid attention.

As the company left the East Gate, Ulla saw a strange thing in the yellow light of the lamps and torches. A line of a dozen men on foot, chained together, shuffled toward the city while two horsemen armed with spears drove them on. She wondered who the men were—thieves or criminals bound for Langvika's gallows—when she realized with a shock that they were slaves being driven to the city's market. She thought of her own folk, bound and chained by the Easterners when she was young, and of her family, lost forever, dead or enslaved in distant lands. Ulla glanced at Siitsa, riding just behind her, who had suffered such things herself, but Siitsa made no sign.

The chained slaves stood by the roadside in silence while they passed. Ulla, feeling their eyes on her, was glad that she could not see their faces in the gloom.

They rode north then, a hard ride, for they pushed their mounts and rode deep into each evening. All felt weary and saddle-sore when at last they stopped at night. They could not take the river back north, of course—the current ran too strong—so they had a longer journey before them. The king's party usually camped each night as far from the villages and farms of the Kotkalaiset as might be. Ulla and Siitsa had a small tent to sleep in, dyed in the pale blue of Etelamaa. Siitsa suddenly became more talkative. Though she always sounded faintly mocking, for the first time she asked Ulla questions about Grankulta and her life among the northern villages. Siitsa even told Ulla a bit about her own life in Keskimaa before it burned.

Siitsa's family had been well off, her father a trader in bloodrock and cloths, so she had grown up in a house with many comforts. But, although Ulla spoke freely about her flight from the Itäläiset, describing in detail how she and Kirsikka had first met and how they were rescued by Väinämöinen, the Seer's servant would not say a word about her own capture. She fell silent when Ulla asked about it.

Väinämöinen's mood had changed, too. He grew merrier, and often rode with Egan on one side and Ulla on the other, amusing them with legends of the Erilaiset and the Seven Clans. The old wizard knew more stories than any other living soul in the Far Northern Land, and Ulla never tired of listening. He told them tales from Akkala about its people's strange speech, and of Unaja's people, the Wolf Folk, who were their close kin. For when the Kaamoslaiset first came to the Far Northern Land, the tall men and women who eventually settled in the west spoke a dialect different than all the rest. Then the Erilaiset taught the people their own language, which became the speech of all the Seven Clans, so that in time they forgot they had ever spoken any other. But even now, centuries later, the Kotkalaiset and Susilaiset still used many words and sounds unique to them, which came from the ancient tongue they no longer remembered.

Teaching Ulla about the speech of the Kotkalaiset made the old man recall a famous legend in Akkala about a king who lived in Langvika when it was still just a trading town and when there was a single round tower where the old castle now stood.

"There was once a king down in Langvika," the old wizard began, "long ago, when the southlands were not so crowded and its woods still grew thick and wild. This king had a daughter named Vappu, who was not only beautiful, with the palest skin and fairest hair in all the land, but smart, too. In fact, she was so smart that the king set her to learning all the tongues of the world, from the east where the Itäläiset dwell, to the mountain halls of the dwarves far to the north, to the tongues of the strange men who live in the south where the sun is bright and hot. Because Vappu was so smart, she learned them all in no time. She had only to spend time with any traveler to soon know their speech.

"Then the king was very proud of Vappu, rightfully so, but she had suitors from many lands and kingdoms and he didn't know how to make the best match for her, which worried him greatly. One day, he finally had an idea. He announced that any man who could bring to her a new language she could not understand would have her hand in marriage, but it must be a real tongue, not fake or contrived, or else he would have the suitor flung from the tower into the Itämeri Sea.

"Now a young shepherd called Timo, who at that time lived in a poor village in the forest, heard of the king's command. Timo didn't have many possessions, but he had sharp wits. He was also a bit of a gambler who didn't mind taking a risk to improve his fortune. Timo told the other villagers that he was going to the castle to win Vappu's hand, and they laughed at him, but he set out through the woods just the same, for he had a secret plan.

"Timo was a great wanderer, and on his journeys he had learned to understand the speech of all the creatures in Tapio's woods—the sparrow and the cuckoo, the squirrel and the fox, the raven and the woodpecker, and all the rest. As he walked through the forest he asked some of his woodland friends to accompany him, and they gladly agreed. When he reached the tower, the guards laughed at him because of his homespun clothes and simple manners. They asked him if he could swim, because the crashing breakers below the tower were cold and dark, but they let him in to see the king and his daughter nonetheless.

"'Now, Your Highness,' he said, removing his simple peasant's hood with its patches and shaking his tangled hair, 'they say you know the speech of all living things, do they not?' 'Indeed I do,' said Vappu, surprised that a humble shepherd boy could be so bold. 'Well then,' said he, 'can you tell me what my friends are saying?' And straightaway the sparrow, squirrel, and woodpecker leapt from his bag. '*Shi shi shi shoo*,' said the sparrow, 'Let me fly away!' and 'Crack-a-crack-brak,' chirped the squirrel, 'Don't grab my tail!' and 'Thunk-dunk-thunk,' knocked the woodpecker, 'Show me the wood!'

"Then Vappu was amazed, for she had never before considered the speech of Ukko's creatures. It was new to her and both she and the king had to admit Timo was a clever boy who had fulfilled the king's commands. And so Vappu happily married him at midsummer, and the shepherd from the forest village became a prince."

The old man spun his tales, the sun grew warmer, and the days stretched on longer as they rode north. Soon they crossed the Akkajoki and passed through the river lands, finally coming to a broad, shallow stream amidst stands of pine and spruce. It marked the border between Akkala and Tavastia in those parts, and Väinämöinen intended to cross the stream and strike a good, well-travelled road that would speed them back to the Singing Valley.

Jarl, Airiki's counselor and advisor, had a large homestead on the Akkalan side called Bredvætten. His big family, and those of his chief men, lived there. Jarl was lord of the lands all about, including several large villages nearby, so Airiki had chosen Bredvætten as the gathering place for his army before they moved north. The king of the Eagle Folk reached Bredvætten three days before Väinämöinen and his friends and was waiting for them.

Three hundred men had already gathered from the nearby districts, and many more would come soon, for the Kotkalaiset were a great people, the largest of all the Seven Clans. The captains and their men-at-arms camped in an open field some miles away, but Airiki and his guards stayed in Bredvætten's long, plain wooden hall, where places were prepared for Väinämöinen, Egan, and the rest. Airiki welcomed them when they rode up, tired and stiff. Servants and maids came out to receive them, guiding them to places where they could wash and put on fresh garments. The cooks had prepared a feast of whole swine roasted in pits after the fashion of Akkala, sour southern bread, and the last of the winter's store of sweet, dried fruit. Airiki sat with Väinämöinen, Egan, and the other chief captains and counselors, and, as pots of dark beer passed among them, the men talked deep into the night.

Ulla sat with the women of Jarl's household, but they said little to her. Perhaps the strange tales they had heard about the witch-child of the Bear Folk raised by the legendary Väinämöinen made them afraid or suspicious. As the night wore on, a woman came to take her to a place in a barn where she and Siitsa could sleep with the Etelalaisen serving women who accompanied Egan, but Väinämöinen refused, telling the Akkalan women that the girls would stay in the long hall near the places prepared for himself, Egan, and the other men. Though this seemed strange to the them—in Akkala, men and women were almost always strictly separated—they did not dare to go against the old man's instructions.

The hall, plain and simply furnished, had a large fire pit in the center and several smaller, enclosed rooms at either end. Airiki and his men were quartered in the rooms at the end nearest the hall's doors. Egan was given the rooms at the other end. Guards and servants slept by the fire pit. The men were still drinking and talking in the cool dark outside when Ulla retired to the little room given to her. Siitsa already slept, rolled in a blanket in the corner, and red coals dimly glowed on the room's small brazier. The girl with dark hair felt tired, weary of Akkala, its strange people, and its strange ways; she missed Kirsikka and Unaja more each day. She wanted to return to the Valley. Though she normally would have stayed awake, listening with her sharp ears for Väinämöinen and Egan to return, tonight sleep overcame her and she quickly drifted away into forgetfulness.

She slept deeply at first, perhaps for several hours, but then she began to dream. As she often did, she dreamed of Grankulta and her old home in the north. She was with her father and brother, walking in the fields of tall rye before harvest. Big Janni, searching for something he couldn't find, kept glancing back nervously at his children. Her Aunt Päivikki, suddenly appearing, reproached Ulla for leaving some chore undone and not behaving as a maiden child should. They walked and walked, and her father went on so far ahead that she could no longer see him. She and her brother were alone. Then the rye parted and a horseman appeared, a tall Easterner with a blazing torch. Ulla tried to scream while the field blazed all around her; cries and shouts broke out from all sides. She could feel the fire's heat on her face as she turned round and round, seeking some escape.

Ulla awoke with a start, only to find her nightmare come true. Dull orange light illuminated the little room. In the hall, people were indeed shouting and screaming. She jumped to her feet and looked wildly about her from side to side. Siitsa was not there, but several others gathered near the entrance to the small room, including Egan, who had drawn his sword.

The long hall was on fire, and bright flames blazed at its far end, racing toward them as the thatching ignited. Black smoke came on before the flames, rolling along the roofbeams, then curling down and choking all within. The doors were lost in smoke and flame, and blazing roof timbers fell near the fire pit.

People tripped over each other in the confusion and panic. Ulla saw the Etelalaisen guards trying to pull Egan to safety through the murk, but he threw them off. The king's eyes suddenly fell on Ulla, still standing in the open doorway of the tiny room.

"Ulla!" he cried, and, coming to her, grabbed her hand and pulled her close to him. "Ulla, listen to me!" he yelled through the din. "We have to get out of here; stay close to me! Cover your face!"

Just that moment, they heard a loud cracking sound. Ulla thought that several timbers burst from the wall beside them, and Egan raised his cloak as a shield, expecting flaming brands to fall down. Then they saw a gaping hole in the wall, and Väinämöinen clambered through it.

"Out!" the wizard cried. "All of you, out through the wall now! Where are Ulla and Siitsa?" Egan pulled Ulla behind him and, passing in front of Väinämöinen, stumbled through the hole and tossed the girl onto the wet, mossy ground outside. Sinio appeared next, then several others, guards and servants. Egan rose and, using *Tarunmiekka* as a prop to steady himself, climbed back inside the burning building.

The heat almost overwhelmed him and he staggered, again using the sword to keep his balance. Väinämöinen appeared next to him, and the shaman raised his arms into the air in a gesture of defiance. Eyes closed, he murmured some words Egan couldn't hear, a chant of some kind in the old tongue of the Erilaiset. Then in a booming voice he cried, "*Paloa Pysähdys!*"

The thick black smoke rolled back as if the north wind blew against it and the fire flickered, recoiling from some unseen barrier. The space about them cleared and the terrible heat diminished even as the rest of the hall burned and blazed.

"Check the rooms!" yelled Väinämöinen to Egan and a soldier who still stood beside him. "Get everyone out at once! And help those folk there on the floor; they may still be alive! I cannot hold this blaze back for long, and even I cannot put it out!"

Egan and the guard did as instructed, but the rooms were empty. They carried out several people who had been overcome by the smoke and heat, then Egan climbed into the hall one last time. His head swimming, he swayed back and forth. Väinämöinen caught him and flung him back outside. Moments later, the old wizard himself leapt through the hole with flames licking at his heels, his long beard singed and smoking.

Outside, amid sounds of commotion everywhere, dogs barking and howling in the dark, the Etelalaiset moved away from the blazing hall to a small stand of nearby trees. There, the guards formed a circle of drawn swords around the king. Two men were missing, a guard and one of Egan's serving men who had been sleeping inside the hall. Shadowy figures ran about, silhouetted against the orange flames, and they could hear shouts and the unmistakable clash of iron on iron.

"Stay here and guard the king—and Ulla, too," said Väinämöinen when he caught his breath. "I am going to find out what is happening and look for Siitsa and the serving women. But be ready to ride swiftly, if our beasts are still here!"

The old man disappeared into the gloom. The others stood about nervously, dazed and in disbelief, while the hall collapsed into a red, glowing mound. Ulla sat on the ground beside Egan and rubbed her stinging eyes. She looked at her bare feet, black and soot-covered, and realized her boots were in the wooden hall. Egan coughed. Before long, however, Väinämöinen returned, even as the eastern sky softened with the first tendrils of the hastening dawn. Airiki came with him.

"What has happened?" cried Egan, jumping to his feet.

"Treachery!" said Airiki. "Treachery and evil. The fire was set on purpose—and by our own folk, no less. They also attacked my men. There was a battle, but the traitors are dead now. Are you all right, Egan? And your people?"

"I am all right," answered Egan. "Väinämöinen saved us. But two of my men are missing, and I fear they are dead. Nor can we find Siitsa of Kyöpelinvuori."

"*Ka*," muttered Airiki, spitting upon the ground. "This news is ill. Never have guests been so abused; I will pay you richly in recompense for your lost folk. Do not judge the hospitality of the Eagle Folk by this evil deed. The guilty ones will be punished and will rue the very day they were born!"

As the light slowly grew, Airiki and Egan went back to the ruined hall with Väinämöinen, Sinio, and Valso; the old man kept Ulla close beside him. It soon became clear what had happened, if not why. Dozens of Airiki's men scurried about, some on horseback and others on foot, and more arrived all the time from the encampment where the alarm had been raised.

On the ground, to one side of the hall, lay five of King Airiki's men slain in the fight; several others had died in the fire. But a ways apart lay the eight attackers, cut down as they fought in and around the burning hall. They had killed the guards who sat in the doorway and poured oil all about before setting the hall ablaze. Yet Airiki had escaped and Väinämöinen returned in the nick of time to save the rest. The old man had been outside beneath the stars, as usual, when the commotion began.

Jarl, the Master of Bredvætten, came up then with Siitsa and a dozen Kotkalaiset. They had two men with them, bloody and beaten but still alive. One wore simple clothes, but the other was clad in a richer garment bound by a fine leather belt with a silver buckle. His blue eyes looked wildly from man to man while Jarl's dogs growled and circled.

"Grels!" exclaimed Airiki, for he recognized the man with the silver buckle, a minor lord of the Eagle Folk who had come to the muster. "So you are the traitor! How dare you raise your sword against the rightful king of Akkala?"

"My men found them hiding in a wood," said Jarl grimly. "The Lady here led us to them. This dog must be the ringleader of the whole stinking lot." He kicked Grels savagely in the stomach and the man slumped to his knees.

"Where were you, Siitsa?" said Väinämöinen. "We were worried about you. How did you come by these men?"

"I was watching the stars, even as you were, my lord," said Siitsa. "But I saw the flames, then saw these two running away in the darkness toward the trees, so I followed them."

"And who are you?" said Airiki to the second man. "Why did you do this foul deed? Speak, or I'll have you burned alive!" The man, his face already broken and bloodied, said nothing. Jarl raised his hand to strike him, but Grels pulled himself up and spoke.

"He is my man; let him be!" he said. "He is loyal to his lord and to his clan. If you lust to burn someone, burn me!"

"Do not tempt me," answered Airiki. "There are many ways to repay treachery. However you die, know that your sons will never inherit your lands and your daughters will be sold in the markets!"

"Treachery!" cried Grels, spitting. "*Ka!* It takes a traitor to name one. You are no rightful king. You have betrayed our clan and brought these sorcerers and magic-users into Akkala against our ancient law. You make common cause with our enemies and lead us into war with this Witch in the forgotten land. And you take this witch-child, this Karhulainen, into your own hall with our men! Is it any wonder that evil spirits afflict our land and all goes ill with our folk? Tuonela take you, and be damned!"

At a sign from Airiki, Jarl drew a knife and would have slain Grels then and there, but Väinämöinen stayed his hand.

"Enough, Airiki! Whatever your law demands later, do not kill him in wrath! And we must know more about these things and why they were done, for I deem he did not act alone—or only with these few men."

"True enough," said the big man slowly. Jarl lowered his knife.

"What have you to say to that, Grels? How many are with you? Who else shares your shame and dishonor?"

Grels smiled, blood dripping from his broken teeth. "Many folk are against you, more all the time. Your day will come—if this wizard and his kind don't kill you first."

"Ignorance excuses many things, Grels," said Väinämöinen. "Lies and deception may excuse others. But what you have done here—trying to kill your own lord and the king of Etelamaa besides—cannot be justified. And you have shed innocent blood and led your own folk to ruin. Who urged you to do these things, Grels? Who put these words in your mouth?

"You cannot bewitch me as you have Airiki," answered Grels.

"I have done nothing to Airiki or any man here," said Väinämöinen. "Nothing other than tell the truth: that Löhi has returned, that these ills come from her, and that we must all stand together or fall separately to her might.

"But you are wrong on another count, Grels. I can indeed bewitch you and you will tell me what we need to know to stop this wickedness. Who else stands against the king?"

Väinämöinen stooped to pick up his staff, which lay on the ground. Then he made a circle with his arm in gesture of invocation. He whispered so softly that the others could not hear his words, but straightaway Grels's face went slack and his arms dropped to his sides. The man closed his eyes as if he had fallen asleep, but said nothing. Väinämöinen gently whispered as the *loitsu* of enchantment took hold and the gathered folk watched in amazement. Grels sighed.

At that moment, the red sun broke through the wispy clouds hugging the horizon, bathing all of Bredvætten in its morning glory. Siitsa suddenly stepped forward and raised her arm, clamping her fist closed as if she squeezed a handful of berries. "Speak!" she cried harshly, "Tell us what you know!"

Grels opened his eyes and gasped before slumping to the ground.

"Siitsa!" cried Väinämöinen, but it was too late.

Jarl rolled the man onto his back with his boot; his eyes, fixed and lifeless, stared blankly into nothingness. "He's dead," stammered Jarl, astonished.

Airiki looked hard at Väinämöinen. "It seems we have chosen a dangerous path. So be it! Let what rats come out that will; all the better to find them and catch them soon. I will not be deterred from my purpose."

"That is well," said Väinämöinen. "But take care and don't be rash. You are strong, Airiki, and your luck is good. That's an important thing. But Akkala's strength is needed, not yours alone."

"Take him away," said King Airiki, pointing to Grels's man. "And call my captains together. I must leave you now, lords, but all is safe. I trust these men, the men of my homeland, with my life. No traitors will come anywhere near you. Already a new place is prepared for your rest and breakfast."

When the Kotkalaiset had left, Väinämöinen looked at Siitsa and then at the dead man, Grels, still on the ground before them. Siitsa trembled, her clenched fist shaking at her side. The old man touched her forehead, and the trembling stopped.

"What magic was that?" asked the singer in a stern voice. "Where did you learn such a spell? Surely not from any Erilainen in Laulavalaakso! He was already under my enchantment and you stopped his heart. What were you doing?"

"I-I only wanted to make him speak," the young woman stuttered. "I didn't mean to—for that to happen."

"And where did you learn that spell?"

"From my mistress. She has an old book in the tower and I have learned to read the ancient letters."

"Then forget them!" said Väinämöinen. "Such enchantments are dangerous and dark—too dangerous for mortals. They are as dangerous for you as for your victim."

Siitsa bowed her head and Väinämöinen sighed.

"Go and rest," he said. "All of you. It has been a strange night and a sad one. We are all weary and tired. Let us meet by that black barn yonder in some hours. Go—even you guards! King Egan will be safe with me and will return to you shortly."

Ulla began to walk with the others toward Bredvætten's clustered buildings, but Väinämöinen grabbed her sleeve.

"Not you," he said. "You stay with me."

"So what do you think, Väinämöinen?" asked Egan, as surprised by the strange events as all the others. He coughed, the smoke and soot from the fire still in his chest. "Were the rebels trying to kill Airiki only? There is always strife among the Kotkalaiset, they say. Or do you think we—or more specifically you—were the real prize?"

"I wonder—aye, I wonder. And I doubt now we will ever know."

Egan looked around at the hall, still smoldering, and the faces of the dead men stretched out on the ground, grey now in the morning sun. He shook his head.

"One thing is certain," said the king. "It is high time we left Akkala and returned to the north. We have passed the whole spring on this journey, and now it's summer, the summer of our hope. Let us ride today!"

The old man smiled.

"So we will, my lad; so we will."

Chapter Seven

The Battle
of the Marshy Gap

Väinämöinen had left the Singing Valley for Akkala even as spring's first blush crept across the Far Northern Land, but summer was well underway by the time he returned. The old man had received messages, as wizardly folk might, from Erilaiset and mortal *tietäjää* in High Länismaa, so he knew that battle had erupted early in the lands of the Karhulaiset. Strong bands of Itäläisen riders harassed villages far south of the Marches, and a larger company had attacked and taken a border fort of the Wardens. Scouts reported that more enemies gathered to the north, Hiisia among them. Löhi had bided her time and rebuilt her strength, and this year, it seemed, she would attempt another full assault on High Länismaa and the lands to the south.

The singer had been home only a few days when two long-expected friends also returned to the Valley: Turi the Changer and Ilkaa. They arrived at night, saddle-sore and weary from the long journey back from the north of Deep Länismaa. Ilkaa had recovered somewhat from his ordeal but still looked worn and thin. His appearance shocked Ulla; he seemed to have aged many years in a short time. His face now bore lines of sorrow and hard experience. But his smile was unchanged, and it quickly spread wide when he saw Ulla again for the first time in many months.

When they had rested and washed away the stains of their journey, Turi told his news—that they had found signs of a camp north of Suommaa and secret paths long prepared where none had ever before existed. They could not know how great a camp or how many men gathered there. It could be hundreds for a raid toward Valkeakosk or thousands to invade Deep Länismaa or even Akkala. But the Witch had plainly prepared an unpleasant surprise for the Seven Clans in the west, even as her servants and allies harried them in the east.

"It is well that we made our foray when we did," said Turi, "though sad that our Warden friends died in the attempt. Let us hope their sacrifice was not in vain. And it is well that you convinced Airiki to join us, Väinämöinen, and you, too, Egan. That is a great stroke against Löhi and perhaps something she never looked for! The swords and axes of the Eagle Folk are a boon to us beyond hope, especially now that it seems Löhi has brought men from distant lands to swell her ranks. Let us hope our allies arrive soon, or they may arrive too late!"

Before long, Airiki himself came to Kyöpelinvuori, where he had not been for many years. He arrived with Bergil and a company of Wardens bound for High Länsimaa and bearing good news for his new allies. A strong force of men from the king's own homelands had gathered in northern Akkala—not the whole strength of the Eagle Folk by any means, for it would take time to assemble and provision such a host, but still many companies of well-armed men, battle-hardened by raids across the Itämeri Sea and battles for the crown of Akkala. Nearly ready to march, they waited only for word from their king. Airiki also brought news that the other traitors who had conspired to kill him—and Egan and Väinämöinen—had been discovered and slain. The short-lived rebellion had ended, though it remained unclear who the actual ringleaders had been.

Thus the leaders of the Kaammoslaiset had gathered at Kyöpelinvuori, for Asikkas had come north again from Tapiola and messengers had come from Teemu, High Lord of the Hirvilaiset. They met in the Seer's old tower, swiftly taking counsel among themselves and deciding how to divide their forces; they had little time left for debate. The main forces of the Etelalaiset and Tavastialaiset, the Folk of the Swan and of the Hare, already camped in High Länsimaa where they fought every summer. Juvari, Egan's captain, would lead them. Together with the Karhulaiset, they would contest whatever force Löhi sent against them. But Egan had kept another army, a smaller force of several hundred, near Pikku Niittuset and south of the *lansikita*; the March Wardens also had new strength coming up from the south. The chief question, then, was whether the threat was now greater to High Länismaa or Deep Länismaa.

Teemu's messengers begged for all possible help. They reported that their lord was fearful, more fearful than he had ever been since the battle at Linnavuori, for he knew of Turi's report. Unlikely as it seemed, he worried that a large force from the north might assail Valkeakosk. The Elk Folk had raised an army and there were also many Wardens in Deep Länismaa, but Teemu's host was not large and mostly camped in the south where the Itäläiset had attacked before.

As fate would have it, an Erilainen came to Kyöpelinvuori even as the leaders gathered. A Haltia of the Enchanted Valley, one of Lúven's folk who scouted beyond the North Marches, he reported straightaway to the tower and quickly gave his account. His news was ill, if not unexpected: all signs pointed to a great invasion of High Länsimaa that summer. Juvari urged that all possible help be sent to Keskimaa.

"And it may be," said the elf, "that this new strength from Akkala will not only save High Länsimaa, but give us the advantage, such as we have seldom enjoyed. If this truly is the Witch's last gambit, as some believe, then perhaps we might rout her servants and score a great victory, one which may cripple her forevermore.

"And there is yet another sign," he continued. "It seems that Löhi has sent a new captain or champion. Rumors of such a one came across the Marches last year, and now many have seen a strange figure leading the Witch's servants. Whether mortal or Erilainen none can say, for he is clad all in black mail and mounted on a black horse and he wears a mask of silver or painted iron, fashioned like the full moon staring blankly into nothingness. So the Bear Folk who saw him first called him Kuupää, the Moonface; now all along the Marches people call him by that name. None know what power or strength he has or what talisman he holds; perhaps he is a Haltia of Työ's folk. Whatever the truth, it seems an ill omen."

Väinämöinen laughed grimly. "Such is the game that Löhi sets out for us," the old wizard said. "A new captain and new strength in High Länsimaa, yet maybe an opportunity for us, too; but the Elk Folk are threatened as well. Löhi is fishing, but what is the bait? Where is she trying to lure us, to trap us? Or maybe there is no trap, no lure, only overwhelming force and all choices likely to run ill."

Then the Seer, who until then had said little, spoke as she stood by the golden Sampo with her hand upon its crown. "All choices may be ill in such perilous times," she said. "Yet in the face of uncertainty, decisions must be made. Dark is all the land north of the Marches where Löhi holds sway. But I have turned my *sight* toward Suommaa and finally pierced its shadows. I have seen the very camp that Turi guessed at and the path long prepared through the wilderness. The enemy's host there is great, and it will soon move on Valkeakosk. So the Witch thinks to surprise us and overrun all the north of Teemu's land before we can react. But Löhi does not yet know that Akkala and Airiki are set against her and the Seven Clans united.

"Let the Witch's trap be sprung upon her own hand! Let the swords of the Eagle Folk surprise her in turn. It is what she least expects, and so our hope is the greater. This is the counsel of Kyöpelinvuori."

"I agree," said Väinämöinen. "For to me, we have little choice: we must help Teemu and his people, no matter the risk. But do not forget that the Witch sent Lovêatar to sicken and afflict the Clan of the Eagle this very winter. It seems strange that she would do so, then be surprised by their enmity."

Nonetheless they agreed that the threat to the Elk Folk was the most urgent and that Airiki's men should go north to Valkeakosk. Indeed, Airiki would have followed the Seer's counsel in any case, for she had aided him greatly and without her he might not have won the crown of Akkala.

Things moved quickly after the council. Egan sent word to his men at Pikku Niituset to move north through the *lansikita* and on to Valkeakosk. Airiki left at once to lead his men into Deep Länsimaa. Messengers were sent to tell Teemu help was on the way. Egan, with the Seer's encouragement, meant to follow his men north, but Väinämöinen would not ride with him. They could not all go to the lands of the Elk Folk and take the chance that Löhi would spare High Länsimaa. If she struck hard, help would be needed there. So the singer made ready to leave with Bergil and the Wardens to do what he could to aid the Bear Folk. King Asikkas of Tavastia would accompany him, for most of the army of the Hare Folk already fought there against the raiders from the east.

Ulla felt for the most part forgotten. She remembered Väinämöinen's promise to take her on the hunt and complete her initiation into the *tietäjää* upon their return to Tavastia, but the old man had made that promise many months ago, and much had happened since then. Ulla knew that, with war again upon them, he would have little time for teaching her the higher arts of wizardry. Yet only the great among the Erilaiset might teach them. She still expected to go with Väinämöinen to High Länismaa and perhaps even return to the North Marches for the first time since her village, like so many others, was laid waste by the Easterners. But when she asked Väinämöinen, he told her no in that curt manner meant to cut off all further discussion. Ulla was to remain in the Valley.

Ulla sat in her *pirtti* with Kirsikka on the day both Väinämöinen and Egan were to leave. She already felt lonely. At least Kirsikka would stay with her, but her red-haired friend had changed. She, too, had grown older, and she thought of little now except Eglano. Eglano, the young duke, had stayed in Tavastia, spending many days and nights at Laulavalaakso while his brother traveled to Akkala.

Kirsikka sang for him and the other visitors several times, her clear voice enchanting all hearts as powerfully as any spell. Afterward, she and Eglano walked through the darkling woods together. On a short summer night just two days before Ulla returned from Akkala, Eglano had kissed her and declared his love. Kirsikka spent half her time absorbed with visions of becoming a true princess and half of it distraught at Eglano's departure—for he, too, would leave with his brother the king for Deep Länismaa and the war along the borders.

Maidens among the Bear Folk did not marry so young, but among the Swan Folk it was quite common. Eglano was now a man fully ready for marriage, by his people's reckoning, as was Egan. The folk of the Seven Clans seldom married for love alone, however; their families, humble and great alike, made their matches for them. Marriages of the sons and daughters of the great houses of the southern clans were carefully arranged for mutual advantage, and never had any prince of any Royal House of the Etelalaiset married a peasant.

Kirsikka fed the *pirtti's* small summer fire with mossy turves and poured out her heart to Ulla, but the dark-haired girl listened with mixed feelings. Ulla had missed her friend terribly on the journey through Akkala, but now she grew jealous of Eglano, who filled Kirsikka's thoughts, and felt guilty for her own jealousy. On top of that, she was angry with Väinämöinen for leaving her again, angry with Kirsikka for her betrayal, and angry with herself most of all.

"He will never come back," said Kirsikka. "Each year they go to the Marches, and so many never come back. He said that he would take me to Etelamaa when they return, but I just know he won't come back."

"He will come back," said Ulla, shaking her head. "They will defeat the enemy. But you are foolish if you think he will take you to the Stone City as his princess. He is the Grand Duke of Etelamaa, Kirsikka, and the heir to the throne after Egan; how can you believe that he would ever marry you?"

"Because he said so," replied Kirsikka sharply. "Why would he lie?"

"It doesn't matter what he says," answered Ulla. "You are Karhulaisen and an orphan, like I am. We have nothing—no home, no family, no dowry; nothing but Väinämöinen, the Erilaiset, and the mark on my shoulder. Don't ever forget that. What happened to orphans in your village, Kirsikka? Who did they marry, if they ever married? And it is the same here in Tavastia and throughout the Far Northern Land. No lord or prince is going to marry a village girl from the North Marches! We are lucky to even be in Laulavalaakso."

Kirsikka stood up and brushed a tangle of red hair from her watery eyes.

"Then why don't you stay here!" she cried. "You can become the Seer's apprentice and live alone in the tower, as befits an orphan from the Marches. But I am not Karhulaisen, I am Tavastian!"

She stormed out of the little cottage, knocking over the birch broom and pail, but Ulla said nothing, staring blankly at the fire until she finally shook her head and sighed. Jumping up, she ran out the doorway and cried, "Kirsikka!"

The sound died on her lips. Kirsikka was nowhere to be seen, but Unaja, the golden-haired singer from Akkala, stood outside the *pirtti*. She carried her staff of dark alder wood in her hand and wore the wolf-fell she had brought back from her hunt about her shoulders.

Ulla stopped short and, feeling guilty, thought, *She knows I have been quarreling with Kirsikka and is angry.* But Unaja's face betrayed nothing of the sort, whatever she knew or guessed.

"She is gone," said Unaja in her strange, thick accent. "I saw her running down the goat path just now—to the hall, I think. Do you wish to go after her?"

"No," said Ulla wearily. "I will find her later." After a moment she added, "In any case, she's upset with me and doesn't want to see me."

"That happens among sisters," replied Unaja. "My sisters and I fought like dogs fighting over scraps from the table. But I loved them no less. Love gives one freedom to say and do things sometimes that are ill considered."

Ulla sat on the earthen stoop outside the *pirtti* and ran her fingers through her loose, unbraided hair.

"You know what she hopes for, don't you?" Ulla said.

Unaja nodded. "I stayed here while you were in Akkala. She spent much time with the Etelalaisen prince."

"She is foolish," answered Ulla. "It can never happen."

"People often do foolish things in the name of love," said Unaja. "Kingdoms have fallen for such."

"What use is love anyway? It only makes things worse when you lose the one you love—or when they leave you. Knowledge and . . . and power. Or strength. These things are forever. That is what the songs teach."

"*Tana*, things are hard enough for women among the clans. You know their lot—our lot, if not for happy chance or fate—is to work and to toil, to wait on others, to be lower than a draught beast in the esteem of men or used cruelly by your husband's mother. Or to bear children and watch them die, one after another, carried off to Tuonela's dark shores by sickness or starvation. To live without hope.

"Do not begrudge your friend her hope, whatever the future brings. She has neither your gift nor your destiny—nor your choices, rare among mortals and most rare among women."

Ulla dug into the damp mossy earth with her bare feet.

"You were almost married, Unaja," she said. "What was the man like? Did you love him?"

The golden-haired woman laughed, a surprisingly merry and lighthearted laugh for one so grave and serious.

"Love him?" she mused, as if talking to herself and considering the question for the very first time. "No, I did not love him. I did not even know him well. And he wasn't really a man but only a boy, a fisherman, as lost and lonely as I was, and as ignorant. Perhaps we would have been happy together, living out our little lives by the waves.

"*Being in love is like feeling the summer sun shine on you from both sides*—but then the dreams began. Night after night they came. Nothing was ever the same again." Unaja fell silent until Ulla looked up at her.

"Väinämöinen is waiting for you," said Unaja. "That is why I came. The Wardens have left, but he is still here. He asked me to find you. He wishes to bid you farewell ere he leaves. He is waiting beside the seidi-stone. Go to him now!"

Ulla leapt to her feet and, without bothering to find her boots or put on her hooded cape, ran down through the trees toward the hall. The few folk about, mortals recently come to learn the songs, marveled as the girl sped through the rowan grove and splashed across the stream. One yellow-haired boy, a Hirvilainen who had only just arrived some few days before, called out to her in surprise, but she didn't stop. Out of breath by the time she gained the other side and began climbing again, she kept running until she reached the seidi-stone. Väinämöinen was still there, sitting atop his speckled grey horse with his eyes closed, face turned up to the sun. The old man's plaited beard looked snow-white against his crimson shirt and cloak, and his tall yellow boots fit tight in their stirrups. Ulla saw that his sword hung from his belt and his staff was strapped to the pack behind him, but he had his kantele still in his hand. Ulla knew the wizard had been singing.

"Nice of you to come," he said without opening his eyes. "I'm already late waiting for you; Bergil left at the crack of dawn and Egan last night. I've got some miles to make up and a hard ride ahead! What do you have to say for yourself?"

"That Unaja just found me, and that I didn't know you were leaving today since you never told me."

"Indeed?" said the old man, now looking at her. "Well, I am leaving today. High Länsimaa awaits, and the lands of the Karhulaiset where you were born.'

"What is waiting there?" asked Ulla.

"Battle and war," answered Väinämöinen. "What else? But we are stronger this year. The Witch will not have everything her own way."

Väinämöinen swung his horse beside the girl and she scratched its ears while it nuzzled her neck.

"Starchaser is a good steed," he said, patting the thick barding, red and green like the colors of Karelia, that covered the horse's shoulders and back. "One of the best I've ever had. He is anxious for the journey." He suddenly reached down and handed her the kantele. "Take this," he said. "Keep it for me and try your hand at practicing. I can't carry it into battle and it's time you learned to play yourself."

"But what about the hunt?" she finally blurted out. "You said that we would make the hunt when we returned from Akkala."

"And so we will, when the time is ripe. High summer is the time for war in the Far Northern Land. Other things come later. When I return—and I will, you know—then we will go on a journey, you and I. Keep that bag packed!"

"And what about the Seer?"

Väinämöinen reached across his belt and swept out his sword, pointing the long blade at the girl's chest while Ulla backed away in surprise.

"I will deal with her later. In the meantime, let it be a lesson for you: answer her without answering! And turn to Turi for help if need be. He will teach the newcomers to the Valley this summer and send whatever messages need be sent. Listen to his songs and tales, for he will instruct you now and prepare you for what is to come."

The old man sheathed the blade. In its place, he raised a fluted, curled black horn. He put it to his lips and let loose a blast that echoed in the woods all about them. Starchaser reared and neighed.

"I'm off, little one! Be good and look for me to return in victory!"

Ulla reached up for his hand and pressed it to her face. "Come back quickly," she said.

"Aye," he said, smiling. "I will; I will!"

***

Egan waved to the approaching riders in the distance. Beside him, his herald raised the royal banner, the white swan on a sky-blue field, the ancient token of the Swan Folk. It was now after Midsummer's Day and hot. The king squinted in the bright sunlight. Sweat trickled down his face. The riders came closer and Egan could clearly recognize them—Teemu, High Lord of the Hirvilaiset, with a small company of guards and his own brother, Eglano, as escort.

The king looked back at his army, six hundred men, some horsed and some on foot, strung out in a long line behind him. Egan had met them at the *lansikita*, the pass into Deep Länsimaa, and together they marched north, first over the River Clearwater and along the Old Trade Road, then past the Blue Lake and Siinisaare, and on into the heart of Länsimaa where the Elk Road sped them toward Valkeakosk, the capital of the Clan of the Elk. Still, they did not come quickly. The men, heavily burdened with arms and supplies, made no more than fifteen miles each day despite the long hours of sunshine. Many folk lived among the woody isles of the lake lands, hunters and fisherfolk, and miners of bloodrock from the marshy fens; they watched the Etelalaisen soldiers trudge northward, spears pointed up toward the summer sky. North of the Blue Lake, however, they met fewer folk until at last they came near to Valkeakosk. Many people dwelled in the town and lands nearby and, most importantly, they had arrived before the servants of Pohjola.

Teemu and Eglano rode up and dismounted, the Hirvilaisen lord bowing low before warmly embracing Egan. They had seen each other only twice in all the seven years since the Battle of Linnavuori, though both young men had fought many battles in that time, growing older and wiser than their years.

"You arrive again in the nick of time, my lord," said Teemu after they had exchanged greetings. "Ill things are afoot. The last scouts sent out did not return and we fear the worst; our wizard says that he can feel a great evil gathering in the north. I do not doubt that our enemies will soon attack us."

"How great is your strength, Lord Teemu?" asked Egan.

"Perhaps one thousand men," he answered, "or somewhat less. We have a force of archers and spearmen, some two hundred light horse, and a company of Wardens with us. I left some men east of here, closer to High Länsimaa, to contest any raid of the Easterners that might come that way; but the townsfolk of Valkeakosk have mostly removed to the Birchwood, where they may hide if need be, then flee south as chance allows. There is much fear and panic among them."

"No doubt," said Egan. "Terrible times afflict us. But I think it good that the town is emptied. If we lose this battle, many can still escape; remember what happened in Keskimaa! Wooden cities are traps for those within them."

"I see that Väinämöinen is not with you," said Teemu. "We hoped that he would come to us, he or another of the great heroes. Surely their magic could save us as it did at Linnavuori."

"Väinämöinen is in High Länsimaa, for it seems Löhi will also attack there in force; Turi remains at Kyöpelinvuori. But I have a singer with me, Nohol, who is a powerful *tietäjää*. And also—" Egan lowered his voice. "Airki is near. His men will greatly increase our strength."

"That is welcome news indeed," said Teemu. "The messengers from Kyöpelinvuori spoke of this, but we have heard nothing more. Does he follow you?"

"No. The Eagle Folk came a different road from Akkala and approach from the southwest, beneath the shadows of the forest. By Ukko's will, they may arrive before our enemies. But, Teemu," Egan said, putting his hand upon the Hirvilainen's shoulder, "let us not speak of this openly. If we have any hope, it is through surprise. Rumor of Airiki's army travels among my men, but only a few know the truth. I know it would hearten your folk, but I fear Löhi's spies will more readily learn our plans if this news is widely published. The Witch may already know, of course, and perhaps even now we merely march into her trap. But let us do all we can to trouble her plans!"

Teemu nodded. "So be it. Let us gather our men and make ready. You are only a day's march, perhaps, from Valkeakosk. I will ride back at once."

"Eglano," said Egan, "go with him and take several swift riders with you, so we may trade messages until we join forces."

So Teemu rode back north, and the king's brother, Eglano, rode with him. But Egan gave orders that the Swan Folk should march as quickly as possible in the bright summer sun and heat. They left the wagons and stores behind with their drivers to follow later. One brief night only, they rested under the stars. On the next day they came to the town of the Hirvilaiset, the northernmost town of the Seven Clans.

Now the fashion of Valkeakosk, the capital of the Clan of the Elk, was like this. To the west of the city was a region of long, narrow lakes stretching upwards like fingers toward the border marches. Between these lakes and the city, the Hirvilaiset had their fields, growing as much as they could in an area of good land, rare so far north. More fields and villages lay also to the city's south.

Valkeakosk began as a trading post and hillfort, no larger than Metsäposti in distant Karelia, but as folk settled on the good land, taming and tilling more fields, craftsmen and artisans came from the south to swell its numbers. The people there prospered, and finally the chief lord among the many small Hirvilaisen clans, called the High Lord of Deep Länsimaa, made his home there, too. Then Valkeakosk became the Hirvilaisen capital, with a new hall for the High Lord and his household, and a great wooden wall and ramparts built around the town to keep it safe from raiders.

Within the city they built many houses, sheds, halls, barns, and smithies, as well as markets. The wandering folk of the Elk Clan, who lived in no settled place but moved every few seasons, came for supplies or to arrange marriages between families. In that way, the Elk Folk were much like the Bear Folk, save that they relied more on hunting and fishing for their livelihood since good land was so scarce in Deep Länsimaa. But many bred beasts and horses, and fish filled the cold, clear finger lakes of Valkeakosk, so the Elk Folk lacked no abundance in good years or bad.

The Swan Folk passed Valkeakosk to the west along a fair road through tilled fields, but they did not enter within. Empty and lifeless, the town had been abandoned when most of its people fled to the forest save for a few watchmen on the wooden walls, gazing while the southerners passed by. Two days' march north of Valkeakosk, they halted. The Hirvilaisen army camped there, too, close to the fens and marches that blocked the town's northern approaches. They hid as well as possible in a narrow, rocky valley with a broad, shallow stream. Egan then met with Teemu and with Tarmo, the captain of the region's Wardens, to make what plans they could.

Ever since Turi's warning that the Witch had prepared a secret way through the wastes and swamps, Teemu's men had watched a gap in the marshes that led deep within, like a spearhead or pointing arrow, growing ever narrower until it ended at last among the bogs. Men had once lived there and mined for iron, but they found little bloodrock, only soft bog-iron, so it had been long since any mortals visited that place, close though it was to Valkeakosk. Indeed, the bogs were so close to the city that when the wind was right in summertime, their reek carried to the town and villages outside the city.

They did not doubt that if Turi's report proved true, Löhi's servants would come through this gap. They would have ample warning if any raiders tried to pick their way through the tangle of the Birchwood to the west; a screen of men-at-arms and horsemen waited to the east where the Easterners had appeared three years before. Teemu would surely know if danger approached from that quarter and might swing his army to meet the attack. But if Löhi's servants came unlooked-for out of the northern swamps, impassable though men thought them, they might swiftly come down on Valkeakosk before any defense could be prepared, attacking the town without warning. So Egan's men camped near to the gap to wait and, if an assault did come, to meet it there, north of Valkeakosk, driving the invaders back into the wastes. Only if the men of the clans were defeated would they fall back upon the town to defend its wooden walls and kill as many of their enemies as possible before the city was sacked and burned.

Not Egan, Teemu, or any other man knew if they waited in vain for an attack that would never come, sitting idle like fools while Löhi ravaged elsewhere, having tricked them into splitting their forces. They did not doubt for long. On the morning of the third day since the Swan Folk made camp in the stony valley, the scouts sent to watch the fens came riding madly back with news that enemies had been sighted in the boggy gap, a long line of armed men on foot and horsemen mixed among them. At once the army of the Kaamoslaiset broke camp. Egan and the other lords led their men northward to meet their foes. Shortly after noon, they came to the edge of the marshlands. The midday sun burned hot and yellow in the clear blue summer sky, making the day as stifling and still as one in the lands away south.

Egan drew his men up directly before the enemy while Teemu and Tarmo arrayed the Hirvilaiset to the right, their archers clustered around a range of short, rocky hillocks and the rest in the gaps between. The Elk Folk were lightly armored for the most part but carried iron-tipped spears, long and sharp, made by the Smiths of Seppälä in exchange for great loads of bloodrock. The archers used longbows from Etelamaa that could shoot foes at great distance.

The Etelalaiset, on the other hand, were strong, war-hardened men, bearing swords and spears, clad mostly in chainmail with helms and shields to protect them. If they had not the numbers of their foes, Egan was with them, and they would fight any terror or lay down their lives to defend him.

Egan sat astride his horse on a rise in the otherwise flat ground with his knights and captains around him and his brother Eglano at his right hand. The young duke, awaiting his first battle, nervously pulled the reins to keep his mount checked. They watched Löhi's servants issue slowly from the sedge like ghosts from the lonely wastelands, line after line—for the Witch had sent an army against them, not merely raiders to harass, burn, and flee back to safety. Eglano raised his arm and pointed north as the Pohjolaiset came closer, separating into several groups.

"Look," he cried. "There are men, many men, of different sort. And there, in the center, are those . . . are those not the Witch's goblins?"

"Hiisia of Pohjola," said Egan. "The Demons of the North! Now, brother, you will see at last what the Witch throws against us!"

"Should we not rush down upon them before they form?" asked Eglano. "Why do you hold back?"

Egan smiled, motioning toward their foes. "Look at the land, brother. Do you see the wet, spongy ground? And how it drops like a bowl before the marshes? That's no ground for horses, and we would suffer great loss of cavalry. Our men on foot would fare little better. No, let us use this high ground and make them attack us at disadvantage. They cannot flank us here, anchored as we are on marsh and hill, but if we break them, we will chase them into the swamp. If things go ill, our horses will screen us as we fall back on Valkeakosk."

Egan drew his sword and held it high for the Swan Folk to see as their enemies came on. To the left, straight at the king and his company marched a mass of strange men, thickset and stocky, with long hair and white skin, bearing spears and spiked clubs. Their shaggy beards looked unkempt to the eyes of the Kaamoslaiset. These were the men known to the Eagle Folk as the Kveni, a wild folk of alien race to the Seven Clans, whose homeland, Kainula, lay somewhere to the north and west. Behind them, several companies of Hiisia carried the banners and tokens of Pohjola, the North Star on sable and blue.

To the right, an army of Itäläiset bore down upon the Elk Folk. Some were mounted, but the chief part, at least one thousand men, marched on foot, for whatever path Löhi had cloven through the wastes and bogs, it was still hard for beasts. Whether the Witch's army expected to find an army of foes before them, none could say. Surprised or not, they attacked swiftly and without hesitation. The Hirvilaisen archers loosed their arrows; men and horses fell, but the Easterners did not waver. Soon they were locked in combat with the Kaamoslaiset.

The Kveni crashed against the line of the Swan Folk, seeking to overwhelm them with their numbers and turn their flanks. Then the goblins attacked as well, pouring arrows into the ranks of Egan's army. Though outnumbered, the Etelalaiset held strong, beating back their foes' attack, keeping their line intact and strewing the ground with their enemies' bodies. Again and again the Kveni massed and charged forward. At last the wild men pierced their ranks, and Egan watched as they pulled down a Swan Knight who sought to rally his comrades, then beat him into the ground with their clubs. The king cried out, rearing his horse as he brandished his sword.

"Stay with me!" he cried to the *tietäjää*, Nohol, who had come with him. "And you, too," he added to Eglano. "Stay close!"

"I will do what I can," shouted Nohol above the din of battle. "But I can feel the magic of our foes already, and it is very strong!"

Egan rode down with the Swan Knights around him and came upon the Kveni even as they tried to flank his men and turn them. He hewed the first enemy he came upon, then, turning to his other side, cut down the second as the man stabbed at him with an iron-tipped spear. With the king in the forefront, the Knights slashed this way and that, cutting their way through the wild men until they broke and fled. Many of the horsemen would have ridden down the fleeing foe, but Egan ordered them back, bringing his men-at-arms together in a solid line.

There were still too many Kveni and Hiisia for the Swan Knights to prevail. Three times the wild men and goblins gathered and pierced the southerners' line. Each time, the king rallied his folk and threw his foes back with bloody loss. The hot sun beat down upon them all as fighting raged across the battlefield.

Despite the Knights' lances and keen swords, the Swan Folk might have been overcome when a fresh company of Kveni arrived with riders of the Itäläiset hurrying to aid them. Egan ordered his captains to draw in the ends of their line to protect his flanks. Even at that desparate moment, a horn call, deep and resonant, sounded across the field from the west.

The Swan Folk pointed and cheered. A long esker wound to the west of the field, and atop the raised ridge, among the scattered pine trees, a thousand men stood silhouetted against the sun. Airiki's men, the Eagle Folk, unfurled their banners and raised them skyward.

Airiki had taken a different road north, through the pinewoods of Akkala and to the west of the Birchwood, marching swiftly with little pause near the forest's eaves. Arriving even before the Swan Folk, the Kotkalaiset had lain hidden in the deep woods until word came that their enemies approached. Then Airiki led them stealthily to the field, marching in the esker's shadow.

Down from the sloping side of the ridge they poured, screaming the war cries of their clan as they ran. They charged into the rear and flank of the Kveni. The Eagle Folk were hardened warriors, fearless in battle. Some wielded great two-handed axes that could fell any foe, mortal or goblin, with a single blow. The battle turned savage as the Kveni, caught between their enemies, Eagle and Swan Folk, soon lost all order, falling by the dozens beneath the newcomers' blows.

Routed, the surviving Kveni panicked, fleeing back to the safety of the marshes. Now only the goblins remained on that part of the field, and they, too, soon withdrew behind a shallow stream bank, well out of bowshot.

Egan secured his bloodstained sword against his horse's barding, then turned to his brother. Eglano, shaking with excitement but unhurt, had fought well, slaying several enemies. The king, spotting Airiki across the battlefield, gathered his men into several companies, commanding some to block the retreat of their enemies and setting others to drive the goblins.

"The field will be ours!" cried Egan. "We will crush the Hiisia between us as between hammer and anvil, then turn to Teemu's aid. But we must not let the enemy escape back to the fens and marshes whence they came; the Pohjolaiset must pay—and pay dearly in blood. We can afford no more empty victories."

"If only we had more riders," said Eglano. "Our horsemen are all in High Länsimaa. What I would give for three hundred knights! We would sweep the field."

"Indeed we might," answered Egan, his eyes lighting up. "But maybe Juvari and Aldon have more need of them now than we. Listen to me, Men of Etelamaa!" He raised his voice so that all nearby might hear him. "Listen to me! March now in good order toward the goblins yonder, and we will take them on one side with the Eagle Folk on the other!"

The words had scarcely died on his lips when a thunderous boom, like the sound of a hundred drummers beating their skins at once, echoed across the field. The hot air before them shimmered strangely, and Nohol the wizard pointed toward the mouth of the boggy gap.

"Your Majesty!" he cried. "Look to the north. I feel a great magic there!"

Egan saw nothing at first, neither men nor goblins, yet a misty glimmer seemed to obscure his view of the mossy earth and green sedge beyond. Nohol raised his staff and called out the words of a finding spell that Väinämöinen taught him. Then he swept his arms back and forth as if clearing the smoke. Whether Nohol's spell worked or not, the veil soon lifted. A terrible thing emerged from the gloom.

The drums beat louder. In the midst of the battlefield appeared a great beast of monstrous form, like a vision from the ancient world returned to life. Its long, serpentine body twisted this way and that as it strode forward on powerful legs. It was covered in green scales, dark along its flanks, bright and vivid about its pointed snout. Wings grew from its shoulders, short and shriveled, that would never lift that huge girth into the air. But it had long, sharp claws and bright teeth like spears glistening between its mighty jaws; a crest of spikes adorned its snakelike head, and, even from afar, its deep-set eyes glowed red.

Trolls and goblins, on either side of it, held the ends of iron chains cast about its neck. Whether to guide it or restrain its wrath, none might say. A sulfurous stench filled the air before it, and, ever and anon, the creature reared its ghastly head to let forth a blast of fire from its jaws. Yellow smoke curled about it, choking its handlers and rising into the air like the issue of a vast chimney of brick and stone.

The men of the Seven Clans gazed at the beast with fear and wonder. None had ever seen such a creature or imagined it living and breathing in the waking world, but all the same they knew its name: *lohikäärme*, a dragon of the north. For the legends of the Far Northern Land told that, in ages past, creatures known as *lohikäärme* had been spawned in mountains of fire and ice far away. These dragons had come to mortal lands and spread ruin among the folk of the Seven Clans.

During the time of the Witch's War, Löhi had gathered the monsters together and used them in her battles, unleashing their dreadful power to serve her own crooked ends. Many men died beneath their mighty feet or burned in their jets of flame, but Väinämöinen and his friends had finally hunted the creatures down and killed them. Lemminkäinen and the hero Eskeli slew the last great dragon, the greatest of all that brood and the most deadly. Then men thought that the scourge of dragons had long since vanished from the world or else only a small remnant survived in the farthest north. Yet Löhi had found at least one to serve her and sent it now to Deep Länsimaa to win the field and, afterward, to ravage and pillage where it would, spreading terror throughout the lands of men.

Egan's heart sank as he looked upon the creature. "A dragon," he said, "Serpent of Fire from the legends of the past. Is there no horror the Witch cannot recall? And we do not have Väinämöinen here or any of the Great Ones of the Erilaiset who might battle this foul thing. How can we defeat such a monster?"

As the beast made its way across the field, a single horseman trailed behind it, slowly loping beside the lines of goblins and trolls that held the iron chains. The rider wore black mail, shining like jet, and a black cloak that flowed like darkness behind him. In his left hand he held a short lance, iron-black, tipped with jagged silver. But his face was covered with a mask and helm; they shone silver-white in the sunlight, shaped like the face of a ghastly winter moon, cold and empty.

Then Egan knew that Kuupää, the Moonface, the captain of Löhi's army and champion of Pohjola, had come. None could tell his race or kind, hidden as he was in his terrible mask, but all sensed that an evil will lurked beneath that disguise. The king felt its power beat upon him. Unbidden, a thought came suddenly into his very mind, a foul message from without that said to him, "I am your Enemy."

The dragon stopped in its tracks. Kuupää suddenly raised his left hand and cried out in the language of old Pohjola. The chains fell away. The trolls and goblins scattered as if in fear for their lives. Immediately, as if on Kuupää's command, the dragon leapt forward. With a speed unbelievable for so large a beast, it bore down upon the companies of the Eagle Folk gathered in the field, moving quickly among them. The mortal men, struck with terror, loosed what arrows they had, then raised spears and swords in defense.

The dragon towered above them. A blast of red flame burned and withered the line of warriors who tried to bar its path. The creature raged among the Kotkalaiset, cutting them down with its terrible claws and batting them aside like strawmen, pausing now and again to rend and devour bodies. Even then, the whiplash of its tail crushed others, spreading ruin wherever it struck. No horse could withstand that horror. The few Kotkalaisen steeds threw their riders or carried them madly away. The Eagle Folk fled in confusion, the ground where they had stood littered with the dead and dying.

When Egan saw the dragon's onslaught, he gathered the riders nearest him and, despite his fear, rode toward the deadly monster. He knew that in all likelihood he rode to his death. Remembering the legends of the ancient past, even in his fright he hoped he might make a stand against the beast worthy to be celebrated in later days, buying time his people to escape; and, especially, he hoped to save his brother.

But Nohol the wizard went before them all, coming to the dragon even as it rested for a moment amidst the carnage. The serpent spied him and roared. Nohol's horse went mad, tossing his master to the ground and galloping away in terror. Nohol picked himself up and, though he had lost his staff, strode toward the creature. He threw his arms open in gesture of invocation.

His voice hoarse, the singer cried, "*Pysäyttää!*" He chanted, swaying this way and that, making the strongest binding spell he knew, a *loitsu* to stop the evil worm in its path. But the dragon was much too large and powerful for mortal magic, and only a ring of wizards or perhaps the Great Ones of the Erilaiset might have woven a spell strong enough to stay its wrath. It almost seemed that the flicker of a smile crossed the dragon's wicked face. Then swiftly it stooped, took Nohol in its jaws, and, throwing back its long neck, devoured him. Red blood dripped from its mouth, staining its livid scales.

So Nohol died, and all seemed ruined. But the wizard's sacrifice achieved one thing. Egan and his riders had closed around the dragon in a ring, unnoticed. Though Egan had not the power of wizards, the strength of his will and spirit held both horses and men to their course. None faltered despite the terror.

Egan had picked up a long lance with an edged blade, like a pikestaff. Raising the weapon, he cried, "Now—strike the beast now!"

From all sides the Swan Folk attacked. Several spears pierced the hoary scales of its flanks, but the dragon twisted about like a snake and belched forth a withering fire, burning the riders in its path. The sweep of its claws felled several more. The attackers panicked, their horses dead or flying, their riders thrown down in ruin.

Egan's steed, maimed, crashed on its side. The king, though dazed, stumbled to his feet, still clutching the lance. He tore off his helm and blinked in the thick yellow smoke. Hot—as hot as if he burned in an oven—Egan stood there, confused and reeling.

An evil presence bore down upon him like a threatening cloud. He looked up. The dragon towered right above him. Steam curled from its nostrils as it glared at him, a forked tongue flicking about the froth of its bloody mouth.

He gazed straight into the dragon's huge, glowing eyes. With a shock he saw that they were the eyes of the Erilaiset, fluted and spiraled with innumerable shifting patterns. Almost he fell under the dragon's spell as he gazed into those yellow orbs. As the serpent reared up, ready to blast him with deadly flame, courage welled in Egan's heart, courage beyond mortal measure, and anger for the weakness of the men of the Seven Clans in the face of evil. Perhaps no other mortal in the Far Northern Land could have withstood that fearsome monster; but Egan, King of Etelamaa and Chief of the Swan Folk, with a sudden strength given him, thrust the bitter lance at his enemy. It pierced the dragon's breast.

"Lemminkäinen!" he cried. Staggering with all his might, like a man struggling to move a great stone uphill, he took one step, then another, driving the lance deep into the serpent's body. The Dragon howled in agony and pain, its spiked head thrown upward. It reared up on its hind legs, lifting the king off the ground. Egan let the lance go and fell to the earth.

With a deafening roar, the dragon crashed full upon him, shaking the earth with its fall. The serpent's tail whipped thrice in a final spasm. The echoes of the fall ebbed slowly away until all was still.

A silence fell across the battlefield as the smoke cleared. The men of the Seven Clans looked on with horror. The beast lay dead, scores of men and horses strewn about it. A wail rose from the goblins who had watched the battle from a distance, lamenting the dragon's loss.

Egan had vanished beneath the fallen monster.

Airiki galloped up and flung himself from his horse. He had been leading his men against the Hiisia when the dragon appeared, too far away to reach Egan in time. Now, with Eglano and several knights, he ran to the steaming carcass. They had no hope for Egan. Even through the sulfurous haze, many had seen the final combat. Be it broken and slain, they would uncover his body. He would be buried with honor.

But Egan was not dead. Though the dragon fell upon him, he found himself trapped in a tiny space between the creature's mighty forearm and its body, a crevice that sheltered him from its crushing weight. Even with his left arm broken and his lungs scorched by the acrid fumes, the young king was still very much alive. Crawling out from his unlikely haven, he stumbled back into daylight before the astonished onlookers, as surprised as they were at his escape. Airiki embraced him.

"By the vaulted heavens!" the big man cried. "You are alive! Alive! And you have killed this savage beast and saved our folk! Never have I seen anything like it in all my life. This deed will be sung in every corner of the Far Northern Land, among all the Seven Clans, until the end of days. Egan Dragonslayer I name you, now and for all time!"

They lifted Egan on a horse to take him to safety and treat his injuries. He paused only to retrieve his sword, *Tarunmiekka*, from the body of his fallen mount. But ere he left, Egan turned and saw Kuupää at some distance, silent and still. He could feel the Moonface's eyes upon him. For a moment they stood like that, gazing at one another across the wrack of war. Whether Löhi's captain despaired at the dragon's fall and the king's escape or else considered both with cold detachment, none could say. But then he turned away, his mask gleaming silver in the sun, and rode slowly back toward the gap. So great a spell of dread hung about him that none dared challenge him.

Airiki took command of the remaining companies of the Eagle and Swan Folk. Still a great army, they drove against the Hiisia. The affray was sharp, but the goblins, now outnumbered, broke and fled. To the east, Teemu and the Elk Folk had been locked in battle with the Easterners. From high ground, Teemu had seen all that transpired and now saw his chance. Leading his riders swiftly to the gap, he made a screen to stop the flight of their enemies. The Easterners' horsemen broke through, seeking safety now and not battle, and so escaped to rejoin the Moonface. Those on foot were trapped by Teemu, save some few who threw down their spears and pled for mercy.

So went the battle, and it ended in a great victory for the Kaamoslaiset. They routed the Kveni and destroyed the Hiisia; many Easterners lay dead upon the field. And Egan had slain the dragon, which might have despoiled the whole of Deep Länsimaa. With Löhi's western army all but annihilated, the dearest hopes of the Seven Clans came true.

A sorcerer named Masku, one of the Tornilaiset of Kyöpelinvuori, rode with Teemu. After he helped tend the wounded, he reached out his mind to the Seer and told her all that had happened, and so from Kyöpelinvuori, word spread quickly of the Battle of the Marshy Gap. To the Birchwood where the Elk Folk lay hidden, to fair Tapiola, to mighty Langvika in the south, to the Karelian Forest, and to the Stone City in Etelamaa where Vendla waited anxiously for news of her sons, came word of the great deed of Egan Dragonslayer, king of his folk and chief of his clan.

CHAPTER EIGHT

THE WEDDING FEAST

Egan did not stay long at Valkeakosk. With his arm set, his ribs bound, and his burns treated with honey and comfrey, he rested in Teemu's hall. The townsfolk came back from the woods and rejoiced in the victory of the Seven Clans over Löhi's army. From the watchtowers, the people of Valkeakosk could see a great smoke rise to the north, where the army burned the bodies of their slain enemies, including the carcass of the terrible *lohikäärme*. But they brought one of its teeth, long as a dagger, to Egan to be made into a talisman by the Erilaiset.

After only a few days, Egan said goodbye to Airikki and Teemu for a time. Despite his hurts, he rode ahead of his army and so came swiftly back to Kyöpelinvuori.

And all the news was good. Two armies of Pohjolaiset had invaded High Länsimaa, one crossing the Marches and coming straight down the North Road, and the other attacking farther west. But the Bear Folk and Wardens had defeated the first army, and the Hare and Swan Folk defeated the second. Many Easterners and goblins had been slain. Then the folk of the Seven Clans rejoiced, for it seemed their losses had not been in vain. The Witch's power would surely fade.

In the golden summer days, the fields grew full and ripe. Hopes rose high, despite the laments of women for their dead husbands and sons, never to return from war. And in the starfields of the short northern nights, the Witch's

Star, red and baleful, seemed dimmer, as if shrouded in mist.

Väinämöinen had been with the Hare Folk, in the thickest fighting, and afterwards stayed some time in their camps, laboring with other *tietäjää* to heal the wounded and ill. But when Asikkas the King returned to Tavastia, the old man came with him and so returned to the Singing Valley. Ulla ran with the others to greet him as he rode up, blowing his horn in victory.

She had spent the summer with Turi, learning chants and *loitsu* that wizards of the Far Northern Land must know. The Seer had not pressed her case any further—resigned, perhaps, that Ulla would never come to Kyöpelinvuori. And indeed, when Väinämöinen returned, the Seer of Kyöpelinvuori announced that she had at last chosen an apprentice: not Siitsa, who was too old, but a young girl from Akkala. Only seven, the slight, silent girl had white-blonde hair and eyes as blue as a northern lake. The girl, named Kilia, was an orphan of Airiki's distant kinfolk. Her parents had died from sickness, leaving her in debt with only an old grandmother to care for her. None knew how the Seer chose the girl, but she came one day with an escort of riders sent by Airiki, went up into the tower, and, after that, was seldom seen abroad. Siitsa moved into the position of Kilia's teacher and protector and chief of the Seer's servants, the Tornilaiset.

The days already grew noticeably shorter by the time Väinämöinen came back. Summer's touch brought life to the Far Northern Land, but it did not linger like a happy guest. Rather it hastened, leaving swiftly with little warning and seldom looking back. It would soon be harvest, then fall. The old wizard felt the passing of time keenly; he had much to do. He wanted to see Egan and learn more about his fight with the dragon, and he wished to speak with Turi of the affairs of Laulavalaakso and the Erilaiset. Most of all, he wanted to see Ulla and Kirsikka, to sit beside the fire with them and sing, and simply be, for he was very tired. But he found a new dilemma waiting. Eglano had proven to be a brave warrior in battle; now he proved headstrong and earnest in love.

He had fallen in love with Kirsikka ere he left Kyöpelinvuori. When he returned, he asked her to be his bride and then announced to all that he would wed her. Now Kirsikka was somewhat young for marriage in the reckoning of her own people, the Karhulaiset, but the maidens of the great southern clans, the Hare and Swan Folk, often wed early. Among the noble houses maidens married even younger, for their matches, made with care and cold calculation, benefited both families.

Eglano, though still young, had come of age. His mother, Vendla the Queen, had been married to Nigan at thirteen, although they waited several years before she lived with him as wife and bore him children. Yet, even if her age presented no obstacles, Kirsikka was no princess of a noble house. Never had a prince of the blood and Grand Duke of Etelamaa married a commoner and an orphan, from another clan no less.

Sons and daughters of the noble houses of the Seven Clans wed for mutual advantage; often the peasants and serfs did too, although they valued strength, health, and quick wits more than whatever meager dowry or possessions might convey. Strangely, only the humblest folk of the Kaamoslaiset might marry solely for love or desire. And Kirsikka, and Ulla, too, had been born among folk just such as these, then lived among the Erilaiset, who prized love highly.

But Sinio opposed the union and argued forcefully against it, advising Egan to cool his brother's ardor. Sinio thought always of politics and advantage; he feared the House of Joutsen would be weakened by this match. If Eglano insisted on marrying a woman outside of their clan, it should be a daughter of a noble house, preferably of the Hare Folk. Sinio always strove to strengthen Etelamaa's ties with Tavastia; already he looked forward to a day when the Witch's power would fade and peace return. Then the Seven Lands and Seven Clans would again vie for what riches the Far Northern Land could offer.

Egan did not shrink from Sinio's counsel. He loved his brother—and Kirsikka, too—and desired nothing more than to see them happy, yet as ruler of Etelamaa and head of his House, he considered his interests carefully. While his heart turned one way, his reason counseled otherwise. He was torn.

The Seer unexpectedly settled the matter. The crone had shown little interest in Kirsikka before, but, with her webs set all about Kyöpelinvuori, she soon heard of Eglano's plight. She summoned the girl to the tower, and reluctantly Kirsikka went. The Seer lavished kind words of support upon her.

"Are you not the adopted daughter of Väinämöinen, Lord of the Erilaiset? What finer pedigree could there be in all the Far Northern Land! And surely the Vanhalaiset brought you together for this very purpose."

Then the Seer counseled Egan to bless the marriage. Väinämöinen did as well. The old man loved Kirsikka and was happy to see her wed Eglano, for she would be well cared for in Etelamaa and his mind could rest easy about her future. Yet, before he gave his blessing, he took Kirsikka walking with him. Together they left the Valley and went into the woods on the nearby bluffs. They were gone one day and night. Kirsikka, quiet when she returned, would tell Ulla only that Väinämöinen had spoken long with her and asked her to search her heart. Satisfied, Väinämöinen went to Egan the King the very next day.

So it was decided that Kirsikka would indeed wed Eglano and, moreover, in Tavastia that very season. Vendla the Queen, far away in the Stone City, knew nothing of what transpired. But in that time of war, such marriages were not uncommon. Death seemed ever present, and folk hurried to draw whatever measure of happiness in life they could.

And Väinämöinen took Kirsikka as his adopted daughter before the folk of Laulavalaakso, according to the custom of the Seven Clans. Egan and Sinio sent messages to Vendla and to all corners of Etelamaa with the news that Eglano, Grand Duke of Kotanrannta, was betrothed to the Princess Cherry Red—for so they called her because of her hair—Kirsikka, daughter of Väinämöinen and Princess of Karelia. King Asikkas, who had long been fond of Kirsikka because of her beautiful voice, made her also a Lady of Tavastia. So Kirsikka entered her betrothal with these noble titles—not as an orphan from the rudest regions of High Länsimaa. When the Swan Folk heard these tidings, they thought their prince had taken a very noble wife indeed.

This flurry of activity left Ulla with a mixed mind. She had never really believed Eglano would return for Kirsikka, and, even if he did, she had felt more than sure that such a marriage would never happen. How could it? A prince wed to a villager and orphan? Kirsikka would be crushed, but Ulla would be there for her friend and comfort her as she always had ever since they lost their families long ago. But that all changed.

Like all the Seven Clans, Ulla rejoiced in Egan's victory, and she felt glad for his return. The story of the battle with the dragon set her imagination ablaze. Yet she could not understand the Seer's sudden interest in Kirsikka. She felt foolish and embarrassed about the many warnings and admonitions she had given her friend over the long weeks while they waited for news of the battles in the north. More than that, though, Ulla felt ashamed of her feelings.

She tried to put it out of her mind, but in her heart of hearts she knew that she envied Kirsikka her happiness, even as she feared being alone and abandoned. Ulla had thought that the red-haired girl, as close to her as any sister could ever be, would go wherever she went. Whatever her fate, she had believed Kirsikka would always be with her. Now that was not to be. The future looked that much lonelier and bleaker.

Ulla grew angry with almost everyone, most of all herself. Why couldn't she share her friend's happiness at her good fortune? To salve her strong pride, Ulla dissembled. She hid her true feelings behind the hard mantle that had served her well so many times in her short life. None knew the full extent of her sadness, though some could guess.

Now the folk of the Seven Clans usually married in spring or at midsummer. Löhi's return turned that custom upside down. Many young men left in spring each year for the fighting levees or else to work as cooks and carters, armorers and fletchers, herders and handlers for the men-at-arms who marched north to face the Witch's wrath. And not all returned. Those who did return often married when they came home. It became common in the little villages for peasants and serfs to wed near harvest time.

In a small village called Tyhää, on the Seer's land not far from Kyöpelinvuori, half the peasants were free and the other half serfs. The Seer had consented for two maidens who lived there to marry boys from neighboring farms. Eglano and Kirsikka would be wed with them, as if they were Tavastian peasants and not the heir to the throne of Etelamaa and his bride.

Indeed, it had become the fashion at that time for nobles and rich merchants among the Hare Folk to seek out villages in the countryside for their weddings. They returned to the ancient traditions that the wealthy had long eschewed but the common folk still practiced.

Egan wished to visit Asikkas in Tapiola afterward, so he was happy to stay. Eglano did not want to wait until he came again to the Stone City, nor to have a wedding filled with ceremony and pomp, so the idea pleased all save Sinio. He only shook his head when told that his duke would marry in lowly Tyhää. The Erilaiset of the Singing Valley were especially pleased, for they loved such festive times among the Kaamoslaiset, and a party of Haltiatar and other *väki* had just arrived from Karelia. The folk of Tyhää had grown used to living near to the wizards of the Valley and accustomed to the princes, kings, and captains who visited Kyöpelinvuori. Unabashed by the high and mighty lords among them, they were delighted that a foreign prince would take Cherry Red to be his bride.

Then came a bright day with a clear blue sky and a mild wind from the north. All the villagers in Tyhää dressed in their finest and the Erilaiset of Laulavalaakso joined them. The two village brides wore white dresses that reached almost to the ground with aprons bordered in red and spirals of bronze woven therein. Fine bronze and copper chains hung about their shoulders and waists, but silver thread graced their fair hair, a gift from the Seer, braided in the elaborate wedding plaits of that part of Tavastia. They even had white flowers set in their hair, and all about them, for the power of the Erilaiset might make flowers bloom whensoever they wished, even late in the season.

Kirsikka dressed in white and red as well, though the fabric of her dress was of finer weave than any that the village brides wore. Chains of silver and gold hung from her neck and waist, and Unaja had braided her flowing red hair in the style of the Wolf Folk. Yellow flowers, shot through with green leaves and spray, made up her maiden's crown, though soon she would take the veil of a married woman.

Traditionally, the bride awaited the bridegroom in her own cottage, but on this day three maidens would be married. So the threshing barn at one end of the village, where the folk kept hay and fodder for their beasts, had been opened and cleaned and set about with more flowers and many fine things. There the maidens waited, with the villagers and Erilaiset all around them. At the appointed time, as the morning sun climbed higher and the air grew warmer, they heard jingling bells and dragging chains.

Three carts came into view in the narrow lane. Eglano and the other two bridegrooms rode in the carts while their families and friends walked behind. Egan, resplendent in the fine clothes of Etelamaa, his broken arm still in a sling, rode with his knights. Ilkka the March Warden went with him. The grooms' families brought food and other needful things to the barns, where they met the brides' families at the threshold. The fathers of the brides gave their daughters into the hands of their grooms as the mothers looked on. Väinämöinen put Kirsikka's hand into Eglano's, while Unaja the Golden and Ulla, dressed in the colors of Tavastia with silver thread twined in her hair, stood by her side.

Then all the people gathered inside the barn and a merry feast began. Two long tables groaned under the weight of many kinds of food, for it had been a good year in the rich lands about Kyöpelinvuori. Plates heaped with fresh salmon caught in nearby waters sat next to bowls of roe; lamb roasted over a firepit vied with pork boiled with greens and yellow turnips. Baskets of apples and sweet fruits made a fragrant aroma, and the village maidens had picked lingonberries and bilberries, some to mix with sweet cream and some baked into pies.

All ate as much as they wanted of blood sausages in their cases, sour milk, bread, and butter. The Erilaiset had baked many loaves of white bread such as only their bakers might make. And Turi had brought several barrels of beer, the strong, dark beer brewed in the Singing Valley with the charms of the Erilaiset upon it, more flavorful than any mortal brew in the north.

The people ate and drank, the children ran about and played, and the gentle northern sun shone down on its sons and daughters at that happy time. When Väinämöinen stood up, wiping the foam from his plaited beard, all turned to hear the greatest singer in the Far Northern Land, and mighty among mortals and heroes.

Väinämöinen wore a sky-blue tunic, a gift from Mielikki, which the Haltiatar had brought him. His long cape was the same hue, as blue as the friendly heavens, and bordered with gold and silver thread, but his boots were yellow and his belt made of gold. He stood tall amidst the gathered crowd.

Then Väinämöinen took up his kantele and began to strum a sweet tune filled with the music of forests and lakes, of woods and swift rivers; the sounds of the cuckoo's call and the wolf's cry and the gulls and terns of the coast he wove therein. The music embodied the quiet calm and melancholy of the Far Northern Land, and it filled the minds of those who listened with fair images and designs. When the wizard sang, his deep voice echoed with windsong. He blessed the couples, calling upon Ukko the Allfather, Ilmatar of the winds, Ahti of the waters, old Tapio in the forest, and mother Akka of the lands and fields. His song called for increase among their herds, life and health for their children, and bounty from the fields, woods, and waters for all the gathered folk, lord and serf alike.

His song finished, Väinämöinen laid down the kantele and went out from the crowd; he sat on a bench nearby and played with the village children. The Tavastialaiset sang and danced, taking delight in teasing the new couples. But then several women from the village came forward, pushing Kirsikka and the other brides before the older women while the crowd gathered around. And, as was the custom in those days, the older women sang laments about the hard life that awaited the brides in their new homes and the sadness and misery to come. Sung in jest, with much laughter from the gathered crowd, the lighthearted, merry songs nevertheless told true: the lot of women in the Far Northern Land was hard, their work never ceased, and their future was always uncertain.

A maiden might be the apple of her father's eyes, her mother's darling, and her brother's love. But when she left home and village to become another's bride, she went as a stranger in her new home. Her mother-in-law might be stern and severe, finding fault in all she did; her father-in-law might be cold and distant. Her sister-in-law might tease and torment her, and the gentle boy she had wed might prove bitter or cruel, given to drink or else quick to raise his hand to her and beat her with no reason.

So warned the older women, and after the laments they gave instructions to the brides for how to improve their fortunes and win the favor of their husband's folk. For throughout the Far Northern Land, they said that, *A new house expects good manners from a new bride.*

And so the women sang, "Rise early, girl, while the Great Bear still shines in the sky. Light the fire and fetch fresh water while the house still sleeps, and chase the dogs into the yard. Feed the cows and pigs and pitch the straw. When the household wakes, wash the benches clean, grind the husks, and bake the loaves with cheery countenance. Follow your new mother's instructions and be quick when your new father calls. Set your husband's bow and polish his traps; bring him beer in the fields when he burns, cuts, and sows. Mend his skis in winter and nets in summer, and keep his boots warm by the hearth."

So sang the women. The brides blushed and looked down, Kirsikka with them—not that she needed to take the instructions to heart, of course. Once she had lived in a village even poorer than Tyhää; toil and drudgery would have certainly been her lot had she stayed. She was no village bride now, but the wife of the Grand Duke of Etelamaa, and her days of washing, milking, and pitching were at an end.

After similar laments had been sung for the grooms, the songs ended. The westering sun dimmed into a quiet twilight. Ulla sat with Unaja most of this time and watched the people dance. She also talked with the elves from

Karelia. As it grew dark and the celebration neared its end, Egan came to her with a cup of cold honeyed milk, which he knew she liked. Unaja spoke with them both briefly, then excused herself.

In all those days leading up to the wedding, Egan had scarcely seen Ulla; he had been much about the lands nearby on urgent errands, taking counsel ere he left again for Etelamaa.

"Why aren't you dancing?" he asked her, sitting down beside her gingerly, careful of his healing wounds. "You are the only maiden here who hasn't joined in."

Ulla laughed, her melancholy lifting somewhat as it always did when she heard his voice.

"Maiden? I'm not sure I am a maiden any longer. But anyway, I don't know these dances."

"When I was young," said Egan, "we often stayed in the Green Vales at a hall near some small villages. The simple folk there had dances such as these, and I sometimes went there with my nurses. I danced with the children, just as if I were one of them. It was very nice." He hesitated for a moment. "I had thought to dance with you, despite my arm, but you have been shy."

Ulla jumped at his words; even in the failing light, she knew he saw her pale skin turn beet red. Still she met his eyes as a smile spread across her face.

"You would have been disappointed," she said. "I told you that I don't know these dances. One of the Tavastialaisen girls would be a better partner."

"I'm not so sure," answered Egan. "They are pretty, but they tend to step on your feet. I've always heard that Karhulaisen maidens dance best."

"Then you are still out of luck," said Ulla. "Because I'm half Karelian by birth and all Karelian by heart."

"Ah," chuckled Egan, "Surely they dance in Karelia too? But look, Ulla—"

However, at just that moment a horn blared and calls rang out; the feast was at an end and the new couples had to take their leave.

The village folk helped the Tavastialaisen brides into the wagons, for they would now go with their husbands to their new homes; the grooms' folk said their goodbyes and prepared to depart. But Eglano and Kirsikka would ride to a fair hall near to Kyöpelinvuori with six Swan Knights as their escort, and this would be their first home together, albeit briefly. Egan embraced his brother, giving Eglano and Kirsikka the gifts he had prepared: two precious jewels, one of dark amber and another of garnet, set in chains of silver.

Then Kirsikka bade her friends farewell, her green eyes shining in the darkness. Even as a child among the rude folk of the North Marches, she had dreamed of being a princess in a castle far away. Now, though she had lost everyone she knew and loved as a child, and whatever little she had owned, her dream came true. Through death and darkness she had passed to be reborn.

When Kirsikka came to Ulla, last of all, the dark-haired girl's heart finally melted and her pride relented. She kissed Kirsikka, holding her close as tears fell from her eyes. They cried together, for they were truly sisters in spirit. Ulla held her sister's hand and helped her into the wagon, then stood blinking, wiping the tears from her face, as the wagons moved off toward the west, black silhouettes against the red horizon.

Many of the people left for their homes then, although a group of village men remained to drink with Turi and the elves until the beer was finished. Egan retired with his retinue. Ulla went and sat by herself a ways apart. Stars appeared in the cool night sky, and she thought to stay in Tyhää for a while before she rode back to the Valley. She had her own pony and enjoyed riding in the dark, fearing nothing she might encounter in those regions. The girl absentmindedly tossed some crumbs to a mouse that dared to dart about, a thief on the lookout for richer fare left unguarded. As she sat there, Unaja appeared, the wolf-fell wrapped about her shoulders and her staff in hand.

"It seems I am doomed to be Väinämöinen's messenger," she said, "at least when he wants you."

"What is it now?" asked Ulla. "Are you riding back to Laulavalaakso? Do you wish me to go with you?"

"Yes and yes," said Unaja. "But it seems that may not be. Väinämöinen is sitting over yonder. He wishes to see you. Go to him now."

"He is probably so drunk he cannot rise," sighed Ulla, getting up. "But let's see." Taking leave of Unaja, she went to where the old man sat in the shadows, his long legs stretched out before him. From the barn, the sounds of carousing villagers wafted on the cool night air.

Väinämöinen's eyes glistened in the starlight. "So it's over now," he said.

"Yes," answered Ulla.

"And Kirsikka is wed to Eglano. She was a beautiful bride. And now the next chapter of her life begins, whatever it may bring."

"Who can say?" said Ulla.

"Indeed," answered Väinämöinen. "And you? How are you, child? I know this was no easy thing for you."

"I am fine," said Ulla. "And happy for her. Yes, I am truly happy for her. But—oh, Väinämöinen, I will miss her!"

"And she will miss you, too, especially in these coming weeks."

The old man rose, grabbing his staff and looking down at the girl in the darkness, but Ulla collapsed into his arms, sobbing. He held her tight, stroking her long dark hair while she cried and not letting go until she calmed herself.

"Do you still have that bag packed?" he suddenly asked.

"Bag? What bag? Do you mean—"

"That is precisely what I mean," he said. "There's no better time than the present. Unaja will see your pony back home; I have a new mare waiting for you and, in any case, bag or no, I've packed all you need. We will leave this very night for High Länsimaa."

Chapter Nine

The Bear Hunt

The black mare Väinämöinen gave Ulla was spirited and strong. Despite its heavy load of supplies, it ran swiftly through the night and had no trouble keeping up with Väinämöinen's great grey horse. The two riders stopped briefly in Piikkimaki to water their steeds, but, in the deep of night, the people all slept, save perhaps herdsmen and watchers.

"Do we go east, Väinämöinen?" asked Ulla.

"Hmm," said the old man, shaking his head. "Not this trip. We'll go north this time and skirt the Wall, then on to the lake lands."

The wizard kicked his horse and they clattered through the tiny square, taking the old cart road north to the lands of the Elk Folk.

Väinämöinen and Ulla rode north and, as summer faded into fall, the days grew milder and the nights turned cold. They slipped past the tumbled hills strung along the western end of the Wall of the Giants and so came into Deep Länsimaa. Then they reached the lake lands and turned east, riding each evening until the sun slipped below the trees. Deep and blue, the lakes of Deep Länsimaa seemed cast like nets in many diverse shapes, some larger, others small.

No stranger could find a way through that watery maze, but old Väinämöinen remembered them well from days of old. He led Ulla on a true path, picking his way round and about, but always finding firm ground for the horses. Ulla enjoyed traveling alone with Väinämöinen, like she had done so many times as a small girl. They didn't talk about the hunt at first, but, as they rode together, they sang many songs about the ancient days and heroes of old like Lemminkäinen or Ilmarinen, the great smith who forged the Sampo. In that merry time, she almost forgot the seriousness of their journey, imagining that they rode to the Enchanted Valley to see Mielikki and their other friends among the Erilaiset. Now and again they stopped at a *pirtti* for the night as guests of the humble folk who lived there. But mostly both Väinämöinen and Ulla preferred to sleep under the stars, wrapped in their warm cloaks and furs beside a crackling fire.

The travelers left the lake lands of the Elk Folk and rode on into High Länsimaa, but Väinämöinen avoided the Old Trade Road and stayed away from the Karhulaisen villages and farmsteads as best he could. Passing the great crosssroad south of Keskimaa, they continued eastward. Ulla began to think more and more about the bear hunt she would make, the last test before she held the staff of a true wizard of the Far Northern Land, just like Väinämöinen and the *tietäjää*. The old man said little about it yet, though. He laughed and sang and told Ulla tales every night like he had when she was young, as if he were reluctant for the happy time to end. He knew a thousand tales about the Far Northern Land, and the dark-haired girl never tired of hearing them.

"There was once a boy up in the pinewoods of Karelia," he might start. "He lived with his old mother on a farm by a little lake. They had been well-off as things were reckoned in those days, with fertile fields and many servants to help them. But his father died and his sister took ill, so they fell on hard times. The boy took to sitting by himself alone at night by the lake and watching the stars reflected in the still waters when the sky was clear.

"One night when the moon was full, he saw nine swans fly in low over the trees. To his surprise, they landed on the opposite shore. He hid himself in the bushes so as not to scare them away. He had never seen swans near the lake before. Suddenly the birds transformed before his eyes into nine beautiful maidens, who took off their robes made of white feathers and left them on the ground. They went down into the water to swim and bathe, while the boy watched as one enchanted. He had never seen maidens so fair before, but one in particular caught his eye, lovelier even than all the others. When the sky began to turn red and light slipped through the trees, they climbed out and took up their feather robes. They changed into graceful swans again, leapt back into the air, and flew away.

"The boy wasn't sure if he had been dreaming or not. The next night and the next, he came back to the lake, but he did not see the swans again until the night of the next full moon. Then the graceful birds returned and shucked off their feather robes, and the beautiful girls swam and bathed until dawn.

"Now, an old woman who lived alone in the woods nearby was a magic-user, so the boy went to her and told her his tale. He greatly desired to have one of the maidens as his wife and plainly saw that they were enchanted, but didn't know how to break the spell. The old woman thought about it for a long time, then took some little bones for divination out of an old sack. She cast them on a stone and stared at them a long time, then chuckled. Bringing the boy near, she whispered into his ear.

"'Just before the sun comes up,' she said, 'make a little fire with pine and tar. Steal one of the feather robes and burn it in the fire! Then the maiden will be trapped and never again become a swan. You can take her to be your wife whether she wishes it or not.'

"The boy decided to give it a try since he had nothing to lose, and waited impatiently all month for the next full moon. Finally it came, and, sure enough, the swans returned and the white maidens went down to bathe in the silent lake.

"The boy waited in the bramble by the shore with his heart beating fast until the first hint of rose bloomed along the pinetops to the east. He quickly sparked the fire just like the old woman had told him. The smoke and reek filled the woods all about. The maidens saw it and panicked, racing over the pebbly shore to where the feather robes lay. One by one they put them on and mounted into the sky: all but one. For the boy had been quicker and had snatched the nearest robe lying upon a stone and tossed it into the fire. The feathers shriveled in the flames. Then one maiden stood alone, naked and shivering on the shore, the beautiful girl that the boy had fancied from the start.

"Now the boy wrapped a warm fur around her and took her back to his *pirtti*, where he sat her beside the fire and brought her food and drink. After she was comfortable, he asked her to tell her story and how she came to be enchanted in swan form.

"'My father is lord of the people north of here,' she said. 'And I have eight older sisters, whom you have seen. But the Witch often comes among us and demands that we pay her in rye and fish, sending much of what we have to her castle far away. Her tribute ruined our lands, and one day my father refused. Then Löhi grew angry and cast a spell upon me and my sisters. We turned into swans forever; only once a month, on the night of a full moon, can we take off our feather robes and swim in the waters of a still lake. So you have seen us.'

"The girl began crying, rocking back and forth. The boy was surprised, for surely he had saved her from Löhi's spell.

"'But why are you upset?' he asked. 'You will stay here now, and I'll take you to wife. I may not be a lord, but these fields are still my family's. Surely it is better to be the wife of a free man, however poor, than to be trapped forever as a swan!' But the girl was not consoled.

"'Perhaps I should be grateful,' she said. 'Yet I am not. For now I will never see my sisters again or my father, whom I love. At least we would fly over his cottages and watch him or swim in the pond beside his barn. But now I will be alone forevermore.'

"The boy, happy to have the beautiful girl with him, thought that perhaps his fortunes were changing. But as the days went by, she remained silent and cold, and clearly forlorn. At last he sighed and saw that the situation could not continue, even though he very much wanted her as his wife. He told his old mother that he was going on a journey, then brought the beautiful girl out and put her in his sled.

"'I don't know where your father's lands are,' he told her. 'But if you'll come with me, I'll try to find your home. Then you can be with your people again.'

"It was a long journey, and they had several adventures and close calls, but at last they came upon lands familiar to the girl and found her father's halls. All the people came out to welcome her. Her father, overjoyed, promised the young man a rich reward. But the boy saw eight swans circling in the distance.

"'Is there no lake nearby where you would swim?' he asked the girl. 'Yes,' she replied, 'There is a still lake not so far from here where we would sometimes go.'

"The very next night was a full moon, and so the girl led the boy to the nearby lake. As the moon rose like a giant pearl, the eight swans appeared and landed beside the dark waters. All through the night the boy and girl waited and watched, for they did not want to frighten the swan maidens away. But when the eastern sky began to pale, they sparked a fire of pine and tar, and, before the eight maidens knew what was happening, the boy snatched up their feather robes and threw them into the flames.

"Then Löhi's spell was broken and the maidens were returned to their own fair forms for good. The boy led them back to their father's home, where they joyously reunited with all their people. And their happy father gave his youngest and most beautiful daughter to be the boy's wife and made the boy his heir to boot. The young man had great wealth and good fortune to the end of his days, and the beautiful swan maiden proved a loving wife who bore him many healthy children."

So they rode on into the lands of the Bear Folk without Väinämöinen ever telling Ulla exactly where they went and without the girl ever asking. She knew the old wizard would tell her all she needed in his own good time. The lands south of Keskimaa had grown crowded with newly built *pirttis* and even villages for the many people who had fled the violence in the north. They passed the camps and depots where the Tavastian and Etelalaisen soldiers stayed in wintertime, but avoided them when they could. Eventually they were obliged to take well-traveled roads and paths, where they met many people and passed long trains of wagons filled with bloodrock heading south for the smiths to fashion into spears, swords, and shields.

They met some refugees from the Marches, Karhulaiset who had once lived in the villages in woods near Grankulta. When Ulla heard their familiar accents and manner of speech, a strange feeling always came over her—excitement mingled with fear and a reluctance to speak with them. Twice she asked people she met on the road if they knew where Grankulta lay or had heard the name, but they did not and had not. After that, she didn't ask again but fell silent. So did Väinämöinen. The old man grew quieter and sang fewer songs. When he did talk, he asked Ulla about the *loitsu* she had learned in Laulavalaakso or the songs and chants that Turi had taught her that past summer. He made her repeat them to him again and again as they rode along. And then Ulla knew they drew near their destination.

At last they reached the White Road and turned north, riding along the western shores of Suurijärvi, the great lake of the Karhulaiset. The villages and farmlands round about the lower lake, swollen with folk from the north, were as bustling and crowded, if not more so, than in Ulla's childhood. People called out to the old man and the girl—the wizard and the witch-girl, as some said—when they rode past and brought them *sahti* or cold sour milk, and oats for the horses. Farther up the White Road the villages dwindled. The Bear Folk of the upper lake had been raided more than once by the Easterners, and a great battle had been fought near Suurijärvi's northern neck. Miners still worked there in the summertime. Each spring, when the waters opened, they came to dredge the rock, for the demand for bloodrock had grown greater. The Verikivens and other merchant families who controlled the trade had grown even richer from the war. Some of the miners were not even Karhulaiset, but Karelialaiset from the forest who, like Big Janni, had left the woods in search of work or pay or a better life, despite the danger.

When they came close to Gamla, only a half a day's ride away, Väinämöinen left the road. The Wardens had taken Gamla and made a fort of it, but the old man did not wish to speak with anyone just yet. They dismounted, and the wizard led the horses into a thick wood of spruce and tall fir until they found a clearing beside a little brook. He let the horses roam free to nose around in the mossy earth for whatever real grass they might find to eat. While he washed his face and beard in the brook's clear water, Ulla gathered wood for their fire. She stacked the wood together as her father had taught her long ago, then sat down cross-legged before the pile and stretched out her hands, palms forward.

From the forge of Ukko's Hammer
to the frozen earth descended,
lit the night with light from heaven,
light from heaven in the darkness.
Spark the match,
kindle flame—
let the light be seen again!

As Ulla finished the song, the woodpile crackled and sparked, then burst into flame. "Good," said Väinämöinen, coming up behind her. "You sing a good fire, child. I can feel the strength in you. You're ready—aye, you're ready!"

It grew colder as night came on. Väinämöinen and Ulla sat wrapped in their cloaks and furs beside a yellow fire while the stars came out into the cloudless sky above the trees. Looking up at the sky, Ulla suddenly remembered watching stars with her father and brother on a cold night. Big Janni told the children that if they could stay awake all night and count every star in the sky before sunrise, Ilmatar would grant them three wishes and they might have anything they ever wanted. Of course, they'd soon fallen asleep. The memory made Ulla think of her home in Grankulta, and, taking a breath, she finally mustered the courage to ask Väinämöinen the question that had been growing on her mind.

"We're near the North Road," she said. "We will reach it tomorrow. The North Marches are not far away. Is that where were going? Are we going to Grankulta?"

"Is that what you want?" replied Väinämöinen.

"No," said Ulla. "No, I don't want to go there. Why should I? There is nothing left, right? The people are gone, the villages are gone. There is nothing left anymore."

"Aye," said Väinämöinen. "All gone now, child. I doubt there are even any wandering folk left that far north. The Easterners prowl those parts each summer."

"Then where are we going?"

"Not quite so far, not so far. It's too dangerous north of Gamla, but we will go to the old heartland of the Bear Folk. Your magic and power will always be greater in your own homeland and near to your totem. Remember that."

"I know. The *tietäjää* who come to Laulavalaakso went back to their homelands for their hunt." Ulla snorted. "Of course, we are hunting bear. It's very dangerous. Most of the others—Swan Folk, Hare Folk, Reindeer—how hard can it be to trap a hare or shoot a swan? There's nothing to it. It hardly seems worth the trouble."

"Oho," laughed Väinämöinen. "So that's what you think? Easy? Listen to me now, little one. It's not the hare of these woods, the elk of these trails—or the bear—that a wizard hunts. You have to leave this world behind, child, and go in spirit form into the forest without colors, the wood that borders Tuone's home.

"Easy? It's the very totem you hunt, child, the spirit-animal that will always be reborn. It is no easy thing to find it and no easy thing to trap it. The hare may lead you down a dark path to an uncertain end or elude you. You may follow the swan's flight too far and find yourself on the other side, in Tuonela, lost among the dead. There is nothing easy about it, child, no matter what your clan or totem. Only the strongest soul with the strongest magic will come back again having completed the task."

"Then we're not going to hunt a bear like my people did?" Ulla asked in surprise. "No one would ever talk about it in the Valley, but I assumed—I thought that—"

"Most assuredly not. How do the Kaamoslaiset hunt? They find a bear's den late in the season, when *karhu* is already sleeping and his fur is nice and thick. Then they rouse him and kill him with spears as he tries to stumble out. It's still dangerous, sometimes. No matter what tales you may have heard, no man in his right mind goes hunting for a bear alone before winter.

"Tell me, child," said Väinämöinen, waving his arms toward the sky. "Where is *karhu* now, and where did he come from?" Ulla knew the answer well. She had heard Väinämöinen chant the tale many times. It was the first thing Mielikki had taught her about magic in the Enchanted Valley.

"There," said Ulla, pointing to the North Star up above. "There is *Taivaantappi*, the nail of the heavens, that keeps the skies from falling. And there is *karhu* shining bright in the north." Ulla pointed to the seven stars that the folk of the Far Northern Land called the Great Bear. As she moved her finger from star to star, faint lines appeared, bluish-silver in the dark, as Lempi had shown her when she was small.

"That's where *karhu* came from, from the moon's shoulder, from the Great Bear's back. Ukko sent him down to earth on a silver chain."

"Aye," said Väinämöinen. "Old honey-paw, king of the forest, and father of both men and beasts. He came first, before any other; even old Väinämöinen doesn't remember it, and neither does Löhi! Only the Vanhalaiset were here, and they were young then. That's where *karhu* came from, and he gives life to this cold place. Löhi hates him, but she can't touch him, she has no power over him.

"That's one advantage we have over her, Ulla. She prowls the spirit world for her own dark purposes, but she can't stay too long in any one place. He's attracted to her, and she draws him. If he ever catches her, maybe our troubles will be over. If you find him and send him back for a time, then she'll have little power over you, either!

"Remember the song, child! Remember where *karhu* came from. Use your strength. You'll find him in the spirit-world and master him, and then you'll be a wizard and mighty singer like old Väinämöinen!"

***

The old man and girl stayed two days in Gamla. Väinämöinen wanted news from the March Wardens, and their tired beasts wanted oats, real hay, and rest. The wizard told the Wardens that their captain, Ilkka, had recovered from his ordeal and would soon be riding north to join them again. And all he heard from the Wardens in return was good.

The Wardens said that, after the summer's battle, a calm had descended along the Marches. Löhi's servants had all but disappeared. No goblins, spies, or scouts roamed the countryside. The grim clouds of the Witch's dark thought had lifted, as if her gaze was turned elsewhere or her reach diminished. New hope sprang up among the Wardens and Bear Folk in the north, even as it did in Tavastia and Etelamaa. When Väinämöinen confirmed that the Eagle Folk had joined the other clans in the fight against Löhi, they rejoiced and lifted their voices in song. But the old man told them to keep their guard up and remain vigilant, for no one yet knew what the future might bring. As hopeful as things now seemed, they had only to look in the sky to see that the Witch's Star still shone close to Taivaantappi.

From Gamla, they struck the North Road. At first they rode with two Wardens, scouts who were headed to the small outpost the Wardens maintained near the Marches. But Väinämöinen soon let them go on ahead. The singer, silent and brooding now, kept his head buried beneath cloak and hood as the horses clopped slowly along. Ulla, too, fell silent; tension grew with each passing hour. She knew the time had come and quivered with anticipation, though she still had little enough idea of what to expect. One night only they camped, in a little thicket near the roadside. The next morning, after riding a few hours, the old man finally stopped his horse and dismounted. He turned around, slowly, pausing at each compass point with his staff held high, then held Ulla's reins while she, too, dismounted.

"We are near," he said. "Can you feel the strength in the earth? The very magic in the air?"

"I think so," said Ulla. "My hair is standing on end and my skin is tingling."

"Good, good. Come on, then! Let's get off the road and into the woods a bit. And then we shall see what we shall see."

They left the road then, going into the surrounding birchwood, a thin wood with white trees and a mossy floor, much like the woods round Grankulta. Their boots sank in the soft turf, and they led their horses very carefully lest they stumble and fall. As they walked, the wizard dug at the ground with his staff and lifted something up: a wiry loop of old horsehair, brittle and stiff, an old snare that had lain there, forgotten and untouched, for years.

"There were some back yonder, too," he said. "Must have been a snare line. Plenty of squirrels and grouse about. Beaver and sable, too, at this time of year."

After an hour or so, they came to a small rise crowned with a stand of tall pines. Väinämöinen stopped and pointed at one of the trees—not far above their heads, a skull dangled from a branch, an animal skull, brown and weathered.

"This is the sign I was waiting for," said Väinämöinen. "A bear-skull pine. *Karhu*'s spirit will always return to such a place; he can always be found close by. This is the place, little one."

The old man slung their packs down and let the horses roam free while Ulla stared up at the old skull in the tree. They gathered wood and made a small fire beneath the bear-skull pine. While Ulla prepared a light meal, the wizard rummaged around in his pack and brought out two items buried deep within.

"Here we are," he said, sitting cross-legged next to her beside the fire. He had a small drum, its skin stretched taut and covered with strange markings and symbols, and an old red leather scabbard with a dagger inside.

"Now listen to me, child," he said. Ulla saw that his grey eyes, the fluted eyes of an Erilainen, were clear and bright. "We're going to sing together, you and I. You will leave this place. Your spirit self, your *etiänen*, will go on before you into the woods without color, the place between life and death. You've been there before. This is where *karhu* is waiting, where his spirit prowls. You must find him, Ulla. Find him and kill him."

Ulla had seen the shamans of both Taikalaakso and Laulavalaakso sing themselves into a trance before, sometimes linking hands and rocking back and forth together. Twice she had sung with Turi and felt her spirit about to take flight from her body, but except for the day that the bear left its mark upon her shoulder, she had never actually gone into the spirit world, and certainly never alone.

"But how can I find him?" she asked incredulously. "How can I trap and . . . kill him? I don't know what I'm doing—I thought you would be with me to show me!"

"I cannot go with you," answered Väinämöinen gravely. "Not on such a hunt. Each singer must do that alone or else try and fail in the attempt. And I must remain here in any case to protect you. Your living body will be defenseless while your soul is not within it. Any passing beast or enemy, even the weakest, might kill you, leaving your spirit lost on the other side. It has happened to more than one singer—aye, it has.

"But do not be afraid! You are strong, little one. You know many spells of binding, of holding. And you know the songs about *karhu's* origin, where he came from and why. You can master him with that. That is the way of the Wizards' Hunt. Your knowledge and power must see you through."

Väinämöinen looked down at the long knife in its scabbard, then handed it to the girl. Ulla drew the blade from its sheath. It was black, black as jet, but so sharp it nicked her finger when she touched it. The blade felt cold, and

Ulla thought she could make out the fine lines of delicately traced runes or symbols upon it.

"What is it?" she asked.

"It was forged in Taikalaakso, by an elven smith, one of Lúven's folk and one of the few smiths left among us. He named it *Pitkälehti*, or *Longleaf.* It was made for you, for this hunt. When you go into the spirit world, you leave everything behind, Ulla—usually. At times you may find yourself with something unexpected, something new—a talisman or charm, perhaps a weapon. And a few singers have enough strength to take something with them, especially on their hunt. Not many have done so, but a few have. Lemminkäinen was one, long, long ago, and your friend Unaja as well. She carried a blade, not unlike this one, into the spirit world and back again."

Ulla's eyes grew wide.

"The wolf-fell!" she cried. "That is how she got it!"

"Yes," said Väinämöinen. "She skinned *susi* and brought the fell back with her through the darkness. A mighty deed that was.

"Perhaps you will manage to take *Pitkälehti* with you or be surprised to discover something even better. It can help you with *karhu*, but only your songs, your spells will find him and hold him. No blade, though enchanted, can do that."

"What if I can't find him?" cried Ulla, feeling a panic coming on. "What if he kills me, or what if I'm lost?"

"Peace, child! Don't be afraid. If you need me, if you truly need me, I will find you and bring you back. You can always call me and I'll hear you. But after that, there's no going back; you hunt *karhu* only once. If you fail or give up, you will never be a true *tietäjää.* There's no shame in that. Perhaps your destiny lies elsewhere; but I don't think so. Call me if you are in mortal danger, child, but, otherwise, be brave and do the deed you came to do!"

The old man's words hardly comforted Ulla. Suddenly, now that the time had come, she felt frightened and unsure—as frightened of the prospect of failure as of death. She seldom doubted herself and had been remarkably carefree about what lay ahead, but now quick thoughts raced through her head. *How could I have been so stupid? Why didn't I ask more questions before? How can I ever do this without him?*

The wizard gathered her into his arms and kissed her brown hair. "I love you, little one," he said. "You will take this with you into the woods, too. Do not be afraid!"

Smoke stung her eyes as she took one last look at the thin, watery sun high above before closing them. Väinämöinen beat the drum now, and the rhythmic *dom dom dum, dom dom dum* echoed all about her. The old man hummed, a toneless, shapeless sound, and then sang:

> *Where did karhu come from?*
> *From the Moon's shoulder,*
> *from the Sun's collar—*
> *that's where karhu came from.*

The drum beat—*dom dom dum, dom dom dum*—and the old man's voice wove a magical melody that filled Ulla's mind as all else faded. She pressed her hand to her leather belt and felt *Pitkälehti* in its scabbard, next to the small pouch with the two little figures of herself and her brother. Then she gave herself up to the enchantment as Turi had taught her. All that remained was the drumbeat: *dom dom dum, dom dom dum, dom dom dum.*

***

Ulla's eyes opened. The drumbeat had stopped. There was an absolute silence about her—no cuckoo's call, no rustle of wind or leaf in the treetops, no sound of life to be heard. Väinämöinen was gone, and Ulla stood alone in a grove of thin birch. She blinked, looked around, and remembered.

She remembered the day long ago when, her life fading fast, she had found herself running through these same woods toward a ghostly voice that beckoned her with soft words. Indeed, she remembered it well. The forests of the Far Northern Land were alive with color, but this wood—no normal wood—was as grey and lifeless as a dim, sad dream. The trees were dun, the moss colorless, and the sky overhead a dull and sickly green. She could not tell whether it was day or night; no sun or star or silver-shining moon ever shone there.

Ulla looked down at her hands and her clothes, as grey and washed out as the woods around her. With a start, she grabbed her belt and drew out the knife that hung there. *Pitkälehti!* Alone among everything else in those woods, the Erilaisen blade gleamed black, faintly glittering as she turned it. She had brought it with her from the other side!

Blade in hand, she walked through the trees, with no clear design or purpose. She reached out to touch the birch bark as she passed and felt a slight electric thrill, but otherwise all was utterly still. After a while, she thought of the bear songs she knew and the strong *loitsu* Väinämöinen had taught her to hold a forest animal still, stopped in its tracks, a slave to the enchantment. The girl reached out her mind to the surrounding woods and called to *karhu* with her inner voice.

Her voice came easily, so much more easily than in the mortal world where flesh and bone encased her spirit! Here, along the margins of life and death, power poured out from her very soul like a torrent, unobstructed and unrestrained by the dams of physical reality. "*Karhu*," she called, and then again. "*Karhu*." She stopped, then cried out with the strange vibrato of her spirit self. "*Karhu!*"

But it was no bear that answered her. As the echoes of Ulla's cry faded, another voice, feminine yet deep and resonant, broke the forest's calm.

"You will not find him that way," it said. "He is clever and dangerous and little to be trusted."

Ulla spun around. A woman stood some ten paces away, tall and erect, her long raven hair spilling over her snow-white gown. Her flawless alabaster skin made her crimson lips startling yet perfect. Her beauty was so singular and unnatural that Ulla couldn't be sure if it was a mask she wore, or her own fair face. The woman stepped forward, and the perfect face came alive, blue eyes blazing with light.

"I've searched long for you," the woman said. "I guessed Väinämöinen would bring you here, Ulla Karhulainen. And I am pleased, very, very pleased to finally meet you."

"Löhi!" cried the girl, backing against the dun-colored birch. Ulla had no doubt about the tall woman's identity. With a shock, she realized that Löhi sparkled with color and brilliance in contrast to the drab forest.

"Yes," said the Witch. "You know me as I know you. But do not be afraid. I did not come to trap you or kill you. If I had, I would have done so already—or else gone to where your mortal body sleeps beside the old man in the woods. No, Ulla. I do not wish to hurt you. I wish only to understand you and for you to understand me. And I wish to show you a path, a new path open only to you, perhaps, in all the world."

The Witch again moved toward her. Ulla perceived a certain transparency, an ephemeral shimmer about her. Yet Ulla's own spirit seemed solid and whole. At once she thought, *It is only a shade, a ghost of Löhi perhaps, and not her true spirit!* But even the shade of a powerful wizard can bewitch the unsuspecting, and how could Ulla really tell the difference?

"Stop!" cried Ulla in a quivering voice. "Leave me alone! I will call on Väinämöinen and—and others, too, and they will come and destroy you. destroy you and your evil forever!"

Löhi, her white face gentle and composed, looked down at the terrified girl.

"And what evil have I ever done to you—to you or any of your folk?"

"What evil?" exclaimed Ulla. Despite her fear, a great anger and hatred suddenly welled up inside her. "You killed my family!" she cried. "My family and my village, all the villages of the north! The Itäläiset and goblins have slain hundreds, thousands, all throughout the Far Northern Land! You have brought ruin to us all! What evil? But the folk of the Far Northern Land will see justice done unto you!"

"A man may name a thing evil when it crosses his interests," said the Witch. "And yet when this same thing pleases him, he calls it good and fosters it. The sun casts different shadows on the stone as the day waxes and fails, but does the stone change? Or is it merely the perspective of those who watch it? When you have more power, Karhulainen, you'll understand that good and evil, right and wrong, are fashioned by the hands of men and women, and by their conceits. This will free you and give you great strength.

"But listen to me now! In truth, many have died in this war, but not by my wish. What you have been taught is wrong. I do not seek the ruin of the Kaamoslaiset. They, too, are my children, as are all the *väki* of mortals and Erilaiset in these lands. Behold, Ulla!"

Löhi suddenly seemed to grow, towering over the girl, and her radiance became so bright that Ulla shielded her eyes from it. From within that light, the Witch's eyes glittered like blue diamonds lit aflame by the morning sun.

"I am the queen of the Far Northern Land, its sovereign and protector! Where now are the Vanhalaiset who once ruled this world? The winds of Ilmatar blow blindly. Ahti sleeps in the sea. They have passed into the earth, leaving their power and authority to me. I alone remain—Löhi, handmaiden of Ukko and his instrument in this world. The folly of Väinämöinen leads you astray, you and all the others. But I offer you—I offer you all—the chance to live free and in peace."

Ulla's heart quickened, beating louder in her own ears than Väinämöinen's drum, but even as Löhi spoke, the girl breathed deeply and mastered her fear as best she could. Quick-witted by nature and wise beyond her years thanks to Väinämöinen, she now noticed several things, details that, oddly, caught her attention despite her panic and dread. Löhi spoke with the accent of the Erilaiset, and she had the telltale spiral in her crystal eyes. Powerful though she might be, the Witch was no goddess, but one of Väinämöinen's own folk.

"You made war on the Seven Clans long ago," Ulla said, "and covered all the lands with snow and ice. Now you would do so again. But men and women cannot eat snow or sow seed in ice. You offer nothing to anyone but death."

"This Far Northern Land is Winterland, Talvimaa, by Ukko's will. But does that stop the ski trails of the Saami with their reindeer herds? Or the dwarves beneath their mountains? And other tribes of mortal men, tribes that you know not, live and prosper in the farthest north. There is land enough below the Wall of the Giants and the great forests for men to grow what they need. Indeed, with my power, the land may become richer still, and the Itäläiset and Hiisia will not trouble it."

"You send them against us!" cried Ulla.

"They seek only what they once possessed," said the Witch. "The Itäläiset lived in these lands before the Seven Clans, whether you believe me or not. And, if the Hiisia are bent and misshapen to mortal eyes, are they not still Erilaiset—Ukko's children, even as mortals? Is it any wonder that they lash out at their tormentors when they have been hated and reviled by all, cast out as monsters into the dark?

"Yet this war and strife may still cease, Ulla. And you can bring this about."

The Witch raised her long hand. Ulla suddenly felt the skin upon her shoulder burn under the Clan Mark; the old scars running down her leg shot with searing pain. Ulla, certain the Witch cast a spell on her, tried to remember the strongest *loitsu* of protection that Väinämöinen had taught her. But Löhi simply smiled.

"Yes," said the Witch. "You bear the Mark of the Clan. You were born to greatness, Ulla, favored child of northern fathers. Well do I know the words, but Mielikki corrupted their meaning long ago. The mark on your shoulder was not meant to make you my enemy, but rather to bring us together. Even as I am Ukko's instrument, I need a helper among the Kaamoslaiset; someone to end this war and bring all the clans together under my guidance. You were born to this task, Ulla.

"What does this mortal, this so-called Seer, offer you? A life wasted in loneliness, locked away in a rotting tower. And Väinämöinen? Even now I would make peace with him, my oldest friend and companion. Long we roamed these lands together! But was he not loath to show you the trail for singers? What does he offer you but a life of strife and no home to ever truly call your own?"

The pain stopped abruptly but left Ulla's mind reeling. She felt no compulsion, but rather revulsion. She couldn't turn away, although she wanted only to flee the colorless world and fly back to her body, forsaking the hunt and all it meant, no matter the consequences.

"Come with me, Ulla!" urged Löhi. "Come back to Sariola. In spirit form we can go, you and I; these things can be done. In Sariola I can show you many things. We may come to understand each other. And after, you may seek your body and so come again in truth to Pohjola—or else go your own way, if you truly wish."

"I would never go with you!" said Ulla sharply. "What could you ever show me?"

"Many things," the Witch replied. "Rising above Sariola is the Kipuvuori, the mountaintop from which springs my wizardry, the wizardry of Pohjola. I can show you a magic stronger than you have ever imagined! With such power, all the Seven Lands can be yours to command beneath my throne. You, who have known hunger and thirst, shall learn to make bread from the very stones and draw clean water from the marsh. And the one you love shall be safe, and loneliness will be a stranger to you forevermore."

"Leave me be!" cried Ulla. She tried to turn and run but found herself anchored to the spot.

"Do these things not appeal to you? And yet there is more. Listen closely, Ulla. What do you hear from yonder wood?" The Witch motioned toward the farther trees with a translucent hand. Ulla's eyes followed her gesture, and she focused her hearing. At first the colorless woods seemed as silent as ever. Faintly, then, as if from a great distance, she discerned a familiar sound— water lapping over rocks and stones.

"That is the Dark River," said Löhi, "the border of the living world with Tuonela, the Land of the Dead. That is Tuone's domain, and there he is lord; there must all mortals go someday, either to pass through and leave only their shade behind or else to become ensnared and wander forever in sad forgetfulness. It is perilous for any wizard, mortal or Erilainen, to go down into that land, though sometimes profitable.

"But that is no concern to me, queen of the Living Earth. I know all the paths of the dead, and many spirits therein worship me. Never can I be trapped in Tuonela, for I am greater than even Tuone. I do not need the White Maiden's little boat to cross. And it may be that I can help you find those souls you have lost and most desire to know again. Maybe together you and I can find them and bring them back to living lands. Is this not your wish, Ulla? Do you not desire this?"

Stunned, Ulla paused for a moment, for the Witch had hit close to the mark. She had never imagined, never thought it possible that in Tuonela's shadowy bounds she might actually find her father, her brother, all those whom she had loved and lost. She considered them gone forever, at least until she joined them in the darkness that awaited. But she had never considered Löhi. The Witch visited Tuonela without fear; she had brought Lovêatar back to the Far Northern Land and other dread spirits besides. Even though Ulla knew Löhi put the idea into her mind for her own purposes, the girl could not help thinking. If the ghosts and shades of Tuonela served the Witch and haunted mortal lands at her command, could she not, perhaps, also find the spirits of Ulla's family and bring them back to her?

"Come, Ulla," the Witch said abruptly, her patience now seemingly exhausted. "Time grows short. Give me your hand and we will return to Sariola! Make your choice!"

With a sudden effort, Ulla broke free of the enchantment and backed away from Löhi's outstretched hand. Tightening her grip on *Pitkälehti*, she cried, "No! It is your time that grows short! Your armies are defeated and your season at an end. Go back to Pohjola where you belong and fade into nothingness! Leave the Seven Clans in peace!"

Ulla turned and ran, stumbling through the dreary wood, willing her spirit form to move through the forest. She ran away from the Witch and the water sounds of the nearby river. She heard laughter behind her, Löhi's laughter, not the measured voice of the White Queen, but rather the terrible cackle of a wicked old crone. She could sense Väinämöinen calling her, warning her, imploring her to return. She desperately struggled to recall the words that Turi had taught her, the words to take her back to her body in the woods beside the wizard.

Just as she opened her mouth to sing, the bear loomed before her.

She had forgotten her task, forgotten all about the hunt and *karhu*, but *karhu* had not forgotten about her. Perhaps he raged against a stranger's presence on his hunting trails in the colorless woods, or perhaps Löhi set a trap, luring the bear near with her own presence and then leading him to Ulla. Perhaps it was chance or destiny. But whatever the design, the girl stopped short. For the second time in her life, she found herself facing a bear in the pinewoods of High Länsimaa. Yet this was no normal bear of the waking world, but the very spirit of *karhu* himself made manifest.

Karhu was huge, at least eight feet tall as he reared up on his legs and roared with his mighty lungs. His eyes blazed with fiery wrath, and his shiny black coat gleamed in that dim wood even as Löhi did. He raised a big paw with spiked claws to bat Ulla aside. She knew not whether the bear might rend her spirit form to pieces and send her soul wailing like a ghost across the Dark River and into Tuone's bleak domain, never to return to the land of the living. But she didn't run. A small child no longer, she remembered what she had been taught and didn't run.

Summoning all her strength, she cried, "*Pysäyttää!*"

She raised her hand with outstretched palm to counter *karhu's* stroke. The claw stopped mid-motion as it hit the unseen barrier. The bear dropped to the ground, shaking his head this way and that in rage.

Ulla's power burst forth like a new-kindled star, its brilliance illuminating the darkling woods, blinding any that might have seen her. She chanted the song she had prepared, the song Turi and Väinämöinen had taught her, to master *karhu* and bind him to her will.

The bear gathered himself and, despite her terrible brilliance, leapt toward the girl on all fours, determined to crash upon her and crush her. Even as *karhu* bore down upon her, she finished the spell. The great beast stopped in its tracks, his face so close to hers that Ulla could see the fluted spirals of his blazing eyes.

Her enchantment held *karhu*, though she could feel his strength bubbling just beneath the spell. It would not last long, but that did not concern her. Grabbing the long, shaggy fur on *karhu's* head with her left hand and exposing his breast, she struck with her right, swiftly stabbing upward and plunging *Pitkälehti* straight into his heart. The mighty beast howled in pain and anger, bloody spittle spraying from his snout. Then his eyes dimmed and went out. Without another sound, he fell sideways onto the forest floor.

The silence surrounded her again. She suddenly remembered the Witch and spun around, wild, feral, and ready to fight—but there was nothing. Löhi had gone; Ulla felt no sense of her presence or power. Her own power, which had burned so brightly only moments before, was spent. The light about her dimmed. It had taken everything Ulla had to hold the bear and slay it.

The girl looked down at the bear as if in a dream. Her head swam and her spirit form seemed insubstantial now, like the wood itself, slipping beyond her control. She took the knife, determined to skin the beast and take the fell back with her as Unaja had. She had skinned small animals before but never anything so large as *karhu* and she had only *Pitkälehti*. She lifted *karhu's* head and began to cut around his neck and jaw.

Red blood stained her hands and quick images flashed before her eyes: the bear, the cub in the woods near Grankulta, her father with ax in hand, coming in from the forest, Egan standing on the parapets above the Stone City as the day's fading light played upon the waters in the bay.

Her spirit flew over the tops of the trees, back to her living body beside Väinämöinen. She knew no more.

***

Her sense of hearing returned first. She thought that she was dreaming a slow, sonorous song. Gradually she became aware that she wasn't dreaming at all but lying very still on her stomach with her eyes tightly shut. Väinämöinen was chanting words of welcome to usher her spirit back into its earthly home. Her body ached and her head rang. Now she remembered everything that had happened: the bear, the Witch, the forest. With a groan, Ulla turned over. The forest leapt out at her: white birch, green canopy fading to red and rust, and blue sky above. The colors of the real world.

The old man beside her reached out to stroke her hair.

"You return triumphant," he said quietly. "Your eyes tell the story. You found *karhu* and trapped him. The journey is complete. You are a *tietäjää* now, a wizard of the Far Northern Land. But that was not all you saw, was it, Ulla?"

She thought of the Witch and jumped to her feet, steadying herself on the old man's shoulder. And someone else was there! A woman stood only a few feet away from the smoky fire with a short, sturdy staff in her hand. Ulla felt a menacing and mysterious aura wrapped about her. Exhausted, the girl tried to speak a word of protection, but something sealed her mouth.

But it was not Löhi who stood there. If it was, the Witch was clad in a very different aspect. The young woman's plaited, light-brown hair tumbled down her back. She wore garments of thick brown cloth covered by a fine skin with many small symbols burned upon it; her narrow boots fit tightly about her legs. A quiver of green-fletched arrows was visible behind her back, and a short knife hung from her black leather belt. No taller than Ulla, the woman obviously was no mortal.

Väinämöinen rose. "It's not Löhi," he said, putting his hand on Ulla's shoulder. "She is a friend. Ulla, this is Tulikki, Mielikki's daughter."

The young woman smiled, a curious smile that stretched slowly across a broad face with high cheekbones.

Ulla was confused. "But how—"

"No," said Väinämöinen. "Tell your tale first, child, and be quick about it. We are in danger here. Did you see Löhi? Tell me what happened."

Ulla drew a deep breath. "Yes. She was there, in the colorless woods. I think—I think she was waiting for me. She said strange things, things I couldn't understand; it seemed a long while. But she didn't attack me. She asked me to go with her to Pohjola and said that she would show me many things there. And then I ran. I was trying to come back to you, and then *karhu* was there. He did attack me. But I remembered the song. I held him, Väinämöinen! I held him."

"Aye, child, you did—as I knew you would."

Tulikki suddenly stepped forward and took Ulla's left hand; the girl had not realized that blood covered her clenched fist.

"Open your hand," said Tulikki. Ulla slowly spread her fingers and, to her amazement, saw that she held three teeth in her palm: long, sharp teeth, the cutting teeth of a bear. She looked in wonder at Väinämöinen.

"I brought them back!" she gasped. "I wanted the bearskin, like Unaja with her wolf, and I . . . I don't remember anything else. But I brought these back."

"Put them away," said Tulikki. "Such things are precious, but now is not the time to ponder them."

"No indeed," said Väinämöinen. "For I, too, have seen Löhi, though she gave me no invitations and offered me no hand!"

"She was here?" asked Ulla.

"Aye," said Väinämöinen. "Not long after your *etiänen* left, I was sitting beside you, listening. A strange feeling came over me, and I suddenly grew afraid. I saw something moving through the trees—Löhi! She wore an aspect terrible to look on, that of a withered hag, the old crone of Pohjola, more evil than even Lovêatar. Whether *etiänen* or flesh incarnate I could not tell, but I knew her. I thought she meant to attack me then and there, but she only smiled, a ghastly, leering smile. Then she was gone.

"I fell into quite a confusion then. Singer I may be, but I can't be in two places at once. I feared for you, of course, and guessed the Witch would go after you while you hunted *karhu*, so I thought to call you back myself. But such things take time. How could I leave us both here, alone and unguarded, while my spirit went out chasing yours through the colorless wood? Löhi might have returned and trapped us both, or her servants might have come upon us. No matter what the Wardens say, the Witch's servants still roam these lands.

"And so I waited, making such spells as I could around this place and hoping for some sign to guide me. I turned my thoughts toward you as best I could. If my hair and beard weren't white already, they would be now, after so harrowing a time! I grew anxious and had just decided to risk it, trusting to fortune, when I saw a shadow in the trees again. I wasn't going to wait to be trapped by the Witch, so I drew my sword and strode forward, my strongest spell on my tongue!"

"And just about took my head off," laughed Tulikki. "If I knew you'd grown so hasty, I would've been more careful. But since you thought I was Löhi, I can forgive you."

"Of all Ukko's creatures, you were the last I would have expected to come at me out of the mists, but so it was. Tulikki! After all these years!"

"But what are you doing here?" asked Ulla. "How did you find us?"

"I was waiting for you," said Tulikki. "My mother told me that you would be coming this way to hunt. I am returning to the Valley, returning to see my mother after all these long years. I've been wandering these trails for some days. So has Löhi. I've seen her twice, at night, searching here and there, it seemed. I don't know if she recognized me or not. I am not afraid of Löhi. As long as she does not surprise me, I know how to slip her nets. But I hoped to find Väinämöinen and warn him before the Witch surprised him. It seems I was too late."

"Indeed," said Väinämöinen. "But I do fear the Witch, and so should you, be you Tapio's granddaughter or no. And so should we all now. I think she sent only her *etiänen*; if she were here in flesh incarnate, she would have attacked at once. But she may still return or rouse her servants. The longer we stay here, the greater the danger. Let us go!"

Ulla felt a wave of nausea sweep over her.

"I am very tired, Väinämöinen. I don't think I can walk right now. All my power is spent, and I feel cold and alone."

"You are never alone," said Väinämöinen. "And my power will do for two. The horses are here now! Mount up and let's leave this place. Don't forget, you are now a wizard!"

Tulikki had a small yellow riding pony, so the three companions left the bear-skull pine and picked their way through the birchwood until they returned to the road. They turned south and made for Gamla, riding through that night and all the next day. Väinämöinen intended to ride to the Enchanted Valley as speedily as possible. It was full fall, with winter well on the way, and he wished to come to the Enchanted Valley before the snows began. The quickest, most direct route meant turning east above Suurijärvi and crossing the Jouksi at the old ferry near to Metsäposti. But Väinämöinen wanted to avoid the empty, abandoned lands above the lake that made a perfect place for Löhi to waylay them. So the old man decided to go back down the White Road through the lands west of Suurijärvi, pass below the great lake, and come to Karelia by a more southerly path.

As they rode through the heart of High Länsimaa, Tulikki told Väinämöinen about her life and adventures for the many years that she had been away. She said much that Ulla didn't understand, and, at times, Tulikki and Väinämöinen used the Old Tongue, of which she knew only a little. But Ulla gathered that Tulikki had left the Seven Lands long ago, not long after Lemminkäinen had died defeating Löhi and the first Seer had come to Kyöpelinvuori. Tulikki had lived at first among the Saami, the strange reindeer herders in the north who lived in no settled place and didn't fear the long winter's dark, but then left the Far Northern Land altogether. The strange, often somber Erilaisen woman would not say precisely where she had gone, only that she dwelt long among folk in other lands who had different names for the Vanhalaiset and knew nothing of Löhi. She saw many things in these lands, some evil and some fair, of which the mortals and heroes of the Far Northern Land knew nothing. Tulikki had lived with such folk for generations, but Tapio had called her back at last. Unable to ignore his summons, she had returned.

The woman bore a fine leather pouch strapped to her pony, embossed with the same symbols as her clothes. Tulikki would not say what it held, even to Väinämöinen. She said only that she would give her message to the old wizard and all the other Erilaiset when they reached the Valley and Mielikki. Väinämöinen, content for the moment, did not press her.

As they rode along, Ulla also became aware—acutely aware—that she had changed somehow. At first, she simply felt weary, but after they rested at Gamla and she regained her strength, she realized that something had indeed happened within her during the hunt. None of the wizards at Laulavalaakso would speak of their hunts; it was taboo among the *tietäjää* and Erilaiset. She had believed the hunts were a ritual passage for those who would be *tietäjää* and little more. But no empty ritual from ancient times had changed her so.

Ulla felt different now, more powerful. Her eyes had always been sharp, but now she saw double or even three times the distance she could before. Her wizardly *sight*, which enabled her to throw her very mind into the distance and see faraway woods, lakes, towns, and towers, increased likewise. The power within her had formerly flowed below the surface, deeply hidden at times, waiting to be called on or drawn out by act of will and concerted effort.

No longer. The girl could feel her wizardly power bubbling over, as if her mortal body could not contain it. She could feel her horse's hunger as night drew on and sense its tiredness, and that of the other horses, too. She knew where the wolf prowled ere she heard its cry and where the eagle circled ere it appeared above her. When they rode some way in silence and Väinämöinen grew restless, she knew the very moment he would break into song. Ulla thought that now she understood what it was to be an Erilainen and to see the world as they did.

Väinämöinen questioned her about Löhi as they tried to stay warm by the fire at night, but she felt strangely reluctant to tell the tale. She only hinted at the Witch's promise that she might find her father and the others she had lost and bring them back to living lands from Tuonela. With her new strength, Ulla dissembled subtly so that the old man seemed satisfied and did not press her, or at least so she imagined.

As she lay awake looking at the clouds and stars, Ulla pondered her feelings. She had never tried to hide anything from Väinämöinen since he first caught her using magic. Had Löhi bewitched her so that she would remain silent?

Tulikki was another story altogether. She seldom questioned Ulla. She asked once to see the Mark of the Clan upon her shoulder, begging her pardon after she had done so. But Ulla felt Tulikki watching her at night, the small woman's bright eyes shining in the darkness.

Väinämöinen had not passed through that part of High Länsimaa for several years, so the Bear Folk welcomed him excitedly wherever they met him. They held Väinämöinen and Egan to be their saviors. Despite his wish for speed, the old man often stopped to help, if he might, the sick or lame folk who sometimes begged them for succor. A kindly soul at heart, he would have liked nothing better than to pass many weeks or months among the simple people of Suurijärvi, but need drove him on.

The Bear Folk didn't know Tulikki, so they said little to her, deeming her an elf from Karelia like those who rode with the March Wardens as scouts. But they knew Ulla, or could guess who she was. Although Ulla's story had spread throughout the Seven Lands, her name had not. Most people called her the Witch Child, Väinämöinen's daughter, or the Maiden of the Mark, and many other names besides. But the Karhulaiset, her own folk, remembered her name: Ulla Karhulainen, she who bore the Mark of the Clan, the totem of the Bear Folk and the first symbol of all the Kaamoslaiset. The people knew the pale girl with long dark hair at Väinämöinen's side, and called to her as she rode through their villages and farmlands.

They passed south of Suurijärvi and turned eastward toward Karelia, then struck a cart path that went more or less in the right direction. They took it, wanting to avoid several large villages along the main way, and came to a small hamlet. The companions stopped to water their horses from a trough for the village animals. The little village, called Rautakylä, lay near the lake's southern banks. The villagers were not fisherman but dug stone and marble from a nearby hill to sell in Keskimaa or Etelamaa. Sometimes they toiled in the nearby marsh raising bloodrock from the pools and bogs. Warier than most of the other Karhulaisen villagers, eventually they gathered around the riders, as the cold autumn rain of a chill grey day beat down upon them, causing rolling mists to gather here and there in low places.

When they realized the mighty Väinämöinen had come among them, they welcomed him with great courtesy. While the old man spoke with them, Ulla threw back her hood and let the rain fall on her face. It was cold and refreshing. She relished the new sensations she felt now, almost as if she were feeling raindrops on her face for the very first time. She shook her head, and water flew from her long dark hair. Just then, a voice from outside the gathered crowd cried her name.

"Ulla, Ulla! Lumikki! Oh, Lumikki!"

Ulla spun around, almost falling off her horse. No one had ever called her that except for Kirsikka—and her own family and friends in Grankulta, of course.

"Lumikki!"

The crowd parted for a barefoot girl, perhaps a year or two younger than Ulla, with fair hair just starting to turn brown and wide blue eyes, clad in a homespun dress with a patched and ragged apron. The girl stopped short of Ulla's horse and stared up at her.

"Lumikki! It's you, isn't it?"

Ulla stared back in confusion for a moment before it dawned on her. The face had grown thinner, the voice somewhat deeper, the limbs longer, but she knew the barefoot girl standing in the wet, muddy lane.

"Siria!" cried Ulla. "Siria! It's Siria!"

To the wonder of Väinämöinen and Tulikki, to say nothing of the startled villagers, Ulla leapt from the horse and wildly embraced the girl. Indeed, she was Siria, Ulla's cousin with whom she lived in Grankulta after her father disappeared. They had not seen each other for more than eight years, not since that fateful day the Easterners attacked the little village.

"I knew it was you!" exclaimed Siria. "I remember the bear in the woods and Väinämöinen! I knew you were the Ulla in the tales, although I've met other girls named Ulla since then. No one would ever believe me!"

So, beyond hope, Ulla and Siria were reunited. The travelers stayed in the village that night as guests in a humble *pirtti* while the cold northern rain poured down from the murky sky. Ulla had no doubt what would happen next; she would not leave Siria behind. For her part, Siria wished to go with her cousin, wherever that might be. Siria had been brought to the village by the March Wardens, who had many such orphans on their hands after the raid. Since her own family could not be found, a village family had agreed to take her in as a serving girl. She had lived with them in the wetlands south of Suurijärvi ever since. Though beaten no more than the family's other children, she still was treated coldly and without love, forever an outsider; and now she was mostly sent to wait on and clean up after an old grandmother, ill and half-mad, who abused her when she noticed her at all.

This strange turn of events hardly pleased the father, one of the quarrymen, for he held Siria beholden to him for food and shelter these many years. But Ulla would not leave her cousin behind, and the man was too fearful of Väinämöinen—and Ulla—to resist. So the very next day, Siria packed her meager possessions and climbed behind Ulla onto the black horse, ready to leave. Väinämöinen tried to give the quarryman and his wife a gold

Tavastian crown in recompense, as much, perhaps, as the man might earn in a year; but when the man saw Ulla looking steadily at him with her hazel-green eyes, he refused the coin, fearing a curse. With no other goodbye or farewell, Siria rode away from the village, never to return again.

"It seems I am doomed to forever collect children," sighed Väinämöinen. "And what's more, girls, who are twice the trouble."

Siria had never ridden a horse before, and had been astride a pony only a few times in her life. Ulla rode well, but a novice rider proved too much for her to handle, so Väinämöinen was obliged to take Siria before him, as he had done with Ulla years earlier. Siria, abashed by the old wizard and especially Tulikki, remained quiet at first. But she beamed at Ulla, and the old man did his best to put her at ease. Soon Siria lost her shyness and proved almost as talkative as Kirsikka.

Ulla found it strange to listen to Siria's speech, so familiar and yet so remote. Her cousin spoke with the accent and dialect of the poor Karhulaiset of the north, and she spoke of the everyday experiences of a maiden of that folk, a life that Ulla had both lost and surpassed, though she well understood it. Siria had seldom left the village near the quarry and did not even know where Grankulta and their old home had been. To her, Keskimaa was a name of legend, and she had never heard of Tapiola, Langvika, or even Valkeakosk.

None of that mattered to Ulla, though. As the two girls huddled together at night before the crackling fire, they spoke of that day when their lives had been separated and forever changed. Siria had been only about five years old, but she remembered it clearly, and tears still came to her blue eyes as she recalled it.

She remembered how her mother, Päivikki, had shoved rye bread into her belt and in her panic, given her a pair of her older sister's shoes to wear, hareskin shoes that barely fit her feet. Then she had run through the trees as fast as she could with the other women and children, always trying to keep Ulla and her sister Meria in sight, but watching them grow smaller and smaller as she trailed farther and farther behind. Then the Easterners came among them, catching some and slaying others. Siria fled wildly, wailing, unsure of where she was or where she was going, caught up in a nightmare she couldn't understand. She lost sight of her cousin and sister and, like Ulla, found herself with a group of people from different villages fleeing south down the road. But Siria's group had several others from Grankulta, including Hebla, whom Siria and her sisters called Aunty. To escape the Itäläiset, who seemed to be everywhere, they had left the road and gone into the marshes, remaining there.

Siria did not know how long she had stayed in the stale swamplands—a week, two weeks, a month. In that evil time, with little food or shelter, many sickened and died from marsh fever, including Hebla's youngest child. Siria fell ill, too, and thankfully remembered little of those days as her head swam in a fever. They had been found at last, not by the Easterners but by March Wardens and men from Keskimaa come to drive the invaders away.

Siria recovered and returned to Grankulta with Hebla and a few others. The village was empty, with no folk dead or alive to be seen, the *pirttis* all burned, and the animals gone. So it was in village after village in the north of High Länsimaa. Pekka the Fat's men took the survivors south. Hebla and her older son went to Keskimaa, but there were many orphans like Siria. One day the March Wardens came and took her, along with several others. She was brought to the village by the quarry. She remained in Rautakylä, never knowing what had become of Ulla, or her parents, or little Onni, or Meria, or Kaisa. She never thought to see any of them ever again.

It was a sad story, yet hardly unique, for hundreds had suffered the same ordeal. Glad to be with Ulla now and no longer so alone, Siria had no more idea where she was going than she had as a lost child, but she was happy.

So Väinämöinen and his three companions left High Länsimaa. As the wind turned colder and the nights grew longer, they came at last to the Jouksi River. On a gentle shore called Kalavesi by the Karelialaiset, at a spot where the river flowed slowly, gathering into quiet bays where the cattails rustled and stirred in the breeze, a ferry paddled back and forth to the opposite shore. Siria stared at the great river in no less amazement than Ulla had years before. Across the way, they could see the eaves of the Karelian Forest clad in the multihued glory of autumn—the greatest wood of the Far Northern Land where the leaves had fallen countless times since the world began.

"That is where we are going, Siria," said the old man with a sigh. "Inside those woods lies my home. And this broad water, the Jouksi, is but the first wonder you'll behold, child. Many, many more await."

Chapter Ten

Tapio's Voice

The Karelian took the horse's reins in his left hand, but with his right stroked the muzzle of Väinämöinen's grey steed admiringly. The man, dressed in typical Karelian garb of rich red and green, had his fur-lined cap pulled down tight to keep out the cold. His round nose was red at the tip, and his blue eyes were almost as bright as any Erilainen's. He was no hero, no child of the gods, but a mortal man dwelling in the forest, from the same clan as Ulla's father, Janni. The Karelian stomped his boots and the great horse stamped in answer, as if anxious to continue until it reached food and warmth at journey's end.

"Now remember what I told you," said Väinämöinen. "That's Starchaser, the best horse I've had in a hundred years, and I want him back. The other horses, too. Three gold pieces is more than fair for a winter's worth of fodder and stabling. But he needs to be run some, snow or not, along the paths. And don't let your wife get any ideas about selling or trading him. When I come for him, I'll be quite put out if he's gone. You'll find your luck turns all bad in that case, and you'll never be welcome in the Valley again."

The man nodded, a smile on his broad, round woodsman's face, and nimbly hopped up on Starchaser. Leading the other two horses with a single line, he moved off down the Forest Road without looking back. He soon disappeared around a sharp bend into the trees.

"Well, that's that," sighed Väinämöinen. "They'll be well cared for. The Reindeer Folk are kind to beasts, even if they're not always to be trusted when trading. But these three will be safe enough with Timo, and we'll see them again next spring. Let's go!"

The three women—Tulikki, Ulla, and Siria—followed the old man off the Forest Road and onto the narrow path leading to the Enchanted Valley of the Erilaiset in the very heart of the Karelian Forest. They journeyed for some days, entering the wood well south of Metsäposti and taking a way new to Ulla through the endless multicolored trees. At times they came to cabins of the Reindeer Folk and stayed among them for a night while the horses rested in places less close. But now, at the edge of winter, they finally came to the magic path that led straight to Taikalaakso.

Tulikki paused beside the white standing stone marking the path's entrance and put her hand on its cool, polished surface. She slid her hand along it and sighed. "Long has it been," she muttered, but the others had gone ahead and didn't hear her. After a moment, she ran to catch up with them.

Ulla and Siria still found it a long walk from the stone to the Enchanted Valley, down the narrow path overshadowed by great trees, but always clean and clear of bramble and bracken. They slept at night beside a fire, peering up through webs of limbs and branches at the dark, cloudy sky, which was only occasionally pierced by moonbeam or starshine. Väinämöinen guided them, and Ulla, now a *tietäjää*, felt no weariness or fear. Rather, she absorbed the strength of the forest around them and the power dwelling at its heart, where the greatest magic in all the Far Northern Land could still be found.

At last, toward the end of a chilly day with the wind whistling high in the trees, the four companions came to the Mustajouki, the dark river that marked the border of the land of the Erilaiset. Before them, the Ankkaportti, the fluted white bridge, shone dimly, as if it held centuries of moonlight captured in its shapely span. On the far side lay the Enchanted Valley.

"Behold, Siria!" cried Väinämöinen. "We've now come to the Valley of the Erilaiset, the land of my people. My home, Väinölä, is not far. We will be there

ere this night is passed. Then you shall see trees the likes of which you've never seen!"

They had just set foot on the Ankkaportti when Siria grabbed Ulla's hand.

"Lumikki, look!" The dark water of the Mustajouki suddenly seemed to boil. Steaming mists rose on both sides of the bridge, mounting higher and higher. Through the haze, they saw black shapes like figures of men, transparent and glassy with pale, glowing eyes, rising from the water.

"Don't be afraid," said Ulla, taking her cousin's hand. "Those are the Näkkiä of the Mustajouki, the guardians of the Enchanted Valley. You are safe with Väinämöinen. If you ever chance by a bridge such as this alone, cross swiftly; do not look at them or listen to their song. If you go down into the water with them, you will never come out again."

Even as Ulla spoke, a shape larger and darker than the others rose up from the water and wavered beside the bridge. Slowly, the Näkki raised its arm in greeting; then the water-spirit nodded first to Väinämöinen, then to Tulikki and Ulla. The wizard raised his staff and a soft light shone from its tip.

"They welcome us back," he said. "Especially you, Tulikki. News of your return has gone before us, and your mother awaits us at Väinölä. But they also welcome you, Ulla. They can sense your power and know you are a *tietäjää*."

Tulikki raised her hand, palm outward; the Näkki, without a word or sound, slipped back down into the Mustajouki while its brethren swayed in the mist. The four companions crossed over the graceful arch and continued down the path, leaving the dark river and its strange folk far behind.

Winter filled the skies of the Far Northern Land with clouds and fog, but stars shone brightly overhead in Väinölä, like netted jewels spread across Ukko's heaven. The Erilaiset waited for them, and as the old man strode into the great circle of lamp-lit trees, they broke into song. Lempi, Ulla's old friend, ran to greet them with open arms. Bowing first to Väinämöinen, he then turned to Tulikki and Ulla and doffed his red cap.

"Now who is who?" he laughed. "You've gotten shorter, Tulikki. Been away from the Valley too long, I guess. Trees can't grow without their roots. But

Ulla, you've shot up like a sapling in Mielikki's garden. How tall you are! And now you are a *tietäjää* and among the Great Ones, by all accounts. You're lucky my magic is so strong and that I started you out in the right direction.

"Who's your little companion? And where is Kirsikka? But wait—we heard the news. She's married off, and to a prince, no less. Princess Cherry Red! Good for her, but my heart grieves, too, because I so looked forward to seeing her."

"She married Eglano, Egan's brother," said Ulla. "She stayed at Laulavalaakso, though I'm sure she will visit the Valley when she comes to Etelamaa. But this is Siria, my cousin, whom we found in High Länsimaa—my own cousin, Lempi. We have never seen each other since the Easterners came and destroyed our home."

Lempi capered about and swept his cap low, but Väinämöinen nudged the little man aside and cleared his throat.

Mielikki had come with many Metsäneitoa from all over the Enchanted Valley. Clad as usual in the colors of the forest, green and brown, Mielikki had a warm cape lined with soft white fur on her shoulders. Taller than her daughter—and fairer, some might say, to mortal eyes—she was the incarnation of the living forest itself, and a luminescence surrounded her, radiant and warm. She walked toward Tulikki, flesh of her flesh and her only daughter, whom she had not seen for years uncounted. Tulikki had left the Enchanted Valley and the Far Northern Land long, long ago, and though Mielikki's sight was long and her knowledge deep, she did not know for certain where her daughter had gone. As she reached out and touched her daughter's hair, the luminescence surrounded them both. All could see that their eyes shone with the same light.

"Welcome home, child," Mielikki said, her voice thick with emotion. "Long you made me wait! But no matter, you are here now and my wait has ended on this blessed night! How I love thee, Tuli!"

Tulikki embraced her mother, saying, "Time has a way of slipping silently past, but my heart stayed with you always."

Then Tulikki took a step back and looked up into the Mielikki's eyes. "And yet, I did not entirely choose the time of my return. I was called, Mother. And I bear a precious burden with me."

"So I understand, "said Mielikki. "And no mere chance brought you to Länsimaa even as Väinämöinen and Ulla came there." She turned to Ulla and took her hand.

"Welcome, daughter of my heart. You have become a singer and shaman, even as you desired. The river flows swiftly on its course. Perhaps the counsels that we soon take will illuminate the paths we must tread, for you especially."

Mielikki led Tulikki by the arm to the Erilaiset who waited to greet her, particularly the Metsäneitoa. The eldest among them, her friends of old, had once roamed the broad woods with her, but the youngest among them, born after Tulikki left, knew her only as a legend of their *väki*. Now they brought a garland of white flowers set with red rowan berries to put on her head.

Väinämöinen smiled as the folk of Väinölä crowded around Tulikki, then winked at Ulla as he nodded towards Siria. Ulla took the girl's right hand and Väinämöinen took the left; together they led her forward while her eyes grew wider and her heart beat faster.

Everything around her surpassed her imagination. She saw the tree Isotammi—the Great Oak of Väinölä, taller than the giants—soaring toward the sky, towering above all other trees of the Karelian forest, and holding Väinämöinen's home inside its living wood. Siria stretched her neck and gazed upward as they came to the doorway, bathed in the silver glow of lamps hung from the lowest limbs.

"It's impossible," she stammered. "It's so big. How can any tree grow so tall?"

"But it's not just any tree," answered the old man. "This is the Great Oak, the heart of the Enchanted Valley and of the whole forest. It was here in the Beginning, and its roots go deep, as deep as the wells of magic that we draw on. It will be here as long as the Far Northern Land exists, right until the End, it will. Not even Löhi can do anything about that.

"Come on, child, let's go inside now. Ulla will show you the way!"

Siria found Väinämöinen's home inside the Great Oak as amazing as its soaring limbs and branches. Like Ulla and Kirsikka before her, she felt bewitched by the Enchanted Valley's magic and its strange and wonderful inhabitants. She marveled at the food they gave her—the white, sweet bread of the Erilaisen bakers, the berries still somehow in season, the honey, the cream, the butter, and the roasted pheasant stuffed with forest nuts and sloe. Daughter of the poor north, the girl had never known such flavors or abundance in her life, nor imagined them possible. She delighted in all the clothes they brought to her, in colors of the living earth, dyed brighter even than Karelian dye: the strawberry's red, the spruce's green, the cuckoo's yellow and gold.

Of course, the Erilaiset themselves enthralled the girl most of all. The tree maidens came to braid her hair, and Ulla's, too, in the elaborate braids of the Erilaiset, shot through with moonbeams and starshine it seemed. The Metsäneitoa left her bashful, but she looked with wide eyes upon the Menninkäiset, especially Lempi, laughing at his pranks and antics and marveling at the illusions he worked for her. She watched the folk of Väinölä at night, sitting in the cold beneath the shining, colored lamps that flicker in the forest's dark, and listened to their voices raised in song here and there among the trees.

The Valley delighted and amazed Siria as it had her cousin before her, but Siria had no mark on her shoulder and no desire to stay in that land far removed from mortal ways. She kept close to Ulla as the winter deepened and snow fell and the wolves howled mournfully in the distance.

***

Little news from the outside world came to Taikalaakso that winter. The season was mild, the snow light and wet, and the lakes froze late. It seemed that all the lands slept and waited, perhaps for some unknown stroke still to come. Winter had become the season of Lověatar in the Far Northern Land, but this year even Tuone's daughter fell silent. She little troubled the folk of the Seven Clans with her ills and pains. Once or twice Turi reached out to Väinämöinen, speaking with him in dreams and visions as men of strength and power might. All was quiet in Laulavalaakso, too. Egan and the Swan Folk had long since departed for their own lands.

Ulla rested at peace for a while, passing the days quietly. Some days she walked through the darkling winter woods with Siria; others, she learned what magic she could from the Erilaiset, for her power waxed and she wished to become stronger still.

On Tulen Yö, the Night of Fire and the longest night of the year, the Erilaiset gathered here and there among their scattered homes in the Valley to light fires and burn tallow candles, singing songs from the past that only they remembered. Väinämöinen gave Ulla a staff that night. Made of rowan wood, fire-hardened and shod with bronze, the short, straight staff resembled the Seer of Kyöpelinvuori's, though it had no carven image. But Väinämöinen had made it himself, putting in it such blessings as were his to give.

The day after Tulen Yö, the wizard told Ulla to gather her things and dress warmly. Leaving Siria with Lempi, they took the old path deeper into the heart of the Valley. Snowflakes fell around them, adding to the branches' burden and making white patches on the forest floor, as they walked through the dusky twilight of the short winter day. But they didn't have far to go to reach their destination. Kukkatarha, Mielikki's garden, was less than a day's journey from Väinölä. Only a few hours after the early nightfall, they came to the bloom-filled clearing where Tapio's daughter made her home.

Mielikki had dwelt at Kukkatarha since time immemorial, even before Väinämöinen came to the Great Oak and fashioned it into his home. Unlike Väinölä, Kukkatarha had no village around it, and few Erilaiset lived nearby save some Metsänaitoa scattered among the trees. No tree was ever felled at Kukkatarha, no glade made by fire nor axe, but, in a natural clearing at its heart, forest grass and berry bushes grew amidst green shoots and bunches of wildflowers: tall stalks of goldenrod, bright-yellow marigolds, blue and purple anemones, beds of white meadowsweet, daisies with pale petals and yellow eyes, and sky-blue forget-me-nots. Most beautiful of all, tiny bell-shaped lilies, white as snow, bloomed year-round beside a clear swift brook that fell from some hidden height and watered the fairylike lawn.

Mielikki, who saw farther than any other living creature, mortal or immortal, in the Far Northern Land, laid her power on Kukkatarha so the flowers there bloomed year-round and the water did not freeze, save when she allowed it. And in a corner of the garden, a low silver door set in a green mound led to Mielikki's house, fashioned like the strange hall at Loulajärvi where Ulla had first been introduced to the Erilaiset years before. While Väinämöinen filled his home in the Great Oak with finely crafted objects of gold or precious stones, from lands far and near, Mielikki chose differently.

To be sure, she had jewels and stones, though she kept most hidden in caskets like the one that held Työ's magical jewel. Yet her home remained simple, filled with things well made yet plain. If time passed slowly in the Enchanted Valley of the Erilaiset, it seemed to stop altogether in the serene simplicity of Mielikki's house under the grass.

Väinämöinen rapped on the silver door with his staff and, without waiting for any reply, stooped low and went inside. Ulla trailed behind. He stamped the snow from his tall yellow boots on the mats and rushes that covered the earthen floor, and Ulla stomped her fur-lined Karelian boots. They both blinked and stared in the smoky yellow light. Mielikki and Tulikki sat cross-legged by a large central hearth lined with bricks, under a round hole that could be opened to let out at least some of the smoke. Satatieto the wizard was there, too, as well as a long-faced elf who sat a ways apart, named Janus. One of Lúven's folk, he had just returned from High Länsimaa.

Mielikki cocked her head toward them and said, "At last! I've been expecting you all day, Väinämöinen; but you've taken your time, haven't you? If Turi were here, I'd have thought you stopped at his home to try the beer."

"More's the pity," said the old man, with a smile. "But it's nice to walk through the Valley with snowflakes in my hair. I have been missing that for all these years. No matter. We are here now."

"Come, then," she replied. "Ulla, come sit beside me. You are a *tietäjää* now, the bearer the Mark of the Clan, and mighty among mortals and Erilaiset alike. It is fitting that you are here."

Väinämöinen and Ulla took off their wet boots, spread their thick cloaks on the earthen floor, and took their places by the fire. Ulla looked at Mielikki and her daughter in the yellow light. As always, Mielikki wore a fine, simple gown, but Ulla scarcely recognized Tulikki, though they had journeyed together for weeks. She had traded her stained traveling clothes for a green dress like unto her mother's, shot through with silver thread. Her clean hair hung long and free, lying gently about her shoulders, and copper rings adorned her fair arms and neck. Ulla did recognize the bag that she carried since the day they met in High Länsimaa, which sat before her on the low hearth.

"I waited long years for my daughter's return," said Mielikki. "But since Löhi came back, I have not only waited—I have expected her. Tulikki often came into my dreams and visions, so I knew—or at least I hoped—that soon she would come home, but I could only guess about the manner of her return. One glad day, she reached her spirit out to me and I saw her again in my mind's eye, close by to that place where Ulla would make her hunt. Tulikki arrived to do her part in the struggle against Löhi, but what that part may be, I could not say. But now she will tell us her tale, the tale that she has yet to tell in full to anyone, even me. For she has waited until this long night, when we all are gathered."

Tulikki fed the fire with sweet-smelling wood and stretched out her hands upon the hearth.

"I have traveled far," she began in her matter-of-fact tone. "Farther even than you, Väinämöinen, in your wandering days. For beyond the Far Northern Land, beyond frozen Pohjola, beyond even the lands of the Itäläiset and their kin, there are other lands and other races that even the Erilaiset know not, save Löhi, perhaps. The strange folk there have different names and images for the Vanhalaiset, and many other gods besides, though doubtless they worship the same beings as all do in this world.

"But for some time now I have dwelt again in our own land, though in its farthest reaches: far west of Sariola and northwest of the mountain of the dwarves where they mine for silver and gold. By a deep lake and a forest of snow-covered trees that looked like candles, I discovered profound peace and solitude. One night, two summers ago, I sat by the lake while the red sun hung for hours on the horizon. Then suddenly he appeared. Tapio, my grandfather, came to me, and his aspect lit the candle-trees with green flame. I was very scared.

"He spoke to me then, telling me that the time had come for me to return. And he bade me go to the Marches, into the lands now called High and Deep Länsimaa, to search for seven things, seven signs, that might put an end to Löhi's madness and end the strife. And I did as he bade me."

She paused and stared into the fire.

"But what are the seven signs?" asked Satatieto.

Tulikki sighed, then slowly unwrapped the bundle that sat before her. Reaching inside, one by one she took out seven objects and placed them on the hearth.

"From the north I come with these," she said. "Behold! The Shards of the Sampo!"

"By the vaulted heavens!" exclaimed Väinämöinen, as the others also cried out in surprise. But Ulla narrowed her eyes and stared closely at the Shards as they lay on the reddish-brown bricks.

They were of different shapes and sizes. The largest was a thin strip of metal almost a foot long; the smallest, a nearly perfect circle of silver, was small enough to fit inside Ulla's palm. Ulla had heard tales and songs about the magical Sampo a hundred times. Forged from different metals by the great smith Ilmarinen, it stood on the green hill of Tapiola, the heart of the

Seven Clans of the Far Northern Land, and brought peace, fertility, and increase to the Kaamoslaiset. Ulla had seen, of course, the miniature golden copy that the Seer of Kyöpelinvuori kept locked in her tower; she didn't know who had made it or how the Seer came by it. Though perhaps worth a king's ransom, it remained an imitation, bereft of power and magic. But these jagged, broken pieces on the hearth were real, perhaps all that remained of the mighty Sampo. Who could guess what power might still be within them?

"Where did you find them?" cried Väinämöinen. "I will never forget that day, if I live another thousand years. Löhi found us—Lemminkäinen, Ilmarinen, and myself—as we sailed down the Kemijärvi with the Sampo lashed to the prow, trying to escape her and bring it back to mortal lands. She came out of the sky and changed into the shape of a giant harpy, big as a dragon, stinking of pain and death. I sang up the strongest storm I could to beat her back! But while we fought her, the Sampo was ruined, broken by song and spell, shattered into a thousand pieces, molten like hot iron, cast into the water and scattered throughout the north like so many grains of precious sand. Never again could we find even a pebble. Where did you find them?"

"Here and there, among the borderlands of the Elk and Bear Folk," said Tulikki. "I sensed them as if I had a lodestone. When I came near one, I would spy a wisp of light, faint and wavering, dancing in the mist. Then I would find a Shard under the ground or else covered in rocks; one lay in a bog, beneath mossy turf. The seventh I found not far from the wooded trails where I met you. When Löhi came, I thought at first that she also sought the Shards, meaning to steal them yet again. But she was waiting for Ulla. She did not know my errand."

Janus touched one of the Shards, smooth and cool despite the fire. In its yellow glow, the metal seemed to change shape and color, flickering from black to gold to coppery red. "But what power do they now hold?" he asked. "Are they talismans or totems, one each for the Seven Clans? Or should we fashion weapons from them, a knife or spear tip that will slay Löhi and send her at last to Tuonela?"

"I wonder," said Väinämöinen. "And who would wield such a weapon?"

"They are not weapons," said Tulikki. "Tapio had a different message: from these several Shards, the Sampo should be reforged!"

At Tulikki's words the fire leapt up high, sending long shadows racing across the room. Ulla felt a rumbling beneath her feet, faint at first but quickly growing stronger. A deep noise, low and vibrating, filled her ears like the distant beat of hundreds of giant drums. The flames crackled and Mielikki scrambled to her feet.

"He is here," she said in a clear voice. Looking down at Ulla, she added, "Now, Child of the Prophecy, look upon the Lord of the Forest who ordained your birth."

Ulla watched as Mielikki spread her arms in gesture of invocation, singing in the Old Tongue of the Erilaiset, learned from the Vanhalaiset in ages past. Her voice rose and fell as she wove the spell. All the air within the room seemed charged and electric. Ulla felt her own mind swim with enchantment. Suddenly the flames died down, as if a cold wind had blown them out. Where the flames had danced moments earlier, a figure now appeared, bathed in its own light, a translucent, greenish sheen.

As the figure grew clearer, Ulla saw now that it had the shape of a man, ten feet tall at least, towering over them, with a crown of leaves and berries on his head that swept the cottage roof. Smoke wrapped about him. His beard hung to his knees, plaited here and there, grey as the winter sky streaked through with brown and black. Beneath a craggy brow, his bright eyes looked down on them, the fluted, spiraled eyes of the Erilaiset. Green and yellow robes covered his massive frame. He lifted his arm to them, palm outward. Pine scent filled the room.

"My children," said Tapio in a deep baritone voice.

Ulla thought that she saw him smile beneath the bushy beard. Mielikki bent to one knee, never taking her eyes from her father's face; Väinämöinen and Satatieto also knelt with bowed heads, their staffs in their right hands. Ulla quickly did the same. The spell intoxicated her; she had never felt a magic so strong in all her life!

"Welcome, Father," said Mielikki. "Tulikki has brought the Shards of the Sampo to us."

"Seven Lands and Seven Clans," rumbled the Lord of the Forest. "Seven Shards to be made whole again. The mortal child has set all in motion and brought the clans together: Bear and Swan, Hare and Eagle, Elk and Reindeer, and Wolf. Raise your heads and hearken to my song, children! For you may hasten Löhi's departure and save the land much ruin."

They raised their heads then to face the mighty spirit, his power beating upon them as a great drum, filling them with awe.

Tapio raised his arms high to the rafters and chanted tunelessly.

From the Cold Land's seven corners,
seven stars to be rekindled,
seven Shards of mighty Sampo
shining lid to earth descended.

Taken once to darkling Northland,
hid in dismal Sariola,
hidden by the old crone's magic,
broken by her wings of fury.

Let the Smith reforge the Sampo!
Bane unto the Witch's fortune,
fade into the northern darkness,
northern darkness everlasting.

Let him forge the mighty Sampo,
brief the Witch's time remaining
for the rising generation—
Seven Lands and Seven Peoples.

The echoes of Tapio's booming voice faded. The fire leapt up again, seeming to swell around him. The Lord of the Forest said no more. In the silence, it seemed to Ulla that he looked straight at her. Her heart quickened as his fiery eyes pierced her very being. Unbidden, a thought came into her mind: *You have done well, child. Indeed, you have done well.*

A blaze of green light dazzled their eyes, his figure blurred, and, when their sight returned, he was gone. The embers in the firepit burned red and low, glowing dimly in the murk.

It was quiet at first, as if none of them wished or dared to speak and break the spell. Tapio's power and presence vanished, as if swept away by a gust of wind or storm. Still they reeled, besotted by the enchantment, striving to focus and return to the waking world. Though the vision had seemed brief, they did not know how long the great Vanhalainen had been among them, minutes or hours.

At last Tulikki sighed as if shaking off a dream and waking from deep slumber. She shook her head, then stretched out her arm to put a dry birch log into the fire.

"So he spoke to me in the north," she said slowly and deliberately, "those verses and others like them. And they came into my dreams. The meaning is clear. We have recovered the Shards of the Sampo so that it may be reforged."

"Yes," said Mielikki. "And at last we see a way to finish what Ulla set in motion. If the Sampo can be made whole again, then Löhi's hope will wither. We can guard it so it will never again be stolen, and she will fade back into the winter's night."

The others stirred as life coursed again in their veins.

"But who can do this deed?" asked Satatieto. "What smith has the skill to reforge the Sampo, whether we have the Shards or no?"

"Ilmarinen forged the Sampo," said Väinämöinen. "Ilmarinen, the mightiest smith this world has ever seen, mortal or Erilainen. I was with him during the long time he forged it. He wove his spells for weeks and worked the metal for months. Then we raised it on the Green Hill in fair Tapiola. But that was long, long ago. Ilmarinen and all his people have long since vanished from the world, slain or driven away during the Witch's War. I know not his fate, but he is gone. Who now could ever do such a deed? I am no smith."

"What of the elves?" asked Satatieto. "Smiths among Lúven's folk forge armor and blades. Might a smith among you reforge the Sampo?"

"None among us has that skill," said Janus. "Few enough remain in any case. Vasara is perhaps the most skilled. When we can, we still make useful things of iron, beautiful things of silver or gold, winterfast blades and knives, but no one among us has the power to match the skill of Ilmarinen of old."

"What of the dwarves?" asked Satatieto.

"They live far away," said Väinämöinen. "Far to the north, beneath their mountain, they hardly notice the troubles of the Far Northern Land, trading rather with the Saami and the men who live away northwest, unknown to the Seven Lands. And Löhi has given them much gold, which they covet, to forge weapons for her. They are skilled craftsmen, but they have not the power we seek. Nor would it be safe to give the Shards to them. Löhi must not find out what we do."

"You speak only of the smiths of the Erilaiset," said Mielikki. "Yet are there no skilled mortal smiths among the Seven Clans? My mind has often turned toward them of late, though I knew not why. Great skill remains in Seppälä, where the famous mortal smiths dwell in their guarded halls, admitting few and loving none, engrossed in their craft. That must be the answer to this riddle. It is the time of the Kaamoslaiset. If the Sampo is to be reforged, the Smiths of Seppälä must do it."

"The Smiths of Seppälä!" cried Väinämöinen. "The Smiths' Guild has become rich beyond measure. They alone among mortals have profited from this war. They craft well, no doubt; but their magic? None of the mortal *tietäjää* who have come through Laulavalaakso have been smiths. None have sought the special arts of Ilmarinen, and, even if they had, none left among the Erilaiset could teach them."

"Who is the Master Smith in Seppälä?" asked Satatieto. "If any within the Guild can do this thing, surely it must be the Master Smith."

"I do not know him," answered Väinämöinen. "I only know he is named Ahjo. I have never met any of the Master Smiths since the Guild was founded."

"And yet they have done great works," said Mielikki. "And they have magic still, do they not? The Smiths of Seppälä learned the secret of making iron winterfast, even the softest bog iron that would break in winter's cold without the spell. If the power does not lie with us here in the Valley, if the Haltiatar cannot make the New Sampo, then the Smiths of Seppälä must be our hope."

They fell quiet again for a while, listening to the fire's crackle. Then Väinämöinen sighed. "Well and good," he said. "I have heard Tapio's words. I do not doubt them, even if I cannot guess how they may yet be fulfilled. I will do what I can. We will see if these mortal smiths can recapture the gift of Ilmarinen."

"Go to Seppälä!" said Mielikki then. "Convince them that they must attempt this thing; the New Sampo must be forged!"

The old man turned to Ulla with a raised eyebrow and an odd gleam in his eye.

"So now you'll see the City of the Smiths in springtime, child, where the waves roll in from the Itämeri Sea and crash against the great white wall."

***

Väinämöinen did not plan to leave the Enchanted Valley for many weeks, not until deep winter had passed and the heavy snows ended. Then, just before spring, he would set out and be well south of the Wall of the Giants by the time the ice thawed, the waters opened up, and the rivers and streams flooded.

Winter was always mild in the Valley, save when the Erilaiset occasionally let the world's weather bring deep, heavy snows into the heart of the Karelian Forest. But that year winter was mild everywhere: in the Birchwood near Valkeakosk; in Keskimaa, where people still labored to rebuild what the

Easterners had despoiled; and in the City of Etelamaa, where the old Keep looked down on its white bay in the moonlight. Folk said that the Witch's power was indeed retreating, though they still feared that, at any moment, she might unleash a new magic to trouble their lands.

Ulla stayed mostly at Väinölä, as did Väinämöinen, though he usually walked all through the Valley when he returned, winter or no. He played his kantele for hours in the Grove by the Great Oak or slept in his own bed beneath the forest floor. Ulla and her cousin Siria walked where they would as Ulla taught her the strange ways of the Valley and the heroes and told her stories out of the past. Sometimes they went with Lempi, who delighted Siria with stories about the forest animals and their funny adventures.

"Now the fox is the trickiest animal in the forest," the little gnome told her. "You have to watch out for him. *Karhu*, old honey-paw, saw him one day and admired how his red coat shone in the sunlight. 'What a grand coat you have,' said the bear. 'Why, it's as red as the rowan berries in Väinölä. How ever did you come by it?' The fox saw a chance for sport and answered, 'Well, it didn't used to be so red. It was as brown and plain as your coat until some farmers helped me out. They made a pile of straw and lit a fire under it, and up to the top I jumped. It was hot, I don't mind telling you, but I let it burn me just a little bit. Ever since, my fur's been as red and glossy as can be.'

"The bear decided he just had to have a coat as beautiful as the fox's, so he begged his friend to help him and the sly fox pretended to agree. They gathered a big pile of autumn straw and the fox lit a fire under it, and the bee-chaser jumped right up on top. After a while, the bear started to get hot and asked, 'How long must I wait, Fox?' But the fox, who stayed well back from the fire, answered, 'Just a little longer!'

"Soon the flames climbed halfway up the straw pile and the bear felt very uncomfortable indeed. 'How long must I wait, Fox?' he blurted out. 'Just a little longer!' said our sly friend.

"Finally the flames reached the top and licked all around the forest-king. 'How long must I wait, Fox?' he cried out in real distress. 'Just a little longer!'

replied the fox. But just at that moment the bear's fur caught fire. He leapt up and ran yelping down the path until he jumped into the Mustajouki to douse himself. The fox rolled about laughing so hard that tears came to his eyes.

"From that day on, the bear's singed coat looked black and shaggy, and that's how he looks to this very day. So be wary, little one, of what others tell you. They don't always have your best interests in mind. Remember what old Väinämöinen says: *The ground is always fertile for fools and there's no need to sow them.*"

Ulla often sat alone with Väinämöinen inside the Oak. In the soft yellow candlelight, he taught her a deep magic that he had not spoken of before, the art of crafting her own spells to do as she pleased and the secrets of working a true change to transform herself into a different shape or form. Ulla learned other dangerous *loitsu*, dark and akin to Löhi's magic, but which a *tietäjää* must still know, especially one with power such as Ulla's. And they pondered Ulla's prize, the three teeth from her hunt, from *karhu*, which she kept close to her in the little pouch that still held the figures of herself and her brother. Väinämöinen could only guess what power the teeth might hold.

As winter finally began to turn, they prepared to leave the Valley. Ulla went to spend several days with Mielikki in her small home before they set out. One day they walked all the way to Loulajärvi and sat on the grey shores beside its deep, frozen water, their furry boots tucked up beneath their cloaks. No one else was about the dark, empty hall. Ulla, quiet and despondent as she always was before reluctantly leaving the Valley, had said little as they tramped together through the forest. Now she removed a thick glove and made a tiny ball from the icy snow. While she molded the ball between her cold fingers, she mustered the courage to ask Mielikki a question she had been pondering, one Väinämöinen seemed too distracted to consider.

"*Seven Stars to be rekindled, Seven Shards of mighty Sampo,*" she mused. "Seven Stars and Seven Shards for Seven Clans, that much is clear. But if Tapio sent Tulikki to find them, why did he wait so long? All the north has been ransacked, Keskimaa nearly destroyed, and so many killed; why could not the

Vanhalaiset have sent us the Shards long ago so that the Sampo could be re-forged before Löhi returned, so that she might never have become so strong?"

"Perhaps they tried to," answered Mielikki. "How can we know what the gods intend, even we who are their servants and children? Our hearing is imperfect. We must listen with our hearts sometimes and not our ears. We are free to choose, each one of us, and the Vanhalaiset will not take away that freedom even if it leads to our ruin. So Löhi differs from them; she wishes for slaves with no choice but to serve her, with no true wills of their own save fear, or maybe greed. And maybe the choice of each person, alone, may still be joined together to determine the course of this world, for good or ill. That is freedom's heavy price.

"But I think the answer to your question, Ulla, lies within yourself. The Seven Clans were not united, and mortals had long abandoned the Old Ways. No Sampo could be forged at such a time, or else a Sampo with little power, like that within Kyöpelinvuori—a beautiful thing perhaps, but no more.

"You wear the Mark of the Clan on your shoulder. You fulfilled the prophecies of old. You more than anything, more even than Väinämöinen, convinced the mortal lords to come together to fight Löhi and honor that which should be honored. Only then, I deem, were the Seven Lands ready for the Sampo to be reforged, if we can but find the smith with the skills and power. You are truly Löhi's enemy."

Ulla thought about it. Indeed, she was Löhi's enemy. If she had not been walking through the woods that day near Grankulta, if the bear had not attacked her, if Väinämöinen had not found her and called her back from the brink of death . . . if those things had not happened, perhaps Löhi would have already overrun the Seven Lands. Perhaps only Egan, besieged within the Stone City, would still stand against Pohjola. Löhi must hate her. And yet the Witch had not killed her when she found Ulla in the colorless wood.

Ulla still had not told Väinämöinen everything about that day, and the old man let it be. But now she told Mielikki all that had transpired, how the Witch had invited her to Sariola and hinted that she might again find her father.

"Why did she not kill me, Mielikki? Even Löhi's *etiänen* must be powerful enough to track me or slay me unawares. Instead, she tried to talk to me, to convince me."

"If what you say is true, she did try to kill you, didn't she? You, who were hunting *karhu*, blundered straight into him, unawares, at your peril. You do not realize how dangerous that was."

"Well, yes. That is true. But Löhi herself might have taken me by surprise and plunged a dagger right into my spirit form. Why didn't she kill me herself?"

Mielikki pursed her lips and sighed, her frosty breath briefly wreathing her in smoke.

"I think she cannot, Ulla—at least not unless she can trap you in Pohjola, where her power is greatest. You are the Child of the Prophecy, the child who united the Seven Clans. Her magic is weak with you, and she fears you. Do not listen to her, Ulla! Only through lies and deception can she ever defeat you. Remain true to yourself. Remember that, my dearest child!"

Chapter Eleven

Seppälä

Väinämöinen sat astride his grey-flecked horse on the snowy height and looked down on the old town of Kotanrannta. Blue smoke from a hundred chimneys and hearths rose into the sky, lazily drifting westward to linger in a distant haze. The wind blew from the east, but weaker now, giving way to gentler breezes from friendlier climes as winter surrendered, as it must, to spring. Between wispy trails of smoke, the towers and gabled roofs of the second largest town in the kingdom of Etelamaa could be seen. A lone horseman made his way slowly up the rocky hill along a winding path. Dressed in blue and white, he bore the device of the Folk of the Swan.

"Here is our welcoming party," said Väinämöinen to his three companions—Ulla, Siria, and Tulikki—who sat beside him on their own mounts. "They looked for us by yonder eastern road, but we fooled them. Not many come to this place anymore, I guess. They used to call it Luntamäki, the Snow Hill. I stood here with Lemminkäinen once, long, long ago. But it looks as if Egan is not here."

The horseman finally approached and saluted them, though his steed, which had other ideas, danced and fought the bit.

"Hail, Lord Wizard," the man said. "And to you, Lady Ulla. We heard you were in these lands and approached the town. You and your companions are most welcome."

"You have our thanks," answered Väinämöinen, somewhat stiffly, as he was wont to do on such occasions. "But what news of the king?"

"I fear you have missed him. King Egan came here a week ago with several others but did not stay long. He rode away with his brother toward Tavastia. I do not know where. But Lord Aldon is in the district and may return in some few days; he may have more news. The king's cousin, Lady Annikka, is in the town with Sampsä, her son, and she would be pleased make you welcome, Lord Väinämöinen, if you choose to stay with us."

"Hmm, I see," said Väinämöinen. "Well and good. We are cold, tired, hungry, and dirty, and we have come swiftly all the way from Karelia. These beasts are tired, too. We will be glad to accept Lady Annikka's hospitality. But we may not wait for Aldon! I, too, have urgent business in Tavastia, and the waters are opening early. We must hurry south and not delay. But I wish I could have met King Egan."

So they made their way down into the town, where Annikka awaited them. A thin, cold woman, the grandniece of Egan's grandfather and namesake, she had been widowed for several years and was silent as snowfall in the early morn of her home in the Green Vales. Her son Sampsä was lively enough, eager to meet the famous wizard and eager to come of age and go to war like his uncles.

Väinämöinen was indeed tired, for the journey from the Enchanted Valley had been a long one. They had left before the Far Northern Land was free from the depths of winter, a dangerous proposition even for a wizard. But the singer would not wait for spring—he wished to bring the Shards of the Sampo to the smiths immediately. So they set out through the woods, the four of them. When they emerged from the forest, they took to sleds—not the working sleds of Karelian reindeer herders, but real traveling sleds, of solid craftsmanship, with runners of black iron and pulled by horses. Väinämöinen had made sure to claim his favorite horse, Starchaser, from its Karelian hosts. After that they went swiftly. They struck a course west, first over the great river and then to High Länsimaa where the smooth winter roads made good sledding.

Väinämöinen drove one sled and Tulikki the other; they sped along the icy paths with the cold wind in their faces while Ulla and Siria, wrapped in cloaks and furs, huddled behind. Before long, though, they came to the pass through the Wall of the Giants that led down into Etelamaa and finally to a road that ran toward Tavastia. Ulla felt sorry to have the wild ride end; she liked the snow-spray flying from the runners, the horses' strong legs pounding on the packed snow and ice, and especially the times when Väinämöinen let her take the reins. She had raced against Tulikki, struggling to control the sled and not turn over as they dashed madly across the white plains.

A large Karhulaisen village sat atop the pass, a wealthy village where the people prospered from the trade across the Wall in summertime. It was the best place to trade the sleds and Väinämöinen did just that, bartering for another horse, a strong sturdy beast, and for fresh supplies. It was not a fair trade, for each sled, made by a master cartwright, was worth more than a horse apiece, but, while it irked the old wizard to lose on the deal, he could do little about it. No sled could manage the narrow pass, and, as the folk of the Far Northern Land said:

> *The traveler cannot choose his food and fire,*
> *but must beg for a place in pirtti or stable.*

No mortal could lead a horse along the narrow, winding pass in winter without peril, but Väinämöinen, Tulikki, and Ulla wove a strong spell of protection around themselves and their beasts, so they met no accident during the descent. When they reached the tumbled foot of the pass, they were in Etelamaa. The days grew longer, the pale sun warmed, and the Witch's season showed signs of ending early and giving way to a glorious spring. Väinämöinen had struck a good road straight to Kotanrannta, passing through Etelamaa's best farmlands and fields.

Now that they had reached the great duchy and found Egan gone, Väinämöinen decided not to wait for Aldon, the king's cousin, to return. They would set out again as soon as their horses rested and the stiffness in their own bodies eased. Siria—unused to travel of any sort, let alone a lightning dash on sleds and horses across the length of High Länsimaa—felt spent. The girl had proved a hearty traveler, though, and would follow Ulla anywhere. Ulla, for her part, was disappointed to miss Egan. She had also hoped to find Kirsikka waiting for her at Kotanrannta, but the red-haired princess was in the Stone City, hundreds of miles to the southeast. They would not take the southern road this time, but rather journey to Tavastia. So they bid Annikka and Sampsä farewell and set out again, not quite as tired if not fully rested. Väinämöinen rode Starchaser with Siria behind him. Striking a road which ran true to the southwest, they followed it through Etelamaa.

Spring, welcome in the Far Northern Land, sometimes had its cost. Snow and ice melted, flooding rivers, streams, and nearby lands. Dry swamps became wet again and roads disappeared. Unwary travelers, finding swollen rivers before them, might blunder into a marshy dead end where they could go no further. The floods were worst on the flat plains of western Akkala and in the deep south of Etelamaa and Tavastia where swift rivers raced to the sea. But they might come anywhere, in any year. So Väinämöinen found it, even as he had feared. When they reached the chain of little lakes that marked the border between Etelamaa and Tavastia in those parts, icy floodwater covered the road, and the rivers and streams were unfordable. They rode around the lakes for three days, picking their way carefully here and there, but could find no ready way through the muck; the few folk they met were not reassuring.

"'Tis a great flood this year, lord," they said. "North to south, the fields are wet and roads unsure. Best to wait till the waters go down to find a way into Tavastia, or else turn north and go up the line to the bridges. But even you, lord, may find it hard to find a way across."

So they said. But Väinämöinen was not content to wait several weeks in the chilly borderlands while the waters flowed on down to the Itämeri Sea. The old man was in a hurry to reach Tavastia and so come to the swift trade road, always open, on which the great wagons of bloodrock rolled from High and Deep Länsimaa to Seppälä.

"We are blind," he said, as they stood beside a cold, quick stream while the horses scrounged for whatever weeds and swamp grass they could find.

"We do not know the lay of this land and where dry places may be, so we poke about like a blind man in the dark, trying to find a pin in a neighbor's *pirtti* where he has never been before. Look at them!" he said, pointing to the little grey piping birds flitting about the rush weeds. "They know where they are, and where we are, too. We need the wings of birds to fly above this place and see all the lands about as with their eyes; then we might find a way out of here." He cocked his head and looked at Tulikki, but she furrowed her brow and shook her head.

"I don't work those changes," she said. "I am not Turi."

"Neither am I," said the old man. "I've never been much of a shape-shifter. I don't like how it feels, but one must do what one must do. I'm going to have a look around!"

The singer gave his staff to Ulla and winked. "Watch and learn, child," he said. "Remember what I taught you last winter in the Valley. You may or may not have Turi's gift, but remember the song just the same. A day may come when it could save your life and more besides."

Väinämöinen began a strange song then, high-pitched and wild, and, among the words in the Old Speech that Ulla recognized, she heard other words and sounds more like to the languages of birds and beasts, perhaps, than those of living men. His voice rose and fell, then all at once, with a sudden flash, the tall wizard was gone. In his place perched a rust-colored hawk with a hooked black beak.

"My goodness!" shrieked Siria in alarm. Tulikki laughed. The hawk opened its beak, screeched at them, and then took flight up into the sky.

The bird flew level straight across the river, then began to climb, describing lazy circles as it mounted ever higher until at last it vanished in the haze. Even Tulikki, with the eyes of an Erilainen, could no longer see its graceful form.

***

Before long, the old man came back. Ulla and Tulikki struggled to make a fire with wet pinewood that wouldn't catch, even with a spell. They never saw the hawk's return, but Väinämöinen suddenly walked up, wet, dripping, and shaking his head. Light bands of grey rain had moved through while he was away.

"That was fast," said Ulla, continuing to try to light the fire. "What did you see?"

"Enough," answered Väinämöinen in a surly voice. "I'm tired. Arms are sore. Too much flapping; had to fly low in this rain. But I found what I was looking for, and—by Ukko's beard, let me do it; I'm cold!"

He frowned, then threw his arms out toward the pinewood. "*Tuli!*" he cried in his great voice. The wood crackled, popped, and burst into yellow flame.

"There," he said. "That's better. A wizard of Laulavalaakso and Mielikki's daughter, and you can't start a fire! But maybe we'll be dry soon enough. There's an ice jam on this river not far south and another in the river yonder. That's what is causing the floods. The water can't flow, so it's spilling out into all the lands about. It will be a while before the ice breaks up, especially since the weather's turned foul. But no matter. I spied a good path not far from here, then a bare esker the horses can climb, rising above the flood. It leads west; we can ford the river in the narrows below the ice jam and come into the Tavastian fields on the other side."

They made camp there that night, since Väinämöinen was weary and needed rest. Even the strongest Erilaiset used such deep magic sparingly, if at all. The next day they mounted and followed Väinämöinen's lead. In a few hours, they had crossed the ice-choked river and come down onto a flat plain, muddy but not flooded, called Leijumaa by the Hare Folk. They were now in Tavastia, in the southern part of Häme. There were many roads throughout that fair region, most of which led eventually to Tapiola. To Ulla's regret, Väinämöinen did not wish to go to that fair city, but straight to Seppälä on the coast of the Itämeri Sea. The wizard soon found the trade road that would take them there.

They were not far from the Singing Valley, of course. Had they turned north, a hard ride of perhaps five days would have brought them home. Tavastia was as enchanted as the Karelian Forest in its own way. As soon as they crossed its borders, Ulla, returning as a *tietäjää*, could feel the pull of Laulavalaakso and Kyöpelinvuori to the northwest, and that of Tapiola, steeped in ancient legend, to the south. Väinämöinen could feel it too. On their first night in Tavastia, he disappeared for some time, taking only his staff and a pot of beer that a Tavastialainen had given them, along with some oats for the horses.

Ulla, sleeping beside Siria as she had done many times when they were little girls together in Grankulta, woke up and rubbed her eyes. The eastern sky was already a deep pink above the pines in the distance, chasing away the last few stars. She rose, the chill air shaking off her sleep, and slung her Karelian coat over her back. She saw Tulikki not far away, standing with one leg on a grey stone, her hair unbraided and loose about her shoulders.

Tulikki was a mystery. They had journeyed far together for months, but in most ways Ulla felt she hardly knew her. The strange woman was polite to her, quick to return a kind word and willing to teach her much magic, patiently explaining the songs and spells. It amused her that Ulla had used her own cloak to hide from Tyë, though she clearly took no pleasure from the story of the elf's final battle. Yet she seldom spoke unless spoken to and revealed little of herself or her thoughts. She laughed at jokes along with the others but made few jests herself. She little resembled her mother, Mielikki, a woodland queen of deep wisdom and majesty, descended from the Vanhalaiset themselves and yet at times as jolly and gay as the Metsänaitoa who served her. Tulikki seemed more like Väinämöinen, moody and sometimes silent and aloof, though not as quick to anger as the singer. She carried great power within her, hidden, perhaps, but present nonetheless, wild and free as the wide lands she had roamed for so long. And Tulikki was as steadfast in her loyalty to her friends as any Erilainen of the Enchanted Valley.

Ulla walked toward her now and the woman quickly turned, as if Ulla had called her.

"Is he still gone?" Ulla asked.

"Yes," said Tulikki. "But I think he will return soon. It is daybreak; rested or not, he will wish to start. If the horses can go, so will we." The two women gazed at the lightening sky for a while, but Ulla felt compelled to break the silence and draw Tulikki out.

"How long have you known him?" she asked.

For once, Tulikki seemed surprised. She turned to Ulla with a tight, strained smile.

"Väinämöinen? Why, my whole life, of course. Even as you."

"I have only known him since that day in the woods, when I met the bear— the day that everything changed."

"You were reborn that day, were you not?"

"Yes," said Ulla. "Nothing was ever the same again."

"Then you have known him your whole life, as I have." Tulikki turned away but, to Ulla's surprise, continued.

"It was different back then, of course," she said. "The Far Northern Land was ours, all of it, from the sea to Talvimaa. The heroes lived and walked where they would, taking little notice of mortals, who were few, weak, and short-lived. We helped them as we could and taught them what they might learn. Always Väinämöinen was foremost among those who love the Kaamoslaiset. Some grew very powerful. Mortals increased, and we did not. You know the rest.

"But Löhi . . . Löhi brought evil to this place. Not the mean, petty, or greedy evil that men do to one another, but evil that would become the very soul of this land, that would poison root and tree, foul lake and river, and stain men's heart with irredeemable sin. She puts herself before the Vanhalaiset and would have folk worship her even before Ukko if she dared.

"And she is Erilaisen! Even as Väinämöinen is, even as I am. She is ours and our responsibility; at least, it is our duty to do what we can with the last of our strength to help defeat her, if that is still possible. Väinämöinen understands that—more than anyone, I think."

Tulikki suddenly put her hand on Ulla's shoulder, the only time that she had ever touched her. "You were afraid that he would leave you. My mother told me your story. You are afraid of being left alone again and afraid Väinämöinen will leave you. Do not be afraid. You are his daughter in heart and soul, if you bear the Clan Mark or no. He will never leave you so long as he is in this world. And if he is slain or lost to us, it will not matter, for all hope will be lost and the ruin of all things at hand."

Ulla, her mouth open, stared at Tulikki, not knowing what to say in turn. At that moment the old man appeared again, coming out of the woods against the red light of the rising sign, a dark silhouette against the daybreak. He stopped when he saw them and waved, smiling broadly.

"I'm back," he said. "And what's more, I did what I went to do."

"You did something besides taking care of that?" said Tulikki, pointing to the empty pot the old man held. Väinämöinen laughed, his ruddy cheeks even redder than usual.

"I did by the beer as was right and proper. But I did more than just drink a serf's winter-brewed *sahti*. I have spoken to Turi. He is in Tapiola, for many things are moving, but we will see to that later. That road is not our road now. We go straight to Seppälä to see the mortal smiths, and Turi will meet us there. And he will tell those few who need to know the nature of our errand— very few, I should think, for, at all costs, Löhi must not discover our secret. Egan, Asikkas, the Seer, and a few others, perhaps, but no more.

"Come, wake Siria and wash the sleep from her eyes, for we are leaving at once!"

The trade road skirted Tapiola and avoided large villages and farms. Built for speed, it facilitated the transport of rock and ore from the north to Seppälä. Great trains of wagons came down from High and Deep Länsimaa. At times, smaller, well-guarded carts passed down the road, too, carrying even more precious ores: silver or gold rock from the rivers near the Marches and beyond. The people they met welcomed them and honored both Väinämöinen and Ulla exceedingly; they saw Ulla's staff and knew she must be a *tietäjää*, young though she still might be. Then word spread throughout the land of the Hare Folk that Ulla Karhulainen, who bore the Mark of the Clan, was now a wizard of Laulavalaakso.

With a good road before them, they put their strength into their tired beasts, for even Starchaser was flagging by now. Soon they reached the sunny fields of southern Tavastia and came to the shores of the Itämeri Sea. As they crested a gentle rise of the road, paved with stone and bordered by gutters, they could see the shimmering water and the town laid out before them, Seppälä, the City of the Smiths.

Seppälä, though smaller than Langvika or the Stone City of Etelamaa, was older, almost as old as Tapiola, which was the first city of the Seven Clans. Built upon a spit of land shaped like a teardrop, it was protected from high seas by barrier islands and a great white wall of smooth stone built along the coast. Its westward side sloped inward at one spot, creating a gentle, sheltered bay, small yet deep. There, boats might easily come and go from the town's docks. The wealth of the Far Northern Land came from its iron, and even in Tapiola's earliest days the Kaamoslaiset had traded ore with the men of distant shores. Smiths from all the Seven Clans eventually settled there.

But it was Ilmarinen who gave the town its fame. Great among the Erilaiset, mighty in magic and song, Ilmarinen had his home and fields near Seppälä. The sound of his silver hammer, made from the precious ore of a star that had fallen from the heavens, rang out from his smithy across all the lands nearby. The great smith came often among the mortals in Seppälä and taught them his craft, including how to use the power and skill of a *tietäjää* to make marvelous things. And Ilmarinen had forged the magical Sampo in Seppälä ere it was raised on Tapiola's hill. Then Löhi stole the Sampo and finally destroyed it even as the three heroes tried to rescue it. The Witch's War began, and many of the great smiths, mortal and Erilainen, were slain. In the Great Battle, before Löhi was at last defeated, almost all who remained perished. Ilmarinen's folk were destroyed or scattered, his *väki* no more, and all his works in ruin. He left those lands forever and either cast himself into the sea or vanished into regions unknown, for no mortal or Erilainen saw him in the Far Northern Land ever again.

But his art and craft did not wholly disappear. Among the Seven Clans were yet some few smiths who survived the war, and as the years wore on, slowly gathered again in Seppälä, though they now had neither wealth nor Ilmarinen's power. They remembered the songs, however, and the sound of hammers beating metal amidst the smoke and heat. And they taught these things to their sons, who taught new apprentices in turn, and gradually their fortunes increased. They found favor with the lords and kings of the Seven Lands.

One matchless skill the smiths devised led all to seek their work. The Smiths of Seppälä had learned to make bloodrock winterfast, so that it would not become brittle in the bitter cold. A hauberk or helm made winterfast might fetch its weight in silver or gold, and a blade made winterfast was the deadliest weapon of all. Lords, princes, and kings from all the lands sought such items for themselves and their chief men, paying heavy prices in precious metals and jewels for the work of Seppälä.

Then the smiths established their mighty Guild, with a great house built in Seppälä near the docks. Boys and young men of promise from all the Seven Lands went to Seppälä, and the Guild admitted those with skill as apprentices who might become master smiths. The Smiths' Guild, not bound to Tavastia or any other land, worked for all who paid them, making beautiful things of gold, silver, and bronze, besides the swords and armor for which they grew famous. And they became partners with the Shipwrights' Guild, and the Mariners' longships took their wares to many shores, enriching them both.

But, as the years went by, the smiths grew ever more secretive. Few passed the fair gate of the Guildhouse save the traders and merchants with whom they did business. In due time, each Master Smith, the head of the

Guild, would die and the rest would choose a new Master from among the greatest of their ranks. The Master Smiths seldom left Seppälä, though they would have been welcome in any town or court. They had no dealings with the Erilaiset, which was strange, for ere Ulla came and the Kaamoslaiset returned to the Old Ways, almost alone in the Far Northern Land, the smiths still remembered the ancient songs and rituals and honored the Vanhalaiset after a fashion.

Ulla looked down at Seppälä now from the hilltop. The bright sun glinted off of the gilded roof of the smiths' mansion. Several people came up over the rise, staring at them in surprise, and a horse-drawn cart rambled past them toward the town, its driver doffing his cap while the old wizard raised his staff in salute. But Väinämöinen kept his horse in check and showed no sign of continuing down the way.

"So... are we waiting for something?" asked Ulla at last.

"Patience is a virtue and will be rewarded," answered Väinämöinen, lapsing into that tone he had used when Ulla was a little girl. "But look, here comes someone you have not seen in a very long time."

Väinämöinen pointed, and Ulla and Tulikki brought their horses up beside his. In the distance, a rider came toward them, a hunched figure dressed in green with a tall, peaked hat. As he came close, they saw he bore a staff across his lap. He didn't look up until he was almost upon them, and when he did, Ulla could hardly contain her delight.

"Turi!" she cried. At her unintended, silent command, her horse leapt down to join him.

"Hey, there's my young lady!" Turi cried in turn. "But I'm forgetting my manners. You've made your hunt and you're a *tietäjää* now, already among the strongest. Welcome, my lady." To Ulla's surprise, he dismounted and bowed deeply to her, then again to Tulikki. "Your mother told me you'd returned. I could scarce believe it! It is very good to look on you again! But who is this little one here that you've strapped behind you, Väinämöinen? Always collecting more, aren't you!"

"My cousin, Siria," said Ulla. A sense of pride surged through her. "We found her in High Länsimaa among the miners. We were together on that day in Grankulta when the Itäläiset came."

"Were you, now? And you found each other again after all these years! So all the news is well and good."

"Not all," said Väinämöinen, swinging down from Starchaser and clapping his old friend's arm. "Not all. But enough, perhaps. Tulikki has the Shards. Our journey was uneventful and mostly unremarkable 'til we neared the town. Have you met the Master Smith yet?"

"No. I arrived here only two days ago, but I have seen Junko, the Lord of Seppälä, whom I have met before in Tapiola. He is a wise man and understands we want no pomp, but rather secrecy; he asked no questions. There is a house at our disposal, and I sent word through Junko that you were coming with Ulla on a matter of greatest importance and wished to meet the Master. Come noon tomorrow the great smith awaits us at the Guildhouse."

"Junko, eh? I remember him. And what about Biril, the young wizard we trained in the Valley? Made his hunt and took his staff four summers ago, didn't he? He was from Seppälä."

"He's away, but it is his house we have use of."

"Beer?" asked Väinämöinen.

"I found two barrels," said Turi. "One's still left."

"Then what are we waiting for?" said Väinämöinen. "We are cold, tired, and hungry, and we don't need to stand up here in plain view for miles around any longer. Let's go!"

They rode down to the town then, mingling with other people coming and going; chiefly Hare Folk, though in a few more weeks, traders from all the Seven Clans would fill the town's streets. A stone wall protected Seppälä, as old as the city, mottled with moss and stonecrop, repaired countless times over the years. The only gate in that wall—tall and made of strong iron and hardened steel—always stood open to the wagons and carts that came from the north, east, and west. The sea roared dimly in the background. Within the gate, they saw many men richly dressed in the livery of Tavastia, red-and-white tunics over shiny mail, with the yellow sun of Tavastia emblazoned in the center. The guards raised their spears and saluted as Väinämöinen and his friends rode past but did not question them. Other folk at the gate stared and wondered what errand brought Väinämöinen of Karelia and Turi the Changer to the City of the Smiths in springtime.

After traveling for more than two months, Ulla was tired, saddle-sore, weary, and so stiff that on some mornings she could barely mount her horse. She had not slept in a real bed since Kotanrannta. Though she was used to roughing it and prided herself on her toughness—she had met many who could never endure the conditions she took for granted—she looked forward to staying in Seppälä, resting, and, most of all, being near the sea. Since she first glimpsed it off the shores of Etelamaa, the sea had entranced Ulla with its ceaseless voice: now roaring, now whispering, endless and relentless, the voice of Ahti. She had been in little boats on little lakes all her life, but she had never been on the open sea. She longed to row to one of the green islands she had seen in the distance; they reminded her of the islands off Langvika.

They passed the evening quietly in Biril's simple wooden house, nestled among the many old stone houses in Seppälä. That night, Ulla gave thanks as she went to sleep beside her cousin on a low bed. But Väinämöinen woke her while the moon still sailed high in the darkling sky. They talked far into the night with Turi and Tulikki, the Shards of the Sampo set out before them on a little wooden table. That, more than anything else, showed that she was no longer a child, but a *tietäjää*. In the past, Väinämöinen would have let her sleep through such counsel, but since the hunt, he treated her differently. Turi, staggered by the Shards, picked them up again and again, feeling the smooth metal slip between his fingers. Tulikki told in detail just how and where she'd found each piece. When she fell silent, Turi and Väinämöinen, enjoying Biril's brew, reminisced about their many adventures together, as they often did when drinking. Then Ulla slipped off to the rush bed where Siria slept and, *tietäjää* or no, quickly fell into a deep sleep.

She awoke late, with Väinämöinen standing over her, shaking her.

"Up!" he said. "The sun's climbing and bright today, too. A good day to meet a smith!"

The singer wore the fine clothes he had carried all the way from Karelia, a sky-blue tunic trimmed with yellow. His gold chain and talisman hung from his neck, and his beard had been neatly brushed, forked, and plaited. As she rubbed the sleep from her eyes, Ulla saw Turi across the room, dressed in rich green, though Tulikki, as always, wore her traveling clothes. Ulla and Siria hurriedly washed while Väinämöinen chastised them, only half-joking, that they had only their travel-stained Karelian garb.

"The Master Smith might as well be a king in these parts," he said, "and you two look like refugees from the Marches. At least braid your hair, Ulla; you look like a wild-haired village witch, and there are enough rumors about you already."

After a quick meal, they checked on their horses, then walked to the town's western side, where the Guildhouse sat on the stone quay. There, men labored to launch a long trading galley now that the ice was gone. They rolled it on logs until it slipped into the water with a splash. A weathered stone gate stood out in the bay, looking as if it had stood there forever, a silent guardian lapped by water since the very world was made. Not far from it, close to the Guildhouse, a squat stone column rose out of the water, holding a wide vessel. Fire burned in that vessel as a beacon to mariners on the seas. Tended day and night, even in deep winter, it never went out.

As they came to the cobbled square before the Guildhouse of the Smiths of Seppälä, Ulla saw its true size. Not one house at all, it was a complex of buildings and sheds behind a high white wall. The smoke from many forges rose black into the sky. The round, gilded roof of the great central house shone in the sun. The front gate, of pure gleaming silver, had been cunningly wrought in an intricate design. The posts and tines were like tree trunks encircled by winding runners and leaves, and each one was unique. Even Väinämöinen sighed when he saw it and shook his head.

"I had forgotten its beauty," he said, blinking as the sun caught upon a silver leaf, twinkling like a star in broad daylight.

"If such skill remains within this house," said Turi, "then perhaps this task can indeed be done."

The guards at the gate saluted them, two clad in the royal livery of Tavastia, the others in similar livery but with a symbol of two crossed hammers, silver on black, on their baldrics. The Guild guards protected the Guildhouse and the wagons carrying its wares. The Guild guards wore the finest high helms, bright mail, and long, sharp winterfast swords. Near the guards stood a short man, blind in one eye and almost bald, clad in simple clothes with black gloves on his hands. He came forward to greet them, speaking in the accent of Akkala.

"Greetings, my lords and ladies," said the one-eyed man. "I am Hanmoku of the Smiths' Guild. You are early but more than welcome. It has been a long time since any Erilainen visited this house; indeed, none here alive can remember such a time, though mortal memories cannot reach back as yours can. Master Ahjo still works at the Great Forge this morning, and the hall intended for you is not yet prepared. But no matter; the Master often meets guests in the forge. Perhaps there you can better explain your desire."

Väinämöinen bowed. "Your courtesy is much appreciated; we are grateful for your welcome," he said. "But we need no special preparations. Lead on, then, Smith Hanmoku! Let us come to your master and see the Great Forge of the Smiths of Seppälä!"

They passed through the silver gate and into a covered courtyard, then through several other rooms. Ulla saw that the Guildhouse was like a small town. Dozens of people lived and worked within its walls: guards and servants, carters and drivers, lads and young men with broad backs and strong arms, apprentices who worked among the smelting pits—and, of course, the smiths themselves.

Some stayed in Seppälä only a short while after being admitted to the Guild, then went elsewhere to make their fortune. Many smiths worked in the Far Northern Land, but a Guild Smith from Seppälä could command his price. Some remained for many years, perfecting their craft and skills. Some never left, but lived their whole lives in Seppälä, filling orders from across the sea and land, growing wealthy, engrossed in their labors. Bronzesmiths among them mixed tin and copper, pouring metal into molds. Silversmiths and goldsmiths made many things delicate and beautiful, but the blacksmiths, the core of the Guild, worked hot iron into chains, anchors, nails, hooks, hoops, and now that the war with Löhi raged, spears, arrows, helmets, shields, and swords.

At last they came into a round hall, the largest in all that mansion. Ulla knew it must be the Great Forge Hanmoku had mentioned. This innermost smithy resembled no other forge in the house. A mighty bellows worked by several boys fired the deep smelting pit, filled with glowing charcoal, and a tall chimney of brick carried the smoke and steam into the sky. Long, narrow windows high on the wall admitted shafts of yellow light but left the hall dark, for smiths gauged the iron's heat by its color. The men and boys who worked there stopped and stared as the visitors entered the hot room. Wisps of smoke curled about their legs and the smell of burning coal and hot iron filled the air.

A man stood at the forge beating and folding a long piece of hot iron on the anvil. When he saw them, he used his tongs to drop the iron into a barrel of water, sending a rush of steam into the air with a whoosh. Dour and heavy-browed, he stepped down from the forge platform and stood before them as a boy hurried up to take his leather gloves. Sweat glistened on the smith's red face and dripped from his short beard.

"Welcome to the Guildhouse of the Smiths of Seppälä," said the Master. "I received Junko's message and have expected you."

Väinämöinen and Turi both struck their staffs upon the stone floor and bowed.

Turi swept off his peaked hat. "Thank you, Master," he said. "I am Turi of Karelia, and this is Väinämöinen Erilainen, greatest of singers. May I present

Mielikki's daughter, Tulikki, and Ulla Karhulainen, the mortal who bears the Mark of the Clan? The child is her kinswoman Siria, our companion on the road. We have come from afar to see you."

The Master nodded, considering them each in turn. When he spoke, his voice was measured and cold, as cold as the water in his cauldron.

"Well met," he said. "But the great usually send an agent when they wish work from us. Few seek to visit our smithies, and we admit fewer still. What errand, then, brings you from afar?"

Väinämöinen looked sideways at Turi. Ulla caught the flash of his eyes even amidst the forge's gloom and glare, but the wizard simply nodded and smiled.

"An errand so important that no other messengers would suffice, and a task so great that all your other works will pale beside it."

The grim smith seemed taken aback by Turi's words.

"Speak plainly," said the dour Master. "What great task brings the Erilaiset south from their forest? Do you need weapons, swords? The smiths among the Haltiatar can make enchanted blades, can they not? I can forge a grim blade of silver-steel that will cut through any other, if you desire—and if the price is right."

"Well and good," answered Väinämöinen. "But that is not my desire. I already have a blade at my belt." With a flourish, he drew *Jääpuikko* from its sheath and brandished it. The sword flickered in the forge's red light. "This is the icicle of the Erilaiset, forged by Ilmarinen in days of old, and his power still dwells within it. Can even the Master Smith do better?"

"But we do not seek swords," said Turi, coming forward. "Should your men leave us ere we speak of this thing? Our errand is not only urgent, but secret."

"We are a brotherhood within these walls and I trust all my folk with my life."

"Very well. Tulikki, show the Master your burden. Then he will understand our errand."

Tulikki raised the casket and opened its lid. The Seven Shards lay on a bed of velvet, and even as Tulikki lifted them up, the clouds drew away and a shaft of sunlight shone through an upper window to fall directly upon her. The Shards came alive, glittering silver and gold, blazing like precious jewels, illuminating the hall as if with a hallowed, holy light. The Master stepped back, mouth agape, as Tulikki raised the casket high above her head.

"Behold the Sampo!" she cried in a voice as clear and powerful as her mother's. "At Tapio's bidding, I have found them: Seven Shards for Seven Clans, the only pieces of the precious Sampo that will ever be found. I gathered them from all corners of the Far Northern Land and have brought them here with his command: let the Sampo be reforged! Let it be raised again on Tapiola's green hill!"

"No!" cried a deep voice from within the forge's shadows. "No, that cannot be! The Sampo is gone and can never be forged again."

Out of the deep gloom in that darkling hall stepped a tall man, taller even than Väinämöinen. His head was bald, his beard cut short, and he wore a leather apron over his bare chest. Muscle knotted his mighty arms; his right hand held a great silver hammer. He gazed on them with the piercing eyes of the Erilaiset, for indeed it was Ilmarinen himself.

Tulikki lowered the casket, and the Shard's light dimmed. For a moment, the only sound was the crackling of burning coal.

"You!" roared Väinämöinen. "You! You are the Master Smith!"

"So I am," said the deep-voiced smith. "Ahjo here is my chief assistant and collaborator. He serves as the face of the Guild to the outside world, whenever it needs a face. But I am the master in these halls and always have been."

"All these years!" said Turi. "And you have been here, hiding in plain sight in Seppälä, all that time!"

"I have an island," grumbled the smith, frowning. "I go there now and again for peace—a year, two. But my work is here, and it is here that I return."

"Leave us," he said suddenly to the others, with a wave of his hammer. "Go; it is alright." At his word, the men and boys left the forge, all except Ahjo and Hanmoku who stood together beside the mighty bellows.

"You betrayed us!" said Väinämöinen, and Ulla could hear the wrath in his voice. "When we needed you most, you betrayed us! Gone without a word, with no farewell, nothing at all—all the Erilaiset, from the Enchanted Valley to the Sea, grieved your loss. We searched for you for years. How dare you!"

"Who are you to accuse me, Väinämöinen?" cried Ilmarinen, becoming angry in turn. "Have you not disappeared for years on end into those woods of yours?"

"You abandoned your folk when their need was greatest!"

"My folk!" exclaimed Ilmarinen. "My *väki* were slain, mortals and Erilaiset alike. Lemminkäinen was dead, my fields barren and abandoned. The Seven Lands were in ruin and the Sampo lost beyond recall—what under Ukko's dome remained for me? I wanted only to be left alone after the War, left to myself and my craft."

"And now?" said Väinämöinen. "When Löhi has returned and made war on the mortal clans for nigh on seven, eight years? And you stand here in shadow watching and say nothing to us, your very brothers? Pray tell, what now is your excuse?"

"I need no excuse! What is Löhi to me? The Seven Clans turned their back on the Erilaiset and the Vanhalaiset long ago, all except for the smiths of this house. If Löhi falls, or if the White Winter comes again, what is that to me? I will weather the storm again, if it be my fate. Besides, we are not idle here. Have not the smiths forged weapons aplenty for the Seven Clans? Spears, swords, mail: our forges never cool, and we go through rock as if it were rye or barley."

"Yes, you stay busy behind your gilded walls," said Väinämöinen bitterly. "And high are your prices. Iron is your servant, perhaps, but gold was ever your master!"

Ulla watched then in amazement as Väinämöinen and Ilmarinen continued to reproach one another. They circled round each other and, as Väinämöinen still held *Jääpuikko* and Ilmarinen his silver hammer, she wondered if they might even come to blows. Meanwhile, Turi threw his own rebukes at the smith, banging his staff down hard on the sooty stones. Tulikki stood as one enchanted, still holding the open casket, her bright eyes all aglitter.

Ulla felt something tugging at her arm—Siria had taken her hand. The girl trembled, and Ulla saw the look of fear, real fear, in her clear blue eyes. Moved as if by some other will, Ulla squeezed her cousin's hand and nodded reassuringly, then leapt forward. Seizing the casket from an astonished Tulikki, she strode toward Ilmarinen and planted herself firmly before him.

"Stop!" she cried. "What is wrong with you? Are you indeed the great Ilmarinen who stole the Sampo right from under Löhi's crooked nose, or are you someone else: an imposter, craven, fearful of the Witch, a hammerer of nails and hoops in the dark where none can find you? The Shards of the Sampo lie before you; does that not even matter to you?"

The tall, bald smith towered over Ulla, anger flashing across his face and furrowed brow. Then his features loosened, and he seemed to smile at her through the murk. He ran his big red hand over his head.

"So you're the child the prophecy foretold?" he said in his deep baritone. "I've heard of you. Stole Työ's glass, did you? And now a *tietäjää*, too, with a staff and all? Good, good. Go to Sariola with Väinämöinen! Strike down Löhi in her own home! That's what it will come to in the end, I'll wager."

"That's no answer," said Ulla. "Are you afraid to look upon them? The Shards of the Sampo lie before you; does that not even matter to you?"

Ilmarinen frowned now and muttered, "Whatever relics these may be, they are not from the Sampo. I looked everywhere for it; I made many spells, the best finding spell I could. Nothing. There was never anything but lonely marsh, silent woods, empty waters. Nothing. The Sampo is gone beyond all recall. That age of the world is passed and will never return."

"I did not find them alone," said Tulikki. "Tapio himself led me to these Shards, and by Tapio's design we have found you. Perhaps they lay hidden all this time for a purpose. Surely Löhi searched for them, too, and all her folk."

"We come at Tapio's bidding," said Turi. "You may forge spears and blades of steel to keep the Witch at bay, but only the Sampo can guarantee the Far

Northern Land freedom from her tyranny. Remake it and raise it again. Then she will surely fade—this time, forever."

"Take them," commanded Ulla. "Surely a smith knows his own craft, even after hundreds of years?"

A silence fell. To Ulla it stretched on and on; no one dared move or speak.

Then Ilmarinen shrugged his great shoulders and tossed his hammer to the ground; sparks flew, and it rang like a bell as it hit the stone. The smith stooped, taking one Shard and then another into his hands, turning them over round and round. He narrowed his dark eyes and peered at the cold metal through the gloom. He saw no sign, no light, no life; even the forge's red glow seemed to dim, leaving them enmeshed in darkness.

Ilmarinen snorted and shook his head, about to toss the Shards away as he had tossed his hammer. But even as he raised his arm, a faint shimmer caught his eye, like the flicker of fireflies on a warm summer's eve. Faint at first, it grew stronger. Then all at once the Shards shone again—gold, silver, white, glittering like stars or like diamonds, until they lit the whole forge with their brilliance. The smith's face was ablaze with their glory. Ahjo and Hanmoku looked away, but Ilmarinen's stern mien melted, and tears welled in his fluted eyes.

"By Akka and Ilmatar the Fair," he stammered. "It is true—true! I can feel the power. I . . . I can perceive the spell, the song I sang so long ago. So long ago! They are pieces of the Sampo! My Sampo!"

Ilmarinen dropped to his knees, clutching the Shards in his hands, and gazed at them wide-eyed like a child. Väinämöinen put a hand on his shoulder and his voice was kind and sad, all anger and remonstrance forgotten.

"This is all that is left, brother," he said. "But it is a gift from the gods. Only you can forge the New Sampo. Only you can remake the shining totem for the Far Northern Land."

Ilmarinen looked up at him. "I cannot," he said through his tears. "That song can be sung only once. It is lost."

"You can find it," answered Väinämöinen.

"I cannot," said Ilmarinen. "The ores that made it came from all the Seven Lands. They can never be gathered again."

"They are already here before you," answered Väinämöinen.

"I cannot. I folded the metal and smote the anvil for a year. There is no time."

"There is time," answered Väinämöinen. "The swords of the Seven Clans will buy that time, and a year is little in Ukko's reckoning."

Ilmarinen stood up and, taking the casket from Ulla, strode to a low step by the bellows. There he sat down with the Shards in his lap. The brilliance had subsided to a gentle glow. The smith wiped his sweaty face and head with a grimy rag.

"The High King hallowed the Sampo as it was raised in Tapiola. But we have no Lemminkäinen among us now."

"Perhaps one among us will be that king," said Väinämöinen. "No Lemminkäinen, maybe, but with a different strength, no less potent."

Ilmarinen fell silent then and sat gazing at the Sampo's Shards, so lost in thought that he seemed to take no more notice of anyone.

Turi gathered his friends and said in a low voice: "Let us leave now; we can take counsel with him tomorrow, perhaps. For now, let us leave him alone. The Shards are with their true master. No other guardian could be safer."

They left the smoky forge with Hanmoku, now as silent as his master, hurrying beside them. When Ulla looked back she saw Ilmarinen still sitting there, head down, the casket on his aproned lap.

After a short while, Ahjo picked up the silver hammer, put it in its place beside the anvil, then departed without a word. But Seppo Ilmarinen, greatest smith of the Far Northern Land, mortal or Erilaisen, sat alone with the Seven Shards of the Sampo in his hands. The burning coals went red and slowly faded while he strove to remember the great song he had woven long ago, when the world was younger, the sun brighter, and hope still alive.

Chapter Twelve

The King's Dreams

They started as soon as he returned to Etelamaa. He might be free of them for a night, or two, or three, but inevitably the dreams recurred and he could do nothing to stop them.

They weren't nightmares, exactly. To be sure, Löhi was always there, her aspect changing from a crone as ghastly and misshapen as Lověatar to a cold and distant queen, beautiful but deadly. Other forms she took as well. But Löhi did not terrify him now as she had in his boyhood. And in the dreams, he always triumphed. Sometimes he watched a great battle from afar, greater than any he had ever fought in. Men battled Hiisia and trolls; wizards fought one another with flashes of lightning, and then he saw Lemminkäinen. The mighty hero, half-mortal and half-Erilaisen, High King of the Seven Clans, struck the Witch down and stooped over her ruined body. But sometimes it was not Lemminkäinen fighting Löhi—it was Egan himself, face to face with the Mistress of Pohjola while the battle raged all around them. He wielded Lemminkäinen's blade, the Sword of Legend, and he, Egan Dragonslayer, struck her down.

It was not a nightmare, exactly. The Witch was always vanquished. But the terribly lifelike dreams left him with a feeling not of triumph and victory but disquiet. They exhausted him, as if he really battled Löhi, night after night without rest. He wished he could share his burden with Väinämöinen, for, though Egan was no *tietäjää*, he understood the importance of dreams, and the wizard was skilled in such matters. But Väinämöinen had gone north with Ulla or else gone back to Karelia and the Enchanted Valley. Turi the Changer was in distant Tavastia; and though Egan spoke of his dreams to Kolkka, the young mortal wizard from the Singing Valley who was now in the Royal Court, it brought little understanding or relief.

At least Egan was busy. He had been absent from Etelamaa from spring through fall, another growing and harvest season, and many men had gone with him. This winter, he had an entire year's worth of matters to attend, not only decisions of war and battle and the constant preparations needed to keep an army permanently in High Länsimaa, but decisions on trade and business, on dealings with the Shipwrights' Guild and the Smiths' Guild, on the guilt or innocence of prisoners brought before him, on their punishments, and on many other matters pertaining to the everyday lives of his people.

Sinio and Toiva came to him daily with such issues and, moreover, urged him to remain in Etelamaa after winter's end. For the first time since the war with Löhi began, the Swan Folk grumbled about the war and its costs and the fact that their young king spent more time among strangers in other lands than with his own people.

All the news about the war seemed good. For two seasons now, the Kaamoslaiset had been victorious and the attacks of the Easterners grown weaker and more scattered. Lovĕatar had not returned to Etelamaa. The invasion of Deep Länsimaa had been defeated, and the king had slain the terrible dragon. It seemed to many that the Witch of Pohjola was already fading—indeed, since Löhi herself had never appeared among them, it might be that her power lessened the farther she was from dismal Sariola.

No one spoke against the king, of course, not even among the lords of the coasts. No whispers touched Egan Dragonslayer, already a legend at his young age—the greatest of all the kings of Etelamaa, some said; maybe the greatest mortal hero since the days of Lemminkäinen. The Swan Folk did not wholly begrudge the aid they gave to others—many Karhulaiset had come among them, bringing tales of fire and terrible goblins besieging men north of the Wall of the Giants. The Swan Folk thought it better for southern swords to fight north of the Wall than on the very plains of Etelamaa.

But had that time not passed? Each year hundreds of men marched north, and each year some did not march back. Sometimes the blacksmith might be told his son died a hero, or children might learn how their father, the village fuller, had been buried in faraway lands after battling a deadly foe. Sometimes the farmer's wife heard nothing, her husband having disappeared, never to return to his fields again. Why did their sons and husbands still need to go to war? Why could the Bear Folk or Elk Folk not defend their own borders now? And if a man wished to go to war, could he not join the March Wardens rather than be forced into the levees? Maybe the other clans must still take to the sword or axe, but could not the menfolk of the Etelalaiset come home at last?

So the people wondered. And so Egan's counselors urged him to stay more than one brief season in his own kingdom. And Vendla, the queen, added her voice to theirs. She had missed her sons and worried for their safety; now she wished them both to remain in Etelamaa. She asked, as her people did, why they could not stay and why Etelamaa must send its sons to battles far away from their southern home.

Vendla had been surprised to learn that Eglano had married and both hurt and saddened not to have seen the wedding or been consulted. She had met Kirsikka, of course, when the girls came to Etelamaa with Väinämöinen. She knew her as Ulla's companion from High Länsimaa. But no more than Sinio did she approve of her second-born son taking a wife both a commoner and foreign. She had planned several matches for Eglano with noble ladies of the Swan Folk, even as she wished for Egan. The queen acknowledged Kirsikka's beauty. Although she was covered in freckles from head to toe, her face and figure were wondrously beautiful, and her rich red hair fell so full and fair about her shoulders that no woman in Etelamaa could match it. And then there was her voice. So Vendla dissembled and opened her heart as she could. A kind woman, she remembered the cold reception her own mother-in-law had given her when she wed Nigan, despite her high lineage.

Kirsikka knew none of this. She had returned with Egan and Eglano to the Stone City in the fall, and though the north wind blew cold, the Swan Folk welcomed her warmly. The people did not know her humble origin as a shoeless girl from the Marches, orphaned and abandoned, her people dead or scattered. They knew only the story proclaimed by Sinio. They knew her as Väinämöinen's daughter, a princess of Tavastia, married to their king's brother to strengthen the kingdom's alliances and security. And she looked the part, dressed in fine clothes with chains of silver and the garnet Egan had given her about her neck. She enchanted all who beheld her, and indeed many believed she was Erilaisen. They called her Princess Cherry Red, and folk cried out when they saw her ride with Eglano through the Stone City's snowy streets.

Kirsikka was happy, happier than she had ever been—even in Bemböle before the raid, when she still had her family and didn't realize their poverty. She loved Eglano and lived each day as if in a dream. If she missed Ulla at times, especially when Eglano went away, she found that her sister-in-law Marjatta made good company. Marjatta, almost her own age, had often played with Ulla and Kirsikka when they were younger. Though two girls could hardly be born into more different circumstances, they shared one thing that brought them together. They both had lost their fathers when they were small, indeed in the same year, one in summer, one in winter. Those memories never faded.

One day, as the wind blew chill outside the Keep, Kirsikka and Marjatta dismissed their maids and went to the Hall of the Swan, where Marjatta taught her friend to dance in the courtly fashion of the noble Etelalaiset. Egan tramped through the corridors with old Orvo. The old man, a little deafer and a little blinder, still insisted on tending the hearthfires throughout the castle, though many other servants could have done it. Egan liked to banter with Orvo; the cantankerous old man still treated Egan as a young boy and not a king.

"Come on, old stone," said Egan. "There will be fine folk in the hall this evening, and it is cold there. They will freeze if the fires aren't lit. You should have done so already."

"A thing done slow is a thing done right," answered Orvo. "I have lit them all in turn, as I've always done. The hall is large, but it warms quickly."

"Well enough, if you'd started early," Egan replied, "and not fallen asleep halfway through the job. Let's get on with it; you're lucky I'm here to help you."

They entered the hall then and saw the two girls before them, dancing while several shaggy dogs chased round in circles. Egan smiled and watched his sister's pale yellow hair mingle with Kirsikka's red mane as they spun about. The hall was warm.

"See, Orvo?" said Egan. "They've beaten you to it. The fire's already been lit while you snored."

"Perhaps," said Orvo. "Or perhaps I did it earlier myself and only remembered it just now. No matter. I have business in the sculleries, my lord. An honest man's work is never done, as you may one day find out."

The old man shuffled off, bowing slightly to the young women. "Your highnesses," he said, then, chasing the dogs with his walking stick, he headed to the kitchens.

"I was teaching Kirsikka the winter dances, my lord," said Marjatta; well-schooled in etiquette, she spoke to Egan the king with polite formality, though he was her brother. Indeed, with Egan's long absences, she sometimes felt him a stranger to her. To Egan, older than his sister and with a longer memory, the princess would always be the little girl he had cared for and played with as a child.

"There will be dances soon at Sunwelcome," continued the princess, "and Eglano has not thought to show her the steps. Kirsikka shows me Karhulaisen dances in return; they are quick and strange to me."

"Eglano does not have the time," said Kirsikka, using her easy, informal way with Egan. "Not with all the errands you've given him. I thought that when we came to Etelamaa, things would slow down a bit. It was quiet in the Singing Valley during winter, but it is always busy here."

Egan laughed. "How many folk live in the Singing Valley? A few score, perhaps? But this is the City of Etelamaa! Many thousands live here, and more nearby. It is always busy. When you live with Eglano in Kotanrannta, you'll have a quieter life. But don't be sad; my sister is a better teacher than my brother. Eglano's a good fighter, but he's never been much of a dancer!"

"And you?" asked Marjatta. "Our mother, along with Sinio, has been giving much thought to the ladies who will come to the City this year. All eyes will be on you—and the one you most favor. Let's hope you, too, dance as well as you fight. And perhaps the one you'll marry will be your last dance of the night."

Egan rolled his eyes, but Kirsikka chuckled. "He doesn't dance much," she said. "He didn't dance at my wedding, either—at least not that I saw. Eglano told me that he asked Ulla to dance, but Turi swore it didn't happen. Too bad. It would have made her very happy. She loves you, of course."

"Kirsikka!" exclaimed Marjatta. The red-haired girl blushed when she realized what she had said, then quickly added, "Well, it's true; why shouldn't I say it? She's loved you since we were still little children. She may not admit it, even to herself, but it's still true. I should know; I know Ulla better than anyone, even old Väinämöinen."

An awkward, silent moment followed. Kirsikka began to regret what she had said.

"I'm sorry," Kirsikka exclaimed. "I really don't know what I am talking about. I know you must marry a high lady of Etelamaa—my lord. And Ulla has gone off with Väinämöinen and is probably a *tietäjää* by now, with a staff and all. I'm afraid such things are beyond me, and I don't know when to hold my tongue." She did him a courtesy and looked down, but Egan took her by the shoulder.

"Don't apologize to me, sister," he said. She looked up and met his blue eyes. "I wish everyone would speak so plainly. Sometimes—well, sometimes I grow weary of guessing what other people really think behind the masks they wear.

You are right about Ulla. I don't know what her destiny is. I'm not Mielikki. But I know the power she has, and the strength—strength and power I could never have, nor really ever imagine. Whatever her fate, it's not to grow old on a throne, I think, even one so fair as the throne of the queen of Etelamaa." One of the shaggy dogs jumped at him, whimpering, and he bent down to pet it. "But you!" he said with a smile to Marjatta. "If our mother has sent you as a spy to sound me out about the ladies of Etelamaa, she'll be disappointed."

"She did no such thing," answered Marjatta. "Your counsel is your own to keep. But still, they'll be watching, all of them. That is most certainly true."

"Hmm," said Egan. "You dissemble well, as befits a true princess. But they will be disappointed. I will take no lady, no wife, no woman of the Etelalaiset or any other clan, while Löhi still makes war upon us."

"Oh, that," said Kirsikka. "But they say it is almost over. After all, you killed the dragon and the battles have all been won. Löhi will soon be gone."

"Not so easily, sister," said Egan. "I'm afraid not. And if she lingers, much evil can still be worked among mortals and Erilaiset."

***

Sunwelcome came and went. The lords and ladies of the Swan Folk came to the Stone City to pay respect to the king: Sunda, Kallas's brother from Harmaaniemi, and Meripäiva and the other lords of the coast; Kontio from the Green Vales, Laso of Poronlinna, and Annika with her son, Sampsä, soon to come of age, and others besides. If Vendla the Queen hoped Egan would choose a wife, she was indeed disappointed.

Egan was not idle, however. Despite the widespread feeling among the Swan Folk that the worst was over and the season of the Witch behind them, the king felt otherwise. *She may be weakened,* thought Egan, *and perhaps her plans have gone awry. But if so, she needs nothing more than a respite.* He could imagine nothing better for her fortune than for the Kaamoslaiset to stand down, lulled into a false sense of security. Then she might gather the last of her strength, strike, and win all in one desperate gamble.

A thought began to form in Egan's mind. The Seven Clans, at last united, had taken up the old songs and stood as one against the Witch. They had healed the rift with the Erilaiset, and each year more *tietäjää* spread throughout the Seven Lands. The clans had more men-at-arms, spears, axes, and swords than ever. The hammers of mortal smiths across the Far Northern Land rang on anvils, beating bloodrock into weapons of war. Never had the Seven Clans been so strong, not since the days of Lemminkäinen, when their great army defeated the might of Pohjola. Yet what did it avail them? Löhi remembered her defeat and had learned her lesson—she spread out what strength she had, striking here and there, destroying what she could, not yet daring any great invasion.

And so each year, even with the clans victorious, more men died, more villages burned, more towns were laid waste, more of High and Deep Länsimaa was despoiled, and more ships were lost on the Itämeri Sea. If the Seven Clans could again raise an army like Lemminkäinen's, they might smash Löhi with one strike and end the ceaseless battles.

But how could they draw Löhi out? How could they make her gather all her allies—the Itäläiset, the Hiisia, the strange men from distant lands—and force her hand so that the great blow could be dealt? Try as he might, Egan had no answer to that question. The Seven Clans could hardly march on Pohjola. And Löhi's allies left for the wastes each year after the battles, disappearing under the shield of her magic, so that even the Erilaiset could not find them.

Another thought grew within him, terrifying and joyous, a thought sprung from his spirit and born of his will. He hardly dared acknowledge it, dared not even muse on it, as if it were a blasphemy. Dreams had come to Egan—vivid, wrenching dreams. Did not the Vanhalaiset send dreams to mortals across the Far Northern Land telling them to go to Laulavalaakso? Did not the Erilaiset learn many things in the night, when their spirits might leave their bodies and journey through the other, unseen world—even to

Tuonela, the Land of the Dead? And yet...if Löhi's army could be finally defeated, what of Löhi herself? Could she not be defeated, destroyed, banished forever to oblivion?

Egan bore the very blade Lemminkäinen had used to strike her down: *Tarunmiekka*, the Sword of Legend. With that blade, Egan had rallied the Swan Folk and slain Työ at Linnavuori. In High Länsimaa, Deep Länsimaa, and Karelia, he had always prevailed. And at Valkeakosk, he had overcome his terror and, alone and unaided, slain the evil dragon, then chased the Moonface from the field.

Why did he dream now of Lemminkäinen? Why? Then the answer came, the answer that set his heart ablaze. Could it be his destiny to take Lemminkäinen's place, to strike down the Witch, to be crowned High King of the Far Northern Land?

At first, Egan scarcely allow himself to think it. He had once doubted himself as king, been unsure, and yet persevered and always succeeded. He doubted himself again now, perhaps as never before; but if such was his destiny, ordained by Ukko himself, how could he deny it? *If such was his destiny.*

Such were the young king's thoughts as the dim winter days passed and the snow fell and no word came from Väinämöinen. Never had Egan felt so alone.

But he was not idle. He prepared for spring and the battles he knew would come. Juvari, his chief captain, seldom returned to Etelamaa now but remained in High Länsimaa with the companies of Etelalaiset quartered there, and in effect commanded the Bear Folk, too. But his cousin Aldon had proved a good organizer and tireless leader. He took a spear wound at Valkeakosk but had recovered well. At Egan's bidding he went throughout the kingdom, ensuring that each district's officer prepared for the coming year, selecting the best men to join the levees or to be carters and provisioners and all such things that men needed at war. Aldon had grown even grimmer since he had been wounded; he believed that the Kaamoslaiset should press their enemies in all ways possible and not relent.

Egan, too, had changed. His arm healed well enough, though it remained slightly crooked at the elbow and turned inward. He wielded his blade just the same, which was his only care. And where the dragon's blood had dripped upon him, a thin white scar ran from the corner of his left eye down his cheek and through his beard, which only reminded men of his mighty deed. So things stood after Sunwelcome and the new year, when Kolkka, the court *tietäjää*, came to the Keep with a strange woman. Middle-aged, short and stout with reddish-brown skin, she was an Etelalainen who went to the Singing Valley two years before to learn the songs. She had not the power to become a wizard, but Siitsa noticed her and took her into the tower's service; now the Seer had sent her back to Etelamaa as her agent. The king had never met her, but she had once called on Vendla on an errand from the Seer and had occasional dealings with Kolkka.

In the Great Hall, Egan had just met with a man from the Smiths of Seppälä. Orders for weapons took longer each year as all the Seven Clans now demanded Seppälä's work, and the smiths' prices had never been higher. Etelamaa had ordered two hundred finely crafted lances for the Swan Knights and paid heavily in gold crowns and amber. A year had passed, and still the lances had not been delivered. The king and Toiva Merikainen were discussing this problem and the smiths' unsatisfactory replies when the chamberlain announced Kolkka.

Though dark outside, the Hall was brilliantly lit, the vaulted white ceiling sparkling in the bright glow of lamps and candles, and the great swan behind the dais glittering. Egan sat on the Black Throne as Kolkka and the strange woman approached; they bowed deeply.

"Your Majesty," said Kolkka. "I thank you for seeing us on such short notice."

"The doors of the Keep are always open to you, Kolkka," said Egan.

"This is Ikä of the Tornilaiset. She came to me last night and said she needed to see you on an urgent errand from the Seer of Kyöpelinvuori."

The woman bowed again, shuffling nervously. Wrapped in heavy, coarse brown robes, she began to sweat in the Great Hall's warmth. Egan noticed the crystal amulet around her neck, round and clear, and the short stick of rowan in her left hand, which the Seer gave to all her folk. He disliked her at once, but she seemed so nervous and kept bowing so awkwardly that he took pity on her.

"You, too, are welcome, Ikä," he said at last. "Any servant of the Seer of Kyöpelinvuori has passage to this Hall. But be calm now, and tell me why the Seer has sent you here."

"Your Majesty is gracious," said Ikä. "It is an urgent errand indeed, but—"

"But what?" asked Egan when she paused.

"Excuse me, my king," said Ikä. "But the Seer, my mistress, bid me give the message to you and you alone. Kolkka is a *tietäjää* and friend of Kyöpelinvuori, but..."

"Do you hear that, Toiva?" said Egan. "She would have you leave us."

"As you wish, Your Majesty," said Toiva, smiling. "I have many tasks to attend to, I am sure."

"And if I want my counselor to remain, Ikä?"

"Forgive me, my king," said the strange woman. "I am only speaking as bidden and do not wish to anger my mistress. In truth, I do not understand these matters."

"And do you fear angering the Seer more than your own king, woman of the Etelalaiset? She is in her tower hundreds of miles away, and I am here before you."

Ikä cast her head down, sweat dripping from her brow. But after a moment she said, "I will do as you command, my king." Egan took pity on her again and nodded to Toiva, who left them. Then he dismissed the chamberlain and guard with a wave of his hand. Only Kolkka remained.

"We are alone now, Ikä! Speak!" said the king.

Straightening somewhat, the portly woman made an odd gesture with her hand and began. "Two nights ago it was very dark, my lord; it rained snow. But behind the clouds, the moon was full. I received the message then."

"How did it come to you?" interrupted Egan.

"I have *sight*, my lord. I cannot see so far as Kyöpelinvuori or Karelia on my own. But the Seer reached out to me."

"What did she tell you?"

"She bid me tell you—only you—that you must leave Etelamaa as soon as may be and not wait for spring. She said that elves have returned from beyond the North Marches of High Länsimaa and found what long they sought: the camp of our enemies, from whence they strike our lands. She, too, has seen this place with her looking glass. She bid me be secret, but to urge you, lord, to go at once to Tavastia and not tarry here nor go first to Keskimaa."

Egan sat with his head bowed, but his heart raced. He looked up at last, his face flushed red, unable to hide his excitement.

"What else did she say?"

"That was all, lord."

"Where is this place? Near the Marches or nearer to Pohjola?"

"I do not know, lord."

"Who dwells there? Only the Itäläiset? Or Löhi herself?"

"There was no more, my lord. Only what I have just now told you. Nothing else."

Egan sat thinking for a moment, then stood up.

"Can you ask her these things, Ikä?"

"I think not, my lord. My *sight* is not so strong, and I cannot make an *etiänen*. I learned the songs of Akka—of fertility, King Egan. Such is my strength."

Egan nodded, then rose, clasping Kolkka's arm.

"No matter," he sighed. "But you have done well to deliver your message, Ikä. Forgive my impatience. Try to reach out to the Seer, whether you fail or not; bring me word at once if you learn any more. But you are wise to be circumspect. Say nothing to any others about this—that is my command as well."

"As you wish, my king," said the woman, again bowing deeply. "I will do as you say."

"And what do you make of all this, my king?" asked Kolkka as the strange woman shuffled nervously from the Hall.

Egan ran his hand through his shaggy hair. "That it is good my brother is returning to the Stone City tomorrow."

***

When Eglano returned, Egan took him into his confidence, telling him both about his dreams and the Seer's message. More frequently than before, Egan left his small, cold chamber and stayed in the larger rooms that housed the royal family of Etelamaa, including the room where his father had died. But if he hoped his father's spirit or memory would bring him peace or counsel, it did neither. Now he sat there with his only brother, drinking a sour brew made with unfamiliar fruit, brought by the Mariners' ships from some far-away southern land.

Eglano, too, had changed. Sometimes, from a distance, Egan scarcely recognized him. Heavier and more muscular, with his dark beard grown longer, he looked much older than his still-tender years. He carried himself with more dignity as well. Indeed, he resembled their father Nigan, while Egan was their mother's child in build and temperament. But with his brother, Eglano could still act as excited as a child.

"How can you doubt the signs?" he cried. "You don't even need to be a wizard to understand them! You are destined to be the High King of the Far Northern Land; you were born to that task."

"I am not sure everyone would agree with you," said Egan.

"Who doubts you? Who would stand against you, after what you've done?"

"I cannot see Airikki or any of the Eagle Folk accepting a High King from outside their clan. And, though my relations with Asikkas are good, I don't know if Tavastia would follow an outsider, either."

"You make no sense," answered Eglano. "If it is meant to be, it is meant to be. The only thing that may hinder such fate is if the fated do not embrace it. Väinämöinen will champion you, of that you may be certain—Väinämöinen and all the Erilaiset. And that is all the support you need."

So they went back and forth, considering the meaning of Egan's dreams, then talking of Lemminkäinen and what they remembered of the stories about his coronation on Tapiola's green hill beside the mighty Sampo.

"But there is no Sampo now," said Egan. "Nothing binds the Seven Clans together, save our enemy, Löhi, who would destroy us all. And therein lies the key. I would give up all I have—life, limb, the throne of Etelamaa—to see the Witch overthrown and peace returned to the lands. And there is no way that I or anyone else can claim to be the High King without first defeating Löhi. But how to find her, to catch her, to draw her out—that I know not. Yet now the Seer has found the camp we have sought for so long; if only it lies within our reach!"

"So you will go to Kyöpelinvuori? At once?"

"It was not my plan," said Egan. "I thought to stay in Etelamaa somewhat longer and visit Harmaaniemi ere I left. Sinio advises me to do so, then to go straight to High Länsimaa. I shared that plan with Väinämöinen before he and Ulla left the Singing Valley, and he agreed. He, too, thinks the Witch far from finished.

"But now? How can I refuse such a summons? And doubtless others have been called, too. Väinämöinen is not here, so we must make our own counsels until we meet him again. I'm afraid you must leave Kirsikka sooner than you hoped, Eglano. As soon as we finish preparations for this summer's campaign, we ride. We will not wait for open water or blue skies! Löhi has never hesitated to strike, and strike hard; neither will we!"

Egan prepared to leave the Stone City quickly, but he told his reasons to few and his full thought to none. Even to his mother, the queen, he said nothing about the Seer's message, only that he had to leave to handle urgent matters in the north. He commanded Aldon to remain in Etelamaa and raise the largest army possible, well-outfitted and provisioned with all they might need for a long campaign. He sent messengers to the Smiths of Seppälä, demanding that the weapons Etelamaa had ordered be delivered at once, especially the lances. If not, he threatened to close the borders to the transit of bloodrock from High Länsimaa or even to hold the wagon trains bound for Seppälä until the weapons were in Etelalaisen hands.

Aldon did his job well, and the king's officers worked tirelessly, but the people wondered all the more. In some quarters, they complained that the levees took their sons and the quartermasters took their horses and livestock, even ordering the oats, barley, and rye they would sow and reap later that year, leaving them with no stores.

Egan's dreams subsided, and he slept better despite his desire to be off again swiftly. He still received no word from Väinämöinen, and Ikä brought no fresh news. Finally, on the night before he left, he met one last time with his chief counselors, then retired to his chambers. Tired, he soon fell asleep, still dressed, on the soft goosefeather bed. It was not long before he dreamed again. The dream was more vivid than ever before, more lifelike. He dreamed a swirl of combat, the confusion of bodies and blades, and the fear. He held the Sword of Legend in his right hand and the Shield of Etelamaa in his left, casting down foe after foe: goblins, trolls, Easterners horsed and on foot. He fought his way forward as if up a steep hillside, heavily mailed and armored, legs aching with effort. At last he reached the top, and she waited there—a wretched crone this time, tall but bent, screaming filth in a tongue he could not understand, the tongue of Pohjola. Egan knew he must strike swiftly, before the Witch could enchant him. With a cry, he leapt forward—but too late!

He stopped in his tracks, feet leaden, his arm frozen midswing. The old crone cackled with delight. She held a crooked knife with a black blade dripping poison. She came toward him, leering, raising the knife to his throat. But then she, too, froze! She was bound! Freed from the Witch's spell, Egan turned. He thought to see Väinämöinen there behind him, but it was not the old wizard. Ulla stood there, bathed in golden light. She lifted her staff above her head, her eyes on fire, and commanded him to strike. The Sword of Legend came down on the crone, and all went black.

In the deep of night, Egan awoke in a sweat, exhausted, limbs aching. He felt none of the exhilaration that victory in battle always brought him, only a cold dread. But Ulla! Why was Ulla in his dream now, saving him, being his shield and partner in Löhi's dispatch? Why did the Karhulaisen girl, the girl who bore the Mark of the Clan, now stand by his side? He thought of the first time he had seen her in Nummela years before—an ugly child, he thought then, pale, wan, rude, and strange. But what were his feelings now?

Eventually he fell back into an uneasy sleep, waking only when Orvo came to fetch him before dawn.

Though tired, the night's phantoms still in his mind, Egan did not take long to prepare. His manservant helped him dress in warm travelling clothes: thick tunic and pants with his tall riding boots and a long, hooded cloak finely woven in pale blue and bordered with golden thread. He ate a bite in the sculleries, as he always did, and walked out into the old castle's small, snowy courtyard, where another servant wrapped a fur-lined coat about his shoulders. The horses, waiting and ready, champed and steamed in the cold morning air, as anxious as their masters to ride away. Egan had often left the Stone City amid a fanfare of trumpets and drums, with an escort of Swan Knights and cheering crowds. But this time he left in the black dawn of late winter, with only four guards to accompany him and his brother Eglano. He wanted no fanfare now and as few eyes to see him as might be.

Vendla the Queen had come out into the snow to wish him well; she seemed older and unfamiliar somehow in the dim light, more drawn and grey. Since confessing to her that he would soon depart, he had avoided her save for a few brief visits. Now their leavetaking felt awkward, but she still came to see him off—to see them both off. Egan and Eglano, her two sons, went to war again. As any woman of the Far Northern Land did, she watched her sons leave, pressing into their hands gloves she had knitted for them as a farewell gift.

Egan smiled. "*Warm is the shirt woven by one's own mother; cold the veil made by a stranger's hand.* Thank you, Mother."

Kirsikka stood beside the queen, openly weeping, and Marjatta, Orvo, Toiva, and others of the household gathered near them. And after embracing his mother, sister, and Kirsikka, the king mounted his tall white horse and took the reins into his hands.

"Fare you well," said Vendla, her voice stoic and calm. "Ukko's blessings upon you. But where will you ride this year, king of the Swan Folk?"

Egan looked down at her and smiled.

"This year?" he said. "Why, to the Land of Victory, my queen! This year my father, Nigan, will be avenged, my father and all our people. Be sure of it!"

Then Egan Dragonslayer reared up his horse and, with a cry, rode forward. They clattered out of the courtyard in a cloud of snow, and then, turning slightly, rode across the bridge and were lost in the dark. Vendla and the others stood still for some time, listening to the echoes on the wind; for all things may leave such echoes, long after they disappear and fade from the memory of everyone save the listeners.

Chapter Thirteen

The Face in the Mirror

The folk of the Thousand Isles saw it first. A flaming star, brighter than any other, trailed a streak of white fire across the southern sky. It rose late and, each night, climbed a little higher. Sometimes it still burned when all other stars had faded, hanging in the sky until the rising sun banished it to regions unknown, only to reappear the following night. On clear, starry nights, the fisherfolk on their tiny, wind-swept islands pointed and stared; but they did not know what it meant, and they had no shamans to ask.

Then the flaming star reached the coast and, from Langvika to the Stone City, folk gazed at it in wonder. Airiki saw it from his castle, Ilmarinen from the Guildhall, and Kirsikka stood atop the Keep with Vendla and Marjatta to watch it shine in the sky. An omen, some people said; a sign from the gods, said others. Some folk thought it an evil portent and looked away, fearing that Lovĕatar would return. Most thought it good, though, a sign to the folk of the Far Northern Land that their time of troubles was over, their enemies weak and scattered. And the Swan Folk called it the Sled of Lemminkäinen, which was hurrying north to fight Löhi or to greet their king, Egan Dragonslayer. At last it was seen even in Keskimaa and High Länsimaa and along the hunting trails of the Elk Folk. But what Löhi's servants made of the fiery star, none could say. The star appeared in Tapiola, too, of course. It was there that Egan first saw it, since the king had gone to the White City to meet Asikkas and the Seer.

Now Tapiola, the oldest, most revered, and most beautiful town of the Seven Clans, had been built on a height with fertile fields all about it. Seven hills surrounded it, named after the Seven Clans: Jänis, Joutsen, Kotka, Karhu, Hirvi, Poro, and Susi—that is, Hare, Swan, Eagle, Bear, Elk, Reindeer, and Wolf. The Tavastialaiset said the town had been built on purpose amidst the seven hills named for the clans, but they were wrong. Before the Seven Clans were ever founded, the Erilaiset had a hill fort on the height nearby, to protect their *väki* from the forefathers of the Itäläiset. So when the Erilaiset befriended the Kaamoslaiset, they took them to that strong place and made a city there.

If there was one thing the Far Northern Land did not lack, it was trees; and if there was another, it was rock. Folk there mined grey rock, slate, black boulders, bloodrock, and marble of many hues. But near to Tapiola—Tapio's land in the Old Speech—men quarried a shallow, stony valley for great slabs of *valkoinen marmori*, a flawless white marble of surpassing strength and beauty. The Erilaiset and mortals built the city with it, and Ilmarinen the Smith put his magic into the masons' work. After a score of years, they finished Tapiola, the White City of the Kaamoslaiset.

Polished streets led to buildings and houses of smooth, white stone. They built tall towers, paved courtyards, and fair bridges to span its streams. In the very heart of Tapiola they fashioned a palace all of *valkoinen marmori*, with many fine rooms and galleries and a delightful hanging garden. Unlike Langvika and the Stone City of Etelamaa, made later when the people had multiplied, Tapiola held plots of green space, with trees, flowering bushes and other blooms. The white wall around the city had a watchtower at each corner, each with a different shape and design. Called Pohja, Etela, Länsi, and Itä—North, South, West, and East—for the directions they faced, the towers were said to stand guard upon the four winds, listening for the tidings they brought, so that enemies might never surprise the city. The great gate faced mostly south, and the road to it ran across a deep moat filled with water.

As the years passed, the Kaamoslaiset increased, becoming the Seven Clans and spreading throughout the Far Northern Land. Tapiola became the capital of Tavastia. They cleared the woods around Tapiola for fields and planted orchards, and, in time, far more people lived outside the city walls than in them, for though fair, Tapiola was not overlarge. And on the hills that were not bare rock, people built houses and towers. But on Jänis, also called Vihreamaki or the Green Hill—the tallest hill and closest to the city's walls— they built no wall or tower. Instead, they chanted the songs and rituals of the Vanhalaiset, welcomed spring, and celebrated summer. The High Kings of the Far Northern Land were crowned there, including Lemminkäinen, the greatest and last. When they brought the Sampo from Ilmarinen's forge and raised it upon the Green Hill, all seemed well throughout the Seven Lands.

But the four towers failed of their vigilence at least once. For the Erilaiset told that when Löhi first returned incarnate in the days of old, she came to Tapiola and walked its fair streets in disguise. She despised the towers and white walls, which she saw as mockeries of her own mountains of snow and ice, all melted away. This made her hate the Seven Clans all the more. Years later, on a night so cold and bitter than none ventured abroad, she came back to Tapiola and, with a spell long-prepared in her dismal halls in Sariola, she stole the Sampo, defiled the hill, then fled, unmarked, back to Pohjola with her treasure before the people were aware. But afterward, Leminkäinen and the Erilaiset hallowed it anew, so it remained green and lovely, though never again did the Sampo or any other magical totem stand there.

Egan had been in Tapiola for less than two weeks when the Seer of Kyöpelinvuori arrived. They expected many others soon, for the Seer and Asikkas had sent messages far and wide to all the Seven Lands, calling a great council of the clans, the first in generations of mortal men. The Seer seldom left Kyöpelinvuori; she preferred others to call upon her, or else to communicate through strange means that not even Väinämöinen fully understood. Yet this time the old woman had insisted that King Asikkas host the council in Tapiola. As soon as she arrived from Kyöpelinvuori with a small retinue, she sent a message asking Egan to visit her at once, discreetly, at night.

It was a peculiar request, perhaps, but Egan was accustomed to the Seer's eccentricity. He thought her a strange, secretive woman and knew that Väinämöinen did not fully trust her. Despite the *sight* her looking glass gave her and despite the undeniable good she had done in the war against Löhi, he knew she exacted a price for everything. She shaped all her policies with her own benefit fully in mind.

The power and influence of Kyöpelinvuori had grown over the past several years. Once a half-forgotten witch in a crumbling tower, the Seer now ranked among the great of the Far Northern Land. She could not be ignored, and moreover, Egan wished to learn the details of the discovery of their enemies' camp, for the elves had not yet come to Tapiola and Asikkas knew little more than Egan.

The Seer's quarters were near the palace, in a low white tower made of *valkoinen marmori*, looking out over a little garden filled with flowers set round a rowan tree. As night fell and darkness deepened, Egan arrived there to see her. He left his guard at the tower's foot with the Seer's guards. The two men in her service wore livery he had not seen before, purple baldrics with the old tower of Kyöpelinvuori stitched in red and white thread. Siitsa met him as soon as he stepped across the threshold.

"Welcome, Your Majesty," the thin young woman said. "My mistress awaits you in the room above; if you please, I will lead you there."

They passed several fair rooms on the tower's lower level, then Egan followed Siitsa up a short staircase that twice turned sharply and ended at an open doorway. In the small, simply furnished turret room Egan saw a light repast set upon a wooden table. Several flickering candles gave the room a bare, yellow illumination. A single narrow window opened onto a shallow balcony which faced south. Siitsa gestured toward the opening, and Egan stepped outside. In the dim light Egan could just make out the Seer's figure on the balcony. As he approached her, she spoke.

"It is bright tonight," she said with her thick Tavastian accent, pointing to the flaming star visible in the southern sky. "The skies have cleared—yet they are often clear of late, are they not?"

"I have watched the star these last few days," said Egan. "It is beautiful, be it a portent or no. But what do you think it heralds, Seer?"

"Ah," she replied, laughing a little in her strange way. "That is the question, isn't it? Great deeds are at hand! But we must decide what those deeds shall be and who shall do them."

"You have heard Väinämöinen's news?" asked the young man. "About the Shards of the Sampo? I just missed Turi as he left for the south, but the Wardens, Bergil and Ilkka, told me the tale. Perhaps the star foretells success. The Sampo will be reforged in Seppälä and raised on the Green Hill."

"Perhaps," she answered. "Or perhaps it tells of other things." After a moment she sighed, then turned to the king at last. A thin smile hovered on her pursed lips.

"Thank you for coming to me, Egan," she said. "Forgive an old woman's folly, but it is better for both of us this way, I think. I wish to speak with you alone before this great council. There are ears everywhere, but my words are for your ears alone."

Egan caught a queer glint in the Seer's eye and hesitated for a moment. Why could she not speak openly, at least to Asikkas? Or Bergil the Warden, who was also in Tapiola? Watching her, he detected another strange thing: she was nervous, she who was always sure of her words, and measured. Now her voice trembled faintly.

"I wish to speak with you as well," he said at last. "Though all should be made clear at the council, when we gather together and Väinämöinen finally returns. But I am impatient and have been since your message came to me through Ikä."

"And what are your questions?"

"Why, about the scouts' report, of course! About the camp. For years we have sought such a place, the camp that shelters them in winter, that sustains their horse herds, and that houses their supplies."

"Then we seek the same thing," answered the Seer, an unmistakable quiver in her voice.

"I don't understand you," said Egan.

"What would you do with this knowledge, King Egan? What has troubled your thoughts throughout winter's dark? For you have been troubled, have you not?"

The young man looked hard at her.

"Yes," he said slowly, "Yes, I have been troubled. I have had strange dreams that would not pass. But tell me, what of the camp?"

"Why? What would you do with this knowledge?"

"I would attack it!" he said with passion, angered by her word-play. "You know that. No more waiting, no more reacting to Löhi's plans while our own people die. I would strike a heavy blow and destroy our enemies. I would end this war—now!"

"Exactly!" cried the Seer. "And now we have both the strength and the knowledge to do so! It is within reach, Egan. The elves have found it, and I, too, have seen it in the glass. It lies within our reach at last and, with it, the war's end and a new beginning for all the Far Northern Land!"

She turned and put her hands on the balcony's rail, looking out over the town. The wind gusted and the candlelight wavered. Siitsa came and stood beside her mistress.

"Look at the fire in the sky, Egan! Tell me now; what were your dreams?"

"I dreamed of Lemminkäinen," he said, and now his voice trembled. "And of Löhi. I saw Lemminkäinen strike her down. Only . . . only sometimes it was not the hand of Lemminkäinen, but my own hand that struck the blow."

"And what else? What else?"

"Nothing else, except that Ulla stood with me. In the last dream she was beside me, and her power bound the Witch while I struck."

"Yes, yes," the Seer softly keened. "So I, too, have dreamed, dreamed and seen in strange visions that the looking glass shows me. And I have had these dreams and visions even with my waking eyes."

The old woman turned, putting her cold, thin hands on his shoulders and looking into his blue eyes. Even in the darkness, Egan noticed that the mortal

Seer's eyes were fluted and spiraled like the eyes of an Erilainen.

"The star is the sign, and the dreams our instructions," she said slowly and clearly. "Now we learn from Väinämöinen that the Shards of the Sampo are found and the Sampo may be reforged. The time is at hand, Egan Dragonslayer. Your time. You will lead the army of the Seven Clans to victory over Pohjola, then you will be made High King of the Far Northern Land. I will make sure all the other clans accept you, and Väinämöinen will help you. You are the Heir of Lemminkäinen."

Egan pushed her away, disturbed by her unwonted intimacy and fervor. He understood the old woman well enough. She would stand behind his throne, behind all thrones, and the Seers of Kyöpelinvuori would be accounted the greatest magic-users in all the Far Northern Land. That could not be helped, nor did it matter. He would always stand beside the Väinämöinen and the Erilaiset.

"I am not Lemminkäinen," he said at last. "I am no mage. I do not have the same power. I can fight; I can lead. But I could never defeat Löhi in the same way that he did."

"Can you not?" said the Seer, her words nearly lost on the wind. "You wield Lemminkäinen's sword, saved from ruin by the gods for this very purpose. And remember Ulla! She bears the Mark of the Clan—the Bear Clan. That was also Lemminkäinen's totem, was it not? Your fate is wound with hers. She will be your queen, if you wish it. I can make it so, Egan. You can be crowned on the Vihreamaki of Tapiola on Midsummer's Day, and none will ever withstand you: Egan Dragonslayer and Ulla the Chosen, destroyers of Löhi, Lord and Lady of the Far Northern Land."

"Is this not what you wish, my lord?" asked Siitsa, almost as if she could not stop herself.

The young man's mind raced, for he had indeed imagined just such a thing. Was it really his to reach out and take? He wished desperately to speak with Väinämöinen and learn his counsel. Before he could answer, the Seer took his arm and led him back inside the turret room.

"Bring it to me, Siitsa," she said softly, while Egan stood speechless beside her.

"Yes, mistress," the strange young woman replied. Siitsa lifted a heavy object covered in gold cloth from a low shelf on the wall, hung above several small chests. She carried it to the center of the room and placed the thing on a small wooden table, nestled in a circle of colored tapestries.

"You know what this is," said the Seer.

"Yes," answered Egan. "It is your crystal ball, is it not?"

"So it is," she said. "The great gift of my mothers, the gift that has been passed down from one to another for many generations. This is my crystal ball, the looking glass of the Seers of Kyöpelinvuori. With it I may read your fortune." She removed the golden cloth, and there, gently reflecting the candlelight, rested a beautiful crystal ball, smooth and flawless, like a drop of clear water from a still northern lake, melted from the purest snow fallen from heaven.

"Many fortunes I have read," continued the Seer, "and many prophecies revealed for princes and merchants, lords and ladies. I read Airiki's fortune, and so now he rules in Akkala. Asikkas sat beside me in this very room. Sit, king of the Swan Folk! The crystal ball does not lie. Let us look into the glass together and see if it confirms what has come to us, to you and me, in our visions and dreams!"

Egan stared at the sparkling crystal in amazement, allowing himself to be seated at the table while the Seer sat beside him.

"You may leave us now, Siitsa," she said. The girl bowed and left the turret room, her bare feet faintly echoing on the smooth stone steps as she went down the stairs. The candles flickered.

"Only one question may we ask," said the Seer. "Only one this time. Such is the spell. Later, perhaps, there will be another opportunity. It is always different. No two fortunes are alike. Come, take my hands!"

Egan took the old woman's hands in his own. They both shook with excitement as she placed their hands upon the crystal ball. It felt cold to the touch, as cold as a snowball, and he shivered. The Seer chanted softly, moving her hands around the globe's smooth surface. Suddenly he felt it: the spell's power, its potency, wrapped around them. He peered into the clear glass, staring at the fractured tongues of flame reflected on its face. It was a beautiful thing, the looking glass of Kyöpelinvuori—a precious, beautiful thing.

"What is the fortune of the king of the Swan Folk?" the Seer said abruptly in a ringing voice. "What crown will he wear?" Then again, with increasing passion, "What crown will he wear?"

No sooner had the Seer asked than the crystal ball came alive with sparkling colors, flashing like multihued lightnings captured inside a tiny world, a little living orb. Egan gasped and looked up at the Seer, but the old woman's eyes were closed.

Then a vision came to the king, more lifelike than any dream. In his mind's eye, he saw things he recognized and some he did not. He saw Väinämöinen and Mielikki sitting beside a roaring fire, then an unknown pale woman with skin like snow and pink eyes. The pale woman raised her hand, and the vision changed. Riders galloped across a grassy field. A green hill appeared; a tall pole was raised upon its crown. People danced around the pole and sang; the sun rose golden in the distance.

The vision changed again. The sun was blotted out; the hill was bare. Towers were raised, and men and goblins fought in their shadow. Two tall men with yellow hair stood together on a rocky height, leaning on their swords. One of the men wore a deep blue cape and a band of colored leather around his brow; the other wore a crown. The crown was black, forged of iron by a man with a silver hammer, and set all about with precious red stones. Then the vision changed for the third and last time. The tall men disappeared; only the iron crown remained to fill Egan's mind, the red gems glowing like burning coals.

The king's heart pounded within his breast; his breath grew labored. Then his vision cleared and he returned to the moment. The Seer had pushed back her chair and risen, pointing her bony finger at him while she panted.

"It rested there, there on your head," she gasped. "Do you know that crown? Have you seen it before?"

"Yes. Yes, I have seen it. In paintings and tapestries. It is the lost crown, the crown of the High Kings of the Far Northern Land."

"It is Lemminkäinen's crown," said the Seer. "And it is not lost! The tower keeps many secrets; Kyöpelinvuori conceals many mysteries. Long ago, when I was young, I found it buried deep within the tower's hoard, hidden. I do not know how it came there. Even Väinämöinen does not know about it, and Löhi cannot discover it. It remains hidden at Kyöpelinvuori until the day I choose to reveal it."

Having mastered herself, the Seer straightened and spoke proudly. "The looking glass does not lie. We both saw the same vision. It is your fortune to become the High King of the Far Northern Land and of the united Seven Clans. It is yours to grasp or turn away from. You dreamed of this, did you not? But beware, king of the Swan Folk! Your choice will determine not only your own fortune, but perhaps your people's as well. Choose wisely."

The Seer placed the golden cloth over the crystal ball; she sighed heavily, her face drawn with exhaustion. Egan, too, felt drained; his head ached. He had too much to think about, too much to take in. The old doubts assailed him as they had done before, sapping his confidence like miners digging beneath the walls of a citadel strong but beset by foes.

"Choose," he murmured. "Choose. But even if Ulla stood beside me—even with Väinämöinen—I don't know that I could defeat Löhi, the most powerful witch in all the world."

"You may not have to," said the Seer, the tension in her voice and in her body relaxing. "I know what you dreamed, but dreams may be interpreted in many ways. The old songs and prophecies tell of Löhi fading away, ebbing, and slipping back into the oblivion of winter's darkness if she cannot divide the Seven Clans and conquer us swiftly. Three seasons of the Witch, say the prophecies: no more. This is her third season, and already she wanes.

"She fears you, Egan! She fears your sword. She remembers Lemminkäinen at the Great Battle. She will not dare to face you—ever—but will send her captain, this Kuupää, whom folk name the Moonface, to challenge you. And you will defeat him and rout her army, sending her back into the darkness forever!

"You were born to this high destiny, Egan, born to join the pantheon of mighty warriors of our people. Songs of glory will celebrate you throughout the Seven Lands, songs of praise lift your name in immortality down the ages; songs of Egan Dragonslayer, the Heir of Lemminkäinen."

The Seer walked out to the balcony, and Egan followed. They looked out over Tapiola as the wind blew low, dark clouds swiftly over the twinkling stars. Sounds filtered up from Tapiola's streets and houses: laughter, voices raised here and there, animals, a child's wail. An ancient bell tower tolled the hour, echoing throughout the night.

"I will think on this," Egan said at last. "And I will speak with Väinämöinen. He should arrive soon with news from Seppälä."

"Do so, then," the Seer replied. "But there is much, very much to be prepared, Egan Dragonslayer. Fate and destiny brook no delay. I have read your fortune. You have my counsel. I will support you among the other clans, and not even Akkala will stand against you. But the choice lies with you . . . king of the Etelalasiset."

Egan turned and left the old woman on her balcony. He paused inside the turret room, running his hands through his hair and softly sighing—only then did he notice Kilia, the Seer's young apprentice, sitting in a little chair in the shadows and playing with a rock of crystal, turning it over and over in her tiny hands. She had been there the entire time. The child said nothing, only watched him with her pale eyes, which gleamed a bit in the candlelight. Disconcerted, Egan quickly walked down the staircase, eager for the cool dark of the garden, but Siitsa waited for him below.

Habitually silent and severe, the thin girl seldom spoke to Egan, though they had travelled far together. He disliked her. But she curtsied to him now after the fashion of Tavastia. A look of unaccustomed friendliness, even joy, played upon her face.

"She is right, Your Majesty," said Siitsa. "The signs are unmistakable. All will follow you."

"Maybe, Siitsa."

"No!" she cried with unexpected warmth. "It is true. You will finally exact vengeance on our enemies: murderers, rapists, destroyers of field, village, and town. Never again will they do so. Never. And those who have hurt us so badly will feel the justice of your sword!"

Egan left the tower then, leaving Siitsa behind him, beaming in the doorway. After speaking briefly with his brother, he returned to his chamber in Asikkas' palace and went straight to bed. He lay awake, thinking—and when he finally slept, he dreamed.

When the young man awoke the next morning, he had made his decision.

***

The important visitors from all the Seven Lands soon arrived in Tapiola: Airiki, Teemu, and Janottu, Lord of the Bear Folk in Keskimaa. Jarko, Lord of Poronristeys in Karelia, came all the way from the forest to speak for the Reindeer Folk, while Bergil and Ilkka spoke for the Wardens.

Master Isku rode to Tapiola from the Shipwrights' Guild, and Juvari, Captain of the Swan Folk, brought several knights and captains from different lands to the White City. Lúven, Chief of the Haltiatar of the Enchanted Valley, came with his elvish scouts, and, lastly, Väinämöinen and Turi returned from Seppälä with Ulla and Tulikki beside them. They had waited only for Väinämöinen's arrival, so the very next day the great council convened to consider all that had happened the past year and debate what might come next.

Much of what they heard surprised Väinämöinen and Turi. They expected more excitement about the Sampo and the news from the Smiths of

Seppälä. The two wizards had seen Ilmarinen many times, speaking with him for hours about all that had happened in the war with Löhi. Ilmarinen had begun work on a mighty spell, a song like no other made in the Far Northern Land, at least not since the days of old. When he finished that song, he might cast the spell and forge the New Sampo, but it seemed to Väinämöinen that the mortals did not fully understand the importance of Tapio's words.

At first Asikkas had suggested to meet on the Vihreamaki, hoping the green, hallowed hill would give them wisdom in their counsels, but both the Seer and Väinämöinen warned against this, since eyes for miles around might see them. Instead the lords and captains gathered in a fair courtyard in the palace, beneath the hanging garden that the Tavastialaiset called *jäninpaikka*—for a carving of a hare, the ancient totem of Tavastia, with its eyes made of shining jet and its body fashioned of *valkoinen marmori* sat there beside a running fountain. All around this place, Väinämöinen and Turi made their strongest charms so that even the eyes and ears of Löhi would be blind and deaf.

The sun shone bright in a clear blue sky, and the breeze was cool and fresh. When everyone had arrived, Asikkas stood forth and addressed them.

"At last we are gathered together," he began, "from the Seven Clans and the Enchanted Valley, from all free folk of the Far Northern Land who stand against Löhi. For eight years she has fought us. She sent the Easterners against us; their riders destroyed our villages and enslaved our people. The Witch has stirred up the wild Kveni and armed them; she has sent her goblins from Pohjola to trouble us. Ghosts and demons haunt the night, and sickness enters our homes on the wings of spirits from Tuonela. She has even loosed a dragon upon us, and were it not for King Egan, the beast would have spread ruin throughout Deep Länsimaa.

"But she has failed. The Seven Clans have suffered but are not ruined. Singly, she hoped to destroy us each in turn, yet now we stand as one. Mortals and heroes are friends once more, and there are *tietäjää* again among the people. Ulla Karhulainen came to us, making the Mark of the Clan manifest and fulfilling the prophecy of old. Väinämöinen has led us to victory, and the Seer's *sight* has been our light in the darkness. Verily, we have suffered, but, for all that, now that we stand together, we are stronger than ever. The question before us, then, is what should we do with this newfound strength? Many things have changed since last summer."

So Asikkas began, and for a while they discussed things that concerned all the clans, especially the situation in Deep and High Länsimaa. Everyone knew that the elves had fresh knowledge of their enemies and eagerly await-ed the tale. Before long they turned to Lúven and asked for his report.

Lúven wore his black mail even to the council, startling some of the mor-tals. They were used, perhaps, to Väinämöinen and other wizards, singers of songs and weavers of spells, wise men with their long beards and magic staffs or sage women of proud mien and bearing. But the Haltiatar looked strange to mortal eyes, even frightening, like wild spirits from the deep forests out of tales of old. Lúven was tall, his face long and thin, and his braided hair fell about his shoulders. His dark eyes seemed to pierce mortal hearts and read the very thoughts of those he gazed upon.

"We have long known that our enemies must have a camp near to the North Marches," began the elf. "How else could they attack us from out of the wastes, and with so many men and horses? Löhi's forces could not do this in the Witch's War. Sariola is many hundreds of miles from the Marches, and the road from Pohjola ends in the swamps long before it reaches High Länsimaa. The lands of the Itäläiset are still farther away. For so many to assail the Seven Clans so often, especially soon after the waters open, they must have a place of refuge, or several such places, to shelter in during winter and to store supplies. Raiders travelling lightly may come out of the wild, but not armies.

"Yet we could never find this place," he continued. "My *väki*, my folk, searched summer and winter. Many Karelialaiset searched, too; some dis-appeared and never returned. As far north as the road to old Pohjola we searched, but the land is wild, full of lakes, woods, and marsh. Not even by working a change and taking the forms of birds or beasts could we find what we sought; few can make such perilous *loitsu* in any case. All that wide land is under the Witch's spell, Löhi's or her servants'. All paths twist and turn. All lakes look the same, all woods impenetrable."

"Aye," said Väinämöinen with a sigh. "Seven, eight years ago, when I first learned Löhi had returned, I went there. I saw no camps then, though I met her servants everywhere. But the Witch's thought lay heavy on those regions, and I grew weary and confused. And that alone is proof enough that Löhi hides a secret in the wastes."

"So it went with us," said Lúven. "And who among us has the power of Väinämöinen or knows better than he the webs of Löhi? But that has changed! Asper, come now: tell your story!" One of Lúven's companions stood forth. Shorter than Lúven, the elf had flaxen hair and narrow eyes, and wore brown and green like the March Wardens or Tulikki.

"For three years I searched the wastes," said Asper in a voice so thick with the strange accent of the Haltiatar that he could scarcely be understood. "Ever and anon I went to Karelia, where my wife yet dwells, but always I returned to my task. The Witch's servants, especially the Hiisia, roam everywhere north of Suonpää. Twice they almost caught me. Lonely months I endured, with many hard days of toil and trouble. But last winter . . . at last I found what I had sought.

"I was journeying south, and I was tired, very tired. The lakes were frozen, but not much snow lay on the ground; it was a mild winter, even in the north. I wanted only to speed my journey back to Länsimaa, then rest and sleep in warmth—such are the dreams of scouts beyond the Marches. I finally came to a place I recognized but had never approached from the north. I found a little river, unfrozen and quick-running, which disappeared into a shadowy defile.

"I followed it," the elf continued, "creeping warily along its banks until I heard a noise ahead, a sound of rushing and churning water. Then I realized I was in a narrow valley, hanging over a deeper vale below. A waterfall emptied down over a glistening black rock face into a broader river, obscured by mist and the dim light—and then I saw it! Luckily enough daylight remained, and I was on the right side of the little river.

"Down below and to the east of the hanging valley, through a haze, I saw the camp of our enemies—more like a town than a camp. Sheds and stables had been built on one side, and I saw horses and cattle in the snowy yards. On the other side, smoke rose from scores of hearths in many long buildings. Across the river, I saw signs of fields or meadows—snow-covered, but they were rye fields, I think, slashed and burned out of the pinewoods. The great camp sheltered hundreds, maybe thousands of horses in the roundhouses of the Easterners."

"How far is that place?" asked Egan eagerly. "Could you find it again?"

"I made my way back up the valley and round again," said Asper. "Then I came down through a range of hills and struck the broad river. I saw the misty falls in the distance but could come no closer. Hiisia patrolled the woods all about. But I knew that place then, and I know my way back. Three by three it is: three rivers and three lakes, and Taivaantappi, the North Star, to guide you. Any other way, and you will be lost among the lakes, but the path is straight to Suonpää."

"Three by three," murmured Turi. "And a misty fall. Maybe . . . maybe I remember now, though it's been centuries. Kivikoinenvirta was the name of that broad river, and Sumuvuori the vale, if it is indeed the same place: the Rocky Run and the Misty Fall. They are far away; yet not too far, perhaps."

"It is the same," said the Seer, who spoke now for the first time. "I, too, have seen it, and Siitsa here found it on the old maps that we still keep in Kyöpelinvuori. Fruitless days and nights I spent gazing into the glass, turning my *sight* to those parts; but little could I see save darkness and confusion. When Asper returned with his report, I looked again. Perhaps Löhi's strength wanes as the fortunes of the Seven Clans wax, for finally I pierced the clouds and saw the camp of our enemies nestled in the deep vale beneath the hanging valley."

"Two other scouts set out at once when Asper returned," said Lúven. "Both found it, even as he described. The Pohjolaiset rest at Sumuvuori."

"Then we have them!" cried Airiki, slapping his broad hand on the table. "Fools! Whatever magic this Witch has, she knows nothing of war if she gathers all her men and beasts together in one place. A perfect trap for them!"

"Whatever else Löhi may be, Airiki," said Väinämöinen, "she is no fool. Mad, crazed by her lust for power, changed in strange ways: all that and more. But Löhi of Pohjola has fought many wars and battles. You do not know the wastes that lie north of the Marches, king of the Eagle Folk. Fair Akkala has good land far up its western coast, but no mortals live in Suonpää. Wanderers come to evil in that land of lake, marsh, and bog. To make such a camp is no small feat, and only thus has she harried us at will for so long."

"But what good does this news do us?" asked Janottu, the Lord of the Bear Folk. "Lake, marsh, and bog: no way for men save scouts and hunters, few and wary. You suggest that we attack this place, but it seems that no army can pass through to it."

"Can it not?" said Bergil. "The Easterners pass through each summer and enter High Länsimaa at many different places. If Löhi can do so, why can't we do the same?"

"That is the decision before us all," said Egan. "We can wait for the coming summer and meet our enemies wherever they strike, as we have always done, or perhaps lie in ambush and hope they don't discover us—or we can gather all our forces, march upon our enemies' camp, and destroy them with one mighty blow."

"But we have no real hope for surprise," said Jarko. "Surely they will have rumor of our coming. How can we be sure that our enemies would fight and not escape us, fleeing farther into the wilderness?"

"They have no choice," replied Egan. "Or rather a hard one. They can flee, it is true, or even fall back to Pohjola, far, far away. This means the timing of the blow is most important. It must come late, as late as possible, after the harvest and just ere winter's first storms. They can flee into the wild then if they will, but if the snow and ice catch them on their long road, they will suffer—and we must burn the camp behind. If we time it well, they must flee wildly into winter's maw or they must stand and fight. Then our strength may prevail."

The men of the Seven Clans murmured then, nodding their heads or rapping their hands upon the table, for they saw the wisdom of Egan's plan. They would be glad to finally take the fight to their enemy and turn the element of surprise against her.

But Teemu asked, "What of Löhi herself? Does she dwell in this place? I have seen Väinämöinen's magic work the impossible and King Egan slay the nightmare creature that no one else could withstand. But dare we hope to defeat Löhi herself if she is there? Can it be done?"

"Löhi will not be there," said the Seer quickly. "She rules her slaves from Pohjola. She fears King Egan and the Sword he wields that vanquished her long ago. She will not face that Sword again, nor the child now grown to womanhood with the Mark of the Clan upon her shoulder and a staff in her hand. Kuupää leads our foes." They all turned to Väinämöinen then, and the old man nodded slowly in agreement.

"It is true," he said. "The Witch fears the king and Lemminkäinen's blade, which he bears. There is no telling what Löhi may do in desperation, but I do not think she will lead her army as she did so long ago—not unless we come to the gates of Sariola itself, which we cannot do. Why has she not led her forces already? First she sent Työ, and now the Moonface. Why has she not come herself, alone, to the gates of every town in the Far Northern Land with ruin and death? Because she is not invincible. She cannot stand alone against an army. The strongest knight may yet be slain with an arrow in the back shot by an old man hiding behind a stone. But before we plan to seek out battle rather than build strong places to defend, let us consider other tidings—for none have mentioned the Sampo or the return of Ilmarinen, though it is a great thing. Listen now to the daughter of Mielikki, child of the gods!"

Tulikki came forward then to tell of the quest that Tapio set her. Strange she appeared to mortal eyes, a slight young woman dressed in traveller's clothes. They marveled to see the grim Haltiatar rise and bow to her, and

Jarko of Karelia, too, for the Reindeer Folk revered Mielikki and remembered her daughter.

Tulikki told how she had found the Seven Shards scattered across the Far Northern Land, met Väinämöinen and Ulla in the woods, then journeyed with them back to the Enchanted Valley. But Väinämöinen stopped her at that point and asked Ulla to report their shared vision of Tapio and his instructions. She did so reluctantly. The girl had remained silent until then, sitting uncomfortably between the two great wizards, aware of the Seer's gaze, and Siitsa's, upon her. But power rang in her voice as she chanted Tapio's words. Those who knew her were amazed by the change they perceived since her hunt. She was no child now, but a strong young woman and singer, stern of mind and purpose.

When Ulla finished, Väinämöinen told of their journey to Seppälä and unexpected encounter with Ilmarinen. Lúven shook his head, clearly vexed.

"I cannot understand it," said the Haltia. "For five hundred years he lay hidden from mortals and Erilaiset alike and only now reveals himself."

"But can we be sure that this is indeed the same smith that made the Sampo of old?" asked Teemu. "And can he truly do it again?"

"It is he," answered Turi. "Väinämöinen and I know him well and remember him, our brother from the earliest of days. And even now he works in his smithy, making the song and watching the fire. Making the Sampo of old took a year; Ilmarinen told us he would need just as long this time, maybe longer. But next year or the year after, we will raise it again on the Vihreamaki of Tapiola on Midsummer's Day, so its power and strength may slowly spread from that green place throughout the Far Northern Land."

"Then Löhi will truly fade," said Väinämöinen, "her life force spent, her spirit weak and houseless. The birth of the New Sampo will be the herald of her doom, and she must not learn of it until it is too late! The people need the Sampo, and the Sampo, too, needs its folk. The folk, the land, the Sampo— together as one. That is Ukko's trail, the path set out for us. It is within our grasp at last."

"Then you think we should not take the offensive, Väinämöinen?" asked Ilkka. "Is this New Sampo all the defense we need?"

The old man sighed and stroked his beard, staring back at the gathered captains each in turn.

"It is a hard choice, and all may go amiss regardless. I say we should follow the words of Tapio. Let Ilmarinen forge the New Sampo, and we will guard it from the Witch's wiles. Let us gather our new strength and make strong places, and weather Löhi's final storms. People will die; aye, they will. But, in the end, the storm may pass and a spring of new hope come again."

Then the Seer of Kyöpelinvuori rose and, taking up her short black staff with its carven wolf's head, stood before them. Dressed all in dark robes of simple yet solid weave, she wore a fine silver chain hung with a pendant like a small crystal globe and gold and silver thread in her white hair. She stood erect, with bright, clear eyes; only her black, rotten teeth marred her impression.

"Wise counsel to be sure," she began. "Ever has Lord Väinämöinen given hope and strength to us all or else we would have failed long ago. But in this, I think, he errs, as indeed we all do. We do not have a choice between acting or not acting, doing or not doing; rather, all things now come together for our common purpose and good.

"Listen to me, folk of the Seven Clans! Can you not read the signs? Look to the new star, Lemminkäinen's Sled, racing to the north! The knowledge of our enemies' camp and the Shards of the Sampo are the gifts of Ukko! Let Ilmarinen forge the New Sampo while you march to victory and destroy Löhi's hordes. And when it is ready, we shall raise the shining pole high on the Green Hill! Then her failure will be complete and our lands know peace."

"Truly spoken!" cried Airiki. "The swords and axes of the Eagle Folk give you new strength. Let us use now what we have and strike as our power swells."

"The Witch ruined my folk; we are more desperate and scattered each year," said Janottu. "We cannot sit by idly, even with this Sampo, and endure attack after attack. If it is within our strength, I beg you—we must strike. But who can lead us?"

Then they debated and argued among themselves as to the right course. None seemed sure which counsel was best: to challenge the Witch, or to build strong walls and towers until the magic of the New Sampo ensured their safety. Egan listened to the debate in silence, troubled at heart, for he saw wisdom in both paths and was loath to reject Väinämöinen's counsel and favor the Seer. But in his heart he also knew that the hour of the Seven Clans, the hour of mortal men, had come. The Kaamoslaiset must take the lead and rid the world of Löhi's menace once and for all. And now he did not hesitate to follow the course he believed in.

The young king came among them and, as he had in Langvika when he first met Airiki, drew Lemminkäinen's sword. It flashed so bright in the sun that it almost blinded them.

"This is the Sword of Legend, Lemminkäinen's blade, given to me by Väinämöinen," he said in a fair, clear voice. All fell silent. "This blade felled Löhi of old. But now I give it a new name and claim it as my own. Behold the sword of Egan Dragonslayer: *Noidankuolli*, the Witch's Bane! And if you follow me, I will lead you beyond the Marches to the camp of our enemies, and we will smite whatever evil we find there! When we return, we will raise the New Sampo on the Green Hill and hold peace and freedom in our hand. Now, men of the Seven Clans, decide! Will you have me? Will you follow me?"

All at that table could feel the power in Egan's call, running like a tremor deep beneath the earth. Though Egan did not claim the crown of the High King of the Far Northern Land nor even mention it, none mistook his words, but none hesitated or opposed him. First Eglano drew his sword and stood beside his brother, then Teemu and the March Wardens, Bergil and Ilkka, then King Asikkas in his own hall; and then all the others stood round the young king. And at the last, but with no doubt in his eyes, stood Airiki.

Then the captains and lords of the Seven Clans raised their swords as one, Väinämöinen and the Erilaiset among them. With one voice, led by Egan

Dragonslayer, they swore the oath afterward known as the Oath of Tapiola or the League of the Seven Clans:

> *As once we were,*
> *let us be again.*
> *One folk to drive the night away,*
> *one voice, one sword, one will—*
> *until Löhi falls or death takes us!*
> *So swear we all by the Mark of the Clan!*

And so they had chosen—they would follow Egan to Sumuvuori and challenge the Army of Pohjola. They embraced each other then and came to Egan severally to do obeisance to him as Lemminkäinen's Heir. The Seer soon departed with Siitsa, and the others, singly or in pairs, retired as well. Egan and Väinämöinen bid farewell to Ulla, Turi, and Tulikki, then went together to a small room in the palace, for they had not spoken before the council. There, Asikkas' servants brought them the sweet berry wine favored in Tavastia.

"I like beer better," said Väinämöinen. Egan laughed.

"Turi's barrels await you at Laulavalaakso," Egan answered. "But speak plainly to me, Väinämöinen. Nigan, my father, is dead and gives no counsel. Since his spirit took to the heavens, you have been as a father to me. I see the wisdom in your words and counsel—but can you see no truth or wisdom in mine?"

"*Two different lakes share the same water,*" said Väinämöinen. "Both lakes have the fish you seek, and both can drown you if you're careless. I gave the sword to you years ago because of what I saw in you, my king. I was right. You are indeed the Heir of Lemminkäinen. I'll rejoice on the day you're crowned on the Hill and the circle is renewed. You saved my life at Linnavuori and have proven yourself time and again. I trust you, and I'll surely follow you.

"He'd have liked you, you know," the old man added. "Lemminkäinen, that is. Not so earnest, not so serious as you, but just as eager, just as bold. He was a very good friend of mine, Egan. Aye, I loved him like a brother and fought with him like a brother, too. He had no sons, but you share his spirit. I see him reborn in you."

Egan stared at the dark purple wine in his crystal glass, thick and sweet, a film already spreading across its surface.

"There is something else," he said less certainly. "I have had many dreams, and—well, it's Ulla. I believe . . . I believe that she should stand beside me. I want her to stand beside me. As we march forward . . . and afterward as well."

The old man stroked his beard and nodded. "No surprise. I've pondered this Egan, aye, I have. Perhaps such is your destiny—yours and hers—and mine was to bring you together. If so—so be it! She seeks a home and always has. Perhaps she will find it with you. But, come what may, she is not ready to stand beside you as an equal and challenge Löhi. The staff in her hand is too green. She must still grow into it, though she is strong. We cannot ask more of her now, unless fate commands it beyond our sight and ken. Of this I am sure."

Egan nodded. "I understand. I would not risk her life. But . . . but I would speak to her all the same, if I may."

The old wizard shut his eyes for a moment, then drained his glass and clasped Egan's arm.

"My king," he said with sudden passion. "My king, if indeed we will do this thing, then let us strike a heavy blow. A heavy, heavy blow."

****

Though they discussed many issues of battle and strategy, the lords, kings, and captains did not stay in Tapiola for very long. They needed to be in their own lands to prepare for the great campaign to come. Indeed, the Seer of Kyöpelinvuori left Tapiola the day after the council, riding out of town in a covered cart with her apprentice and Siitsa. Väinämöinen and Turi wished to return swiftly to the Singing Valley. Väinämöinen had been away for almost a year, and the mortals who came each year to learn the songs would soon arrive. The old man did not wish to neglect them amidst the excitement. He stayed a few days in Tapiola, taking counsel with Lúven, Jarko and Bergil. Then the Erilaiset took leave of King Asikkas and prepared to depart.

Ulla, too, wanted to return to the Singing Valley. She missed Unaja and her other friends. To add to that, she felt out of place in Tapiola, although in the past she had enjoyed her stays in the White City. She was well known and popular in Tapiola; the townsfolk sang songs about the Mark of the Clan and Väinämöinen's daughter, made a princess of Tavastia by their king. When they saw her in the streets, people shouted to her or bowed and did her courtesies as if Ulla were a real princess of noble blood. But all else seemed strange to her now. She had hunted and returned a *tietäjää*, a woman of sight and power, a wizard of the Far Northern Land, yet she took no part in all the weighty counsels. No one talked about the Clan Mark; no one debated what she, Ulla, meant to the folk. The League of the Seven Clans had become a reality. Everyone focused on wars and battle now, planning musters and marches for armies of hundreds and even thousands going off to battle. Even the Sampo seemed almost forgotten.

What was her role in all this? What part did she play in this story? Not for a moment did Ulla doubt Egan; he would be the High King of the Seven Clans. She trusted Väinämöinen's instincts, but the Seer's words, and Egan's, moved her. She did not fear death, at least not her own; Ulla had seen death in many forms for all of her short life. When her own time came, she only hoped that it would be swift. She did not want to linger, stricken by illness or injury, living half a life as her body and mind withered. But she also knew the tale of Lemminkäinen. That hero had sacrificed his life to throw down Löhi, and she feared that Egan would share his fate. Whatever else happened, she did not want Egan to die.

Ulla had a fair room in a house of *valkoinen marmori* near the palace, the same room where she often stayed with Kirsikka. Siria shared it with her now, and they mostly stayed within or walked in the small courtyard garden.

A maid waited on them, and when word spread that Siria was Ulla's kins-woman, others came. They dressed the girl in fine clothes like a Tavastian noblewoman, and braided her fair locks after the fashion of the Hare Folk, entwined with silver thread. Such treatment amazed Siria, like Kirsikka be-fore her. She had never imagined being doted on like the child of a rich fam-ily rather than an ignorant orphan. But, unlike Kirsikka, the attention made her uncomfortable; she felt foolish and lowly even as they pampered and dressed her, and Ulla understood her cousin's feelings and took pity on her.

The night before Ulla planned to leave Tapiola with Väinämöinen, she and Siria were alone, having just dismissed their maidservant. Egan came to their room, bowing as he lightly rapped on the open door. He had not seen her since the council. He and his brother Eglano planned to return to Etelamaa soon before riding to High Länsimaa and the war.

"Good evening to you both," said Egan. "I have heard much about you, Lady Siria, and am glad to make your acquaintance. I hope you will soon have the opportunity to visit us in the south.

"I'm sorry if I have disturbed you, Ulla—but I think this may be our last chance to talk for some time. You leave tomorrow, do you not?"

"Yes, we do," answered Ulla. "At the break of dawn, as Väinämöinen pre-fers; at least, that is the plan."

Egan hesitated for a moment.

"Siria, will you not leave us for a bit?" he finally asked. "I must speak with your cousin alone on urgent matters. It is a fine, clear night tonight, and the breeze is from the south. There will be much singing and merry-making in the town, and my maid waits outside to escort you wherever you will."

Siria looked unsure, but Ulla smiled and nodded. "It's fine; do as the king wishes. His people will go with you."

When Siria had left, Egan came inside, and they sat down together on fine Tavastian stools fashioned out of southern oak. Ulla wondered what urgent matters Egan wished to discuss. When he did speak, he began with trivial things, then fell to talking about the Stone City. That caught Ulla's interest. She was eager for news about Kirsikka, so Egan told her all he could remember.

They laughed about how Kirsikka had adopted the dress of the Swan Folk and now had a wardrobe that almost filled her room. They both enjoyed talking of how the townsfolk cheered when Eglano and his wife, Cherry Red, rode through the streets together. Ulla smiled, glad for her friend, and proud that she could feel happiness untouched by jealousy, for she missed Kirsikka greatly. After a while they fell silent, and Egan suggested they go into the garden for a breath of cool night air.

In the southern night sky, clear as it had been of late, they could see the fiery star. It rose higher now, slowly making its way to the north and east, charting its own path among its shining cousins. They watched it for a while, listening to voices singing in the distance at some happy gathering.

"It shines bright tonight," said Ulla. "Your star is ascendant. That is what Väinämöinen says."

"Perhaps it is not my star," said Egan.

"No, it is yours. You are the Heir of Lemminkäinen, without a doubt. You will defeat the Witch and be High King of the Far Northern Land."

"But perhaps it is not only my star, but ours."

Ulla turned quickly toward him and felt the blood rush to her face.

"The mark is mine," she said. "Not the star."

"I do not believe it," said Egan. "Have you had dreams, Ulla? Have you not considered Ukko's will?"

"I do not know Ukko's will, save what we all know, man and woman, in our hearts. But I know Tapio wills that the Sampo be reforged. Beyond that, all is dark to me. I have had no dreams."

"Then let me tell you mine. I have seen us standing side by side and the darkness lifted. A new light shone throughout the lands! There was increase among the folk, the harvests were good, and the waters open and abundant. The Child of the Prophecy and the Hand that Wields the Sword were as one.

"Lemminkäinen's Heir I may be, but I have not his gift, his power. I am no singer. That is your gift, your role, chosen by the Vanhalaiset. Of old there was but one, but now there are two: you and me. And together, perhaps, we may heal the Far Northern Land of its ills and make the Seven Clans as strong as of old."

Ulla turned away, even as the breeze blew her long, dark hair, and said, "I am not Kirsikka."

But Egan took her by the shoulder and turned her around. Before she could speak, he gathered her into his arms and kissed her upon her lips. She almost pushed him away in surprise—almost. But then, like a panicked child lost in the woods who stumbles into her mother's waiting arms, she surrendered to her own feelings, her own unspoken love. The release swept through her very being. Egan slowly pulled away. They stood like that, look-ing straight into the other's eyes, Ulla as tall as Egan.

"Let us see what happens," he said. "Let us see what this summer brings. And if the star we both see in the sky tonight wins through, if it holds its true course, then we may stand together on the Green Hill beneath the Sampo. Believe in me."

For a moment only she paused. "I believe in you."

Without another word, Egan touched her pale face and kissed her again on her forehead. Then he turned and left the garden, even as Siria returned.

Siria found Ulla in the garden, among the flowers and starlight, entranced.

"There you are," she said. "I didn't know where you were. I saw him, the . . . the king. He is gone now."

But Ulla did not respond, or else said a few words soon forgotten. Siria left her presently and went to sleep. The mild southern air blew through the garden and into their chamber, but Ulla stayed outside in the pleasant dark-ness for a long time. When the clouds obscured the moonlight, she sighed and went inside to lay down in the little bed that she shared with her cousin.

She couldn't sleep, though a great weariness spread all throughout her body. A sense of enchantment followed the weariness, as strong as any *loitsu* she had ever cast. Joy mingled with fear in equal measure, coursing in her veins, driven by her beating heart. Ulla enjoyed this feeling, as if she were drunk on *sahti*. She savored her emotion, choosing not to think of what had transpired between her and Egan nor ponder his words. And so the minutes passed, and the hours, and at last she fell into a light but untroubled sleep. Some time later she opened her eyes, just before dawn. The sky was still dark, but morning's cool scent rode on the breeze, bringing the feeling of possibility and expectation that all people know. *Perhaps today will be different.*

Ulla turned over, watching the dim outline of her cousin's sleeping face and the gentle rise and fall of her chest. She thought of how Siria's gaunt features had filled out, then thought of her aunt, Päivikki, and uncle, Reiko. What would her aunt think, what would any of them think, if they could see her now? How could they ever begin to understand? Then, beyond Siria's sleeping figure, Ulla noticed a light.

No red glow of embers or yellow candlelight, this light shone white, transparent and clear. She threw off the blanket and rose from the low bed, her bare feet on the cold stone floor.

In a shallow alcove on the chamber's far side, a small stand held a basin and other such needful things. Above the table hung a looking glass—not like the Seer's crystal ball or the glass Ulla stole from Tyë, but a piece of glass crafted to reflect an image. It held no magic, although such things were rare enough in the Far Northern Land. When Ulla first saw such a glass in the Keep in Etelamaa and first saw herself clearly, it amazed her. Of course, no such glass existed in Grankulta or anywhere in the north. Ulla had only seen her reflection in pools of clear water or on a lake's untroubled surface, like any village child. In the Far Northern Land, one's appearance was known by what others said. It still made Ulla uncomfortable to look in such glasses; she thought herself very ugly and half feared the glass might trap her soul. But in Etelamaa and Tavastia, such things were prized by the wealthy.

Now light came from the looking glass. Ulla approached it slowly, shivering a little in the chill air, then stood before it. But she did not see her own reflection looking back at her. Another face filled the glass: cold, white, and flawless, as if carved out of stone save for ruby red lips. Ulla knew the face, had seen it before: Löhi.

Her eyes darted to her staff in the corner. She thought to grab it, to defend herself, magnifying her magical power. Yet Ulla sensed that this was no *etiänen* and that it had no power to harm her. As she stared at the image, transfixed, the Witch's blank eyes came to life.

"Ah, so I've found you at last," said the Witch's voice, distant as an echo, yet in a strange sense terribly present and clear. "I've been seeking you for a long time, Ulla of the Karhulaiset. All through the winter I've watched for you. Did you hide in Karelia with Väinämöinen? And now . . . yes, now you are . . . in Tapiola, are you not? The White City. Still riding with Väinämöinen? On your way back to the Singing Valley?"

Ulla, wiser now, knew not to answer the Witch's questions. Löhi sought information, from Ulla or from any lie she detected in Ulla's voice. Instead of answering, she questioned Löhi in turn.

"Where are you?" asked Ulla. "And by what magic can you so appear?"

Löhi's face shifted and smiled, her cold, metallic laughter ringing out.

"You would question me? Very good. I have nothing to hide from you. I don't wish to harm you at all, only speak with you. I am not so near, yet not so far, Ulla. Does this answer your question? And my magic can do many things. No, Ulla, I do not wish to harm you. Will you not come to me?"

"You do not seek to harm me? Do you think me a fool? You tried to kill me in the wood with no colors."

"No! Unless you believe that Väinämöinen, too, tried to kill you. You hunted *karhu* as a test of strength—and you passed the test, did you not? And both Väinämöinen and I knew that you surely would."

The white light from the looking glass grew brighter, illuminating the chamber. The Witch's face grew terribly clear.

"You are a *tietäjää* now," said Löhi. "Your power waxes strong. I was right in choosing you. Together we may yet stop this war, this senseless killing. How many more need to die without reason? Listen to me, Ulla! Do you know a rocky hill, a few hours ride east of Tapiola? *Kiurunmäki*, the Lark Hill, they call it now in Tavastia. Go there tomorrow as the sun westers; my servant will meet you and bring you to me. These things can be done by those with power.

"Then we may talk, you and I. I will show you wisdom and strength, Ulla. Power and possibility."

"I will never come to you," said Ulla. "What could you possibly show me? Your time grows short. Your season is at an end. All the Seven Clans stand as one against you. Leave us alone and go back to Pohjola! That is your dominion, not the lands of living folk!"

"My dominion is the Far Northern Land," the Witch said more sharply, her cold voice resonating in the room's still air. "The Far Northern Land and all the world under Ukko. I am his vehicle and vessel, as you, too, were meant to be.

"And what can I show you, Ulla? Many things—chief among them, perhaps, how to protect those whom you love and cherish. Is that not your heart's desire, child of the north? Will you not come to me?"

The girl with dark hair stepped back from the ghostly face in the glass. Taking a silver cup from the stand, she hurled it with all her might, shattering the looking glass into a thousand pieces.

CHAPTER FOURTEEN

THE LEAGUE OF THE SEVEN CLANS

Summer was passing when Turi the Changer returned to the Singing Valley.

"What did he have to say for himself?" asked Väinämöinen without looking up as Turi walked into the smoky hall. The old man sat beside a low fire, winding a string of fine sinew on his kantele.

Turi stooped, taking a pull on a pot of birchbark liquor that sat at the wizard's feet.

"When did Ilmarinen ever have much to say?" answered Turi. "He was grim as always, and dour. Only when he spoke of the Sampo did his eyes light up with a bit of the old fire. He has joined the Seven Shards together into a golden lid like a shield. I saw it. And he melts it and remakes it every day. The spell will be finished by fall, then cast in winter's gloom. By spring, the New Sampo will leave the forge."

"Spring then?" sighed Väinämöinen. "Well and good. At least it will be ready for Egan's crowning on Midsummer's Day."

"The Smiths of Seppälä have been busy while Ilmarinen gazes into the fire," continued Turi. "I left the town with a train of spears bound for Deep Länsimaa. Spear, sword, and shield—they have forged enough to fill a great armory this summer. But I heard no rumors among the people, no talk of any march to Sumuvuori nor of the Sampo. The secrets stay secret still."

"That's better," said Väinämöinen, brightening somewhat. "They need stay secret but a little longer. I was up at Kyöpelinvuori last week with old Mechtil; she'll want news of Ilmarinen. But it can wait a bit," he added, offering the pot again to Turi.

With Turi's return, the Erilaiset were ready to leave the Singing Valley and join the companies of the Seven Clans gathering in the north. Few mortals had come to the Valley of late to learn the songs; indeed, only four had come to Laulavalaakso that past spring. Of these, one had grown impatient and left the Valley, going instead to Kyöpelinvuori where he entered the service of the Seer. But one boy, at least, showed promise. A young Hirvilainen from the the west of Deep Lansimää where few now dwelt, he had arrived in the Valley just after Egan slew the dragon. Unlettered, he knew nothing of magic, battle, or the wider world around him, but once taught, he remembered all and thirsted for more. He had a natural affinity with earth, wind, and water, and could feel the spirit of all living things. His folk called him Kaukomieli—*Farmind* in the tongue of the clans, after an old hero from legends and tales—and the name fit him. Väinämöinen spent many long summer days with him, then sent Ulla to teach him songs and the ways of a *tietäjää*.

For the first time, the war seriously affected lands near Laulavalaakso and Kyöpelinvuori. The Tavastian crown called on all able men to join its levees as soldiers, drivers, carters, and such; few were excepted. Half the serfs on the Seer's land went. All the women and children, except for the oldest and youngest, worked the harvest, doing their share of what the men would have done. The king's officers came from Tapiola and organized the menfolk into groups, sending them here and there as need called. A dozen worked the road to Tapiola; another dozen marched eastward to the great encampment in the Neck of Tavastia; and ten or so, the strongest and most hardy, who had fought along the Marches before, donned arms and mail to rejoin their companies, marching in the ranks of the Tavastian men-at-arms. The serfs paid a tax as well, yielding some of their store of rye flour and cattle to be driven away north toward High Länsimaa.

As all made preparations in the lands about, one day Ulla and Unaja went and sat on the seidi-stone. The friendly sun shone down all around them, blessing the green leaves with its warmth and commanding all living things to grow. The seidi-stone itself felt cool; it always felt cold to the touch, in warm and cold weather alike. The spirit trapped inside had been restless throughout the summer. The two young women sat on the strange grey stone, swinging their sunbaked bare feet back and forth while squirrels ran about beneath them, looking for all the world like two village girls off in the woods alone.

When not with Siria or instructing Kaukomieli and the other novices, Ulla spent most of her time with Unaja. Her strength continued to grow. She knew the songs of the seasons and all the magic spells any *tietäjää* must know. Ulla knew where iron came from, where *karhu* was born, and where the stars were kindled; she knew how fire first sparked, where the rye seed came from, and whence the barley seed sprang. She could strike a fire with a word, flint or no, and banish a fever from a sickly child. She could enchant mortal and Erilainen alike or bind an enemy with unseen cords that only the strongest magic-user might escape. She worked all spells save the change-spell and a few others that Väinämöinen would not teach her, since they came from the dark magic of Pohjola. He felt her too young to be burdened with the Witch's *kalma*, the opposite of the *loitsu* of the Erilaiset. But in all the rest, Ulla had become as strong as any Erilainen.

Unaja had grown stronger, too. Wise and far-seeing, a *tietäjää* after the manner of wizards of old who went on perilous quests or fought great beasts, she crafted her own songs and spells. Väinämöinen and Turi, well-pleased with the golden-haired Susilainen, smiled when they heard her sing. They had planned to send her to Mielikki that summer to learn prophecy and the deep understanding that only Tapio's daughter might teach. Unaja knew of the Great League, though, and the plans to march on their enemy's camp. She refused to go to the Enchanted Valley if it meant missing the coming battle and leaving her friends. So Tulikki left for the Valley alone, and Unaja stayed with Väinämöinen and waited, just like Ulla.

"Where is your cousin today?" asked Unaja in her peculiar western dialect.

"With the bakers," Ulla answered. "It seems to be the one thing she really enjoys."

Siria lived with Ulla now in the little *pirtii* on the hillside. Sharp and quick-witted like her older cousin, she had swiftly adapted to the dress and customs of the Tavastialaiset around her, though she kept her Karhulaisen accent. She still seemed most comfortable with the common folk who lived nearby, and had made friends with a few girls her own age.

"They are baking loaves of white bread, the kind the Erilaiset favor," Ulla continued. "Dozens and dozens of round loaves for the journey northward. Siria's a good baker now," she added.

"She has grown this summer, has Siria—even as you have," said Unaja with a smile. "I can see you now in her face: her nose and her mouth are like yours. Her limbs are long. These things came to both of you from your grandparents. Tell me, did Siria's mother look like your mother?"

"I don't know," answered Ulla. For some reason, Ulla felt at ease with Unaja and spoke to her without hesitation about things she rarely discussed with anyone else. "My mother was younger than Aunt Päivikki. I remember people saying that. But she died when we were born, my brother and I. I have no memories of her. My father told me that her eyes were green like mine. I don't remember anything else."

"Ah, yes," sighed Unaja. "You were only a baby; that is right. Alas, many lose their mothers young in the Far Northern Land. And did your brother look like you?"

Ulla paused for a moment. "I suppose so. They said we were twins. He came first and they thought it was over, then suddenly I was there. Little Janni had green eyes, too. Dark hair and green eyes."

"Madness or magic," said Unaja. "So they say in western Akkala about green eyes. You have told me many stories about your father but very little of your brother. It's strange that you speak of him so seldom. But perhaps this is painful and I should be silent."

Ulla considered what Unaja said and agreed with her. She seldom mentioned her brother. She thought about her father much more often. Her memories of her father remained sharp and clear, but those of her brother had faded, although she had spent virtually all her days with him until the fateful trip to the Marches. And, while she had kept alive her secret hope that Big Janni would somehow, improbably, return to her one day, she anticipated only his return, not Little Janni's too. Yet she had loved him no less than her father and still did. Even now, she sometimes took out the little wooden figures and looked at them in the dying light of a westering sun: Little Janni and Ulla, the young twins of Janni the Cartwright from Karelia.

"We were very small," said Ulla at last. "And I think, maybe—maybe because we were twins, he is still here with me, a part of me somehow. Not so my father. He is lost, like all the others. I will never see them again."

"But one day you will, Ulla. So will we all—see those whom we have lost. And they were not all lost, were they? Against all odds, you found Siria."

Ulla grinned from ear to ear, so that Unaja laughed. "Yes, I have Siria. That's an amazing thing, isn't it? If only she weren't so bent on becoming Tavastian!"

A horn sounded suddenly in the distance, high and shrill. The Erilaiset called their mortal pupils to the wooden hall.

"How many days until we leave?" asked Ulla.

"I thought to ask you the same," replied Unaja. "Not many now. Four? Five? I think Väinämöinen will tell us tonight. Are you packed?"

"I've been packed for weeks."

"So sure are you that he will let you ride with us?"

"Quite. From the first, even in Tapiola, he included me in all he said and did. Turi has taught me the *kalpaloitsu*, the spell to wield a blade as if it were my own arm and hand."

"That is good, then," said Unaja. "You should go on this march as a *tietä-jää* and the one who bears the Mark of the Clan. But don't talk about the *kalpaloitsu*! Väinämöinen does not wish you to be a fighter. For that reason, he was loath for you to start down the trail for singers."

Ulla felt a chill pass from the seidi-stone to her body, and her shoulder drew tight where the claw mark was.

"I am scared, Unaja," said Ulla suddenly. "I don't know why. Tell me—do you think Egan can really defeat Löhi?"

Unaja narrowed her eyes and stared at the the fair-faced girl with freckles sprinkling her nose. "What did she say to you this time?"

Ulla started. She had told only Väinämöinen about Löhi's ghostly specter in the looking glass, and she had told him only a little. She had said nothing at all to anyone about Egan's last words to her in Tapiola.

"What do you mean?" she exclaimed. "How do you know about—you enchanted me and read my mind while I slept!"

"I have read your mind, alright," said Unaja, "but not while you slept, and only that part you wished me to read. You told me about Löhi's *etiänen* in the woods, and Tulikki told me more. From your hints and half confessions, it was not difficult to know you saw the Witch again in Tapiola and had converse with her. Keep your secrets if you wish! Sometimes it is better so, and if Väinämöinen feels satisfied that you gave nothing away to the old crone, nothing that will harm us, who am I to press? But if you seek solace or counsel, you must meet me halfway."

Then Ulla told her all that happened without hesitation: the apparition in the glass, powerless yet terrible, and Löhi's chilling voice. She even told Unaja now some of her conversation with Egan, though she kept his kiss to herself. Unaja listened intently to all she said, her expression serious, but then, smiling, hugged Ulla so tightly they both almost fell off the seidi-stone.

"My poor little sister," she sighed. "So much seems to depend upon one so young. But you are wise; you did well with this Witch, I think. Something connects you to her, to be sure. How else could she find you, in all the Far

Northern Land—and see you through this glass, even when she did not know that you were in Tapiola? That is powerful magic. She fears you, that is plain enough. Do not go to her!"

"What will happen at this place, this Sumuvuori?" asked Ulla. "You have not answered me. Do you think Egan can really defeat Löhi?"

"He is brave and strong," said Unaja. "He wields a mighty blade. He bears scars on his face since he killed the worm, but courage comes with those scars. Who knows what he may do? But I agree with those who say she will not face him. Why should she, while she still has others to fight for her? Löhi is powerful, wise, and cruel. She fears her own death, though. Perhaps more than any other creature under Ukko's heaven, she fears death. That is what drives her.

"We may destroy her army in this battle or even slay the new captain she sends against us, the Moonface. But I fear she will only escape again and trouble the Far Northern Land for a long time to come."

Ulla lay back on the stone and felt the warm sun on her face.

"Then perhaps I am like her," she said. "I didn't used to be afraid of Löhi or Pohjola . . . or even of dying, really. I feel differently now, and I don't know why. Maybe the Witch's ghost put a spell on me across all the long miles. I do not want this battle to happen."

"You used to seek peace," answered Unaja. "Rest. Safety. A truce with life, at best, not victory. I know it well, indeed I do," she said, shaking her head. "But that has changed now. It is not peace you seek, but happiness. That is a very different thing, a quest full of danger and risk. You may be afraid, Ulla, but is it not more for Egan—or for the two of you together—than for yourself alone? A troubled girl seeking peace has little to lose, but one who sees happiness within her grasp knows both hope and fear, the two sides of the coin."

"You sound like Väinämöinen!" said Ulla, and the golden-haired young woman laughed again.

"Well and good!" Unaja said, imitating his deep voice. "But do not worry overmuch or look too far beyond the task at hand. Let your fear make you cautious and wise, and do not despair! It is the summer of our hope, Ulla. Remember that!"

In fact, only three days passed before Väinämöinen came to Ulla and told her to be ready the next morning. All was finished, and a company of March Wardens approached Kyöpelinvuori from the south. They would set off to High Länsimaa and beyond together.

Ulla had already gathered her small kit: extra clothes and, sewn tightly into a small badger-skin pack, a long, hooded cloak from Karelia, deep red like Väinämöinen's and lined with thick fur to keep out even the most bitter cold. Apart from her staff, she had *Pitkälehti* at her belt, the three teeth she had taken from *karhu*, and the little figures of herself and her brother. She wore the jewel she took from Työ as a talisman around her neck, and in its leather scabbard was *Pohjanpiiki*, Työ's sword, given to her by Egan. That left little enough inside the *pirtii*, for Ulla kept few possessions. Siria was to remain there, angry and disappointed. She wanted to ride with Ulla wherever she went, to the Marches and beyond, but Väinämöinen would not allow it, nor would Ulla risk her cousin's life in any way.

They gathered at daybreak before the hall, Ulla on her black mare named Midnight and Väinämöinen atop his big grey horse. The old man had forked and plaited his beard, and his red travelling cloak hung down to the top of his high yellow boots; *Jääpuikko* was strapped to his saddle. Turi, dressed all in green and with a peaked green hat on his head, sat beside him on a good mount. Unaja sat next to him with Jarko of Karelia and several other Erilaiset and mortals. Indeed, only Satatieto and a handful of others would remain at Laulavalaakso. That place of song and teaching was silent and nearly deserted. They said their farewells, and Satatieto blessed them with words of protection and safety. Ulla kissed her cousin one last time—Siria wept, distraught—and then the little company followed the stream out of the folded valley in the direction of Kyöpelinvuori.

They reached the road just as the March Wardens appeared around the bend, coming from the direction of the bluffs behind. The Wardens emerged from a cloud of dust: two hundred men on horses and ponies with Bergil, Lord Captain of the March Wardens, at their head. Bergil had brought virtually all of the Wardens from the south to meet Ilkka, who was marshaling the companies in High and Deep Länsimaa. The Wardens, clad in their traditional green and brown, went well-armed with swords at their belts and spears on their shoulders. Some wore coats of ring mail over leather jerkins, and round wooden shields hung at their backs. They bore a new device on their banners, however: a white circle on a field of green, the new symbol of the League of the Seven Clans. The Wardens represented the alliance of the Kaamoslaiset well, for they hailed from all the Seven Lands, from Akkala to Karelia, and had pledged oaths to serve all their folk.

Väinämöinen turned to his little group. "Remember that these men believe they go to the forts along the Marches. Only Bergil and a few others know the truth. Do not speak of the enemy's camp or our plans. It must remain secret as long as possible and come to Löhi's ears late in the season, if at all."

The long line of Wardens came upon the Erilaiset and halted, and Bergil removed his helmet. He squinted as he faced the rising sun in the east.

"Hail, Väinämöinen!" he cried. "Punctual as always!"

"Did you expect anything less?" said the old man, bowing. "But you are dusty and travel-stained as if coming from the Marches, not riding through the farmlands of Tavastia."

"It is dry this year," answered Bergil. "A poor harvest in these parts, perhaps. But one challenge at a time. Are all your folk here?"

"Aye," said Väinämöinen. "All from Laulavalaakso. The Seer's people await us further down the road at the tower."

"Then let's ride!" said Bergil. "Though fair and cool now, it will turn hot as the sun climbs higher."

They reached Kyöpelinvuori after a short ride of maybe an hour. Ulla had not seen the Seer for several weeks, having avoided the old woman though she knew the mortal witch desired to speak with her alone before she left. Now, as they came under the shadow of the old mottled tower on the hill,

Ulla saw that the Seer had come down and stood upon an outcropping of grey stone just above the road. Siitsa and Kilia stood beside her. Waiting in the road were two riders, the Tornilaiset whom the Seer would send to battle: Maanavilja, second only to Siitsa and a powerful sorcerer, and his companion. Siitsa would remain with the Seer at Kyöpelinvuori.

They stopped just below her perch; Väinämöinen's horse reared and whinnied. The old woman, clad in dark robes, looked down at them and raised her short black staff. Ulla could see the glint of her eyes in her bone-white face and bloodless, pursed lips.

"All the news is good, Väinämöinen," she called. "The summer raids of the Easterners were beaten back. Ride now to battle! Go forth and defeat our enemy! And return in victory to the new glory of the Seven Clans!"

Starchaser reared again; Väinämöinen took up a horn from his saddle, and, putting it to his lips, he let out a great blast that echoed throughout all the lands about Kyöpelinvuori and beyond.

***

All things now ran swiftly toward their appointed end.

Throughout the summer, the chiefs and lords of the Seven Clans had gathered as many men as they could. They had sent great stores of rye and barley to Keskimaa and Gamla. Brick ovens built there could bake a hundred dark round loaves at a time. Women and children took the place of fathers, sons, and brothers in the fields or with nets and traps in lake and forest. Horses were sent north, too, paid for with gold and silver in Etelamaa and Tavastia or levied as taxes in Akkala. The smiths in Seppälä and across the Seven Lands busily forged swords and spears, helmets and shields, arrowheads of steel to pierce the thickest leather, and many other things a great army needed. Despite all this, the clan folk did not know what awaited them.

For the plan to work, trapping Löhi's servants in their winter camp unawares, the Witch could not guess their design too early. So the leaders of the Seven Clans spread rumors that they believed the Witch would make a final attack as her strength lessened. Her mighty strike would come late in the season somewhere along the Marches, to finally destroy High Länsimaa and take it for her own. So it was that they gathered their own great army in the guise of manning new forts being built for the Kaamoslaiset to weather this coming storm, and few were the wiser.

Indeed, Egan and all the other leaders feared more than anything that this rumor might prove true. As the army of the League of the Seven Clans formed, they spared few men to guard the Marches and fight the summer's battles. The March Wardens stayed in their hill forts, and the Bear and Elk Folk stayed on guard as they always were, but few men from Tavastia and Etelamaa joined them. If Löhi had launched all her forces south for a great invasion, she might well have overrun all of Länsimaa before help arrived, but the leaders of the Seven Clans accepted that risk.

But she did not invade. The small summer raids, meant to harass and plunder but not conquer, told the chiefs and captains that the Witch's power diminished. Predictably, Löhi's servants marched on the old North Road that ended in the wastes, a road now called The Gate since they so often came that way. Bands of Itäläiset harried the Wardens and others came down east of Suurijärvi, burning the few small villages that remained there but avoiding pitched battles and fleeing when the Karhulaiset fought back. Only to Karelia did a larger force come, some five hundred riders, well-armed and fell-handed.

The Easterners crossed the Jouksi and swept down upon Metsäposti, even as the Karelialaiset gathered men for the League. The people followed Väinämöinen's advice and fled into the forest, leaving almost all their goods behind. The Easterners defeated the small band of Karelian warriors who tried to stop them, slaying them almost to a man, then rode straight away to Metsäposti, looting at will, taking whatever slaves they could capture, then burning most of the town to the ground. But they did not push on. While the embers still smoldered, they turned back north, pillaging a few small villages and farms they had bypassed, then disappearing as swiftly as they had come.

Many died among the Reindeer Folk, hitherto largely spared attack and assault. But the attack still fell far short of their worst fears. The Seven Clans had survived the summer—and now it was their turn to strike.

And this is the plan that was decided on by Egan and the other chiefs. It would do less good to march on Löhi's camp in the summer or early fall, for their enemies might flee to other places, even to Pohjola or the lands to the east, suffering little loss even if their camp burned behind them. Or Löhi might have time to summon new forces and make the battle more terrible, its outcome unsure. Instead they decided to march late in the season, after harvest and just before the winter snows began.

Then their enemies would face a hard choice. They would have to do battle, even if outnumbered, or else flee into barren lands at the worst of times, with the plants failing, game scarce, and food and shelter hard to come by. The cold north wind would freeze them, and before they could reach Pohjola or their own lands, snow and ice might catch them in the wild. They would lose many horses, a great loss impossible to recover. Only the goblins might not fear the northern wastes in winter, for they made light of the cold and endured when mortal men and beasts perished. But an army of mortal men would fare ill in the wastes in winter.

Ulla and Väinämöinen rode with the Wardens now across the Neck of Tavastia, taking little-used paths and veering south. A few days after they left Kyöpelinvuori, the old man told Ulla to follow him while the others rested their horses beside a little lake. Turi and Unaja went with them.

They rode a ways, came over a rise, and reined their horses. A broad green field dotted with stands of tall pines spread out before them; thicker woods grew some miles to the northwest. Sedgegrass and wildflowers swayed in the southerly breeze, bringing a rustling music to their ears, accompanied by the buzz of insects and birdsong. Peace filled that place, a peace as idyllic as any in the morning of the world long ago, when the first men and women of the

Seven Clans had found hope and plenty in the Far Northern Land. On a hillock to the east, however, stood an old rust-colored tower built of piled stones and brick. Unlike the straight, narrow old tower at Kyöpelinvuori, built so as to survey all the surrounding lands, this was shorter and squat, a round war tower built to defend a strong place, with few windows and an irregular parapet on top. Dark stonecrop stained the tower's red stones. The wall and parapet on one side had crumbled, exposing the ruined interior to the winds and rain and making it the abode of birds and beasts. Black ravens now lived there, nesting in rocky cracks and fissures or perching amidst the rubble.

"That is Taistelukenttä, the field where the Great Battle was fought," said Väinämöinen. He sighed.

Ulla had never seen it before, even though it lay close to the Valley. She remembered that that old wizard had taken Egan there once years before.

"Can you feel it?" asked Turi quietly. "The power . . . the strength. So many lie beneath the flowers and grass. So many . . ." And then, with a rush as of cold water unexpectedly thrown on her face, she felt it: the spirits of the dead, the shades of their passing, almost she perceived them as thousands of voices echoing dimly from the distant past. Midnight stirred beneath her, troubled by the ghostly vision.

"I stood on those walls," said Väinämöinen, pointing to the rusty tower. "The walls of Tavanlinna, the old castle. Late in the day, as the sun sank in the west, our foes made one last attempt to take the tower. But the king came from those woods yonder, where our last strength lay hidden. He marched straight to that rise, cutting through our foes. There stands the Witch's Knoll, where he besieged her and threw her down. I was too late . . . too late. So Löhi passed for that time, and Lemminkäinen with her. The world was never the same again."

For a moment Ulla heard horns blowing and the clash of arms on steel; the harsh cries of men and goblins filled the air. Then a gust from the south swept the noise before it, and the sun shone again while butterflies chased one another among the blooms.

"The third time pays for all," said Turi.

"So it does," answered Väinämöinen. "So it does."

"Come, let's go!" he cried, pulling Starchaser around. "It must end otherwise this time—and it will!" So they left the battlefield and returned to their companions, though none spoke of what they had seen and felt.

Soon they turned north and rode up through the gap of the *lansikita* into the lands of the Bear Folk. They often encountered groups of men marching north. Once, for several days they traveled with a company of Tavastian pikemen: tall men, one hundred in all, carrying long-hafted spears and halberds, with bronze helms on their heads and breastplates to match. Ulla rode mostly beside Unaja, for Väinämöinen kept quiet, wrapped in his own thoughts, or else talked with the Bergil and Turi. But from time to time he joined her and spoke of battle: how to bind an enemy with a word and ward off his blows, how a wizard might enchant his cloak or armor to turn any shaft or blade, save a very heavy blow indeed.

They passed south of Keskimaa on a cart road, making poor time but seeing few folk, as Väinämöinen desired. The men of the clans traveled in smaller groups to deceive the Witch and her spies and traveled along back ways, but from all across the Far Northern Land they came, even as the first hint of fall crept into the woods and trees, turning the night air cold. At last no back road would suffice. The Wardens came to the White Road and sped north swiftly, passing long lines of Etelalaisen men-at-arms and Karhulaiset with wagon trains of supplies.

When they finally reached Gamla above Lake Suurijärvi, they found no peasants lived in the town any longer. It had become a great camp, and many thousands of men from all the clans gathered there. King Egan Dragonslayer waited there with his brother and captains, and all was nearly ready for the great march to Sumuvuori.

Egan had been in Gamla for some time. After the great council in Tapiola, he returned for a while to Etelamaa, but did not go so far south as the Stone City. He rode to Kotanrannta and gave necessary orders there, sending greetings to his mother, Vendla. Finally, leaving Sinio in charge, he departed again for Keskimaa. There he took counsel with Janottu and Juvari, waiting anxiously as the summer's battles unfolded, ready to drop all their plans and march his men at once to High Länsimaa, if needed. But it had not been necessary, and as summer waned he moved his banner to Gamla, the Wardens' great camp, and began all preparations in earnest. It was at Gamla that an unexpected message reached him from Etelamaa.

Vendla had sent a trusty manservant to Kotanrannta with a private message for the king and his brother: Kirsikka was with child, the baby expected ere winter fell. Egan and Eglano had already left Kotanrannta when the message arrived, and since Egan traveled in near-secrecy, the messenger had only rumors to guide him. He soon heard that the king rode for Tapiola, and, as he carried a confidential message only for the brothers, he set out for Tapiola himself. Thus he went first to Tapiola, then on to Keskimaa, and, after nearly three months journeying, he at last found Egan and Eglano in Gamla.

If the news brought Eglano joy, it made Egan even happier. The king's counselors had opposed Eglano's going to war and leaving only Sampsa as the last male of the House of Joutsen in all the kingdom, since Aldon always fought alongside his cousin. But if Kirsikka gave birth to a boy, the kingdom would have a new heir, even if Egan never married. Egan told his brother to return to the Stone City at once, for he did not wish to risk any ill chance with Kirsikka expecting and the battle looming. When Eglano refused, Egan did not press. He understood his brother's loyalty, valued it, and felt glad to have him by his side. Eglano wrote a letter to Kirsikka, enclosing three spring blossoms from a bird cherry tree, enchanted by a *tietäjää* so that they would never fade but remain forever fresh and fair. The messenger, rested and refreshed, left Gamla on a new horse but did not reach the Stone City until all the great events had come to pass.

Many men already camped at Gamla when Ulla and Väinämöinen arrived, and thousands more came in the days that followed. Their multi-colored flags and banners flew everywhere, planted wherever men pitched their tents or beside the long halls and cabins the Wardens had built. All the accents of the Seven Clans could be heard throughout that place. Egan sought out Ulla the very day she arrived and told her of the coming baby. Kirsikka's news astonished Ulla. She had not seen her friend in more than a year and could hardly believe that the baby would be born before ever she saw her again.

But then he took her aside and looked into her hazel-green eyes, now level with his. "Let us not speak of what the future may hold, but think only of what waits in the hard days before us. It may be that, triumphant or not, we both may fall or suffer grievous harm. But if we triumph and return unscathed, there will be time to consider all things. Remember when things seem darkest that I love you."

And to these words Ulla agreed, and they spoke of it no more, but all that they had said and all that might yet be stayed in her mind and heart.

Väinämöinen spoke mostly with Egan and the other chiefs, since Teemu, Asikkas, and the rest now camped in Gamla with their men. But the old wizard set Ulla a great task, surprising her. She had expected him to leave her alone, as he always had, while he went about his business. Now he told her to take charge of the men who fell sick or were hurt, since in so a large host some always met with unhappy circumstance.

Embarrassed at first and reluctant, Ulla was abashed by the way the men watched her, Hirvilainen and Karelian, Karhulainen and Etelalainen. Perhaps a few of the soldiers, especially among the Tavastialaiset, knew her by sight. Most of that host, though, had no experience with women of power or action. They knew women only as wives, mothers, maids, and servants, unless they glimpsed a lady or princess from afar, dressed in many colors like a cuckoo in a gilded cage.

The soldiers looked askance at the pale, dark-haired *tietäjää*, scarcely come of age, with her staff and long sword, talking and walking as an equal with Väinämöinen, Turi, and the other great lords. They whispered of Väinämöinen's daughter, a half-breed like Lemminkäinen, or else a witch like the Seer of Kyöpelinvuori, but avoided her gaze and spoke seldom to her. When Ulla overcame her fear, as in all else she put her mind to, she swiftly mastered the task at hand. She had Wardens prepare small shelters away from the camp so that the sickness and fevers would not spread. Then she and Unaja worked among the afflicted, using such knowledge and healing magic as they possessed. The men watched, amazed by her skills, and did obeisance to her, and soon it seemed natural to her to command them. And Väinämöinen saw this with pleasure, for he knew she had come into her own as a singer and *tietäjää*.

The fall came early, the leaves soon turned, and the host of the League of the Seven Clans made ready to depart. Ilkka returned from the North Marches, where most of the Wardens waited, and reported that all was ready there. The Erilaiset arrived from Karelia—a small company, only four hundred of Haltiatar, Menninkaiset and other such *väki* who hated Löhi. Then each of the kings and lords went to their folk and spoke to them. For the first time, their leaders explained why such an army had been gathered. For the first time, they learned that they would march on their enemy's camp, though most had long since guessed that great things were afoot. Väinämöinen went with each of the lords to speak of the Sampo on Ilmarinen's forge in Seppälä. He told the men that even as they struck the great blow to their enemies, the Sampo would be remade and raised in spring, and though Löhi's winds might blow and frost might fall, never would she take their lands. The Seven Clans would know peace and prosperity again. The men of the clans were glad then, and hope ran high. They sang about the time to come and made new songs about the heroes among them: Väinämöinen the mighty wizard and Turi the Changer. But most of all they sang about Egan Dragonslayer, the Captain of the League of the Seven Clans. From all the Seven Lands they hailed him as lord and said that indeed, he was the Heir of Lemminkäinen, the spirit of the ancient hero returned to life in mortal form.

The host moved out of Gamla and up the North Road, where it stretched for miles. King Egan rode at the head of the host, with Juvari, his captain, always beside him. Only the Eagle Folk were missing, for Airiki had marched by a different route and would meet the main host at the Warden's north-ernmost camp. The *tietäjää* and Erilaiset wove such spells as they might to dim their enemies' eyes and obscure the army's numbers and nature, but they could not hide the great army from wizardly *sight* or the eyes of scouts and spies, birds and beasts. They did not put their hope in secrecy now, but in speed. Löhi would soon know, if she did not already, what they intended. But the season was late, the days ever shorter, and she would have to decide swiftly whether to meet them in battle or flee.

Every horseman carried two extra packs slung across his mount. One carried bread, hard and dark to last many weeks, and the other carried dried fish. Thus every rider carried food for himself and for another who marched on foot. But the many pack animals and wagons carried still more supplies, and they drove a herd of cattle and sheep before them so the host had no want of provisions. More awaited them in the north as well, with the Wardens and Eagle Folk. But, for all that, they still marched swiftly and with purpose.

Ulla rode with Bergil's company of March Wardens, enjoying the time with her friend Ilkka. Lúven and the Erilaiset of the Enchanted Valley rode near them. They soon came to that part of High Länsimaa where Ulla and her folk had lived, now empty and desolate save for the Wardens or Löhi's spies and servants. In the days after that first great raid, some refugees had returned and tried to rebuild their lives, but they were few and their days were hard. When the Easterners raided again in force, those who survived abandoned their homes at last and fled south. Save for some secretive, wild Karhulaiset hidden deep in the woods, no mortals now dwelt there.

Ulla's heart fluttered as they passed through empty lands where once so much hope and life had thrived. She spied the grass-grown remains of tiny paths and small cart-roads here and there along the main way leading to the ruined villages. One of them led to Grankulta, the tiny village of rye farmers and fishermen among whom she had begun her life. Ilkka, riding beside her, read her thought. When they had ridden a little apart from any others, he asked her in a grave voice, "Do you wish to know?"

Ulla, startled, looked at him—and understood. Of all people on earth, only Ilkka and Väinämöinen might remember where Grankulta once lay and which half-hidden path might lead to it. But the girl with dark hair answered without hesitation, "No."

Soon they came to the border of High Länsimaa and the end of the lands of the Seven Clans, now called The Gate. The March Wardens had made a fort there: a small hill fort, solidly built, with food stores, cattle pens, and shelter for many men against the onset of winter. They had built two others much like it elsewhere, similarly stocked. The forts would resupply the host as needed or men might find food, shelter, rest, and protection from their enemies there in defeat. Väinämöinen and Ilkka had planned their construction and also ordered that the foundation for a huge stone building be laid nearby as a ruse, as if they meant to build a tower or keep. Airiki met them at The Gate. He embraced Egan, laughing, when he saw the size of the host. He was eager for battle and felt sure that a force this strong could not be defeated.

"Never have I seen such an army," he marvelled. "I had four thousand men behind me from all my father's homelands when I defeated Torvald at the Battle of Niemi, and I thought I would never see a greater force! But surely this League rivals even those in the old tales."

Despite Airiki's wonder, the chiefs of the Seven Clans did not march with all their strength. They left men in Länsimaa to guard against any foray by the Witch. None believed a winter attack likely, but they still took thought to protect the lands behind them. A Hirvilaisen force, chiefly horsemen, remained in the north of Deep Länsimaa to cover Valkeakosk and the approaches to Siinesaare. Four hundred men, Bear Folk and Wardens, defended a strong place in the west of High Länsimaa, and another two hundred Wardens would remain at The Gate, manning the hill forts. But no more did they spare from the great adventure.

The Kaamoslaiset rested and tended to their weary horses. They left some cattle in the pens and slaughtered others to have enough meat for several days. They remained only two days at the fort, however, for Egan and Väinämöinen wished to push on. The success of their plan depended upon speed as much as chance. They crossed the border into the wastes, the companies of marching men first and the mounted men behind with the baggage train. The North Road continued for a while, then dwindled; as soon as they had left their own lands, they could feel the Witch's power, for her thought had been heavy on those parts for many years. That could not readily be dispelled.

Through the wastes of Suonpää they passed, near where Turi had found Työ and the Army of Pohjola years before. Scouts who knew the area led them through marshes and lakes, always finding firm footing for man and beast. In places they saw signs of their enemy: trees felled and paths cut through the woods by the Easterners and, at one place, a ford built of earth and logs to make passage across a swift stream. They traveled slowly through the wilderness, but never an enemy did they see. The wind turned colder, blowing from the north out of a slate-grey sky that threatened snow.

When the northern sky cleared and they could see over the treetops, men noticed that the fiery star was gone. All summer it had traveled from east to west, climbing higher until, when fall came, it seemed to dive as if their march outpaced it. Now, as they crossed the North Marches, it disappeared altogether, lighting still the sky, perhaps, in gentle southern lands, but lost to wanderers in the bitter northern wastes where Löhi's voice sang on the wind.

Three by three and Taivaantappi to guide you, the elvish scout had said in Tapiola, and so it was. The host forded the three rivers easily, but not so the lakes. The first lake they came to could not be skirted. The great lake, deep and blue, ran north-south, as did many northern lakes. Its southern end spilled down through thick woods into a swift river. The northern end petered out into marsh where horses could find no footing, a tangled wilderness where men could not go without becoming scattered and lost. The broad, deep lake lay right in the way of their march, yet the Pohjolaiset clearly had come this way, for signs of their cuttings and passings were everywhere.

No one knew how Löhi's servants crossed the deep water. The scouts could find no boats, and horses could not swim so far. If Löhi's magic had grown so strong that she could weave a spell for her armies to pass as if on a frozen solid lake, then her magic was great indeed. But the men of the Seven Clans were resourceful, and Egan himself had come up with their plan.

Many of their horses pulled sleds across the sedge; some pulled long wooden planks behind them. These planks, enchanted by the heroes, when joined together by woodcraft and magic, made great flat-bottomed ferries pushed and steered by long poles. A hundred men might cross on one ferry and still it would not sink, or many horses with packs of food and supplies. Seven such ferries they made now, and in them the host of the Seven Clans passed over the lake and gained the other side. It took all of one day and most of the next ere all had crossed the broad lake; and they slaughtered the last of the cattle, since the animals could not take to the boats nor move through the more difficult terrain on the other side.

Deep into the wilds they had passed, deeper than any army of mortal men had ever gone, and still they found no enemies. Then Väinämöinen called Ulla to the gathered lords and captains and, for the first time, asked her to use her glass.

"Many wizards and singers are with us," he said, "some of the most powerful in the Far Northern Land. But, as you know, dark enchantments have been set about these woods and no wizardly *sight* will avail us. Even I can see little. Maybe Löhi herself makes these spells to trouble us; maybe her sorcerers and servants do. Little does it matter. It could be that our enemies will set a trap and ambush us unawares as we approach their camp. I would do so in their place. Take your jewel, child, the jewel that you stole from Tyë to his ruin, and gaze upon it. Pierce this darkness and warn us if danger awaits."

"But why don't you take it?" she asked. "Your *sight* is stronger than anyone's."

"No," replied the old man. "The jewel is yours, and you are attuned with it now. It is your talisman. You are strong, Ulla. If your will does not prevail, none other can."

Then Ulla went into the little *maja* that she used and took the jewel from around her neck. She had seldom used it since the Battle of Linnavuori; now she felt a heavy weariness settle on her as she stared at its smooth, pale pink surface in the dim light. She pushed her mind and will into it as only a wizard could. She saw their camp in its reflection and the woods around them; then all went dark as she encountered the webs of their enemies. Ulla pushed on, summoning all her strength, like a woman in deep water struggling to hold her breath until she surfaces. Just when it seemed she could go no farther, she broke through. She could breathe again, the glass cleared, and, with her mind's eye, she espied all the lands about with a special *sight*. Deer ran free. Squirrels scampered from tree to tree. Woodpeckers knocked. But she saw no goblins, no creeping evil things, no men in Löhi's service lying in wait. Nothing moved in the woods for miles about. Then the vision failed and the jewel went dark, for, though it gave clear *sight*, it could not see far from its bearer. She could not see all the way to the camp of their enemies, but, for now, the way seemed clear, so they moved on, warily, deeper into the wilds.

After two days, the host came to the second lake that they could not go around. Again they used the ferries. They passed over this lake, not so broad as the other, more quickly, although they lost some horses and men in the crossing. Väinämöinen called upon Ulla for the second time to use her glass—still the way looked clear.

At last they reached the third lake, dark and cold, with two pine-covered islets in its midst. They guided the ferries between the islets, carrying the men and horses across the lake. At Egan's command, they left most of their supplies on one isle and the carters, porters, and some few guards on the other. When the last of the army had crossed the lake, the guards poled the ferries to the island. The army neared their journey's end and needed no large store of supplies in battle.

Now only two days' march from Sumuvuori, the host of the Seven Clans felt the forest close in around them; songs that sounded hopeful under bright sunlight in Gamla now seemed doubtful in the cold, darkling woods. A clear path lay before them, a well-trodden path made for horses. They found many small boats and other signs of their enemies on the third lake's far shore. They knew that eyes watched them from all sides, though they saw no one. Then Egan and Väinämöinen summoned special scouts to them: Sá of Lúven's folk, and Asper, and several others besides. They called twenty scouts altogether, ten Haltiatar and ten mortals—Wardens and Karelialaiset. They charged the scouts with going before the host, spying on the enemy's camp, and bringing back news to the lords and chiefs, for they still did not know what awaited them at Sumuvuori: an enemy prepared to fight, or an abandoned camp.

The men of the clans, wary and on less certain ground, marched slowly now. Yet as the dawn broke the next day, they took heart. The sky cleared and the pale sun shone down through the trees. The threat of snow retreated, and with it a great danger. A heavy snowfall might imperil all their plans and make battle hard, even threaten their lives. They hoped for their enemies to be caught in the wastes without shelter when winter came, but winter could not come too soon, lest it imperil their own plans.

They followed a broad path cutting through a thin pinewood, still fragrant even in the cold. Frequent trails branched off from the main way, but they had no doubt where their objective lay. When the pinewood failed, the ground opened up and they found two cleared fields before them, separated by a rocky river, broad but fordable. That river was indeed the Kivikoinenvirta, the Rocky Run, which came down a narrow defile past Sumuvuori where the sparkling waterfall cascaded from the hanging valley. In those two fields, the host of the League of the Seven Clans made its last camp. They pitched tents, built shelters, and picketed the horses in the sedge grass.

Then Egan called all the captains and lords to his tent for a final council. Väinämöinen and Unaja, with their strong *sight*, bent all their power upon the enemy. Though so close to Sumuvuori, they saw little. Magical, wizardly nets lay over the land, and they could not tell how many enemies awaited them.

"I do not feel Löhi's presence," said Väinämöinen. "But the Witch has many servants. Pohjola is filled with Dark Erilaiset, in whom the old magic runs strong. Perhaps a great sorcerer, perhaps this Moonface, weaves the spiders' webs that cloud our vision. Come, Ulla, and tell us what you see. Our food will not last, and we must strike now or else our strength will fade."

For the third time, Ulla looked into the jewel, and straightaway she pierced the gloom, for they drew near the camp of their foe.

"They have not fled," she said when her awareness returned. "Hiisia and other evil things fill the woods. I turned my *sight* toward Sumuvuori and descried our enemies. I saw several thousands there, men mostly, and almost as many horses, but the Easterners do not have our numbers. And I saw the Moonface, who leads them. He rides a black steed and oversees all things as he would for their defense. Most of the men seem to have crossed the Rocky Run from the great camp in the falls' shadow, but I saw others struggling with carts and sleds as if preparing to leave."

"So it is," said Sá. "We saw the same thing from a distance before we fled from the goblins. It seems they propose to make a stand in the meadow and fields south of the river, an open space where their cavalry may be used more readily."

"Then we have them!" cried Airiki. "They have taken the bait and stayed too long in the trap. Now it is too late to flee! Let winter come on now, for it will be their death in the wild after we have won the field!"

"So it seems," said Egan. As excited as Airiki, he struggled to contain his emotion. "But no field can be so broad in these tangled wastes as to allow us to easily flank horsemen. What do you make of this, Juvari?"

All regarded Juvari, Captain of Etelamaa, as the chief among all the captains. He had won more battles than any other mortal alive and knew the strengths and weaknesses of the Itäläiset like no other. They turned to him now, and he fingered a long, Itäläisen dagger, jewel-encrusted, when he spoke.

"It will be a hard fight," he said. "King Egan speaks truthfully. They may block our numbers with a stand between the river and the woods and have no flank for us to turn. But King Airiki speaks truly, too, for when we break them, they are trapped. They can only flee into the wastes or die upon the field. No retreat is possible."

"If only we had more horsemen," said Asikkas. "Such has ever been our want in battles with the Easterners. Let us hope the pikemen prevail, as we have long prepared."

"What is your counsel, Juvari?" asked Egan. "Tell us now your mind." Juvari did not hesitate.

"Let us steel ourselves to meet them head on, pushing with all our strength straight to their camp. And let us march south of the Rocky Run, not through the narrow defile, which may be long held against us."

Then they all agreed to the plan and parted with gestures of goodwill and good luck before returning to their own folk to prepare for the coming day. But Väinämöinen and Turi remained behind and, with them, Ulla and Unaja. Eglano, too, stayed with his brother.

Egan and Väinämöinen looked each other in the eye for a long while. Then Egan smiled.

"So at last it comes to this, Väinämöinen," said the king. "All the years, all the battles may end with our victory, if luck is with us tomorrow and if it be Ukko's will."

"*Fortune favors the bold*," said Väinämöinen.

"And come what may," said Turi, "Ukko All-father will always look down in kindness upon the children of the Far Northern Land, whether we glimpse his design or no."

Egan nodded. "Will you ride beside me tomorrow, Väinämöinen?" he said. "I will need your strength and wisdom."

"I will always be at your side, my king," said the old man. "And my own folk are here, too, the Erilaiset of the Valley. Small though our company may be, they will stand with you. Together, we will never fall."

Egan embraced the old man and all the others in turn, one by one, and so they departed, until only Ulla remained, standing by the pole on which hung the king's mantle and armor. Few words had passed between them on that march save for counsels of war and battle, but now they regarded one another in the yellow candlelight.

Then Egan took Ulla into his arms and held her tight, brushing away the tangle of long, dark hair from her pale face.

And he said, "Tomorrow comes the morning of our hope. And if fate does not cheat us, I will take thee unto me and cleave to thee. And all our folk shall truly know thee as the sign of their peace and content."

But Ulla answered, "And what of Löhi?"

"Väinämöinen says that she is not here. What is thy belief?"

"I cannot sense her as he, the eldest hero, does. Yet, here or not, no power can withstand thee, Heir of Lemminkäinen. That is my belief."

The he kissed her and she clung to him; but after a while, without another word, she went away to sleep, for using the jewel wearied her. And Unaja awaited her outside, yet Ulla met his eyes one last time as she slipped away into the darkness.

Egan called his brother to him then and spoke for a while, instructing Eglano on the coming day. When Eglano retired to rest, Egan took a dark cloak and wrapped it all about him. He slipped out the back of his tent without his servants or guards being aware and walked down into the great camp where thousands of men awaited the morn.

Campfires and lights twinkled all about, like *Kekri* in the Stone City. Some men slept and others stood guard, but many sat around the fires, talking among themselves or singing songs from all the Seven Lands. Egan the king went down among them, wrapped in the cloak so that none knew him. He crept into a wide circle of soldiers, staying just outside of the fire's glow in the shadows. He sat among the Swan Folk, his people and the men of his homelands, and listened to their tales and songs by the firelight. In the clear sky above, amidst all the gathered stars, Taivaantappi shone white and bright while her companions wheeled around her, hurrying on their way. So Egan sat beneath the North Star as the night slowly passed, and he sat there still when the pale dawn stretched its fingers up from the rim of the world toward the heavens.

***

Siitsa waited a long while inside the Silver Gate of the Smiths' Guildhall in Seppälä for Hanmoku to return. The Guild guards in their fine mail looked askance at the woman dressed in long black robes, hooded, with a golden talisman that she frequently fingered: a mortal witch from Kyöpelinvuori, they thought. She had arrived unexpectedly, bearing a message from the Seer for the Master—the True Master, she said—and stressed its urgency. The Seers of Kyöpelinvuori seldom had dealings with the smiths, although from time to time over the years a special order reached the hall. After Väinämöinen brought the Seven Shards to Seppälä, the Seer sent a single, simple message of greeting to Ilmarinen, along with a gift, a silver brooch of exquisite craftsmanship, wrought like the shape of the great fish in the Itämeri Sea. And indeed Ilmarinen had made that brooch long years ago before Löhi's first return and before the Sampo was ever forged.

When Hanmoku came back to the Silver Gate, he bowed low.

"You are welcome, mistress," said the one-eyed man. "The Master is within, at his forge. Come with me now, and I shall take you to him."

Hanmoku led Siitsa through the Guildhall past the many smithies and courts, but the silent young woman hardly noticed them. She stared at the ground, lips pursed, as if intent on her own thoughts or the message she would deliver. But if she wondered how to politely request to speak with Ilmarinen alone, she need not have bothered. The Great Forge was empty save for Ilmarinen himself. Hanmoku bowed again and left them alone.

Siitsa looked around in wonder, with the wide eyes of a child, marveling at the mighty bellows, the great pit, and the round room with its high, narrow windows. But the bellows were silent, the hall darkened. Only red coals burned in the pit, casting an otherworldly light. The red light fell on something that sat on a stone block beside the anvil—a great shield or lid, it seemed, and it glowed with a cool radiance all its own. And at that moment Ilmarinen stepped toward her from the gloom.

"I am the master of this place," said the tall Erilainen in his deep voice. "You came here seeking me. Tell me, girl, what message do you bear from the Seer of Kyöpelinvuori?" He stood before her with his gloved hands and arms crossed over his apron-covered chest.

Siitsa hesitated for a moment, then spoke at last, her voice proud, though it quivered.

"My mistress sends her greetings, Lord Ilmarinen," she said. "I am Siitsa, her handmaiden. And she would know when this great thing, the Sampo, will be made ready, for it is long now since Väinämöinen brought news of its forging to Tapiola."

"Is that all?" asked Ilmarinen. "She asks a question of me but has no news in return? I had hoped, Siitsa Handmaiden, that perhaps you bore tidings, good tidings, from the north. It is cold outside. Fall passes into winter. Months have passed since the Tavastialaiset marched away, marched north, to join this great League of the clans. Surely they must have done battle by now if Löhi did not flee. But I have heard nothing here, no news and no reports. And there is little for us to do. There is no rock; we have used it all on spears and swords, and no new trains come south."

"Perhaps no news is good news," replied Siitsa. "But I do not know. There is no word yet from the League, and little wonder, since they have left their own lands and entered Löhi's domain. Perhaps few will return from the wastes. If so, then your work shall be all the more important."

"Your faith in your folk is impressive," answered Ilmarinen. "Are those your thoughts or the Seer's?"

He turned without waiting for her answer and stepped back up to the anvil. Siitsa followed, stopping beside the glowing lid, in which she could now, at close quarters, see her own reflection. The smith watched her glittering eyes.

"Yes," he said. "That is it. I have joined the Shards and folded the magic lid. The spell is ready and will soon be cast. And when at last it comes out of the fire, it will be strong, strong and tall: a mighty Sampo to raise on

Tapiola's Hill, much to the Witch's dismay. But, for my part, I do not doubt that Väinämöinen and the young king will return. Löhi will not face them. I deem her fate lies elsewhere."

"And how do you know that?" asked Siitsa. "The Seer has her crystal ball. She can see many things, can read many fortunes by looking within it. Do the fires of your forge tell you the future? Does the Sampo have the power of prophecy?"

Siitsa reached out her hand to touch the shiny object but quickly drew it back, for though it was cold, she could indeed feel its power.

"Are they all—all of the Seven Shards, I mean—blended in this one thing?"

"They are seven no longer," said Ilmarinen, "Only one. But you have many questions for a messenger. Is that all your errand? Have you nothing more?"

"There is this. My mistress offers her help, if you desire it, to finish your task as soon as possible."

Then Ilmarinen laughed, a deep, rich laugh that boomed throughout the hall. When he stopped, he shook his great head and frowned. He had taken a dislike to this strange girl from Kyöpelinvuori.

"Does she?" he replied coldly. "Does she indeed? And how does she purpose to help me? Tell your mistress what you have heard here: the Sampo will be finished soon and raised at Midsummer's Day. But I do not need the help of Kyöpelinvuori."

He turned as if to dismiss her, stooping to pick up his silver hammer, which lay beside the pit. But Siitsa said, "Oh, I will certainly tell her."

From beneath her dark robes she drew a long knife. The jagged blade had saw-like teeth and evil runes from Pohjola engraved upon it; it was poisoned and enchanted with doom and ruin for the Erilaiset. Long had been its making in the fiery forges of Sariola, and Löhi herself had crafted the evil spell that bound it. Now Siitsa, with a gasp, stepped quickly aside and thrust the knife at Ilmarinen with all her strength, burying the blade to the hilt in the Master Smith's belly.

"Thus she purposes to help you!" cried Siitsa. Ilmarinen staggered and sank to his knees, and their blue eyes met. The hammer slipped from his hand and fell to the ground, its ringing echoing throughout the forge. But the smith reached out and seized the girl by the shoulders.

"Why have you done this?" he coughed, as red blood flowed from his mouth and his face twisted in pain. "Why have you done this?"

But Siitsa released the knife and pushed him away with a savage kick. Her hands shook and her eyes were wild, but she took up the Sampo from beside the anvil and hid it beneath her robes. Speaking a word to give her strength and speed, she fled the forge back toward the Silver Gate.

Now the knife of Pohjola was quick to do its foul deed. The poison already coursed through Ilmarinen's veins. The smith lay beside his forge and wrenched the blade from his belly. He cried out in a great voice, swelled by pain and anger, which sounded all throughout the Guildhall and even into the streets of Seppälä. All his folk hastened to the Great Forge. Hanmoku passed Siitsa even as she fled and called out to her, but when they found the smith, they could do nothing. He died in their arms, Erilainen though he was and mighty hero of old. And his dark blood ran in pools across the floor and could never be washed clean from those stones ever again.

Siitsa did not run out the Silver Gate, which was guarded by well-armed men, but took a marble stair upward. After many turns she came to a high courtyard on the Guildhall roof, beneath the open sky. Breathless, the tall, thin girl collected herself and threw back her dark robes. She closed her eyes and, with both hands on the Sampo, began to chant a song. She chanted in the Old Speech, laced with words from the language of ancient Talvimaa. A flash of light, bright as the sun, dazzled the eyes of watchers below. People in the street gaped, for the girl was gone, but on the edge of the parapet perched a great beast, winged like a bat but with many-toed claws, black as the night in the farthest north in wintertime.

The creature cried out with a terrible voice, its ghastly, mottled beak open wide. It gathered itself, then leapt from the parapet into the open air, wings spread and beating as it took flight from the city. But not all of the guards had run inside the hall at the sound of Ilmarinen's cry. One yet stood outside the Silver Gate with bent bow, staring up at the shadow that passed over him. With a shout he loosed his arrow at the horrid thing and fled within the gate's lee. The arrow sped true, straight into the belly of the winged beast. The creature shrieked again, this time in pain and agony. It fell from the sky, crashing in ruin onto the cobblestone square before the Guildhall, while all the nearby people screamed in terror and ran away.

Then there was silence. And when the folk dared return and crept back to the square, the creature was gone. Where it fell lay a small shape like a tiny black bundle: the broken body of a girl, pale and wan, shot through with an arrow. And blood spilled from her dead, ruby lips. When the people came closer, the look on her face was of such inexpressible sadness that those who saw it turned away, shaken, as if struck by a blow to their very hearts. But the Sampo was gone, and neither cast nor shards were seen ever again in the world of living men.

***

Bright dawned the day upon the Kaamoslaiset. When all in that host were marshaled and arrayed, at a signal from Egan they began their final march. The king rode a grey charger, its rich coat shot through with speckled white beneath steel barding, and its proud head held high. Its silver headstall, festooned with feathers and precious stones, looked regal in the sunshine. The king, clad in the armor of the royal house of the Etelalaiset with the White Swan on his breast, shone brilliant in the morning light. He wore a tall helm of silver steel and had a blue shield slung at his back. Eglano rode at Egan's side, as did Väinämöinen of the Erilaiset, looking like the very image of Ukko descended to earth. With them went all the lords and princes of the Far Northern Land, mortal and Erilainen alike.

They followed the broad path to Sumuvuori, where the misty falls dropped like rain from the hanging valley. The Easterners had come this way countless times; the goblins had marched the route at Löhi's command to trouble the folk of the Seven Clans. But now that path gave speed to Löhi's foes. Before long they reached the pass that opened out onto the wide plain before the Rocky Run. Then a scout appeared in that pass, a green-clad Warden galloping madly toward them with black-feathered arrows in his kit. He stopped before the king, dismounted, and bowed.

"Your enemies await you on the field, Your Majesty," he said when he had caught his breath. "Their numbers are great."

"Good," the king replied. "Let us not keep them waiting."

The host of the Seven Clans then passed onto the field and at last saw their enemies in the distance. The companies and regiments now arrayed themselves for battle as planned, and they covered all that wide plain. Not since the days of Lemminkäinen, since that fateful day long ago when Löhi's first strength was defeated, had ever a host of the Seven Clans been assembled as strong or fair as that host. All the folk of the Seven Clans were represented, their banners and devices fluttering in the new day's breeze. Spears were long, swords were sharp, and faces proud and grim; the hearts of many an Erilainen beat swiftly to remember that terrible and glorious day long ago and see in Egan that same strength and majesty.

Now this was the order of battle of the League of the Seven Clans.

Upon the left flank rode the Folk of the Eagle. Their banners bore the device of an eagle in different fashions, and they bore the banners of their many homelands as well. The Kotkalaiset, a great folk, made up the League's largest army, but in their midst a small company of men, tall and fair, carried a single sable banner with a white wolf's head: for these were the remnant of the Susilaiset, the Lost Clan, the Folk of the Wolf. And all that host, armed with swords and axes, wore helms and mail or carried round shields. Dogs rode at their stirrups, brave and loyal, ready to fight to the death to protect their masters. The number of that army was some three thousand and five hundred. And it was led by Airiki, King of Akkala, and Biorn, his thane.

Next in that line came the Folk of the Elk. And the banners of the Hirvilaiset were black or dun. Their army was smaller, for they had left many men in Deep Länsimaa to guard the Marches. But from their herds, the Hirvilaiset had outfitted a company of five hundred light horsemen to vie with the riders of the Itäläiset. The Elk Folk, well armed with iron-tipped spears and swords, numbered one thousand and five hundred. And they were led by Teemu, High Lord of Deep Länsimaa.

To the right of the Hirvilaiset marched the Folk of the Hare. Their red-and-white flags snapped in the breeze; their bright mail, helms, and shields, forged by the Smiths of Seppäläa, shone in the sun. There were pikemen and spearmen among them and knights with winterfast swords. The Hare Folk fielded a strong company of archers armed with great bows of yew and arrows tipped with iron. The Tavastians, hardened and bold, the veterans of many battles, made up two thousand and five hundred. And they were led by King Asikkas of Tavastia, and his captain Kalpa; and the men-at-arms were led by Lukka.

Beside them stood the Folk of the Swan. The countless banners of the Etelalaiset sprang up like trees in the forest, blue and white, with the fair device of the White Swan of Etelamaa upon them. The Royal Guards, clad in flowing capes of silver and blue, bore the tokens of the House of Joutsen. They carried fair weapons of many kinds: spears and swords, maces, steel hammers, and deadly pikes. Four hundred Swan Knights, each bearing a long, bitter lance and in full mail, sat on steaming horses beside the lighter horsemen; and with them were the soldiers of the Swan Folk, brave and strong, men of honor and duty, the flower of the Far Northern Land. The number of that army was three thousand men. And it was led by Egan Dragonslayer, King of Etelamaa, and the Grand Duke Eglano; and Aldon of Kotanrannta, and Juvari, Captain of the Etelalaiset; and the Swan Knights were led by Valo, the brother of Satou who was slain at Linnavuori.

On the other side of the Swan Folk, the March Wardens formed their own companies of men from all the Seven Lands, standing proud beneath their green-and-brown banners. Men from the Mariners' Guild and the Smiths' Guild stood among them. Well armed and outfitted, some mounted and some on foot, the number of that army was eight hundred, more than half of all the Wardens in the Far Northern Land. And they were led by Bergil, Lord Captain of the March Wardens, and by Ilkka.

Next came the Folk of the Bear. The Karhulaiset had suffered great loss from Löhi, more than any other clan. Grim now and silent, at last they saw a chance to defeat their enemies and save their people. And if they had been a gentle folk of farmers and fishermen before, they had become warlike now, eager to avenge their families and friends. Armed with spears and swords, only a few wore mail. Yet there were many bold men among them, a cold fire burning in their eyes and resolve lining their faces. Their green-and-yellow banners bore the token of a bear's claw, the Mark of the Clan, and some held long poles upon which bear skulls, hallowed by *tietäjää*, were hung. The number of that army was two thousand, for almost every Karhulainen who could bear arms had marched to war. And they were led by Janottu, Lord of High Länsimaa, and Janni, his captain.

Then came the end of the line, and it was held by the Folk of the Reindeer and the heroes. The Karelialaiset, a small people, unused to such battles, had sent all the men they could muster. From the Karelian Forest they came, under many-colored flags and banners. On tall poles they had set great antlers and skulls. They had helped their kinsmen greatly already, for they knew the ways of the wastes and wilds better than other mortals. Armed in diverse ways, they wore leather rather than steel.

The Erilaiset made up the smallest company, for the *väki* of the Enchanted Valley had dwindled to a small folk; but they were clever, sorcerers and wizards, and wielded powers unknown to mortal men. Some of each of the *väki* of the Erilaiset marched among them, but, for the most part, they were Haltiatar, elves of the deep woods. With their strange and varied banners bearing ancient tokens and forgotten symbols, they stood mingled among the Reindeer Folk. The number of that army was six hundred Karelians and four hundred Erilaiset. And the Karelians were led by Jarko and Turi the Changer; and the Erilaiset were led by Lúven of the Haltiatar.

And the number of all that host was over fourteen thousand men, the green-and-white banners of the League of the Seven Clans scattered among them. But it was commanded by Egan Dragonslayer.

They planned to march ahead boldly, crossing the meadow and tilled land to attack their foes. On their left was the defile whence issued the Rocky Run; a white mist rose from the river in the morning light. To the right sat a tall bluff that fell drunkenly on its southern side. The bluff's tumbled rocks and uncertain grade made it easy for spies to hide yet difficult for any large force to surmount. As they approached the field, a small company of elves went to scout it. Spies fled at their approach, but though they found no hidden enemies waiting to ambush them, the elves discovered something else.

On the bluff's far side, away from the plain, an old trail ran its length. Made, perhaps, so that horsemen or carts might skirt the fields where the Easterners' slaves grew rye, it was broad enough for many to march abreast. The sunken path, overgrown with grass, issued at the plain's eastern end, almost directly in front of the great camp, though open field still lay between. The captains thought then to guard the trail's near end, the western end, so that no Easterners surprised them and attacked their rear. But when he heard the report, Väinämöinen had other ideas. Even as the host deployed on the plain, he came to Egan and Juvari.

"Now is our chance," he said quickly. "This trail seems empty and little guarded. Our enemies probably think, even as we do, that since it is narrow it can be easily blocked with only a small force until help arrives. But they reckon without the Swan Knights! Let us send the Knights down the trail, with the Bear and Reindeer Folk marching behind. We will sweep away their guard and attack their rear, or else pass straightaway across the river and burn the camp. Either way, they will be caught between hammer and anvil and thrown into disarray. But send the main force straight across the plain at once. As the Pohjolaiset fix upon it, they may not see us slip behind the bluff."

Egan and Juvari swiftly agreed, for now they saw a way to outflank their enemy. They extended the line, and Unaja sang a song of cloud and mist, for she was skilled in such arts. Unaja could not hide all that army from sight, for it was far too great, but she obscured the way to the bluff while the chosen men—the companies of the Bear and Reindeer Folk, and the March Wardens—withdrew behind their kinsmen and made for the trail. The least heavily armed of all the host, they might pass quickly through. But the Knights of the Swan went before them.

Väinämöinen turned to Egan with a sudden doubt in his eyes, but the king spoke first.

"You must go with them, Väinämöinen. They will need you."

"I know it, my king," said the old man. "But I would stay by your side."

"Let us meet in the middle, then," answered Egan. "Swift be your onset, and then ride to the banner of the Swan!"

Väinämöinen smiled and clasped Egan's arm.

"May Tapio's blessing be with you," he cried. "Lead us to victory, King of the Far Northern Land!"

Ulla sat some ways away on Midnight, watching as the captains debated and prepared. As Väinämöinen spurred Starchaser, he called out to her. When she hesitated, he checked his steed and spun round.

"Ulla!" he cried. "Come with me! There are no *tietäjää* among the Karhulaiset; they have need of you. It is fitting you should ride with the clans of your parents, the Bear and the Reindeer. We will meet the king on the battlefield, but we have work to do first!" So, with a last look back at Egan and Eglano, Ulla kicked Midnight with her heels and followed Väinämöinen, galloping across the very front of their great line with her hair flying behind her until they joined the Swan Knights and took to the cut around the bluff.

Egan looked left and right. Seeing that all his folk stood ready, he drew *Noidankuolli* and held the glittering sword aloft while his horse reared and snorted. And at that signal, the king's herald, Dane, set his lips to a silver trumpet and blew a mighty note. All the trumpets of the Etelalaiset and Tavastialaiset then sounded together, with the ox's horns and drums of the Hirvilaiset and Kotkalaiset. All that plain and valley rang with the sound; the goblins spying from the bluff covered their ears and hid, while the spies in the hanging valley above thought that enemies were upon them. The host move forward across the plain toward the waiting army of Pohjola. Now they descried the smoke of many hearths rising from the camp and a great mist where the waterfall fell into the river, cascading over shiny black stone; they could hear the roar of its troubled waters. The sergeants shouted to their men to keep their ranks together, and the riders held their nervous beasts in check. War dogs ran about the host, eager for battle.

At last they came before their enemies and halted only some few hundred yards from them. Egan and all those in the front ranks could see their foes clearly for the first time. Then the king's heart sank, for he saw their array and numbers. In that moment he knew that he, not Löhi, had been deceived. Line upon line, rank upon rank, the enemy awaited. The men of the Seven Clans had not imagined that Löhi could still raise such an army; they had counted on outnumbering their foes. But the wizards had been misled; Ulla and the scouts had been wrong.

The Pohjolaiset stood before them in close serried ranks: Itäläiset, Kveni, and men of strange race as yet unencountered. Their horsemen alone numbered in the thousands; more still were on foot, and goblins gathered into black battalions. The servants of Löhi, clad in red and black, bore many strange devices on their flags and shields, and they carried great poles with skulls and chains or ghastly faces fashioned of wood and bone; but the banners of Pohjola were sable with the North Star set within.

As numerous as the host of the clans, maybe greater, the Pohjolaiset looked well fed and well armed—a forest of spears and spikes. Indeed Egan knew in his heart that he had been lured deep into the woods to a battlefield of Löhi's choosing, far from the safety of their homelands.

At that moment the ranks of the Pohjolaiset opened, and out rode the Moonface all alone. His leering silver mask seemed to mock them. His mail was golden from the neck down, and a long black cape trailed behind him; his gloved hand held an iron-tipped spear, while a great shield hung at his back. When he raised his spear, all that deadly host erupted in answer to the clans, with drums and harsh horns and screams in many tongues, a dreadful cacophony that shook the very ground so that the horses of both hosts reared and snorted. None knew who hid behind that mask, what race of man or monster it might be. The Moonface, so similar in height and build to Egan, seemed a very mockery of the king, a counterfeit made by the Witch's magic.

And then a terrible thing unfolded. The Moonface gave another signal, and from within those ranks goblins appeared, driving a crowd of people—men and women—out onto the plain between the hosts. Naked, shivering in the cold, they huddled together, some trying to cover themselves in their shame. They were slaves of the Easterners, captured in raids and made to slash and burn the woods near Sumuvuori. Their lives were hard, hopeless, for even if they escaped the camp and the goblins in the forest, what chance had they alone and in the unknown wastes?

The poor folk crowded together, yet none sought to flee, as if the Moonface's magic bound them in an unseen cage. Then Kuupää gave a great cry in a terrible voice, and from that army came a pack of wolves, white and black, with ice-blue eyes: the wolves of Löhi of which old tales told. Released from the spell, the people cried and ran in terror, but there was no escape. The men in the front ranks watched in horror as the wolves attacked and mauled the slaves, tearing them limb from limb in a frightful frenzy. The few who escaped the wolves were shot down with arrows so that not a one was left alive.

Then Egan turned to those nearby, seeing fear and doubt on the faces of his brother, Juvari his captain, Asikkas of Tavastia, and Teemu as well. Throughout the front ranks, those who beheld that evil host now murmured among themselves as if bewitched. "Let us flee from this place," they said. "Let us flee while we can and seek the safety of the woods. For this host is too great and too fell."

Now Egan, too, was shaken, but mastered his fear. And he laughed then, in a voice both bold and grim, so that all who heard him marveled.

"Do not lose hope, men of the Seven Clans!" he cried. "You see only our enemies' despair! For we have trapped them, and they know it. They have no hope but to frighten us with cruelty. What does it matter if their host be as large as our own? For when has any army of Pohjola ever been the match of the Kaamoslaiset? *As once we were, let us be again, one voice, one sword, one will.* Look not to our enemies' host but to your own! Then you will see why the Pohjolaiset tremble and bluster!"

Then the men in the front ranks turned and looked upon their own host; and their despair turned to newfound hope. For they saw that their army, too, looked great beyond measure, stretching the length of that plain, row upon row, line upon line, iron and steel gleaming in the sunlight, flags and banners streaming in the morning wind. They turned back to the army of Pohjola not with fear but with resolve, determined the war would end on that very day.

Egan brandished *Noidankuolli* and cried aloud, and the host of the Seven Clans leapt forward. The Moonface was gone now, the ranks of the Pohjolaiset closed. Flights of arrows darkened the sky, and at last the armies came together. The ring and clash of iron on iron sounded greater even than the cry of the trumpets and horns. The men of the Seven Clans drove into their enemies, and their onslaught was fierce. The Eagle Folk pierced the ranks of the Easterners who stood before them, and they broke. Then the Easterners' cavalry, at least one thousand riders, seemed to give way and withdraw, and a legion of goblins that battled the Elk Folk did the same.

In that brief moment, even at the battle's outset, it seemed Egan's prophecy would come true and the might of Pohjola crumble before the host of the clans.

And at that same moment, the Swan Knights swept through the bluff with Väinämöinen and Turi at their head. Two rings of goblin archers guarded that exit, and a third line of goblin spearmen lay in wait behind them, for they had set a trap and thought to pour arrows into any who went that way, choking the path with death and confusion. But the mail-clad Swan Knights, their horses well-protected by barding, had wizards to dazzle the goblins' white eyes with magic. The arrows bounced and snapped, and the knights charged through with no loss. Straight through the first ring they drove, then broke the second ring, and then they were among the spearmen, chasing them across the field. Behind them, free now from peril, the soldiers marched onto the field in good order and arrayed for battle.

Väinämöinen looked out upon the plain. Just like Egan, he saw the thousands upon thousands of foes that faced them and, at his own front, along the line of the river, thousands more. The old man understood then that they had been tricked, their *sight* blind and confused, the jewel's vision false. They had no chance of driving into their enemies' rear now, no thought of raiding the camp. With the strength of the Pohjolaiset far greater than he feared, he saw only a deadly and uncertain fight before them.

Then Väinämöinen noticed a strange thing. Across the field, Egan saw it, too. From the misty falls, a cloud rolled across the river and gathered over the battlefield. Grey it was, boiling within as if heated by fire and steam; wisps of smoke like trailing tendrils lashed about its margins. Men held their blows and shouted, pointing skyward at the troubled mist that suddenly seemed to blot out the sun. To their horror a face appeared within it, like the aspect of a mighty god peering down from the sky. That ghastly face, a wizened, gap-toothed crone, cackled now in a dreadful voice that chilled their hearts. For behold! It was Löhi, Löhi of Pohjola. The Witch of the North was upon them! And at once a spell of despair fell upon all the folk of the Seven Clans. Wherever men stood on that field, which stretched some miles from end to end, it seemed that Löhi's ghost hung just above them, for the Witch was skilled in such arts of seeming and could change her aspect at will.

And this is what she said:

"Look now, men of the Seven Clans, look upon thy doom! For all thou hast done was at my bidding. Now thou hast followed those fools thou callest kings and lords to certain death. The wolves and crows shall devour thy bodies, while my servants take thy souls to Tuonela; and from its black maw there is no escape, even unto the end of the world. Flee then to the woods if thou can! For perhaps some few may survive and gain thy homelands. And there thou shalt do obeisance to me and tell thy folk that Löhi alone is queen of the Far Northern Land!"

And there followed a hideous laughter, a crone's dry cackle. And lo! Horns and drums sounded from across the river. From the tangled woods on the Rocky Run's far banks appeared an army of Hiisia, legions of goblins that no scout had ever seen. They had lain hidden in the trees or in holes long prepared. Even as the grey mist faded and Löhi's visage disappeared, the goblins emerged from their hiding places, dragged hundreds of small boats from the woods, and swarmed across the river. On the banks stood a thousand goblin archers armed with bows of horn and bone, darkening the sky with black-feathered arrows, where minutes before had shone clear sunlight. The goblins in those legions alone were as many as the Kaamoslaiset, yet many more thousands of Easterners, Kveni, and strangers remained unfought.

Old Väinämöinen put forth his *sight* now and descried Löhi across the field. Löhi incarnate, neither spirit nor *etiänen*, stood on a rocky height near the river's southern banks, opposite the foaming falls. The Moonface stood beside her with her other generals and captains. The Witch, at once aware of Väinämöinen's gaze, smiled, her aspect now that of the flawless, alabaster-skinned queen. Then Löhi drew him in and opened her mind to him, for she wished to fill him with dread and despair; and she showed Väinämöinen how everything had proceeded according to her design.

For Löhi, bold and fearless, had been willing to risk all on one throw. She had not forgotten Lemminkäinen or his sword, and hated Egan above all her foes. When she saw that she could not defeat her enemies singly and in turn, and might spend all her strength in vain assault while her season upon the earth grew short, she made a desperate plan to bring her enemies together and lure them into the wastes, then destroy them with a shattering blow. She feigned weakness then and lessened her assault, withdrawing her power to fool the Kaamoslaiset. She had attacked Valkeakosk chiefly to trick men into thinking it her last, great threat, though she had hoped the dragon would spread wider ruin. Almost she had achieved Egan's death in Akkala, almost

Ulla's in the woods, but what did it matter? For the Vanhalaiset remained silent, their prophecies empty, and she alone now was a god unto the world.

And then there was Siitsa. The Witch had come to her on a time and seduced her. Secretly she entered the service of Pohjola, for Löhi promised the unhappy girl that the old tower at Kyöpelinvuori would be razed and built anew, tall and fair. In place of the Seer, Siitsa would rule over all the lands nearby. But most of all, she promised the girl that those Itäläiset who had tormented her and killed her folk would be delivered unto her, that she might do with them whatsoever she desired and take her revenge.

All the Seer's *sight* and wisdom had been only what Löhi allowed her to see—the Witch laughed at the foolish mortal who fancied herself the equal of an Erilainen, the queen of the north. So all the counsels of the Erilaiset and the Seven Clans swiftly came to Sariola, and Löhi set her trap accordingly while Siitsa whispered in the Seer's unwitting ear. Last, and most cruel, she let Väinämöinen glimpse Ilmarinen; his heart sank like bloodrock in a lake, for he knew that the smith, who was like a brother to him, was dead and the Sampo gone beyond all recall.

He came back to himself then as Ulla shook him. Violence erupted all around.

"Väinämöinen!" the girl cried. "Väinämöinen, can't you hear me? Väinämöinen, what shall we do?" The horror did not leave his face, but the old man steeled himself and steadied his frightened horse.

"We fight," he said. "That is what we do, with hope or without it. Who knows what change of fortune the wind blows on its wings? We must cut our way through this brood and join the king. But listen to me, Ulla! If things go ill and all is lost, then flee! Put on the cloak you weaved at Linnavuori and make for Länsimaa. Go to Mielikki! You must save yourself at all cost!"

"I will never flee!" she cried, pulling Midnight sharply away from him. "Do you think I'm afraid to die? But if I can find Löhi, I will slay her!"

"No!" the old man cried. Ulla was amazed at the power and compulsion in his voice, which moved her against her will. "No! Think not of yourself, foolish child, but of your folk! As long as she who bears the Mark of the Clan lives, there will be hope! Tapio chose you; it is not given you to seek release in death. You will flee, if flee you must!"

Across the battlefield, hard against the river, the Eagle Folk bore the brunt of the goblins' attack. Airiki called to his men to hold close to the banks and throw the goblins back as soon as their boats hit the shore. Their numbers were too great, however. They made one, then two bridgeheads, and soon the sheer press of numbers forced the Eagle Folk away from the Rocky Run. The men, though taller, stronger, more skilled, and better armed than the goblins, were shocked by Löhi's apparition and filled with dread, while the goblins were spurred on by the evil will of their mistress. Their curved scimitars and spears hacked at the mortal warriors. They threw themselves at their enemies in frenzied attack, heedless of their losses. Riders of the Itäläiset now joined the assault, followed by hundreds of strange men with black locks, painted faces, and tattooed skin from head to toe. And always the goblin archers across the river shot flight after flight of arrows at the ranks of men just behind the line.

The Kotkalaiset fell back. Itäläisen horsemen drove between them and the Elk Folk, trapping the Elk Folk against the river. Teemu rallied them, and they made a wall of spears and swords, bringing their horses inside to save them from the wolves. But though the Eagle Folk loosed all their dogs now, and the loyal beasts leapt upon the goblins and fought savagely with the terrible wolves, it was to no avail. Even as Airiki tried to rally his people in the rout, an arrow struck him between neck and shoulder, where his mail did not cover. The men of his household carried him from the field to the rear, but a bloody froth came from his mouth and he did not speak again. So perished the lord of the Eagle Folk on that dark day.

In the center, where the Tavastialaiset and Etelalaiset stood, the fighting was thick and deadly. The soldiers and knights of Tavastia and Etelamaa were the best men the Kaamoslaiset had, the flower of all that great host. Shaken though they were, even tempted to flee the field, the will of King Egan held them true. Egan refused to despair in the face of darkness. He mastered his men, and even the horses and beasts of burden, with the calm strength that flowed from his very being in that black hour.

Löhi's captain, the Moonface, knew that the Pohjolaiset must defeat these men to win the day, and threw his greatest strength against them in all-out assault. An immense force of four thousand Kveni came against the Tavastialaiset. Another great company of mail-clad Easterners, armed with spears, axes, and iron swords, marched against the Swan Folk. Their banners waved in the wind like a billowing sea of red and black.

But before the foot soldiers attacked, a mass of Itäläisen riders—over a thousand horsemen in three lines—charged, aiming at the junction where the armies of the Hare and Swan Folk met; for so they hoped to break their foes with one terrible blow. And the Easterners had long prepared for that attack, the greatest cavalry charge ever attempted during the whole war. Their horses' hooves pounded the ground like thunder; dust rose from the earth like mist from a lake. Yet the pikemen and spearmen of the clans stood firm and did not falter, their bitter spikes pointed toward the enemy. Great was that clash; the screams of men and horses filled the air. Men fell, pierced by lances or trampled beneath horses' hooves. Easterners tumbled and crashed through gaps torn in the line. But the Kaamoslaiset did not break. They closed the gaps, trapping and throwing down the riders within; then a terrible slaughter followed.

The soldiers of the clans had broken and scattered the first two lines of riders when the third line rode hard after their fellows, ready to chase their enemies down and attack their rear; but, seeing a solid front still held against them, they wheeled and turned, shouting curses in the harsh tongue of the east. The attack's dismayed survivors, on horse or dismounted, fled with them.

Still the Pohjolaiset did not stay their assault. The Kveni and Easterners attacked on foot. Climbing over the piles of the dead and dying and the twisted bodies of horses crying out in agony, they came on. The battle turned into a frenzied melee. Blow after blow rained down. Men on both sides fell, slain or sorely wounded. Egan, ever at the forefront of that fight, rallied his men, led charges, and struck down enemy after enemy. So the savage battle raged all day, yet neither side could gain the advantage.

To the east, the Bear Folk covered a broad front, with the Wardens to their left and the Karelians and Erilaiset on their right. And a great force was arrayed against them. An army of Easterners and goblins assaulted them, and the fighting was fierce. On their right, a company of Dark Erilaiset from Pohjola attacked, sent especially by Löhi to challenge the folk of the Enchanted Valley. There was much enmity between those *väki*: trolls, dark elves, and other races mingled together who hated Väinämöinen and the heroes. Strong magic-users fought on both sides, and the Reindeer Folk would soon have come to grief had the Erilaiset of the Valley not protected them. But Turi led them, and his power outshone their enemies'.

As the fighting raged, a tall figure emerged from the fray—a sorcerer who sang a mighty spell of orbs of fire, white like lightning, which he cast at the mortal men, engulfing them in flame. And that sorcerer was named Saarelon. A Dark Erilainen who had championed Löhi of old, he was evil and delighted in the arts of pain and suffering. And on his hauberk, he bore the device of a death's head.

Then Lúven, Lord of the Haltiatar of the Valley, did single combat with Saarelon of Pohjola. The two elves had fought one another long ago at the Great Battle, and neither had forgotten—or forgiven—any blow. Back and forth they parried with sword and shield, dealing each other many wounds. At last Lúven spied a break in Saarelon's defense. He ran his enemy through, and Saarelon died there, cursing Taikalaakso with his last breath. But in his death throes, Saarelon rolled on Lúven's sword, wrenching it from his grasp. Two trolls then set on Lúven as he struggled to regain his folk. Grievously wounded and burned, he defied his enemies, armed only with his shield. The shattering blows of their clubs overwhelmed him. They beat him to the ground and slew him, leaving his mangled body for the wolves to despoil.

Ulla stayed behind the lines of the Bear Folk, laboring with a few others to help the wounded. She sang of faith and hope, though she felt little of either in that dark hour. But she was skilled in such spells, and Väinämöinen had charged her to counter the despair that Löhi wove all around them. All the *tietäjää* not trading blows in battle did the same. Ulla stayed at her post, doing as the old man had bid as long as she could. But, despite Väinämöinen's words, she saw only ruin all about her, and her own life seemed to matter little in the balance. When she could wait no more, she sprang to her feet, whistled for Midnight, and swiftly mounted.

Ulla drew her sword. She rode well, having been instructed by Väinämöinen since she could first ride a pony. Egan had taught her how to handle a blade, fencing with her atop the Keep in the Stone City, and Turi had taught her the sword *loitsu*: the spell that gave her the strength and skill to wield any blade as if it were part of her own body, her own arm. She closed her eyes, shutting out the noise and tumult around her. Chanting softly, she wove the best spell she could. Then, with a cry, she kicked her horse and galloped toward the battle. Two mounted Wardens passed by bearing Bergil, sorely wounded by the Easterners. They called to Ulla, but she sped away to the fight, her cloak and hair streaming behind her, blown by the cold north wind.

Ulla had never drawn blood before; she had never done battle. Death she had seen, death and war unrelenting, but in a war between men and monsters, not women—not even women of power. In that moment, Ulla changed. She became a wild thing, wild and untamed, like the little girl in the woods near Grankulta, fighting for her life when the Easterners came.

Now the Swan Knights, heavily armed and armored, battled Easterners on a fallow rye field. The great host of Itäläisen riders outnumbered them; the Easterners' small, swift horses cut through the Southerners' lines, scattering them into many smaller groups. Each group fought desperately to ward off their enemies and fight their way back to Egan. Väinämöinen, Ilkka, and many Wardens on horseback struggled to do the same. Ulla galloped straight for the wheeling riders, cutting down two screaming goblins in her path, and came upon a group of Easterners who had encircled several knights.

Heart racing, blood pumping, she struck down one rider from behind, knocking him from his horse. Another Easterner passed by, slashing her arm with his curved sword, but she rode past him. Now they saw her—a wild witch of the Erilaiset, to their eyes. Two riders came toward her. They aimed to pass Ulla on either side, their favorite tactic for slaying mounted foes. Ulla, with no time to think, acted on instinct. A surge of fear and power welled within her. She cried, "*Pysäyttää!*"

She bound the legs of one horse, throwing its rider to the ground in ruin. Drawing Midnight close beside the second man, she avoided his spear thrust by inches and brought *Pohjanpiiki* down upon his helm. The long sword, Tyë's sword, felt as light as a feather in her trembling hand. Wheeling about, Midnight scarcely under control, Ulla saw yet another Easterner riding hard at her. His pale skin, lank hair, and long mustaches made him the very image of the Easterner who had caught her in the woods near Grankulta. With a single stroke she swept off his head. His horse galloped away, its dead rider still holding the reins like a ghost from Tuonela.

The circle broken, the Swan Knights rallied, driving at their foes in turn. Ulla sat gasping atop Midnight, shaking and gazing at *Pohjanpiiki*, now stained red with blood. For the first time, the lust of battle came over her, woman and *tietäjää* though she was. Looking up, she saw Väinämöinen at a distance, standing in his stirrups and staring at her across the field. But the old man said nothing and gave no sign.

Ulla pulled hard on her reins and brought Midnight around, seeking new foes. The battle raged back and forth as the riders hacked and chopped at one another in cold fury. But their foes were too many, and even with Väinämöinen and Turi to lead them, the eastern wing of the host could not find a way to drive through their enemies' ranks and reach Egan.

The short day waned; clouds gathered in the sky. As Löhi put forth all her power, snow began to fall. Again and again the Pohjolaiset drove against the Seven Clans and were thrown back. The dead lay in mounds across the field. Teemu rallied his men and finally broke through their encirclement. Coming from their rear, he and his men attacked the goblins who still pressed the

Eagle Folk, rescuing their kinfolk from destruction. Though that restored the line from north to south, they could do no more.

The goblin archers crossed the river now with more Itäläiset, reserves that Löhi had held back to harry her defeated enemies—for the Witch grew impatient. For all her great strength, she saw that her forces might soon be spent, and wanted nothing unforeseen to mar her plans.

Egan the king looked then at his host, beset and desperate: men falling or fleeing, riderless horses running in terror. He saw the ruin of his war and held himself responsible, he who had been deceived by Löhi, he who wished to be High King of all the Seven Clans. He thought of his folk now, cursing his name and memory. He thought of the survivors becoming slaves, the North Star of Pohjola flying even over the Stone City, and he wondered if even the New Sampo could protect them, for he knew not of Ilmarinen's death and Siitsa's betrayal.

Then rage, rage and anger, built within him: anger at his failure, anger at the Witch, anger at the hopelessness of mortal men set on earth without choice in the face of illness, disease, misfortune, and evil. He tore off his lofty helm and wiped the gore and grime from his face. Turning to Eglano, he grasped his arm, his bloody hand sliding down the steely vambrace.

"Brother," he said as tears welled in his eyes. "Brother, we cannot leave the field without rout, and if we stand here, we will finally be destroyed. Let us take all those men left to us of our own folk and attack the enemy. And if we fail, at least we shall avenge our father and cover this accursed ground with the blood of our foes."

And Egan called Juvari to him and Lukka of the Tavastialaiset, for Asikkas was wounded, his sword arm cut off, and Kalpa his captain was slain. He told Lukka to hold off the enemy with the Hare Folk. But the rest of the army of Etelamaa would charge the enemy, turn on his flank, and then drive to the river. So they might throw their foes into disarray and rejoin Väinämöinen and the eastern wing. And it was a desperate plan, but they had no other.

As fate or chance would have it, a respite came then. New Pohjolaisen forces relieved their exhausted and bloodied comrades, and the Witch's servants jumbled together in confusion. The trumpets of the Swan Folk sounded for the second time that day, and amidst swirling flurries they moved forward. The thin line of goblin skirmishers shot their arrows and ran. Egan raised high his sword. His brother, Eglano, rode on his right, and on his left, his cousin Aldon; and it was later said that no one fought more bravely on that field than Aldon, save the king alone. The lines of the Swan Folk followed *Noidankuolli* and slowly turned in perfect order. And then they had flanked the enemy and looked north.

The men of Etelamaa drove forward, and behold! The plain filled with foes hurrying to close the breach. First they came upon legions of Hiisia, the green-skinned goblins clad in leather over tunics of thick black cloth, white eyes sparkling with hatred for all other living things. Swords rose and fell, cut and parried, and savage spear thrusts skewered man and goblin alike in frightful slaughter. But it seemed that a white light shone about Egan; neither spear nor dart could pierce him. And the goblins were stricken and slain, their champions thrown down and their valor gone. Those that yet lived ran shrieking in terror from the wrath of the Swan Folk.

The men of Etelamaa drove forward. Next they met an army of Easterners, fresh to the field, a clan from far to the east, newcomers to Löhi's wars, eager for battle and for the rich spoils they had been promised. A tall, cruel Haltia of Pohjola led them. The fighting grew fiercer still, frenzied and savage. The Easterners, strong men armed with iron, asked for and gave no quarter. They hated the king of their enemies and knew that his overthrow would deliver unto them all the lands and treasures they coveted; and the Haltia who led them, a great sorcerer, used his magic to inflame those passions all the more.

They surrounded the Swan Folk and drove them into smaller groups, attacking with reckless abandon. An Itäläisen sword ran Aldon through, and many others fell beside him. But Egan rallied his men yet again, calling out to them in a great voice that rang across that bloody field. First one, then another of the sundered companies flocked to him. Then the rest came as they could. And lo! The tide turned again, and the Kaamoslaiset now attacked, tearing the Easterners' lines and dividing them, hacking them down with fury; and Egan slew the elf who was their captain and cut off his head, lifting it above the fray for all to see.

Then Löhi, from her rocky vantage point, saw him clearly, for the Swan Folk had fought more than halfway across the plain. And it is said that for the first time that day, doubt entered into her cold heart and she grew afraid. The Sword of Lemminkäinen flashed before her, wielded by the boy who would be his heir. Väinämöinen remained unfought, and Ulla rode wild upon the plain. The Witch felt her strength almost spent, her mighty host shaken and in disarray. She turned to Kuupää, ordering him into the combat with the command to slay Egan at all costs; and all her evil will was bent upon him.

The Moonface called on his last reserves: a legion of goblins, stiffened by great trolls and a final company of his best horsemen. With that, Pohjola's strength was spent. He could not withdraw the soldiers from the other fronts, or else all his host might collapse and be trapped against the river. So the Moonface cried out in the tongue of Pohjola and rode down into the battle himself, for he had become the Enemy of Egan.

The men of Etelamaa drove forward. They faced a mixed force now, for the eastern clan from far away had been destroyed. Soon the goblins and riders fell upon them, but still the Swan Folk swept aside the first line of their enemies and crashed into the second. Suddenly Egan descried Löhi in the hazy distance, standing atop the rocks. For a moment, hope rose in his heart like a falcon rising swiftly from an opened cage. He thought that his dream was come true, that he would indeed throw her down, even as Lemminkäinen long ago; and in his hope, he looked about him wildly for Ulla, as if she might suddenly appear at his side—but only for a moment. For, as the king called out to his men to make for the Witch's rocky height, he perceived the ruin all around him.

Too many were slain, too many, and the rest wounded or scattered. Their strength was at last at an end, even within sight of the Witch of the North. Horsemen rode down his soldiers. Small groups made valiant stands, fighting back to back against the goblins, even as the blue-and-white banner of the Swan was cut from its pole and stamped into the earth. Then Egan stood with his guard, surrounded by enemies, and they made a ring of slain foes all about them in the snow. And Eglano fell, a troll's mighty club beating him to the ground. The king stood over his brother, thrusting *Noidankuolli* madly all about. But Egan grew weary, exhausted, and his light dimmed. His shield shattered; his sword arm felt heavy at his side.

The Moonface came upon him then and put forth all his power. His silver mask shone as if the moon had descended from the heavens; his golden armor glittered like treasure in a secret cave. He stood before Egan and, with a word in the language of Pohjola, bound him; and even then Egan did not give up, but struggled toward his enemy like a man swimming against a swift, strong current.

And when at last they met, the Moonface thrust his spear at Egan, piercing the ancient armor with a thousand glittering sparks and driving deep into his heart.

And behold! Egan said nothing as he sank to his knees, his blue eyes looking skyward. And it seemed to some on that field that they saw a white bird take flight from the carnage, never looking back, mounting swiftly toward the pale, setting sun or toward the *Linnunrata* far above, where the souls of men may go. But across the field, Väinämöinen cast down his head and Ulla felt a blow to her heart, for they knew in truth what had happened.

Thus died Egan II, Dragonslayer, King of Etelamaa, Chief of the Swan Folk, and Heir to the High Crown of the Far Northern Land. And *Noidankuolli* was never found, nor did any ever know his body's final resting place. For he was vanished forever, a memory of what might have been, perhaps, had fate and fortune ruled otherwise.

Now the disaster was complete; the battle was lost. For all the mounds of slain, the Pohjolaiset still outnumbered them, and the host of the Seven Clans was weary and hopeless. The army of Etelamaa was no more, a broken mass of leaderless men. The survivors streamed southward toward the bluff. In that last hour, even as Egan drove on Löhi, Ilkka had finally broken through the front dividing the host's western and eastern wings. With all the men that he could muster, he had struggled to come to Egan's aid and to attack those who assailed him. No longer. The Moonface came down upon them and swept them away; some fled west with Ilkka and reached the Tavastians, while others broke and fled back to where Väinämöinen and Ulla still fought.

The old wizard had done all that he could. He knew now that hope was lost, nor was there any way to reach their friends and kinsmen still fighting to the west. His anger blazed high; weary and wounded though he was, he thought to work a change and come at Löhi across the field to challenge her to single combat. He had been late coming to Lemminkäinen's aid long ago, and he was now too late to help Egan. He saw only downfall and failure all about him. But Turi came to him and restrained his reckless despair with harsh words.

"Master yourself!" said the Changer. "What right have you to throw your life away while you counsel others elsewise? The girl needs you! Do you want her to perish, too? Look about you at all those who may yet be saved. Sirkka of the Menninkaiset has scouted a way south of here, round lakes and bogs, which might lead to the Marches. No way for an army, but a way of escape, maybe, for fleeing men. All of us are needed, or they will never make it. Think of your folk and cast off your pride, because it is your pride that fuels your rage and despair!"

Väinämöinen grasped his shoulders as if to strike him; Turi's eyes shone with fire in reply. But just as swiftly, the old man's expression changed, his face sagged, and his tired, grey eyes welled with tears.

"Come, my friend," said Turi, more gently now, "My oldest friend and brother. Help me now. I cannot do it alone."

Then he and Turi gathered those men left near them, for half of the Bear Folk still lived and others besides. Ulla slumped on Midnight beside the old man, cold and silent, but she did not protest his instructions or try to ride away. Indeed, it seemed she had no will of her own.

Most of their foes drew off and turned away, summoned by the Moonface for the destruction of what remained of the host's larger, western wing.

Löhi's captain deemed the survivors on the eastern side would make for the old trail again and be trapped. But, with the remnant of the Swan Knights, Väinämöinen made a screen to cover and protect all those on foot. They fled into the wastes as they could, carrying the wounded and injured with them, save those beyond hope of healing; and the cries of the men left behind pierced their ears like knives as they fled. Then the knights stripped off their horses' barding and armor and, with Väinämöinen to guide them, plunged into the woods behind their kinsmen. The Pohjolaiset, blinded by Turi's magic, thought that they took to the trail as the Moonface expected, and did not pursue them. And Löhi's gaze was elsewhere.

Night came; the snow ceased. Stars appeared at the edges of the jagged clouds. The waxing moon began to rise, bathing all Sumuvuori in a yellow glow, the glow of death and the tallow candles of Tuonela.

Swan and Hare, Eagle and Elk, all that remained in that ragged, weary host fought on, crowded toward the line of the river. Ilkka took command of the remnant, still several thousands; Teemu and Lukka of Tavastia fought beside him. Juvari, Captain of Etelamaa, though grievously wounded, yet begged to be laid nearby for their last debate. Ilkka could see their enemies massing for a final assault, and knew his own men were spent. The Warden decided to form all who could still bear arms into a square, put the wounded within, and so fight through the night until at last they were slain. For he deemed that if they broke and fled, few would ever reach safety, nor was it possible to withdraw in orderly fashion with the Easterners at their heels.

But Unaja the Golden came to them then, she of the white skin and golden hair. Now the mortal *tietäjää* had been scattered throughout the clans, each with their own folk, striving to counter the great *loitsu* of despair that Löhi wove or to help the wounded. Some did battle, binding their enemies or sending darts like lightnings from their rods and staffs to afflict their foes, challenging the sorcerers of Pohjola to duels of power and magic. Few were left to return to the Seven Lands afterward. Unaja had bid farewell to Väinämöinen and gone with the Eagle Folk. She had been with Airiki when he died and held Biorn's hand as his life slipped away. She had helped Teemu surprise the goblins as the Elk Folk broke free from their trap, and now she came to the remaining captains, speaking so sternly and with such authority that none dared gainsay her.

"The battle may be lost, but our enemy, too, is shaken and exhausted. Take now the path through the defile, alongside the Rocky Run. For if there be any hope for the future, these men must live to defend their homelands and fight another day. I will hold this foul brood back until you gain the fords, which are not far away; you must leave a guard there to halt your pursuers. But cross the lake as swiftly as you can. Do not wait for dawn, no matter the loss! Thus may many yet be saved and come again to the North Marches and the lands of the Seven Clans."

Such was her power that her words swayed all who listened, strange woman from a strange folk though she was. And, while some broke and fled to be ridden down or lost in the wastes, Ilkka quickly put most in ordered ranks. Then the ragged, tatterdemalion host began to pass into the long defile.

Unaja stood before them, facing their enemy, and set her staff on the ground. Both her own eyes and the blind eyes of the wolf-fell that twined about her shoulders sparkled in the darkness. She raised her hands skyward, palms open, and sang a quick, rhythmic chant. And lo! A sheet of flame, a great wall of fire, rose all around her, from the river to the outer edge of the defile. The red and yellow blaze lit the night, climbing higher and higher, as tall as the tallest pines. And that wall encircled the Kaamoslaiset within, keeping all their enemies without.

Now the Pohjolaiset had been poised to strike even as Unaja made that spell. Night-eyed goblins were prepared to attack and break through the defenders; the last companies of Itäläisen riders would come behind them to ride down and slaughter the rest. But the flames panicked the horses, and their riders could not control them. They ran away and would not come near that place. The goblins shrieked and yelled, the fire reflected in their white eyes. They shot arrows through the wall and launched spears with truncheons, but to no avail. They could not see Unajaa and knew not what happened; but the wizard kept up her spell and did not waver.

The minutes passed and the night wore on—and that spell was known forever after as Unaja's Wall. At last a group of goblins steeled themselves and, with bowed heads, charged through the fire in a desperate attempt to gain the other side. But that flame was the flame of Ukko. As they passed through, they burned. Some fell dead; others ignited as if doused with burning oil and danced madly toward the river, where they threw themselves into the water in their agony and drowned.

Then the Moonface came with two other sorcerers, dark elves of Pohjola; they mastered their steeds with magic and sat before Unaja's Wall, sensing the woman and her spell. And they began their own song, a *loitsu* of wind and rain and water. It swirled about the Wall, scattering wisps of flame into the sky. The fire's circuit drew ever smaller, scarcely covering the mouth of the defile, but it did not break. It burned steadily. Slowly, the counterspell faltered and faded. The elvish sorcerers slumped exhausted in their saddles; the Moonface threw down his golden rod in anger, and it shattered as it hit the ground. Yet they could not defeat that spell, nor did they dare ride through the Wall. And, all that time, the Kaamoslaiset passed through the narrow gorge toward safety.

And at last came Löhi. Even in the fire's harsh glow, a silver sheen wrapped about her; her aspect remained beautiful and flawless, a snow-clad goddess made of ice, come to life in the waking world. Her white garment remained unstained by that field of horror, and in her right hand she bore a black staff of iron. And yet the Witch's anger kindled like the fires of Hell, for she saw her chance to destroy the last of her enemies slipping away; and still she hoped to find Ulla ere the girl fled but knew not where she was in all that wreck.

Löhi approached the fiery Wall and raised high her staff. All her servants that yet cowered nearby shrank back or hid their eyes with their hands; and even the Moonface, her captain, bowed his head and turned away.

Thrice she cried out in the tongue of Old Talvimaa. Each time the Wall flickered and wavered and less certain became. Unaja staggered at Löhi's spell but did not fall. And at the third cry, the Witch strode forward into the fire and it turned to silver, then to blue; and then, as suddenly as it had come, it disappeared.

Without breaking stride, Löhi walked straight to Unaja. The tall mortal woman, she of the golden hair, even now sought to stay her with a mumbled spell. But Löhi reached out with cold hands and took hold of her, looking into her deep blue eyes. A sheet of white flame twisted itself around them, hiding them both. And Unaja's cry was heard across all that place, and in the hanging valley above, and throughout the wastes for miles and miles. But then the white flame burned out and the Witch stood alone, and there was nothing left at her feet save the sizzling wolf-fell and a charred staff.

In all the great deeds of those evil times, the deed of Unaja, the wizard who kindled Ukko's Fire to hold the darkness at bay, is perhaps the most renowned, for the hour that she sang that spell gave her folk precious time to escape. Yet still she paid with her life.

And so the day at last ended. The moon's sickly glow reflected from the groaning earth and tortured fields. The dead and dying lay in heaps upon the ground: mortal and Erilaiset, Easterner and clan folk. Carrion fowl descended upon them and the wolves of Löhi came among them, and it seemed that the Gates of Tuonela had opened and spilled their horrors into the waking world.

But where Löhi came, the birds and beasts fled. She walked among the dead as a queen among her folk, a white, upright figure suffused in a pale, misty light. Now and again she paused, looking at some twisted face or body that perhaps she remembered or which caught her fancy, as she searched for the enemies whose death she most desired. So Löhi spent the night, giving no more thought to battle or pursuit, and when at last she returned to her tent, she clutched a great bundle of things picked from the field and wrapped in a black cloth. And on her expressionless face now hovered a smile, thin and cruel, which still did not mar her preternatural beauty.

But the dead were too many to be buried. The Hiisia and Kveni who yet lived stripped the bodies, gathered them into piles, and burned them, friends and enemies mingled together in the smoking earth. They pushed others into the marshes or threw them into pits as chance allowed.

And there was no mound or stone to mark the spot where Egan the Young lay with his brother, cousin, and kinfolk in sleep everlasting. Never again was his fair form seen or his voice heard in the Far Northern Land. But in later years, the woods and trees returned to the battlefield and the echoes and cries of that terrible day were forgotten by all save the wind and stars.

Chapter Fifteen

The Lonely Woods

Great was Löhi's triumph. All her designs had borne fruit, and her gambits and lies found fertile ground in which to blossom, bringing ruin unto her foes.

Egan, the one she most feared, was dead, never to be crowned High King in Tapiola. Eglano was slain, never to see the child born to Kirsikka on the very day of the battle. Aldon was killed, and Valo dead, and all the valor of Etelamaa left to rot and wither on the cold field of Sumuvuori.

King Airiki of Akkala lay dead alongside Biorn, his thane, and Kalpa, Captain of Tavastia. And though Asikkas lived, carried away from the wolves of Löhi, his young son and standard-bearer, Pekka, never saw the green hill of Tapiola again.

Bergil the Warden and Janottu and Janni of High Länsimaa were dead, and the strength of the Bear Folk destroyed. And Lúven of the Erilaiset and Unaja the Golden perished, and most of the mortal *tietäjää* besides.

Of all the great host that unfurled its banners at Sumuvuori beneath a bright morning sun of hope, more than half were slain. The rest returned a mass of broken and spiritless men, refugees fleeing ruin and despair, their pride and purpose forgotten. The League of the Seven Clans was broken, never to unite again. And in far-off Seppälä, Ilmarinen lay dead on a slab of stone while the smiths mourned, and the Sampo was lost forever.

And Tornilaiset, seduced by Siitsa and loyal to Löhi, had set fire to the tower at Kyöpelinvuori. It blazed throughout the night while evil spirits and ghosts wailed round it and the wind blew like a gale. When the frightened villagers finally returned, they found the Seer dead in her chamber, a look of horror upon her bone-white face. And Kilia her apprentice lay dead beside her.

Great indeed was Löhi's triumph. And yet, for all the ruin and despair she wrought, she failed in her main purpose. For her own injury had been enormous, far greater than she had ever imagined. She had emptied Pohjola to raise her grand army, calling on clans of the Itäläiset and their kin from the farthest east to make her master stroke. Now she had no strength to pursue her fleeing foes or invade the Seven Lands, as she had planned, to affect their final and utter defeat.

It was said that eight out of ten parts of the Hiisia of Pohjola fell on that field and their bodies lay there by the thousands, for Löhi had thrown them into battle like logs into the fire. Never again would the goblins march in varied legions at her call. And the Kveni were crushed, and thousands of Easterners, her strongest servants, slain or scattered. Moreover, the Easterners' might lay in their horses. Their herds had all but been destroyed, their twisted carcasses choking the Rocky Run like an evil dam. Though the Easterners were hard men, they loved their beasts as their kin and grieved greatly, nor could those losses ever be made up.

Most of all, Väinämöinen and Ulla had escaped alive, so Löhi still knew fear deep within her cold heart.

But Väinämöinen knew little of all this, and Ulla less. The Kaamoslaiset who fled south separated into small groups, no larger than a hundred or so together, and the Erilaiset led them. Each band picked its own way through the lakes and trees, back toward the safety of the Marches. Turi and some few others went ahead to scout the way. Most of the refugees were Bear and Reindeer Folk with some Wardens and Swan Folk mixed among them, including a few who had marched with Egan on his final charge and afterward escaped.

It was an evil journey with little food, the wounded crying in pain, and the dying with little succor. The way was impassable for beasts, so in their need, the Swan Knights slew the horses they had left for their meat. Only Ulla and Väinämöinen saved their mounts, Starchaser and Midnight; for such was the wizards' power that they might make a way for their loyal steeds.

One night, Väinämöinen and Ulla sat by a small campfire amidst a thicket of short, stubby trees. In the darkness around them, more fires had been kindled by the mortals Väinämöinen guided, a hundred or so ragged and weary men of the Bear Folk, wishing only to return to their homes and families. The weather held cold and clear, the one blessing they had. It had not snowed or blown a winter gale since the flight from Sumuvuori. Yet this was small benefit to set against all their pain and loss.

Ulla said little for days after the battle. When the old man had told her about Ilmarinen and the Sampo, and what he had read of the mind of Löhi, she fell silent and spoke no more. They hurried through the woods, searching for solid ground among the marshlands, always fearing pursuit by Löhi's servants. Without bidding, Ulla did what was needed for the hurt and the sick and spent such power as remained to her to sustain their little company and speed it southward. Now, they camped in lands that Väinämöinen remembered, perhaps only a few days from the Marches.

Väinämöinen held a stick with bits of rabbit on it, turning it this way and that before the fire, but the young woman refused the meat when he offered it.

"Eat," said the old man in a gravelly voice. "You called them, didn't you? If they gave their lives for you, don't waste them."

He coughed and wrapped his thick coat tighter about him, stretching out his leg that had been wounded by an Easterner's curved sword. He set the meat aside.

"Do not waste lives!" said Ulla suddenly. She laughed a little. "Not a hare's—oh no! But ten thousand men are yet a bargain!"

"The silent speak!" replied Väinämöinen. "To what do I owe such an honor?"

"Don't mock me!" Ulla cried with a flash of anger, so that men nearby turned toward her in wonder. The old man coughed again, then laughed, unperturbed.

"Well, you're not addled, I see," he said, taking the stick again and poking at the fire's glowing embers. "*Quick to anger, quick to fail.* It lets others perceive your thoughts, and that's not always wise."

Ulla fell silent again, leaning back against the rough bark of a pine and staring up at the night sky. There was no moon, but the North Star shone bright overhead. She thought that it, too, mocked her.

"If we gain the Marches," said Väinämöinen suddenly, "there will be a fort nearby with Wardens and Karhulaiset, waiting. These men will have food and rest there. But news of all that has passed must come swiftly to Mielikki. I want you to go with the Erilaiset at once to the Enchanted Valley."

"No," said Ulla, her voice flat. "I'm going to Siria."

"I must soon go myself to Kyöpelinvuori, and—"

"No. I am going to Tavastia to get Siria."

Väinämöinen peered at her through his long, tangled hair and nodded. Then there was nothing but the fires, the forest, and the wild dark around them. The stars twinkled overhead, seven stars, the Great Bear of the Far Northern Land.

The wind whispered in the trees.

"Where is *karhu*?" asked Väinämöinen.

"There is *karhu*," answered Ulla.

"Where did *karhu* come from?" he chanted.

"From up there in the sky, on a silver chain," said the woman.

> *From the Moon's shoulder,*
> *from the Sun's collar—*
> *that's where karhu came from.*

FINIS

The Far Northern Land Saga concludes with

Book III: The Queen of Pohjola

Seven more years have passed. Village by village, Löhi has laid waste to the Far Northern Land, until only the southern kingdoms remain free.

Ulla's power has grown. She is strong, pitiless and relentless, her sole measure being utter devotion to the seemingly hopeless cause. Accompanied by Kaukomieli, the last wizard to win his staff, she prowls the Marches, ambushing Löhi's servants. The young man obviously loves Ulla, but she is fervently devoted to Egan. The wizards journey in spirit form to Hell to bargain with its lord for a weapon to slay the Witch, and Ulla and Väinämöinen trek through Pohjola toward a final confrontation with Löhi.

Regardless of the battle's outcome, she fears the future. She is, after all, still a child inside, longing for love and home, but cold and hard on the outside: the very personification of the Finnish heroic spirit.

What does an author stand to gain by asking for reader feedback? A lot. In fact, it's so important in the publishing world that they've coined a catchy name for it: "social proof." And without social proof, an author may as well be invisible in this age of digital media sharing.

So if you've enjoyed *The Heir of Lemminkäinen*, please consider giving it some visibility by reviewing it on the sales platform of your choice. Your honest opinion could help potential readers decide whether or not they would enjoy this book, too.